until
now

until now

a novel

JENSEN PARKER

Made for More Publishing, LLC

UNTIL NOW

Cover Design: Jensen Parker

Beta'd: Grace Rose, Kate Gegas, Becky Taylor

Editing: Kate Gegas

ISBN (e-book) : 979-8-9879868-0-6

ISBN (printed) : 979-8-9879868-1-3

Published by Made for More Publishing, LLC

https://www.jensenparker.com

Playlist

Before You - David J
Rome - Dermot Kennedy
Breathe - Breaking Benjamin
Watching Airplanes - Gary Allan
Room to Breathe - You Me At Six
Love is Gone (Acoustic) - SLANDER and Dylan Matthew
Costume Party - Lauren Duski
I'll Be - Edwin McCain
Strangers - Jonas Brothers
Over and Over - Three Days Grace
Mr. Brightside - The Killers
Everywhere - Fleetwood Mac
Whiskey Colored Eyes - Little Big Town
What Have I Done - Dermot Kennedy
Leave - Matchbox Twenty
She - Elvis Costello
Full Circle - Miley Cyrus
I Want More - Kaleo
Selfish - Nick Jonas (feat. Jonas Brothers)
More Than A Feeling - Boston
Before You Go - Lewis Capaldi
Backroad Therapy - Alexandra Kay
Payphone - Maroon 5 (feat. Wiz Khalifa)
Back to Me - 3 Doors Down
Whiskey Side of Me - Emily Brooke
How Do We Go - Alexandra Kay
Dance in the Rain - Jana Kramer
I Won't Back Down - Tom Petty
If You're Gone - Matchbox Twenty
Let You Down - NF
The One - Jeremy Renner
Surrender - Angels & Airwaves
Godsend - Riley Clemmons
Nervous - Nick Jonas
When You're Gone - Shawn Mendes
Love You Anyway - Luke Combs
All I Wanted - Paramore
Over You - Daughtry
Fearless - Taylor Swift
If You Love Her - Forest Blakk
Apologize - OneRepublc (feat. Timbaland)
Never Too Late - Three Days Grace
Waffle House - Jonas Brothers
He Said, She Said - Ashley Tisdale

Apple Music

Spotify

*for the girl who was scared to share her words
with the world...*

we did it.

Part One

"Life isn't about waiting for the storm to pass, it's about learning to dance in the rain.

- Vivian Greene

one

THIS HAS GOT TO be a joke.

I gasp as the mix of ice, liquid, and sweet cream soaks my chest — coffee meet romper. Fuck me. I don't have time for this. I'm already running behind, but won't make it through my meetings without coffee. The stain has already started settling into the white stripes, no way to hide it from—

"Maybe you should watch where you're going."

I look up from the crime scene to see what, or should I say who ruined my favorite romper. The smirk on his lips irritates me, but the lack of coffee on his own clothes irritates me more. "You think this was my fault?"

"You did just walk without looking, so yeah."

"Testa di cazzo."

His whiskey-colored eyes hold a warmth that the rest of him doesn't. Something in them feels so...familiar. Wait, do I know him? Tapered dark brown curls match the stubble on his sharp jaw. Not to mention the way his white T-shirt displays very toned arms, skin bronzed from hours spent in the southern sun. Guarantee if I wasn't in heels, he'd stand at least five inches taller. "I'll take that as your apology."

"Apology? Scusa? Tu sei quello che non ha guardato, tu..." I scoff. "You know what, I don't have time for this."

"Nina?" Lucy calls from the pick-up window, a fresh iced coffee in her hands. "This one is on the house as long as you promise not to spill it on anyone else."

"See, even she knows it was your fault." I can hear the smirk in his voice.

Taking the new coffee, I make sure to avoid the stranger when I step off the patio this time. I need to get to the office before Kathleen. Crossing Sparrow Street, I survey the damage done — a light brown stain has infiltrated the white stripes settling in for what was sure to be a long battle for my dry cleaner. Naturally, this would happen the day after I take my extra clothes home from the office. I'm going to have to buy something else to wear for my meeting.

"What happened to you?" Michaela asks when I walk through the front door. Michaela Davis — friend, assistant, and intern. We met in college at Rosecliffe University — a public university near the Carolina borders, mostly known for its architecture and business programs. Michaela was a freshman who had placed into a higher-level calculus class, I was a junior who had avoided it as long as possible. She came to work for me as an intern when I opened my interior design firm, DV Designs, but more recently she has been handling designs on her own.

"Oh, I thought it could use a little color. You don't like it?" I glance at the clock. Shit. I have one minute before Kathleen is supposed to be here. "Some guy ran into me at Java."

"Was he cute?"

Yes.

"No, Michaela, why is that the first thing you ask?"

"I'm just curious."

I roll my eyes. "Kathleen is going to be here any minute to go over samples, I need to go get something else to wear. Can you handle her for ten minutes?"

Michaela huffs, "Fine, but you owe me."

"Not like it's part of your job or anything, but sure, I'll buy lunch today."

"You're a saint!" Michaela yells as I race back out the front door. Kathleen is not the type of person who would approve of a coffee-stained outfit. She would prefer me to be ten minutes late with clean clothes than show up with a large stain across my chest.

Approaching Sparrow Street again, I can't help but glance at the patio of the Java Fountain. No sign of him. A small ball of disappointment settles in the pit of my stomach. Why do I care? It's not like he's going to apologize and offer to buy me a new outfit. We aren't going to swap life stories and fall in love. This is real life, not a Hallmark movie. I will probably never see him again, but I can't shake the feeling I know him from somewhere. And, I almost wish I could see him again — if only to return the favor and add a splash of color to his white T-shirt.

two

"THERE YOU ARE!" A blonde girl shouted over the music grabbing ahold of my arm. Wait, when did I get to the kitchen? And, when did I get another drink? Tobias stood next to me talking to Jonas and a different guy I don't recognize. "I've been looking for you," the blonde said. Lydia Holt — English major at Rosecliffe. We became friends on the first day of welcome week.

"Not hard enough," I said downing the rest of my drink. Some kind of tequila and fruity mixture.

"One minute we were talking and the next you were just gone."

"You found her!" A dirty blonde boy broke through the crowd. His baby blue eyes matched the color of his shorts. Lee Madigan — business major and my "boyfriend," if you could even call him that. We had never put an official title on things, mostly because I never wanted to. I was content to stay friends with benefits if only to get under the skin of my so-called best friend, Teagan Kennedy. Needless to say, it's complicated. "What are you doing in here? I thought we were gonna hang out."

"Stavo cercando di stare lontano da te," I huffed.

"English, please."

16

"Why are you so concerned about what I'm doing?"

"I got worried when Lydia said she couldn't find you."

"Well, you seemed pretty content with that redhead from Kappa."

"That's not fair, Nina."

"Fuck off, Lee. I don't need a babysitter." I had been adamant about not wanting to come out that night, but Teagan wouldn't stop begging. The only way to get her to shut up was to come along. And now, Teagan was off doing God knows what with God knows who. When Lydia finally showed, I decided to stick by her, it would keep me out of trouble. But, I didn't count on the drinks being so strong.

As the alcohol coursed through me, the air grew thick, the music too loud; I needed to breathe. Catching a glance of the side door closing, I found my escape. "I need some air," I said, heading for the door without looking back.

§

I've come a long way since then. After that night, I stopped going to parties. If I did show up, I was gone within thirty minutes. Enough time to show my face, say hello to a few people, and leave. My focus turned to my studies and securing an internship. But, what surprised everyone most of all... I started dating Lee — officially. Long gone was the party girl. Now, I own a successful interior design and decorating firm, DV Designs.

My current project: a penthouse in Manhattan. It features floor-to-ceiling windows with 360-degree views of the city from Central Park to the Chrysler and Empire State Buildings. I used to dream of living in the city, maybe in a penthouse just like this, but that dream ended almost two years ago. I've been avoiding New York ever since, unwilling to deal with the memories around every corner. I can't deny it has been nice being back in the city — even if I've been on edge the entire time. Constantly looking over my shoulder when I go into my old coffee shop. Scanning every face on the street. All in the hopes of avoiding one person. I don't have to do that back in Winchester. Even though his parents still live in the low country, he hardly visits.

I triple-check every detail of the penthouse: re-fluff couch pillows, re-stack coffee table books, and re-straighten the blanket on the chaise. Wipe invisible dust from the marble table in the gallery, rearrange the candles on the dining table, and put a bottle of champagne to chill in the kitchen. I've done projects for celebrities without an ounce of nerves, but this one felt different. This one is personal. Lydia is moving to New York City to be with her boyfriend, Jack, a wall street guy; and she refused to move without my help. I was more than happy to oblige, even if it meant coming back to the city.

"You're late," I say without looking, hearing heels echo against the floor. Michaela. Late, per usual.

"I am so, so sorry!" Michaela practically begs. This is the one time I asked her not to be late. "I met this cute guy and we got to talking and before I knew it, it was three!" Michaela hands over a fresh cup of coffee from Second Cup on 58th Street. "I brought a peace offering."

"I guess I can forgive you...this one time."

Michaela breathes a sigh of relief and glances around the penthouse. "You've outdone yourself, Nin. I'm gonna go chill the champagne!"

"Already done." I laugh as the blush creeps into her cheeks and she ducks into the kitchen anyway to see what else she can do.

I check my appearance in the mirror: I comb through my waves, push my shoulders back, straighten my peplum top, and wipe some dust from my black jeans just as the elevator dings.

A squeal of excitement follows Lydia through the double doors, a blur of blonde and pink. She moves from one thing to the next, unable to decide where to look first. Finally, her eyes land on me and she practically tackles me. A tall redhead trails in a moment later, behind him the doorman wheels an overfilled luggage cart. He's not as interested, but he acknowledges Lydia whenever he hears his name as she flits around the first floor. "It looks great, Nina," he finally says before disappearing upstairs with the luggage.

I loop arms with Lydia leading her towards the dining room and kitchen, "Let me show you around."

§

I salivate as the waitress sets a plate of seared scallops in front of me and a plate of pan-seared branzino in front of Lydia. I've been dreaming of these scallops from Butter since I landed at JFK, but I promised Lydia I would wait to indulge until she arrived. "How was your trip?" I ask, cutting into asparagus between us.

Lydia's hands wring together underneath the table. "Well, actually, I have some news." She waits another second before stretching her hand across the table. A sparkle on her finger practically blinds me under the light.

Holy shit.

I grab her hand and examine the rather large diamond sitting on a very important finger. "Quanti carati?"

"After all these years, I still don't understand you when you speak Italian."

"Sorry! I'm just excited. How many carats?"

"Eight."

"Little blue box?"

"Naturally." Lydia admires her ring under the dim restaurant lights. "It was everything I wanted. He took me to this cliffside restaurant and..." I take an extra large sip of wine. I'm happy for Lydia, really I am, but I can't deny the sinking feeling in the pit of my stomach. Was it jealousy? Regret? No...I don't know. I don't think so. If things had gone to plan, I'd be married with a kid or two and a townhouse on the Upper East Side. But, things never seem to go as planned, do they?

"Sounds perfect," I say quickly, realizing I have yet to comment.

There's sympathy behind her eyes. "You probably don't want to hear about this."

"Of course, I do."

A smile spreads across Lydia's face before an uncomfortable silence falls between us. She pushes food around her plate, tapping the fork along the rim trying to find the right words to say. We haven't talked about this, not really. I haven't talked to much of anyone. I don't want to. I don't—

"Nin, are you okay?"

"I'm fine." A suspicious look. "I am!"

"I just worry about you. You never gave yourself time to get over everything that happened with Lee. You didn't give yourself time to process."

"Listen, Dr. Phil—"

"I'm just saying. I don't think it's a bad idea to take a break."

"I'm too busy, Lyds. I have so much going on, I don't have time." How am I supposed to take a break when I have projects lined up for the next year? I've become one of the most sought-after interior designers. Before I started my own company, I worked at the best firm in Charlotte, North Carolina. I've worked with celebrities, companies, investors, flippers, and everyone in between. And sure, some people only recognize my last name, that's bound to happen, but I have worked hard to build my business from the ground up. I can't just walk away...

But, Lydia is right. I have thrown myself to the wolves,

more than usual.

"Why don't you go talk to someone? Get things off your chest."

"I don't need a shrink, Lydia."

"I'm just saying, you need to do something. You never let yourself go through the motions. It was a serious break-up, Nin. A big life change and you're staying busy to avoid what happened. Four years is a long time to be with someone and then have it end so suddenly." Lydia covers my hand. "Just promise, you'll think about it." She stops me before I can object, "Promise."

"Well," I sigh. "I was thinking about going to the Haven house this year, but I don't know if I want to deal with my family."

"You love Haven!"

I do love Haven, it has always been that...a haven. A small ski town in central Colorado where my family had purchased a vacation home years ago. We used to go to Haven for most summer vacations and the occasional Christmas break when we weren't in Greece or Italy.

"I'm just saying, it's not a bad idea," Lydia pushes further, but I've already let the conversation go. Right now, we should be celebrating the ring on her finger, not my lack of one.

"Okay, tell me more about your trip. I want all the gossip." As Lydia begins to relay the details, I think back to the last time I was in the city. It seems like a lifetime ago, but it had only been a year and one hundred sixty-four days, not that I'm counting.

three

I CAN'T HELP BUT think of the stranger who spilled coffee on me just two weeks ago every time I'm at Java Fountain. That poor romper, it didn't stand a chance. Taking my coffee from Lucy, I almost ask her if she knows anything about him, if he frequents the cafe, what his name is… But, I simply take my iced coffee and make sure to look both ways before stepping off the patio. I don't want to risk losing this dress, another one of my favorites.

My office is located in a two-story brick building on Pearl Avenue in the middle of town square. I picked the location based on the fact it is within a two-minute walk to the cafe. Winchester, South Carolina, is a small town in the northern part of the state, near the Carolina borders. It's considered a bigger suburb of Charlotte, but with the small town charm — somewhere you wanted to raise a family. Most people come from wealthy families, native to the area, but my family moved here in 1992. Daddy didn't want us to grow up in the city, but Mother refused to live somewhere with a population of less than five thousand, so they compromised on Winchester — population 6,020 in 1992, but has grown significantly to closer to thirty-thousand in recent years.

The office is still locked which means Michaela is running

late, shocker. I could lock the door behind me, let her think I'm running late, and give her a good scare when she gets in — maybe next time. I have a lot to do before I leave for Haven next week and not enough time to do it: pull samples for a meeting later today, print off sketches for another, make suggestions on a design Michaela submitted, and review the schematics we've needed for two weeks. And that's just before noon.

I finally sit down at my desk to finish another design now that the morning necessities are finished. Sunlight streams through the two large windows that separate a black accent wall behind my desk. Between the windows, a Monika Luniak painting and a cabinet with intricate hand-carved floral designs holds two bouquets of hydrangeas. Design books, certifications, and photos scatter the shelves of a bookcase along the left wall.

Before I can get started, my phone vibrates across my desk. *Mother.*

I ignore her call. Whatever she has to say can wait until I get to Haven. Almost immediately, it rings again. I send it to voicemail and turn the ringer off. This time, my office phone rings. Without looking, "Yes, Mother?"

"I was starting to think you were ignoring me."

"Kind of the point of a voicemail. I send you there, you leave a message, and I can decide whether to call you back or not."

"Davina Bay."

"Busy."

"Well, I just wanted to make sure you were still coming this year. You never gave me a definite answer. And after your little hiatus, I just—"

"I already told you, I'm coming."

"No need to get snippy. I'm just trying to keep track of everyone's arrival." I roll my eyes. "So, what day will you be arriving?"

"Wednesday."

"Wonderful! You'll arrive the day before Lee."

The stylus in my hand clatters to the floor. I'm sorry, did she just say—

"The Madigans will be arriving Thursday afternoon, just like always. And, I don't want you to make this difficult for them just because you broke up with Lee. They're our friends and they're able to put differences aside, I think you can do the same."

"Have you forgotten *why* I broke up with him?"

Five hundred and twenty-six days. That's how many days it has been since December 17th. The night the universe took all my plans and knocked them off kilter. Christmas time in New York is nothing short of magical. It had been two months since I had managed to get away from the Low Country, but there was no better time.

Lee lived in a high-rise across from Rockefeller Center, the one I had picked because of its location. The one I had picked because he was too "busy" to do it himself. The one I picked because he wanted me to be comfortable when I was in town. I walked through the door of the residential tower and wiped the snow from my boots, declining the doorman when he offered to take my bags. Stepping into the elevator, I greeted the older man already there. "Buonasera, G!"

"Good to see you, Nina. It's been a while."

"Been pretty busy, but I wanted to surprise Lee." I scanned my elevator badge and pressed P4. 'G' was the first neighbor I met when Lee moved in. Lee couldn't have cared less, but I enjoyed getting to know some of the neighbors.

When the doors opened to his floor, G gave my shoulder a brief squeeze. "Good luck with everything, young lady. I know you'll do great things," he said with a wink and the doors closed between us. And for some reason, it felt like a goodbye.

The doors reopened moments later to Penthouse 4. It was

dark and quiet. I checked my watch, too early for Lee to be in bed. And, he wouldn't be out on the town, he had a big work presentation the next day. I shouldered off my long black coat resting it on top of my bags and dusted off my chiffon ruffled shirt. My boots echoed against the oak floors walking further into the darkness. A light flickered from the kitchen. Candles?

Candles, indeed. From the doorway, I saw the evidence scattered across the granite countertops: a bottle of Dom Pérignon, two champagne flutes, and take-out boxes surrounded by candles and rose petals.

A laugh echoed from upstairs. It wasn't his, but I recognized it.

Up the stairs to the master bedroom, whispers filled the air. Just as I threw open the door, another laugh from the bed.

I cleared my throat. Lee popped up from under the covers, his blue eyes looked like they might explode. The gears already turning as he tried to find an excuse. There wasn't one. I wasn't completely shocked. I had suspected it for a while, but he had reassured me nothing was going on — we had been talking about rings just the week before.

Lee chased after me, but I ignored him and slammed my hand on the button closing the elevator doors between us.

"Oh, Davina, you need to let it go. It was years ago! It's time to move on," Mother cuts through the memory. I can practically hear her eyes rolling on the other end of the phone. She has always loved Lee; correction, she has always loved the money Lee's family would bring to the table. When I broke up with him, she was devastated because it meant less chance for the Madigans to join Villa Inc. "You know, I could set you up with that neighbor boy, he has always seemed nice and very interested in you."

"No."

"Well, it could get rather awkward if you show up alone, don't you think?"

"Last time I checked, their last name isn't Villa. So, forgive me if I don't give a fuck how it makes them feel."

"The least you can do is let the neighbor boy come around to ease the awkwardness. We don't want our guests feeling unwelcome."

"Stop trying to pawn me off because you invited my ex-boyfriend to our summer house." There's a heartbeat forming inside my skull. Maybe this isn't a good idea. I wonder how much it would cost to book a last-minute trip to Greece instead.

"They're like family."

"Good thing I'm not dating him anymore, otherwise that would be incest."

"Oh for the love of— Enough. Don't be so dramatic, Davina."

"I need to get back to work."

"Wait! Before you go, I'm going to let Lee and Teagan have your room since you'll be alone. You'll be fine in one of the smaller rooms."

"You're joking," I scoff. Why would I be okay with them taking my room? It's my room. It has been my room since we bought the house. "You know what, I was gonna wait until I got there, make it a surprise. But...I'm bringing someone."

I regret the words the moment they leave my mouth. Why would I say that?

"What's his name?"

"You don't know him."

"Where did you meet?"

"I have to go. Goodbye, Mother." I slump back in my chair with a frustrated sigh. What in the hell was I thinking? There isn't anyone I can bring they wouldn't recognize and call my bluff immediately.

A knock on the door. Michaela stands with a shy smile.

"Well, look who decided to show up."

"I said hi when I got in, but you didn't hear me. Didn't want to bug you while you were in the zone." I vaguely remember hearing her when I was finishing the suggestions on her design. She falls into one of the blue velvet chairs across from me. "Eleanor needs to reschedule tomorrow, she said she could be here Monday."

"I'm thinking you should meet with her instead."

"She is so excited to see you, I wouldn't want to disappoint her." I roll my eyes. Eleanor is a pain in my ass, but she's a good client who brings me a lot of business. I really shouldn't complain, but right now, she just wants to meet for coffee and conversation. I don't have time for coffee and conversation. Between work and now this thing with Mother... "You okay? You're looking a little more stressed than usual."

"Ho appena detto a mia madre che stavo portando un ragazzo a Haven."

"I got something about your mom and Haven, but I have no idea what you just said."

"I just told my mom I was bringing a guy to Haven."

"And who, may I ask, would that be?"

"The guy I've been seeing the last six months."

"You've been seeing someone?" Michaela's voice rises two octaves.

"No!"

"Then, why did you—"

"She invited Lee! And to make it 'less awkward' for him and Teagan, she wants to set me up with the neighbor kid."

"You could always hire someone."

I choke on my coffee. Hire an escort to bring on my family vacation?

"What? People do it in the movies all the time!"

"This isn't a movie, Michaela. This is my life. I can't bring an escort to meet my family."

"I didn't say escort."

"Well, what do you call some random guy hired as my boyfriend for the summer?"

"Why don't you say he got stuck at work? Some guy with a big corporate job, that's believable. I mean, look at your dad. He misses stuff because of work all the time."

And, when Daddy goes asking around and finds out this "boyfriend" doesn't exist... Yeah, I don't think that's a good idea.

"You know tons of guys, why don't you ask one of them?"

"Who do I know, that they don't know, that I could ask?"

"What about your cute neighbor from the condo?"

"Married. Baby on the way."

"Come on, you're Davina Villa! I'm sure you know someone."

I roll my eyes. Yes, I'm Davina Villa, but that has nothing to do with this. "Thanks, but I'll figure this one out on my own." As much as I appreciate her help, this is not Michaela's area of expertise. "Can you call Claire and let her know the samples are ready?"

four

ELIZABETH RUBS THE SCARS on her arms, her mind somewhere far beyond the conversation happening around her. I meet her and Michaela for drinks at Fitz's Bar — my favorite local spot, even before it should have been. "You okay?" I ask, but Elizabeth doesn't hear me. "Elizabeth?"

"Huh?"

"You okay?"

"Yeah, of course. Why do you ask?"

Elizabeth Cain — best friend, and practically my sister. We were born exactly two years and two days apart; our fathers were best friends which led us down the same path. She has always been optimistic, innocent, and somewhat naive, always wanting to see the good in everyone. Her brother, Nate, not so much. Nate was ungrateful, irrational, and conceited. He refused to learn the value of hard work and their father, tired of Nate's reluctance to grow up, decided to cut Nate off seven years ago.

In the fall of her sophomore year, Elizabeth came home from a football game to find her parents laying in pools of blood before her brother turned the knife on her. After a fight with my mother, I drove to the Cain home and found the home consumed by flames. I hardly registered the lifeless

29

body on the front steps. Miraculously, she hadn't suffered any major burns, but she was bruised and bloody from the attack. It didn't take the police long to figure out who had attacked them and where he went. After she was released from the hospital, my family took Elizabeth in.

"I don't know why you went to see him," Michaela says. And if looks could kill… "What? You don't think it was a good idea, either."

"It doesn't matter what I think. If she wants to see Nate, she can."

"Well, it doesn't matter, he still refuses to see me," Elizabeth interrupts us. She has been trying for years to see her brother, to talk to him about what happened. She hoped giving Nate some time would make him want to see her, Elizabeth wants to tell him she forgives him. Something I can't understand. Elizabeth waves her hands, "Enough! Tell me more about this conversation with Brina."

"You told her?" I smack Michaela's arm.

"I was just informing her that you may or may not have a boyfriend," Michaela casually shrugs behind her wine glass.

"Michaela!"

"Come on, spill. Who is it? Who are you taking?" Elizabeth pushes.

I groan, "I'm not taking anyone."

"You're just gonna tell your mom you lied about having a boyfriend to keep your room? That'll go over well," Michaela says and I want nothing more than to smack the smirk from her face. "I just can't believe she invited Lee to begin with."

"I can," Elizabeth disagrees. "Brina has always had a soft spot for him. Did Lee go last year?"

"Karol and Jack did, but he skipped, too," I say.

"I told her to hire someone," Michaela interjects.

"I can't hire someone. They're not stupid, Michaela."

"Well then, I'm all out of ideas."

"Hiring an escort is the only idea you've had!"

"It's not a bad idea," Elizabeth says behind her martini. "I mean, it could be fun in a no strings attached kind of way."

Hiring someone wasn't exactly how I imagined starting my next relationship post-Lee.

"What if we found you someone?" Michaela's eyes light up at the idea.

Oh, no.

"Yes!" Elizabeth practically shouts, earning a few glares from other patrons. "Let us pick someone for you."

"That's a scary thought..."

"I kind of wish Josh and I were going now. I can't wait to see how this plays out." I wish they were going too, it would alleviate some of my stress about this trip.

"Look, I appreciate you guys trying to help, but no. I'll just go alone."

§

Hushed whispers come from the front of the office. Is there someone here? Did Michaela forget to tell me about an appointment? Turning the corner, I see Michaela taking a large paper bag from a man with shaggy brown hair. Josh Davis — Michaela's older brother and Elizabeth's fiancé. Michaela regretted introducing us almost immediately. Josh became the older brother I had always hoped Kai would be and we clicked instantly. Introducing him to Elizabeth, I never imagined they would get together. Actually, they couldn't stand each other when they first met — Josh thought Elizabeth was stuck-up and she thought he was a no-good troublemaker. Oil and water. Until her ex-boyfriend broke her heart in front of the entire Christmas Ball and Josh stepped in...but, that's a story for another time.

Josh and Michaela aren't alone, another man stands with

his back to us. He stares at some of my older designs lining the wall. Before I can get a good look at him, Josh pulls me into a bone-crushing hug. "Short-stack! I was hoping you'd be here."

"Hey Bub, what did Elizabeth make this time?"

"Some pies for an event Mom's hosting tonight."

"And she let you drop them off without sending me one?" I touch my heart, half-offended. "Tell her I'm rescinding my RSVP."

"I think she'd hunt you down and drag you to Savannah anyway."

We laugh because it's true. They're getting married in three months and I better be dead — not dying, just dead — if I don't show up.

My laugh dies as soon as the other man turns around. "What are you doing here?"

"You know each other?" Michaela looks between us.

"He's the guy who spilled coffee on me."

"You're coffee boy?"

"Coffee boy?" Josh asks.

"Nick ran into Nina two weeks ago and spilled coffee all over her."

So, his name is Nick.

"Correction, she ran into me," he interjects. I don't miss the small smile that spreads across his full lips before fading into a smirk.

"Well, allow me to re-introduce you... Nina, this is Nick, our cousin, and apparently the guy who spilled coffee on you the other morning," Josh finally introduces us.

"Are you ready to go?" Nick doesn't try to hide his annoyance. "I need to get back to the shop. Pop has 'em lined up."

"You're such a workaholic," Michaela teases earning, an eye roll from her cousin.

"Make sure you take these to Mom right after work, if not

I'll never hear the end of it," Josh instructs his sister walking towards the front door. Elizabeth would have both of their heads if Jenny didn't get the pies on time. Now that I think about it, why wouldn't Josh take the pies to their mom himself?

"Yeah, yeah. I know. Now go before he throws more coffee on my boss." Nick glares at her before Josh ushers him outside.

"Is your cousin always so friendly?" I ask when they're finally gone.

Michaela turns with an apologetic smile. "I am so sorry, I had no idea."

I shrug. "Has he been here before? He looks very familiar."

"I mean, you did meet at the coffee shop." Always the smartass, Michaela glances into the brown paper bag ignoring my glare. That's not what I meant. "He went to RU. Studied architecture for a while, maybe you had a class with him."

Josh finally pulls onto Pearl Avenue and an idea forms. Maybe her idea wasn't so bad after all — if it was the right person.

five

"I'M SURPRISED, HE AGREED to come," Michaela said walking into my office with a wide smile. She had been more than happy to make the phone call — seemed a little too excited, in my opinion. Confirmation that my chance second meeting with her cousin was, in fact, a setup. "I think his curiosity got the best of him. But, I told him, I wasn't taking no for an answer."

That was two days ago.

That's how I ended up here... Eyes bore into my back from across the patio. I'm waiting for Lucy to finish my coffee while she tells me a story about something that happened on her way into work, but I'm not really listening. My focus remains on trying to calm the butterflies that haven't left my stomach since Michaela told me he had agreed to meet me. "Isn't that the guy you ran into a few weeks ago?" Lucy glances around me at where Nick sits. "Oh my gosh, are you dating now?"

"No."

"Well, I'm happy to be of assistance in your meet cute."

"We're not dating!"

"Not yet," she singsongs.

"Go back to your coffee, Luce."

Taking a deep breath, I turn to face him for the first time

34

since arriving. As I suspected, he's staring right at me. His eyes hidden behind a pair of sunglasses, but I can feel the intensity. Deep breath. This is nothing. Just a friendly conversation.

In.

Out.

I chew on the end of my straw sitting across from him and we sit in silence for a few moments before, "Look, I need to get back to the shop. So, you gonna tell me what this is about?"

Harsh.

"Yeah, of course. Sorry." Deep breath. "You are going to think this is crazy. I mean, it is…" He sits up a little straighter, interest peaked. "Normally, I wouldn't do this. I don't like doing this sort of thing, asking for help, but I need a huge favor. I mean, it's big." I chew on my bottom lip, considering my words. I wish he would take those damn sunglasses off. "I need a boyfriend."

"Not sure what that has to do with me."

"A fake boyfriend." I wait for some kind of reaction, but he remains stoic. Baiting me. "Someone I can bring on vacation to get my mother off my back. I leave Wednesday. I'd pay you, whatever you want." I visibly cringe at my own words. "Obviously, I will pay for all the expenses while you're there. But, I can't do this alone. My ex is going to be there and I refuse to let my mother set me up with someone. And, she will if I don't bring my 'new boyfriend' as promised."

Still nothing.

"I know this is weird, really weird. But, I can't take anyone my family would know. They'll see right through it. Michaela suggested hiring someone. When you came into the office the other day, everything just seemed to fall into place."

"Even after I spilled coffee on you?"

"So, you admit it?"

Nick's lips twitch, but he restrains the smile. "You're insane." He leans forward on his elbows. "Okay, let me get this straight. You want to pay some guy, me apparently, to be your boyfriend because your mom invited your ex on vacation?"

I squirm under his stare. "I'm glad you find this amusing."

"Forgive me, but it's not every day the Princess needs help from the peasant boy."

"Princess?" I scoff. "You know nothing about me."

"Oh, but I do. You and every girl just like you." Nick stands from the table ready to leave. Before I can say anything, he continues, "I'm not an escort and I wouldn't feel comfortable lying to your family."

"You don't know my mother."

"Guess I never will."

"But, this could help your family! It could pay for your brother's school or give you and your dad a break from the garage."

That stops him.

The family card wasn't something I wanted to play, but Nick was my one shot at making this work. According to Michaela, Jimmy Davis is your typical blue-collar family man. Still lives in the same house he grew up in — a one-story, brick ranch home with a big magnolia tree in the front yard. His dad ran an auto body shop out of the small garage next door. When Jimmy took over, he renovated the garage to handle more than one car at a time. Jimmy was the ultimate role model, but he always wanted more for his boys. Wanted them to do the things he couldn't, live the life he couldn't.

Jimmy hates that Nick let his degree at Rosecliffe slip through his fingers, but Michaela said Nick was content to work in the garage if it took the stress off his father's shoulders. The younger Davis brother, Alex, is enrolled in the law program at Boston College. That's why Jimmy works so much, to help his son pay tuition to avoid a lifetime repayment of loans.

Nick considers his next words and when he finally responds, his words are clipped, "Sorry, Princess, but I'm not your Prince Charming."

six

I SHADE MY EYES stepping out of the plane, a faint bead of sweat forms on my hairline. Summer in the low country is not for the weary. I pull my bottom lip between my teeth containing a laugh when Nick practically jumps out of his skin. He hadn't been expecting to see Andrew standing there. Andrew Collins — Villa family pilot for as long as I can remember, he's more like an uncle than someone on payroll. I've always told him to call me just Nina, but he refuses. Mother would never allow it, but that doesn't stop me from trying. Andrew hands the cabbie money for the fare and retrieves Nick's bags from the trunk. "Please, Mr. Davis, it's no trouble," Andrew says when Nick tries to stop him. "Go ahead and get settled, we'll be leaving shortly." He hands the suitcase to Phillip by the luggage compartment. Phillip Gable — Villa family pilot in training for the last three years.

"Thanks, Andrew," I say when he passes by me.

"He seems nice," he smirks. What does that mean? Andrew winks before disappearing into the plane to finish preparing for departure.

"Do you ever dress like a normal person?" Nick asks climbing the stairs.

What is that supposed to mean? I am dressed like a normal

person. Navy polka-dot skirt, cream satin tank top, booties... What's wrong with that? When I look up, he's there. Dressed in his normal jeans and a T-shirt. Mere inches from me. No sunglasses, his warm, whiskey-colored orbs stare back at me.

"Didn't think you were coming."

"I wasn't." The slightest smirk tugs on his lips.

Great, this is going to be...fun. Why did I think this was a good idea again?

"Andrew seems nice."

"He said the same thing about you."

Phillip bumps into Nick's shoulder to enter the plane before politely excusing himself to move past me. Nick glares after the younger pilot before looking at me. What does he want me to do?

I turn into the plane, "Andrew?"

"Just waiting for clearance, Miss Villa. Once we get up, should be a pretty quick flight." I'm almost back to my seat when I hear Andrew give Nick some advice, "Don't worry too much. They're actually very nice. Her mother, Brina, can be a little rough 'round the edges, but Nina can handle her. You'll be fine as long as you keep your story straight." Andrew closes the entry door before he closes the cockpit door leaving just me and Nick in the main cabin.

My attention remains on the email in front of me when he finally strolls inside, but I don't miss the way he pauses briefly taking everything in. His eyes roam every inch of the plane, you'd think he's never seen one before. Michaela did say his family rarely takes vacations, maybe he hasn't ever been on plane a before. Well, here's to hoping he doesn't have a fear of flying we're about to discover. The thought tugs at the corner of my lips just before I hit send and we're racing down the runway.

So far, no new fears of flying have been unlocked. Peaking over my screen, I wait for any kind of reaction when the wheels lock in place...Nothing.

When we reach an appropriate altitude, Nick peels himself out of his chair and into the one across from me. I expect him to say something, but he remains silent. Without looking, I motion behind me to the kitchen. "You can have whatever you want. It's all back there."

"Seems like you have just about everything in here."

"Mother wouldn't have it any other way."

"Whatcha doin' over there?"

"Working."

"Do you want—"

"No." I don't even notice his hand reaching across the table until he has already closed my laptop. "What the hell?" A glare. "Look, you made it very clear you had no intentions of helping me, so I'm not sure why you're here."

"The money."

A smile tugs at my lips. "Honest, I like it."

"I like to keep it real."

"Hopefully, not too real."

"I promise not to expose you too early."

"Buono." I open my laptop, "Now, can I get back to work?"

"Actually," Nick closes the laptop again. "I was thinking we should figure out what's going on between us."

§

I'm trying to ignore the constant feeling of someone watching me as we climb the private drive through thick forest. My focus has been on my phone from the moment we touched the ground in Colorado. The day I go out of town is the day everything wants to go to shit on one of our job sites. So yes, I've been on my phone trying to help Michaela resolve the issues. I'm just hoping the entire trip isn't like this. I did warn Nick, I may have some work to attend to, but I'm sure he thinks it's just an excuse to avoid him when we're away from everyone. Then again, he probably doesn't care.

On the plane, we set the boundaries for our arrangement — holding hands and small touches in obvious areas are okay; kisses on the cheek are acceptable, but not on the lips; and we met at Java Fountain, the only thing about this whole arrangement that wasn't a lie. Since we will be sharing a room, with only one bed, he will sleep on the floor. "We have plenty of pillows and blankets, you'll be fine," I assured him. And the final term? He should in no way feel obligated to entertain me when behind closed doors. I don't care what he does when we're alone. "Just don't give us away."

After what felt like hours to climb the mountain, the car stops in front of the house. Scratch that... It's more like a mansion. Secluded and surrounded by acres of untouched land, no sign of anyone for miles. The house towers over us and I smile stepping out of the door held by Phillip. I've missed this place. I almost forgot how grand it is... Large windows litter the four-story home. Brown roofing contrasts white stucco. Pale logs accent the home making the modern design not seem out of place in the mountains. The garage and first two stories are built into the earth. Rocky steps on one side lead from the driveway to a patio and eventually a rooftop. Another leads further into the mountain, curving into an open door, a small garden along the way.

"È la mia bambina?" A deep voice walks down the front steps.

"Daddy!" I jump into his arms. Alaric Villa — patriarch of the Villa family and mastermind behind Villa Incorporated. A barrel-chested man, Daddy stands well over six feet tall. "Mi sei mancato!"

"I missed you too, Piccola. And, I see you brought company."

A blush creeps into my cheeks before turning to find Nick helping Andrew pull our bags from the car. Andrew whispers something earning a chuckle from both men. "We'll take it from here, Mr. Davis," Andrew says as I approach. "You have a show to do."

"Ready?" I whisper.

"Do I have a choice?" A warmth spreads through my fingers when he takes my hand. It's probably just his nerves making his hands feel warm. Curious green eyes carefully watch from the front steps. "Daddy, this is Nick…Nick, this is my dad, Alaric Villa."

"Ric is fine. It's nice to meet you, Nick."

"It's nice to meet you, sir," Nick stammers. He slips his free arm around my waist and uses the other to shake Daddy's hand.

"Don't be nervous, Nick." Daddy clamps down on his shoulder. "Save that for her mother." A booming laugh echoes as he pushes Nick towards the door.

Daddy leads us past a mirage of hallways and bedrooms. Everything looks the same as it did two years ago. Stepping over the threshold of the third floor, I'm greeted by one of my favorite parts of the whole house: a wall of windows showcasing unobstructed views of the luscious green landscape surrounding the house. Breathtaking. Nick's eyes grow wide at the sight.

"Pretty cool, huh?" I ask.

"It's nice to not be the only outsider for a change," a dirty blonde greets us. Eileen Eberly — my brother's girlfriend and the reason we have any sort of relationship. "I'm Eileen. I was surprised when Brina said Nin was bringing someone. She's never mentioned you before." Eileen glances at me, "How could you not tell me about *this*?"

"Hands off, Lina." I lean into Nick's side and as if acting by instinct, he wraps his arm around me. "I'm not into sharing anymore."

I hear her before I see her. And, I feel myself grow rigid

against Nick. I hope he doesn't think he did something wrong. No, this has nothing to do with him and everything to do with the woman walking inside from the kitchen patio. I haven't seen my mother in almost a year and I can't say I'm upset about it. Seeing her... I'm instantly reminded to stand up taller, straighter. Don't talk too loud. Don't smile so big.

Brina Villa — matriarch of the Villa family. Per usual, she is extremely overdressed for the mountains in a stark white pantsuit and high heels. Her pin-straight blonde hair held by a clip. Her face fully painted, she still doesn't look a day over thirty even though she's almost 50. She holds an empty martini glass and uses her teeth to slide olives from a plastic sword. "Davina. You're finally here!" An awkward pause where there should be a mother-daughter embrace, but we don't move. Her stare matches the icy color of her eyes when she turns her attention to Nick, "You must be Nicholas."

"Just Nick is fine. It's nice to meet you, Mrs. Villa."

"Davina, how on Earth could you keep such a handsome young man a secret?"

"Bri," Daddy warns behind us.

"I was sparing him the torture." I roll my eyes.

"Nina."

Mother and I share a look, but don't continue. Instead, she tears Nick from me and loops her arm through his. "Come, I'll show you around. Get you acquainted with the house."

"Mother, please. It's been a long day, we can do this later."

"Oh, Davina, he doesn't mind. Do you, Nicholas?" Nick hesitates. Stuck between not wanting to be left alone with my mother just yet and wanting to make a good impression. "See, he's fine." She leads him towards the separate staircase leading to the fourth floor, the master bedroom. Before they're gone, she throws a smirk over her shoulder to me.

"Welcome to the family," Eileen whispers once they've disappeared.

seven

"WHERE'S YOUR BOYFRIEND?" MY brother asks when I join him and Eileen in the kitchen. Kai Villa — my older brother and my mother's pride and joy, to anyone who knows our family, it's obvious she favors him over me. We never got along growing up and we're still trying to navigate the brother-sister thing. We have only one thing in common: being a workaholic. Kai finally pulled himself away from some last-minute work twenty minutes ago. Daddy has been putting more on his plate lately — I think he wants to start the transition to Kai sooner than expected. Kai is dressed in gray slacks and a blue button-up, his dark brown hair combed back. He looks like he is about to walk into the boardroom at any moment. I can't deny Kai is handsome, but handsome in a men's aftershave commercial kind of way.

"Mother has been holding him hostage for over an hour," I say, taking the glass of red wine Eileen offers.

"If he survives this trip, you should marry him." I roll my eyes. "If he can survive Mom for this long, you better not—"

"Nick!" Eileen interrupts as Nick walks in from the patio. "How was tour al la Brina?"

"It was…great."

I laugh at his hesitation.

44

"Don't worry, she can be a little much, but you'll get used to Mom." Kai extends his hand, "I'm Kai Villa, pleasure."

Eileen offers Nick a glass of wine, but he declines, "I'm more of a beer man."

"Dad keeps some in the garage, come with me."

"He seems nice," Eileen says when Nick and Kai are gone.

"I guess," I shrug and count plates pulling them from the cabinet. I hand part of the stack to Eileen to set the table for dinner. I will never hear the end of it from Diana, the personal chef Mother always hires, but I enjoy doing small things to help out.

"He handles your mom well, that's a huge plus."

"A treasured skill, for sure."

"Davina, what are you doing?" Mother's shrill voice interrupts our laughter. Mortified at the sight, she slams the patio door and marches into the dining room. "Stop this. The help will be here soon." She slaps my hand. One of the navy blue plates clatters against the black tabletop before falling and breaking into three pieces on the floor. "Now look what you've done!"

"What I've done?"

"You just broke that plate. How could you be so careless?"

"Sai una cosa—"

"Nin," Eileen stops me. I threaten to say more, but she gives me a warning glance. A classic Brina-Nina fight is the last thing anyone needs on the first night in town.

"I can't believe this. Stronzata," I huff before leaving them upstairs to find a quiet place to cool down.

§

"Diana says dinner will be ready soon."

I look up from my book to see Nick in the doorway, hands deep in his pockets. After the altercation with Mother, I needed to be alone. Away from the questions I was sure to face from Kai when he found out what had happened. I decided the best way to cool down was to sit on my bedroom balcony and finish my book. "Thanks, I'll be up in a few."

I turn back to my worn copy of *The Shining* by Stephen King with no sign of moving any time soon, but Nick still stands in the doorway unsure of what to do.

"Are you okay?"

"Bene," I say without looking.

"What does that mean?"

I crack a smile. "It means, fine or good. Sorry, sometimes my Italian slips. I don't even notice. I'll try to refrain while you're here."

"Italian?"

"My grandpa was from Italy, he taught my dad, Daddy and Nonna taught me."

Nick turns the new information over in his mind. "Eileen said something happened with your mom. Is everything okay?"

"Nothing out of the ordinary." I can tell he wants to ask more, but he doesn't push. "Guess we better go, Diana won't be happy if I miss dinner on the first night." I shove my bookmark inside and leave the book on the side table, glasses on top of it. "Thanks for checking on me."

eight

ANY SIGN OF THE earlier altercation gone. A delicious scent flows from the kitchen where a middle-aged woman dressed in a chef's coat plates dinner. Diana Edwards — private chef and by far one of my favorite things about Haven. The first summer Diana worked for us she almost quit. Mother kept referring to her as the help and always had a comment about the menu or the food or the wine... It finally boiled over one day and Diana told Mother exactly how she felt and walked out in a huff. Daddy managed to get an apology out of Mother and convinced Diana to come back. Now, it's normal for the two of them to take small jabs at one another. Working for my mother requires a thick skin, but the tolerance of those who make it doesn't go unnoticed or unappreciated — Daddy pays them a little extra on the side.

Diana quietly scolds me for pulling out a bottle from the wine fridge built into the island. "Wouldn't want to upset your mother again, would we?" She winks.

"Oh no, wouldn't want that." I fill a glass with Chardonnay and return to join the group in the dining room.

The dining room is situated in an open space between the kitchen and living room on the third floor, separated from the kitchen by a knee wall. The back wall painted a faded earthy

47

green, a stark contrast to the neutral colors coating the rest of the floor. Atop a white buffet cabinet, a large gold-framed mirror leans against the wall. A pale oak table runs the length of the room — six rattan chairs on either side and two beige armchairs on the ends.

"Place cards?" Indeed, around the table, small cards with our names written in precise calligraphy designate our places at the table. "Seriamente, Mother?"

"I thought they would be a nice touch, that way Nick knows where he can sit," Mother shrugs.

"This isn't one of your fancy, bullshit dinners, it's family dinner. He can sit anywhere he wants."

"Nina," Daddy warns. "Drop it."

I flick the card to the middle of the table. "I don't think he meant literally," Nick whispers, pulling my chair out. A smirk tugs at the corner of my lips from behind the glass.

"So, Nick, tell us about yourself," Daddy says as Diana sets a plate in front of him. Herb-crusted lamb chops with mashed potatoes and a vegetable medley. For dessert, we'll have New York Style Cheesecake with fruit, Daddy's favorite.

"Well, there isn't much to tell. I grew up in Bridgeport, my family owns a garage out there," Nick says following my lead cutting into the lamb. I wonder if he's ever had lamb before? I can only assume not as he takes a timid bite testing the waters.

"Do they do well?" Mother asks jumping right to the important stuff.

"It pays the bills. My brother and I used to help out when we were younger, but I can't help as much as I would like to with work."

"Where did you go to school?" Daddy cuts her off from asking more about finances.

"RU."

"Oh?" Mother glares at me. "You know, Nina and Lee attended Rosecliffe. Is that where you two met?"

Nick doesn't respond right away, he slowly cuts a piece from lamb chop and chews on the inside of his cheek. Did he already forget what we talked about on the plane? We didn't meet at Rosecliffe. A brief tug at the corner of his lips catches my attention, but the others miss it. "Nope, we must have run in different circles," he finally says and takes a bigger bite of the lamb.

Mother spent the rest of dinner gushing about her latest finds in an estate sale in Napa last week. She has recently gotten into antiquing, but it's just a phase, something for her to spend money on. She goes to auctions and swoops things out from under people just because she can. Then turns around and sells them back to the same person for double the price. Sometimes, not often, but sometimes she keeps them and finds a place for them in one of the family homes. Only if she really likes the piece, though. It's obvious Daddy is not a fan of her newest activity, but it keeps my mother busy and out of his hair, so he doesn't complain too much.

§

The living room is a mixture of whites and grays. White walls match the rest of the house. Gold pillows stand out against the light gray fabric of the couch. A marble coffee table separates the couch from two rattan chairs, two white stools sit on either side and a white rug covers the wood floor. An artificial succulent and two black covered coffee table books rest atop the table. The rooms look as if they've been taken straight from a home and garden magazine — staged and unlivable.

Eileen and I sit on the couch discussing my latest trip to New York. She wants to know every detail, especially if I ran into a certain someone or someones. Daddy sips whiskey from one of the rattan chairs across from us vaguely interested in the conversation himself. But, he pretends to be scrolling through a news article on his phone. Nick is about to join him when Kai beckons from the balcony door.

"He's cute, Nin," Eileen grabs my attention. I hadn't even noticed I was staring at him through the window. "Where have you been hiding him?"

"I just wanted to have him to myself for a bit."

Kai looks over his shoulder and gives me a small smile through the window. I wonder what they're talking about. I'm sure he's apologizing for our mother probing into Nick's family financials at dinner. That's just who she is, always has been. They laugh at something Nick says — that's a good sign. I can live with Mother not liking him as long as Daddy and Kai do. Their laughter is cut short when Mother rips open the balcony door. "Boys, I'm so glad you're bonding, but you should wait for Lee. Don't you think?"

"We're good." Kai rolls his eyes. No one misses the tight smile that pulls over Mother's lips when Kai doesn't comply. She hates it. Hates that he doesn't jump to do what she wants anymore. Kai refuses to look at her, his eyes trained on the sunset. Nick looks between them, unsure what to do.

Finally, she says, "Well, won't you come in? The rest of us would like to get to know Nick a little better, too."

Kai downs the rest of his whiskey before he finally follows Mother's orders. She smiles brightly before taking Nick's arm leading him back inside.

nine

MY ROOM IS OPEN and airy, it's one of the larger rooms just behind the master bedroom which encompasses the entire fourth floor. A large picture window overlooks a balcony with views of the surrounding mountains. A warm, earthy pinkish-brown color coats the walls — in-between a dark blush and muted terracotta shade. White sheets and comforter cover the bed, with a cream knitted throw blanket and decorative pillows matching the walls. The TV hangs on the wall above a white double dresser with intricate hand-carved floral motifs. In the corner opposite the balcony door, a solid wood accent chair with white cushions. The closet and bathroom on the left side of the room, and a private laundry room on the right. This room holds a certain level of warmth the rest of the house lacks.

Rays of morning sunlight filter through off-white curtains casting a soft glow on the wall and a gentle breeze carries the scent of morning dew through the open balcony door. With my second cup of coffee, I step around the sleeping landmine on a pallet of blankets and pillows. A sliver of sunlight sneaks through straight on his face, I adjust the curtain if only to give myself a few more minutes alone. A glance at the clock reads 6:55 A.M.

It seems like mere seconds between when I sit down and he emerges from the room. The sound of feet padding across the tile shoots a twinge of familiarity through me. The first time Lee came to Haven as my boyfriend, he had woken up each morning and greeted me with a kiss before starting his day. That didn't last long. He began staying in bed longer, leaving me alone most of the day. There were plenty of days I wouldn't see him until dinner.

I don't dare steal my attention away from my book when I feel him stare. I lazily trace the words in my lap. Finally, I look up to meet his stare and his eyes grow wide realizing he's been caught. Without a word, he turns away to look at the structure of the balcony — walls mostly made of stucco, but the far left side made entirely of glass, like the living room. It is identical to the balcony of Kai and Eileen's room on the other side of the house, but their view is blocked by fir trees. Hands run across the metal top of the banister, examining the way everything fits together — how the unnatural meets the natural in the middle of the woods.

I finally join him. "Morning."

"What no silk set?" He motions towards my choice of pajamas — an oversized RU sweater and shorts. "You strike me as a silk set kind of girl. You know, the ones who like to wake up looking like they just walked off the runway. Can't have people thinking you don't look made up all the time or anything."

"Quite the morning person, aren't you?"

"Normally, yes. But, normally I'd be waking up in a bed."

"What do you want? An air mattress? How am I supposed to do that without them hearing it every night?"

"Sounds like a you problem." Nick retreats inside slamming the bathroom door.

Lifting my mug to my lips, I groan when the cold liquid touches my tongue. Dumping it over the edge of the balcony,

I make a mental note not to talk to Nick first thing in the morning. Despite what he says, I disagree that he has ever been a morning person.

§

"Those are for later!" Eileen smacks my hand away from the freshly baked blueberry muffins, but I'm able to snag one.

"But they're fresh, I can't help myself." I pick a piece of the muffin and stick it in my mouth with a smirk. "It's a compliment, Lina. You're just such a good cook, I don't want to wait."

Eileen rolls her eyes and sticks another tray of muffin batter into the oven. "Plans today?"

"I should probably give Nick the fifty-cent tour."

"Do not take him to Sopris."

"It's not *that* bad." Eileen's glare reminds me of the last time I dragged her to the mountain. While it's one of my favorite trails, it is not for the weary and has been known to be difficult even for experienced hikers. "Okay, okay. You're right, it can be a little difficult if you're not used to it." I pop another piece of muffin in my mouth. "So, when does…" But, my words falter, the question stuck in my throat when I see Nick step up to the third floor. His hair still damp from the shower, I find myself wondering what it would feel like to run my fingers through the dark brown curls. The sleeves of his black T-shirt showcase the strength of his biceps. Is that from working out or does that come from working on cars? His blue jeans hug the shape of his lower half and —

"Mornin," Nick says, joining us in the kitchen. My attention quickly turns to the muffin in my hands.

"Good morning, Nick," Eileen says with a smirk. "What were you saying, Nin?" She's not stupid, she knows what caused the sudden halt in my question.

"Hmm?" I look up from my hands. "Oh, I was just wondering if you knew what time the shit show began?"

Nick chuckles from the coffee maker.

"Sometime this afternoon. Wasn't really listening when your mom told me, I was too focused on your super secret boyfriend."

"We just wanted to keep things quiet for a bit." Nick wraps his free arm around my waist. His touch hot as his thumb rubs a bit of exposed skin on my side. We exchange a small smile before he turns back to Eileen, but I'm still staring at him. There's a small dimple — of course he has a fucking dimple — in his left cheek when he smiles I never noticed and it's the cutest thing I've seen. "We're still getting to know each other."

"You know, Kai and I kept it on the DL for about four months before he told the fam."

"Lina!" I can't help the outburst. "You never told me that."

Eileen shrugs, "We all have our secrets."

"Apparently." I untangle from Nick to refill my coffee. "I'm going to join Daddy outside." It wasn't an invitation and I'm thankful when Nick opts to stay in the kitchen with Eileen.

Every morning Daddy drives into town to get a copy of the newspaper and a cup of coffee from Sal at the gas station. When I was younger, I used to go with him before we'd come home and eat breakfast together on the living room balcony. I'm not sure when, but eventually, I stopped going for those morning rides and started enjoying mornings on my own balcony.

"Good morning, Daddy," I join him outside.

"Buongiorno, piccola." He looks up from the newspaper, an article about some proposal for a new building downtown — a.k.a. the urbanization of our small town. It'll never pass. Haven isn't exactly a small town, but it's not a big city, and the people here like it that way. "You're in a better mood this morning." I mumble an agreement and he folds his newspaper giving me his undivided attention. "Are you doing okay?"

"Of course, why do you ask?"

"Well, for starters you didn't even tell me you were dating again. Imagine my shock when your mother told me you were bringing someone. And not just anyone, the guy you've been dating."

"Daddy..."

"Look, you don't have to tell me every little detail, but a heads-up would be nice."

"I'm sorry, but after Lee—"

"I told your mother inviting them was a bad idea, but you know how she is." Daddy offers a sympathetic smile. He does his best to manage Mother, but he can only do so much. "If it was up to me, we'd never see that boy again."

"I'm sure we know someone who can make that happen."

"I plead the fifth," Daddy laughs. Standing from his chair, he presses a kiss to the top of my head putting an end to our conversation. Knowing Daddy, he's about to lock himself in the office and put in a few hours of work before the Madigans show up. It's not unusual for him to sneak away and handle some business while on vacation. It was something Kai and I knew better than to question growing up. "Good morning, Nick," he says, opening the door.

"Morning sir." Nick grimaces when Daddy clamps a hand down on his shoulder.

"Relax, boy! You're stiff as a log. You sleep on the floor or something?"

"Or something," Nick mumbles, earning a warning glare from me.

"Well, if you're looking for a place to unwind, this is it." He turns to me, "Go easy on your mom, Nin. She's happy you're here."

"That's why she invited the Madigans, right?" I pop the final piece of muffin into my mouth.

"Have fun today, Nick. But, don't let her take you out on those trails, wouldn't want to run you off just yet." Daddy shares a smile with Nick before going inside.

"You are pretty stiff," I say when Nick sits in the chair.

"So are you."

I roll my eyes over my mug. "You don't know me. I am not—"

"Daddy's girl, gets everything she wants, just say the word and it's yours. Hell, you were probably handed Rosecliffe on a silver platter."

"I was not." Nick raises a suspicious brow. If I had a penny for every time someone accused me of buying my way into college, I'd double my net worth. "I did well in school. Really well. Everyone is so surprised by that... Now, don't get me wrong, I liked to have a good time and I went to my fair share of parties. And sure, the life comes with some perks, but I don't live off my family name. I've worked for what I have."

"That doesn't mean—"

"My dad did not buy my way into school."

"He didn't pay for it?"

"Of course, he paid for it, that doesn't mean he bought my acceptance letter." My tone is clipped. "I learned how to balance work and pleasure."

"Whatever you say, Dee."

"Dee?"

"Yeah, thought I should come up with a nickname for you. Honey and Dear just sounded too synthetic, and it's too early for baby. So, I thought why not call you Dee."

Dee? That's a new one.

"Short for Davina?" He nods and a smile spreads across my lips, I kind of like it.

"I can go with babe if you want." He tossed the last piece of his own muffin in his mouth. "What's on the agenda today, *babe*?"

"Let's just stick with Dee, okay Fossette?"

"Fossette?"

I just smile.

"Whatever you say, *Dee*."

ten

"OH, YOU MUST MEET Nicholas!" I hear my mother as we walk through the front door. The Madigans must be here. I touch Nick's arm getting his attention and hold my finger up to my lips. I'm not ready to face our guests just yet. Despite our attempt to go unnoticed, we've already been discovered. As we reach the second floor, Mother calls down the stairs. I ignore her continuing down the hallway to my bedroom, but Nick is stuck between playing the good boyfriend to my family versus me.

"What are you doing?" I hiss when he begins walking up the stairs. "If we go like this, she will murder us in our sleep." We're covered in sweat and dirt from the trail. Not Sopris. No, I promised I wouldn't take him there unless he asked. But, I was pleasantly surprised at how easy conversation came to us on the trail.

"But isn't your favorite pastime pissing her off?"

My eyes widen when my laugh echoes through the awaiting silence. Shit. I didn't mean to laugh so loud. Now we have no choice, we have to go upstairs. Mother will be furious if we don't.

"C'mon," Nick reaches his hand out to me. "I'll be right there with you."

With a heavy sigh, I take it.

§

It's obvious Mother is biting her tongue. Her murderous gaze zeroed in as we reach the third floor. "Oh good, you're here! Come, come." She ushers us into the living room where two of our guests await us. Lee Madigan — my ex-boyfriend, financial analyst, and sole heir to the Madigan family fortune. He looks like he just walked out of a frat house, the Vineyard Vines plaid button down and matching pink shorts nauseating. His blonde hair doesn't match the thick, dark beard growing on his face — was he still dyeing his hair? I can't remember it being so blonde. But, the raven-haired girl beside him looks exactly the same. Short dress. Full makeup. No curves. Black hair hanging just past her shoulders. Teagan Kennedy — former best friend, college dropout, and professional nuisance.

Nick takes a small step in front of me, shielding me from Lee's roaming eyes and I squeeze his arm in thanks.

"Lee, this is Nicholas, Davina's new friend." Mother introduces them, looping her arm with Lee just as she had done with Nick yesterday.

"Lee Madigan," he extends his free hand, but Nick doesn't reciprocate it. Without missing a step, Lee turns his attention back to me. "It's good to see you, Nin."

"Oh, Davina! It's so nice to see you." Teagan pushes Nick aside, embracing me tightly, but I push her away. "Oh wow, you smell awful."

"We just came back from the trail," Nick gains her attention.

"Oh," she purrs and grips his bicep.

The action stirs something inside me. Jealousy? Wait — am I jealous? No, I can't be jealous.

"Brina said Nina brought a friend, but she didn't say how handsome you were. Where in the world did she find you?"

"Enough, Teagan. If you want a man to grope, look behind you," Kai says when he follows Eileen into the kitchen from the patio.

"Kai, don't be rude! Teagan was just being friendly." Mother smiles apologetically at Teagan who retreats to Lee's side.

"My mistake, I must be thinking of a different Teagan. The one who slept with Lee for three years behind her best friend's back. You're right, this Teagan is very friendly."

Teagan rips her hand from Lee storming off to the corner guest room. At the same time, Mother huffs off to join Daddy and the Madigans on the patio.

Nick stops Lee when he tries to approach me, "I think it's best if you don't."

Lee ignores him. "Nina, come on, can't we talk? I don't want this to be weird. I mean, when did you start dating again?"

"It's not any of your business, is it, James?"

"James? So, we're on a first-name basis now?" I don't respond. "Let's talk about this, Davina. Like adults."

"I'm good. This was supposed to be my vacation and I refuse to let you ruin it."

"I suggest you take the hint. Stay in your space and we'll stay in ours." I grip Nick's arm a little tighter as he sets the boundaries.

Lee continues to stare at me. I don't think this was how he imagined things going. His eyes never leave me as Nick wraps around me. Holding me, protecting me...from him.

"And, I think that's your cue," Eileen says when Teagan calls from the bedroom.

§

The only light comes from the fire at my feet, I stare out into the dark, the wilderness calling to me... *Breathe.*

And I do. For the first time in hours, I can breathe. The

fresh mountain air dances in my lungs, counting to three as I exhale.

To say I was shocked when we came up from dinner would be an understatement. Actually, I wasn't that shocked. Nothing surprises me when it comes to Mother anymore. Where there had once been an eight-person dining room sat a brand new ten-person table she had ordered to accommodate all her guests. Mother wanted to make sure everyone knew she could drop that large amount of money within a moments notice.

After another Diana prepared dinner, the group moved to the living room to enjoy cocktails and the evening breeze from the open balcony doors. I kept my distance sipping wine from nearby waiting for the right time to sneak away. Mother made sure to put us in the hot seat again, but the topic soon switched to one of Karol Madigan's party stories we've heard a million times. When it seemed like everyone was totally engrossed by the slightest change of detail, I took the opportunity to run.

Footsteps falter just before the final step up to the rooftop. I smile to myself, to the wilderness… I wonder if he truly knows what he's gotten himself into by joining me this summer. I don't know why I thought this was a good idea. How am I supposed to explain to my family that we simply broke up at the end of the summer? What explanation can I provide that will suffice when we're supposed to appear picture-perfect? We've been under a microscope since we arrived. One wrong move and—

"You okay?" He stands next to the couch now.

"You didn't have to come up here."

"Wanted to make sure you were okay." Nick sets the wine bottle I'd been drinking from earlier next to my feet on the edge of the fire pit.

"Peachy." I finish the small amount of wine in my glass and we reach for the wine bottle at the same time. A familiar warmth spreads through my fingers when they brush his. The fire dances in the reflection of his eyes when I meet his gaze. "I can pour my own wine," I say, but don't fight when he takes the bottle and empties it into my glass. "I'm not a damsel in distress."

He laughs and I can't help but smile, "You really are something else, you know?" His arm drapes around my shoulders to pull me close. "Not a damsel in distress, yet you needed someone to come and save you on this trip?"

"Shh! They'll hear you."

"Oh, come on, Nina. You could've done this."

"And listen to my mother tell me how pathetic I am? No thanks. I get enough of that without being here. Besides, I really didn't want Lee and Teagan sleeping in my room. That would be...weird."

He stares a moment too long, but I pretend not to notice. Clearing his throat, he tries to change the conversation. "He still seems into you."

"Lee?" I scoff. "I'll never do that again."

"Sure?"

"Oh, absolutely."

"Well, your mom seems to *really* like him."

"It's the money." I swish the red liquid in my glass. "She and Karol have been planning our wedding for as long as I can remember. When we finally got together...it was the first time I'd ever seen my mother take remote interest in me." My eyes close and I take a deep breath. When they reopen, they're wet, but I blink it away. "It was destined, the Villas and the Madigans...And, I ruined it all."

"She knows he cheated on you, right?"

"If my dad can forgive her, I should be able to do the same." I don't hide my smirk as he slowly starts to realize what I just said. "Every family has their secrets, Nick. From the outside, I'm sure we look perfect. She wouldn't have it any other way. But, if there is one thing you'll learn...Brina Villa only cares about two things: money and my brother. And, I always seem to get in the way of both."

"Have you ever told her how you feel?"

"My mother knows exactly how I feel. I've never tried to hide it."

Nick treads carefully as he digs deeper into the secrets of the Villa family. Of Nina Villa. Secrets people would pay for, have paid for.

"If it was my mom—"

"Well, it's not your mom. And, it's not any of your business." I finish my wine. "Look, I am not paying you to be my shrink. So, stay out of it." Without another word, I leave.

eleven

"**WHAT HAS YOU SO** tired?" Eileen wiggles her eyebrows as we leave the yoga studio. We had gotten up early to enjoy a girls day — breakfast, shopping, and yoga.

"Not what you're thinking." I suppress another yawn walking down Park Avenue where we parked earlier this morning. I tossed and turned most of the night, finally giving up on sleep around three in the morning. I resorted to working on a sketch that has been stuck in my mind for months — my dream office in New York City. Before my alarm could go off, I turned it off and quietly got ready. I didn't bother leaving a note for Nick, I told him the night before he would have to fend for himself for a few hours. I just hoped he wouldn't slip up anymore.

Two days ago, he had managed to confuse everyone when he asked where I had gone on a Sunday morning. I left him a note...

Back @ 12:30... don't get in trouble without me. - N

But, it wasn't enough to keep him from asking questions. The first thing he did was ask Kai and Eileen where I had run off to. "She sneaks away to Church most Sunday mornings," my brother told him skeptically. He should've known that. To be fair, I can't remember if I actually told him or not. So, I guess it's partially my fault, but that small slip was enough for Kai to question me.

"So, how is it?" Eileen pushes.

"Lina, we are not discussing this. My sex life—"

"Not that!" She laughs. "I mean seeing Lee."

"A blast. Loving every minute of it."

"How's Nick feeling about all of it?"

I don't know. We haven't talked about it. Not that we need to. He has no reason to feel any type of way about Lee. But, Eileen doesn't know that.

"It won't cause problems, right?"

"Lee and I are done, like *done* done. Why would it cause problems?"

"Does your mom's infatuation with Lee bother him?"

"He's mentioned it, but I don't think it bothers him. Personally, I don't care who she likes."

"She is your mom, Nin."

"That means something?"

"Now, hear me out before you get mad. Maybe it's not a bad idea to have Nick try and appeal to her. Who knows, maybe it could change your whole relationship!"

"I won't hold my breath." I roll my eyes and unlock the Wrangler. "Besides, who knows if it's even gonna last."

"Why would you say that?" Eileen asks, rightfully confused. "Are you guys having problems?"

"No, nothing like that. I don't know, I just—"

"Usually, bringing someone home to the family is a good sign, right?"

"We just started dating, Lina. I don't know what's going to happen. I'm still trying to figure a few things out."

"Eileen!" A shout echoes behind us. I see my brother waving

us over from across the street on the patio of the Haven Tap Room and Brewery. I just want to go home and take a shower. I don't want to deal with entertaining anyone else right now, but it's hard to say no to the pleading look Eileen gives me.

"What are you boys doing here?" Eileen asks as we reach them.

"I had to pick up a few things in town for Mom, figured I'd bring Nick since you were having some girl time."

As much as I want to stay annoyed, it's hard when Nick winks at me. He pulls the chair out next to him and brushes his hand over the exposed skin of my shoulder. I fail to hide the smile forming on my lips.

"That's cute, you're having a little bro-date," Eileen coos as she sits next to Kai.

"Perché la mamma non l'ha semplicemente presa da Diana?" I ask my brother. Nick looks to Eileen for clarification, but she only shrugs.

"I told her I'd do it since I was already going into town."

"We're gonna stop by the parts store, he's been hounding me about cars," Nick says.

"Dad never taught me," Kai defends himself.

"You were too busy being Mom's errand boy. Just like now!" I laugh at my own joke.

"Shut up."

"Truth hurts, doesn't it?"

"He never taught you either."

"I learned the basics, it's called Youtube, Kai. You still don't even know how to change a tire. At least, I can do that."

"That's what he has me for." Eileen pats the top of Kai's hand.

"How was yoga?" Kai tries to change the subject.

"It was great, after Lina stopped talking." I steal a fry from Nick's plate.

"You girls hungry?" Kai offers a menu.

"We don't want to intrude on your date. Besides, I'm sure Nick has enjoyed spending some time with someone other than me."

"Typical Nina, never wants to share."

"Can you blame me? I got tired of it after all these years." I laugh, but there's still a twinge of hurt deep inside. I wonder if I'll ever be able to totally get over what happened. I made up my mind a long time ago, I would never get back with Lee. No matter what he said or did, I had finally freed myself from something I never wanted in the first place. I had refused to date him for so long, but at some point, it felt like my only option. And soon, testing the waters had turned into four years and talks of engagement rings. I had done everything to make him happy, but it still hadn't been enough. I wasn't enough.

Rough fingers graze my own bringing me back to the moment. Blinking back the tears, I see Nick's thumb rubbing across the back of my hand. He offers me a soft smile and I return it, thankful to have him here with me.

twelve

I PACE THE BALCONY listening to Michaela explain how a client wants to change the entire design four days into construction. This cannot be happening. Trying to get them to agree on the current designs was hard enough and thinking of the hoops I'm going to have to jump through with the city and county and then— No. This is what Michaela is supposed to be doing. She is supposed to be handling this while I'm gone. "No, I don't want to talk to him. If you're ever going to do this on your own, you need to learn how to handle these things. I'm gone, which means you're in charge." I'm greeted by a suspicious Nick when I walk into my bedroom. "Look, I have to go, Nick just—"

"OMG. How is that going?" Michaela shrieks on the other end.

"Fine, I guess."

"Tell her you have to go, your boyfriend requires some assistance," Nick says loud enough so Michaela can hear.

"What did he say?" Michaela's voice echoes through the receiver.

"He said, my boyfriend requires some assistance," I laugh.

"What does that mean?"

"Goodbye, Michaela." I hang up and toss my phone on the

bed with a sigh.

"Doesn't working on vacation defeat the whole purpose of a vacation?"

"It helps take my mind off things." I feel like I have to be available to some degree. I've worked too hard for something to go wrong just because I'm on vacation. A phone call here or there won't kill me — seems to be a Villa family trait. Daddy and Kai have been working some every day too. "So Fossette, how was my brother?"

"Didn't even realize we'd been gone so long 'til Eileen called to see if we ran off together."

I'm glad that Kai has been able to find a friendship in Nick. Kai normally hangs around the stuffy guys from the office or old school friends. It wasn't until he met Eileen that he finally started to branch out and get to know other people, but this is the first time I've seen him enjoy himself. A sinking feeling settles in my gut thinking about what is going to happen at the end of summer.

"Don't worry, I made sure to keep our story straight."

"I'm not worried."

"Sure about that?"

"I'm more worried about how he's going to take it when we break up."

"Doesn't mean he and I have to break up."

"Doesn't it?"

Nick sighs. "Your brother is a cool guy, Nina. Just because you and I can't make it work, doesn't mean he and I can't."

Pretty sure it does. Doesn't it? I don't want to think about it anymore... "Hey, you know, I was thinking about something,"

"That's not good." Nick laughs and dodges the decorative pillow I throw at him. Picking it up, he sits on the bed next to me.

"I was thinking...you should sleep in the bed tonight."

He raises a questioning brow.

"I can take the floor."

"Dee, I'm not letting you sleep on the floor, this is your house."

"You've been sleeping like shit. I can tell. It's not a big deal, we can take turns."

"Or, we can share."

Or, we can share?

"Or not, whatever you're comfortable with."

"No, it's not that, I just…well, I guess we can."

"Real couples share a bed, right?"

"Right." I didn't notice until then just how close we had gotten. Looking down at the bed, his hand brushes mine. This is new territory, in the past, we have only touched when others were around. This is definitely outside the boundaries. "We're adults, right? I think we can manage."

A knock at the door causes me to jump away. "Diana said to drag you upstairs, dinner is ready!" Eileen chirps when she walks in.

"We'll be up in a minute, Lina," I say without looking.

Eileen looks between us with a small smirk, I think it's pretty obvious she just walked into the middle of something. "Everything okay?"

"Great," Nick says and reaches for my hand again.

Eileen checks the hallway and steps further into the room, closing the door. "I heard you and Teagan had a little reunion earlier. I overheard her telling Lee all about it. Said you were being a bitch to her for no good reason."

I roll my eyes. "We'll be up in a minute. Cover for us, please?"

"Don't take too long," Eileen winks.

When Eileen is gone, I rip my hand from his and push off the bed.

"You wanna talk about it?" Nick asks.

"No." My tone has extra bite as I walk into the bathroom.

Shit, he didn't deserve that. He's just trying to help... I sigh. Stepping back into the bedroom, "Thank you, but I'm fine."

§

I had been in the kitchen trying to return Michaela's call from earlier that morning, but naturally, she didn't answer on the first or second try. As I turned to leave with a fresh bottle of water, I'm face-to-face with Teagan. "Aw, poor Nina. Is your boyfriend ignoring you?"

I did my best to contain my eyes from rolling out of my head. "Can you put on some clothes?" I motioned to Teagan's outfit — booty shorts and a green ruched crop top. Did the girl have to dress so provocatively all the time?

"Don't want Nicky to see what he's missing?"

"Trust me, he's not missing anything."

"Rumor has it you're celibate now."

"That happens when you don't have a boyfriend for a while and when you don't jump every guy you see."

"Never stopped you before."

"That's the pot calling the kettle black."

"What's that supposed to mean?" The smile on my face infuriated Teagan. "You better watch it, wouldn't want Nick to go in search of a real woman."

"If you're a real woman, then I don't want to be one."

"Davina Bay!" Mother exclaimed from the back stairway and Teagan smirked knowing she had won this round.

"Wonderful," I mumbled.

"I am so sorry, Teagan," Mother said, making her way to the kitchen. "You will have to forgive Davina for her behavior."

"It's no trouble, really, Mrs. Villa. I know how she can be." The smile on Teagan's face was sickening.

"She does have a bit of a temper, doesn't she?" Mother started to pull out ingredients for a martini. "Come, Teagan.

I was just on my way to enjoy a drink on the roof, would you like to join me?"

"That would be delightful!" They took the ingredients leaving me alone in the kitchen as my phone rang, Michaela finally calling back.

§

I scan through the words of the book in my hands trying to ignore the butterflies in my stomach. The thought of what is about to happen makes me more nervous than when I used to sneak around with John. This was one of the rules we set in the beginning, but I can't let him sleep on the floor one more night, it's too uncomfortable. And, he refuses to let me sleep down there, so... We're adults, right? We can manage this.

I keep my eyes on the page when the bathroom door opens, but I can't focus on the words in front of me. I've reread the same sentence ten times at this point. I am accurately aware of exactly where he is as he moves around the room — bathroom...closet...laundry room...bed. He hesitates at the bed. It's brief, but it's there. He's considering sleeping on the floor, unsure how this is going to work.

"It only works if you actually get in it," I say pretending to read.

"I know."

"I don't bite." Finally, I meet his stare. "Unless you want me to." I'm not sure where the small bout of confidence came from, but it does the trick. We share a small laugh before Nick climbs under the covers and almost instantly his muscles relax against the plush mattress.

I reread the same sentence for what must be the fiftieth time before finally giving up. Turning off the light, I settle further into bed and the Grand freaking Canyon could fit in the space between us. I haven't shared a bed with someone in over two years, but I'm pretty sure it doesn't work like this.

I think we've both been dreading this moment since I suggested it earlier, but neither of us wants to be the one to break the silence. It's not until I hear his soft snores that I realize we're doing it — sleeping in the same bed, at least one of us anyway. Turning my side, I stare at him in the dark. His features are softer when he sleeps, he almost looks younger without the weight of the world on his mind...

Listening to the sound of his breathing, I feel my body finally start to give in to sleep.

thirteen

"YOU WENT TO SEE him again?" I walk into the bedroom trying to find a private place to talk to Elizabeth. She called on her way home from the prison where she tried to see Nate again. Personally, I think she wants to find some closure before she opens the next chapter of her life. She's happy with Josh, happier than I have seen her in a long time, but I think she's scared to open herself completely to his family after what happened with her own. "Elizabeth, I know you want him to—"

"You don't understand, Nin."

"Nate has made it abundantly clear he doesn't—"

"I lost my parents, Nina," her words soft. She doesn't like to talk about it, not really. "They're gone. I'm getting married without two of the most important people in my life because of him. Don't you think I deserve some kind of explanation?."

"He hasn't given one in seven years, I don't think he will now."

Elizabeth says something, but I don't hear it. My attention is on the half-naked man in the middle of my room. Maybe it's because I've been trying to respect his privacy until this exact moment, but I never noticed the tattoo on his left pectoral — an intricate design of the Tree of Life with birds flying from it like leaves falling off the branches. When I finally meet his stare, his smirk lets me know I've been caught. All of the sudden, it's ten degrees hotter. "Hey Elizabeth, I uh…I gotta go." I hang up without giving her time to respond. "I didn't know you were here. I thought you were still with Kai in the garage." The words come out less confident than I wanted, but I'm trying my damndest not to stare at his bare chest.

"Your dad offered to help, so I gave them some space."

"That was sweet." And, it is. I'm happy to hear my brother is getting some bonding time with Daddy. Something that rarely happens — most of their time spent together revolves around work.

"Don't tell anyone. Wouldn't want to ruin my reputation." A smile lights up his face when I laugh. His smile is gorgeous. It's a bit crooked, but it radiates his face. And that one dimple on his left cheek tells me it's a real smile.

I feel the heat radiate off his tanned skin. I swear this man is a natural radiator or something. If I wanted to, I could easily reach out and touch his chest. And, I really want to, especially after this morning — let's just say when I woke up we were no longer on opposite sides of the bed. Looking away, I ask, "Do you think you could put a shirt on?"

Nick smirks. "I was actually about to take a shower."

"Oh…I can go. I was just trying to talk to Elizabeth about Nate and—" Without warning the door opens as Lee barges into the room. He looks between us, acutely aware of how close we are, Nick still shirtless. "Sure, Lee, come on in. Thanks for knocking, by the way," I say.

"I didn't think I'd be walking in on an afternoon delight." Lee laughs at his own joke, but we don't find him as funny. "I was just dropping by to see if Nick was free, but I can see he's got his hands full."

"My boyfriend is not here for your entertainment. I'm sure my mother or Teagan would be happy to oblige, though."

I won't admit it to anyone, but saying 'boyfriend' makes my heart flutter.

"I just want to get to know him a little better. Besides, I'm sure he could use some pointers when it comes to dealing with you. Am I right?" Lee turns to Nick with a smirk, but Nick doesn't return the favor.

"Puoi andartene ora, Lee." I try to push Lee from the room, but he doesn't budge.

His focus still on Nick. "You know, you look really familiar. Do I know you from somewhere?"

"Couldn't tell ya," Nick says, clearly not amused by Lee's intrusion.

I can see the wheels turning in Lee's head and I don't like it. If Lee is anything, it's determined. He always gets what he wants and if he thinks something is off, he will do whatever it takes to find the truth. "He lived in Bridgeport. You probably saw him around town."

"No, I don't think that's it." Lee studies Nick a little longer. "You went to Rosecliffe, right? Were you in a fraternity?"

"Nope. Guess, I just have one of those faces." Nick shrugs off the questioning glare from Lee. I'm glad he doesn't feel the need to answer any of Lee's questions.

"Well, as fun as this has been, you can go now, Lee." I push Lee towards the door, but he plants his feet again.

"How about we have breakfast tomorrow, Dove?" I immediately notice the difference when Lee takes my hand in his, thumb caressing my skin. His hands are too soft. I like the callousness of Nick's hand — the way it warms my skin when he touches me. "Say, nine o'clock?"

"I'll be sure to tell your girlfriend when she's looking for you." I step away from him, straight into Nick's arms. "Bye, Lee." With a huff, Lee finally leaves the room, shutting the door a little too hard behind him.

"You know, I get the feeling he doesn't really like me," Nick says.

"Good, that means you're doing your job." I pat his chest, my fingers lingering a moment too long before I look up to meet his eyes. The next words catch in my throat, mesmerized by the molten honey staring back at me. The air around us thick. I can feel the heat from his bare skin through my clothes — a satin camisole and jeans. Goosebumps erupt over every inch of my skin. When had we gotten so close? I glance down at his lips before meeting his gaze again. Slowly, he leans forward and lowers his head...

fourteen

I CAN'T GET THAT moment out of my head. I can't stop thinking about what would have happened if his phone didn't ring. We wouldn't just be taking a small step over the boundaries we had set, we'd be jumping with both feet. Neither of us moved as his phone continued to ring, even when it stopped. The ringer immediately started again. He took a deep breath before finally stepping away. I didn't move, almost cemented in place. Adrenaline coursed through me as I watched him pick up his phone. "What do you want?" He asked through gritted teeth and slammed the bathroom door.

Since, I've started making two cups of coffee each morning — taking one out on the balcony and leaving the other on his nightstand. The smell rousing him from bed to join me. My book long forgotten in my lap as we spend mornings talking and laughing until we decide to join the rest of the world. Each day finding a new adventure.

One day, we hiked a trail further out from the city. The trail was long and tiring, but the views made it worth it. Along the way, I caught him staring from five steps behind — tall grass and wildflowers at my sides. My fingers grazed the flowers. The sun cast a warm light on my skin. I don't think he even noticed he had stopped walking until I called his name, but he pretended to look for something when we made eye contact. A blush rose in my cheeks, I turned back to the trail hoping he didn't notice. That day was the first time we had taken a picture together.

The second time was at the Haven Brewing Company. We spent the afternoon at the Haven Art Museum, and while I was busy looking at the art, Nick was busy looking at me. Catching him for the third time, I slipped my hand into his and smiled when he intertwined our fingers. We might Kai and Eileen that night for a brewery tour and dinner. There was a collective groan when Eileen asked the waitress to take a photo. But, Nick's protest ended when I leaned into his side, my hand resting on his thigh where it remained the rest of the night.

The third time was at Ghost Town nestled in the mountains about an hour from Haven. Ghost Town had been one of my favorite things to explore growing up. There were so many stories and legends, with new ones to hear each time you visited. The town featured the restored remains of several buildings from an old mining town that no one knew the name of, hence the name Ghost Town. I pointed out the different buildings and shared the stories I remembered from years ago. We stopped to take a photo in front of the old motel, and this time an elderly couple offered to take the photo for us. "Such a lovely couple," I heard the wife say as they returned to their tour. I couldn't help but agree.

The fourth time was on a trip out to the lake. Eileen had booked a private horseback tour that would lead us up the mountain to the lake, where we would set up camp and spend the night. Nick was surprised when I jumped at the idea. Apparently, I didn't seem like the type to rough it in the wild, but I assured him I was more than capable. I've spent plenty of nights under the stars throughout the years in Haven. On the ride, Eileen and I hung back from Nick, Kai, and the tour guides who spent most of the day bro'ing out. "It's like they've never seen guys before," Eileen giggled. Once we reached the lake, Nick helped me dismount. I didn't need the help, but let him anyway. The tour guides took a photo when we posed in front of the lake. But, it was the photo later in the evening that really mattered. Eileen showed me a candid she had taken of us sitting by the fire — a smile lit up my face as Nick leaned in close and whispered in my ear.

After the night under the stars, I suggested a quick detour to Elk Camp for Tuesday night dinner. Farm to Table is a local tradition where you ride the gondola up the mountain and enjoy dinner prepared with farm fresh foods accompanied by live music and activities. We've always made it a point to go at least once a year.

Nick rejoins the table with a fresh bottle of wine. He refills my glass before pressing his lips to my temple, the simple action speaking on the recent change in our relationship. We still haven't talked about that day in our room, how close we had been... But, there has been a noticeable shift in our relationship. I always have some kind of hold on him, and he feels more comfortable pressing a kiss to my cheek or temple. Last night, I think it surprised both of us when I leaned in for a quick, noncommittal kiss by the fire. Ever since, I have been trying to ignore the desire to do it again, minus the quick and noncommittal part.

"So, Nick," Eileen starts as Kai refills her glass. "How has your trip been so far?"

"You've really never left Winchester?" Kai is still dumbfounded by the idea.

"Not really, we went to Boston to drop my brother at college." Nick shrugs, "We didn't travel much growing up. Dad felt like he couldn't leave the garage. And, Mom didn't work, so the garage was our only income."

"If you haven't noticed, most people aren't like us, Kai," I say. "Vacationing in Greece, Barcelona, Haven...it's not the norm."

"Tell me you at least got to go Disney World," Eileen pleads.

"Nope," Nick says behind his beer.

"Che cosa?" I'm shocked. "Well, we have to go then."

He presses a kiss to the back of my hand and smiles at me. But, it's not the same one I've seen the last few days. It doesn't quite reach his eyes. No dimple. He thinks I don't mean it... He thinks this is all for show. We only have a few weeks left and after that — Nick will be back at the garage and I will be... A heavy weight settles in the pit of my stomach at the thought.

"Hey babe, can you and Nick go grab some water? They're going to be closing up soon and I'm parched," Eileen asks my brother. Kai looks between her and the table confused, why did she need more water? There is a pitcher on the table and she has a full glass of wine. When he doesn't get up, she kicks him under the table.

"Okay, okay, I'm going. C'mon Nick, wouldn't want her to kick you too." Kai rubs his shin. "Damn, she's ruthless."

Eileen chuckles watching them leave and when they're far enough, she turns back to me. "So, when are you going to tie this one down?"

"Lina!"

"It's not like you haven't thought about it. He's nice, charming, not to mention incredibly handsome." Eileen sips her wine. "And those eyes!"

I laugh when Eileen fans herself. I can't deny his eyes are gorgeous, the perfect combination of a warm whiskey and golden honey. When he stares at me, I just melt.

"He gets along with your family. But, above all else, he is totally in love with you."

"Love?" I scoff, "Lina, I think you've seen one too many Hallmark movies."

"Don't believe me?"

"We just started dating!"

"Your brother told me he loved me after three months. When you know, you know!"

"He told you he loved you before introducing us?"

"What can I say? Kai James Villa is a romantic."

Nick doesn't love me, it's all part of the act. But, his acting is better than I thought it would be, he's almost had me convinced a few times. "I don't think we're there, yet."

"Keep telling yourself that."

"What did we miss?" Kai asks, handing out fresh bottles of water.

"Just a little girl talk," Eileen winks at me.

fifteen

I LEAVE A CUP of coffee on Nick's nightstand before retreating to the balcony hoping to get a few extra minutes to myself before he joins me. I haven't had any alone time and I can't stop thinking about the conversation with Eileen two nights ago. She is utterly convinced Nick and I are just like her and Kai — a love-at-first-sight scenario. Which is definitely not the case. I don't believe in insta-love. How can you know you love someone if you don't even know them?

I'd be lying if I said I didn't consider telling Eileen the truth. I hate lying to her, she's one of my closest friends. It's getting harder and harder to keep this secret. But, what would Eileen say? Would she be mad? Would she judge me? Surely, she'd understand, on some level. Right?

I hear someone skipping down the stairs winding along the side of the house. There's only one person I can think of and I hope I'm wrong. I carefully sip the steaming coffee and scan the pages of the book in my hands. Hearing footsteps approach, I don't have to look up to know my suspicions are correct. His cologne permeates the fresh mountain air — Ralph Lauren Polo Black, the same one he's worn for years.

Lee clears his throat, but I turn a page refusing to acknowledge him. "Oh come on, Nina. You're not going to ignore me, are you?"

Yes.

"You can't just avoid me."

Actually, I can.

"We can't keep acting like we don't know each other."

"I would prefer it, actually," I finally say without looking up.

"Come on, Dove."

"Don't call me that." I sigh heavily, bookmarking the page. "What do you want, James?"

Lee rolls his eyes at the use of his formal name. "Well, I was going for a walk, enjoying the morning breeze, and I thought—"

"And that walk just so happened to lead you right to my balcony, where you know I sit every morning. Interesting."

"Would you like to join me?"

"No."

"Can't we at least try to be friends?"

"Hard pass."

"Look, I just—"

"Everything okay out here?" A shirtless Nick steps out of the bedroom with his steaming cup of coffee. His muscles flex and his jaw tightens, eyes hard on Lee before he leans down to kiss the top of my head.

"I was just asking if Nina wanted to join me for a morning walk."

"Take the hint, Lee." Nick's tone is stern. He's tired of Lee's attempts to corner me. Honestly, I'm a little concerned what it might have been like if I had come alone.

When Nick doesn't stand down, Lee storms up the steps and I can hear the door slam above us.

I pull the blanket aside and Nick gently lifts my feet before letting them relax in his lap. "If I have to keep saving you, you might need to take back the whole, 'I'm not a damsel in distress' thing."

"My Prince Charming." I roll my eyes over my mug.

"Not Prince Charming," Nick says repeating the same phrase he used when I invited him. He gently squeezes my leg. "You okay? You kept tossing and turning all night."

"Fine, just stressing over this job."

"Nina—"

I put my hand up. "I'm letting Michaela handle it, but the client is a lot. He's not happy. He's one of those people who have to find a problem in everything." Rubbing my eyes, I yawn. "What did you want to do today, Fossette? I figured you might want to decide since Eileen and I have kept us all pretty busy. I'm starting to run out of things. At this rate, I'm gonna have to take you over to Mt. Sopris."

"Whatever you want, Dee. I'm just here to have a good time and get paid."

My heart wrenches. *To have a good time and get paid.* I have to remind myself that's all this is to him. A job. "Biggest payday of your life." I try to smile, but it doesn't quite reach. "You know, I think I'm gonna work on this project today, you should see if Kai is busy."

"Nina, I don't want to leave you to work."

"Duty calls." I reach my arms up into a long stretch letting my spine align. I close my eyes and take a deep breath feeling more of my vertebrae click into place. Just before I open my eyes, I feel the ghost of his touch at my sides. Heat radiates through me when his fingers graze the bare skin of my sides and I can't contain my laughter as his fingers tickle me. I try to push him away, but his hands are bigger than mine and slip out of my grasp with ease. I can't hold off their assault. And then, tickling turns into a soft caress. His grip tightens on me and he pulls me close. I try to catch my breath, but my heart feels like it might beat out of my chest as he leans forward and runs the tip of his nose along my jaw. His breath dances across my collarbone.

My breath hitches and I feel him smirk against my skin. The cool morning breeze like ice as he moves his lips up my neck. I try to suppress a moan but fail.. Just before our lips meet, he stops. His eyes like molten honey stare into mine, asking for permission. He wants to know I'm okay with crossing this line. Because once we do...

I don't care. I'm tired of the games. Every time he touches me, I find myself wanting more. The small sensations up to this point have left me unsatisfied. I need more. I need to know what it's like, so I close the space between us.

sixteen

"**WHERE ARE YOU HEADED?**" Kai asks when I meet him at the bottom of the front steps. He is carrying...logs? Wait, Eileen was serious about Daddy asking him to bring some logs in for Diana? He's never done manual labor in his life. I wonder if Mother knows about this. She'd probably have a coronary. The thought makes me giggle. "You seem pretty dressed up."

"I'm not dressed up." I glance down at my outfit — a black T-shirt tucked into black jeans. A coffee brown colored cardigan over my shoulders and my hair is pulled into a loose bun.

"You've worn leggings almost the entire time you've been here. *That* is dressed up."

"At least I own something besides dress pants." I point toward the gray slacks he wears.

"Some of us like to be prepared."

"For what, a board meeting? You're in the mountains, Kai. Do you need me to buy you a pair of shorts while I'm in town?"

"Ha. Ha." Kai wipes a bead of sweat from his brow setting the logs on the steps. "You and Nick heading into town?"

"Daddy and I are going to lunch."

"You leaving Nick here?"

"That's what I said."

"No, you said you and Dad were going to lunch."

"Yes, Kai. I am leaving Nick here." Finally, Daddy pulls one of the Wranglers from the garage at that exact moment. "If you would like to take him on a date, be my guest," I say, climbing into the passenger seat.

§

I sigh as we pull into town wishing it was a longer drive. When I was younger, drives down the mountain felt like hours. They were filled with laughter and singing. Daddy kept a collection of old CDs in the center console for us to shuffle through: Tom Petty, Led Zeppelin, AC/DC, The Police, Fleetwood Mac, Def Leppard, Carpenters, Rod Stewart, the list went on. But, my favorite was always Tom Petty.

Daddy turns onto Peake Street and parks in one of the open spaces across from The Vintage House.

"Can we sit outside?"

"Always." Daddy wraps his arm around my shoulders as we walk towards the little white house on the corner of Main Street. The Vintage House is a small cottage that had been converted into a restaurant by the Hicks family. Esther "Grandma" Hicks was known for her delicious homemade meals. She would invite people off the street to enjoy dinner with the family almost every night. The house was passed down from generation to generation until it reached the great-great-granddaughter and current owner, Esther Hicks-West, named for her grandmother. The patio offers many entertainment options from people watching to stunning views of the mountains at the end of Peake Street to live music on the weekend.

"Welcome to Vintage House, how many?" The hostess asks without looking and I recognize her almost immediately. Her eyes widen when she finally looks up from the reservation book. "Oh my gosh, Nina!"

"Hi, Sarah." Sarah Wilkes — a local girl who I spent most of my summers with. We spent many nights finding ways to keep entertained throughout the years, but I haven't seen her in almost four years.

"Outside?"

"Please." We follow Sarah out the front door. "How have you been?"

"Working this summer to pay for the rest of school. What about you? I haven't seen you for a while."

"Yeah, I've just had a lot going on. Starting the company and all..."

"She has a new boyfriend, Sarah. Don't let her leave that out," Daddy says.

"No more Lee?" Sarah has never liked Lee, she made that obvious before and after I started dating him. If I'm completely honest, I think that's part of why we grew apart.

"Finally." Daddy's smile is large as he sits down and glances at the menu. Daddy has never commented much on my past relationships. I suppose I always assumed he was okay with the idea of me and Lee, but maybe I had mistaken his silence for acceptance when it meant something else entirely.

"What's his name?"

"Nick," I answer before he can. I can't help the smile thinking about our kiss this morning. But, the more I think about it, my smile falters, and I turn my attention to the menu in my hands. I don't need the menu, I get the same thing every time, but I'm looking for a way out of the conversation.

"She'll bring him in before they leave," Daddy says.

I hum in response and Sarah excuses herself. Closing the menu, I watch people walk along the street. I love coming into town — the food, the shopping, and the people. It's all so inviting. The Vintage House is my go-to spot with Daddy. We always make it a point to sneak off and enjoy a father-daughter meal at least once. But, today I can't get my mind off the events from earlier this morning.

The kiss is only going to further complicate things. We aren't supposed to cross the boundaries. Boundaries set to keep us from being able to walk away unscathed at the end of the summer. Sure, I wanted it, especially after the way he's made me feel with every touch. The warmth that spreads through me just from his hand in mine or a touch on my back… It makes me want to know how it feels when every part of him touches me.

But, I have to push those thoughts aside. It cannot happen.

Daddy says something catching my attention, but I don't hear him. "Sorry, Daddy. What?"

"Are you okay?"

"Fine, ho solo molto in mente."

"Wanna talk about it?" I shake my head. "C'mon piccola, you can talk to me."

I know I can, but I don't want to. Not when I can't tell him what is really going on. "It's nothing," I sigh. "I'm just confused."

"About?"

"Tutto."

"Well, that certainly narrows it down." Before he can push further, our waitress arrives to take our order. She's new, at least to me. Daddy seems to know her. He doesn't have to order his usual burger and fries, but she looks at me expectantly. I order the kale salad and club sandwich. When she's gone, he wastes no time continuing the conversation. "Does 'everything' have to do with a certain boy?"

You have no idea.

"He didn't hurt you, did he?" Daddy leans in lowering his voice. "Because, if he did, I—"

"No," I quickly interrupt him. A small laugh. "Daddy, no. Nothing like that. Our relationship is just…complicated."

"It's only complicated if you make it that way."

"You have no idea," I whisper.

"Care to elaborate?"

"Not really. I mean, this is kinda weird, right? You're my dad. I'm not supposed to tell you these things."

"Davina, there are a lot of things I know about that I probably shouldn't. And, at this rate, anything you tell me isn't any worse than you've done before."

"Ci baciammo."

"Oh, my goodness. You're right, that seems very complicated." He laughs as I roll my eyes. "No, no, you're right. Kissing your boyfriend is definitely on that list of complications."

"Ha. Ha. Very funny, Daddy."

"I'll be here all night."

"I'm serious! This is..." I sigh. I don't even know what it is. The agreement with Nick seems like it has been thrown out the window, but something about him just feels... "Different."

Daddy squeezes my hand, "I know what you mean, I felt the same way when your mother and I started dating."

Yeah, okay. I can't even imagine Mother being different. I can almost guarantee she was born this way.

"Life has a way of changing people. You should be able to understand that."

"Sometimes for the better, sometimes for worse."

"Nina," he laughs.

I'm not wrong, he knows I'm not wrong. Mother is different, even Kai says so. Personally, I can't say whether she is or not, she has always been this way with me. It breaks my heart to see the way Daddy loves her, but I don't think she feels the same way. Maybe she used to, a long time ago, but I think she loves the idea of him, what he can offer her.

"Your mother has a strong personality." That's one way to put it. "It's demanding and forceful. But, she has always known what she wants and she'll do anything to get it. It's one of the things I have always loved about her."

I roll my eyes.

"You remind me a lot of her, you know."

"I resent that."

"It's not a bad thing. You're both ambitious, passionate, disciplined, and independent. There's nothing wrong with any of that." He got one thing right, she's definitely ambitious — she'll sniff out any way to bring more money into her pocket. "Look, I never said anything because I wanted you to make your own choices...and your own mistakes. But, I feel like it's time." He takes a moment to gather his thoughts before he continues. "Your relationship with Lee, it was never going to last."

"What's that supposed to mean?"

"When you were with Lee, you were a different person. Nina, you changed, and not for the better."

"No, I didn't."

A sad smile. "Nina, you weren't happy. That was obvious to everyone."

"Except Mom."

"She has her own ideas of how a relationship should work," he shrugs.

That's one way to put it.

"When you were with Lee, you worried so much about what that boy wanted, it was never what you wanted. Don't you remember that one Christmas? You spent your entire break with him and his friends out in Washington."

How could I forget? I remember that trip vividly. Lee guised the trip as a Christmas getaway for the two of us, leaving out the fact we would be sharing a chalet with six of his buddies. I thought about leaving, I would rather spend Christmas with Mother and Kai than seven college frat boys. But, Lee kept promising things would get better. I should've known better. That year, I spent Christmas Day alone in the chalet with a book by the fire.

"You were miserable. But, you thought it was going to be good for you guys, help get you on the right track. Was it?"

"No."

"You gave him everything and he gave you nothing. Your studies slipped, you stopped going to Church, you just weren't happy. You acted happy, but you weren't. You were so worried about making him happy, you forgot to take care of yourself. You became who your mother always wanted you to be. You weren't my little rebel anymore."

Tears burn my eyes. Everything he said was exactly how I felt, but I pushed the feelings down for so long. I actually started to believe I was happy with Lee. I had been willing to ignore the signs, willing to get engaged, willing to take my degree and do nothing with it. Just like Mother wanted.

Until I was finally free.

"Your mother sees an opportunity for you to have in Lee what she has in her relationship with me. It's reliable and safe, but I know that's not what you want. It's not what I want for you. I want you to find someone who won't just take care of you, but who loves you. And, that isn't Lee. Dumping his ass was the best thing that ever happened."

"Daddy!"

"And, when I see you with Nick, I see you, the real you. The free-spirited, fun-loving, rebel that used to keep us on our toes. You say it's complicated, but this is not the same as Lee, or John, for that matter. That's a win in my book."

I wipe a stray tear that falls down my cheek. "Thank you, Daddy."

"I can see how much you care for each other. So, whatever is making it complicated, figure it out."

I promise him I will, and while I feel one weight lift off my shoulders, another still holds me down. He makes it sound so easy, like I can snap my fingers and everything will be okay.

But, I don't even know the first step in un-complicating things.

seventeen

"YOU JUST CAN'T STAY away from me, can you?" Lee says when he sees me walking down the hallway.

"Oh, fuck me," I mumble.

"If you insist."

Oh for the love of God, I am not in the mood for him today. "If you'll excuse me," I try to make a quick escape up the stairs, but he follows.

"So, where did you and Alaric go earlier?"

"As if you have to ask," I chuckle. "Where are you coming from?"

"I ran into town to grab a few things that I forgot."

"Typical."

"What's that supposed to mean?" Lee touches his hand to his heart. Under his stare, I tuck a strand of hair behind my ear. It's small moments like this I missed most after we broke up. In moments when Lee isn't trying to put on a show, he is kind and funny. He seems genuinely interested in me. When Lee acts like this, it makes me nostalgic for the old days when we first started dating.

Lee motions for me to go ahead of him. I oblige but keep my distance. "See? We can get along!" He moves closer as we walk upstairs. "Are you sure we can't catch up?"

"Don't push your luck."

"Just a coffee, nothing else. You owe me that much, don't you think?"

"I owe— Non ti devo merda."

"Lee, is that you? Did you get the stuff?" Teagan appears at the top of the stairs and her face drops at the sight of me and Lee together.

"I'll be right there, Teag," Lee assures her and turns back to me. He's trying to fix this problem before he worries about the one upstairs. "Nina, I didn't mean it like that. Please, don't take it that way."

"Fuck off, Lee."

Lee grabs me when I try to walk by him, but I rip my hand from his grasp pushing past Teagan.

"What was that about?" Teagan hisses just before I exit out the kitchen patio.

Outside, Eileen and Kai swim in the pool. A natural-infinity hybrid, the pool combines the natural landscape of the mountain it's built into and an infinity edge that overlooks the surrounding landscape. This is actually my favorite part of the house.

"There you are!" Eileen shouts from the water. Clearly, she's been waiting for me to get home. "How was lunch?" She untangles herself from Kai and swims to the edge.

I lower my feet into the water. "It was good, Daddy took me to—"

"Vintage House, we already know."

"Why don't you join her, Nin?" Kai climbs out of the pool and dries off. "I was about to go inside anyway, gotta jump on a board call."

"You're leaving me?" Eileen pouts.

"Sorry, babe, duty calls."

"Do you love me enough to make us some margaritas before you go to work?"

"How about I pour you a glass of wine and call it a day?"

"Deal." Kai leans down and kisses her. When he closes the door, Eileen turns to me, "Everything okay?"

"Bene. Perché?"

"Just curious. Seemed like something was bothering you the way you were bursting at the seams to get out of here this morning. Not to mention, Nick was acting weird before he left."

"Yeah, where is he?"

"Went for a run, is what Kai said."

I nod letting my fingers dip in and out of the water.

"You sure everything's okay?"

"Just figuring some things out, Lina. You know how it goes."

She doesn't believe me. I wouldn't believe me either, but I'm thankful when she lets it go. "Go change, I'll get the wine from Kai and we can soak up the rest of the sun before dinner."

I push myself up from the edge, and the ground falls from underneath me. Kai's laugh echoes in my ear just before I land in the water with a SPLASH! "Porca puttana, Kai!" I laugh and splash him as I resurface.

"I told you to change!"

"I was going!"

"Took you long enough to bring the wine," Eileen says, taking a glass from him. "You could've made us margaritas in the same time."

"You'll take what you get and like it." Eileen sticks her tongue out at him and ducks when he sends a wave of water her way.

"Well, no sense in changing now," I toss my soaked cardigan on the edge.

"That's a good look for you, Nin," Kai says.

"Don't you have the board's ass to kiss or something?"

§

I try to avoid dripping water as I carry my pool-soaked cardigan to my room. Eileen and I swam until well after Diana started to cook dinner. I swiped a few asparagus pieces on my way through the kitchen but regretted informing Diana I wouldn't be joining them. I don't want to be around everyone, but mostly I don't want to be around Lee. As I descend the stairs, I see Nick approaching from the foyer. He's covered in dirt and sweat from the trail, I wonder if he looks this good after working on cars all day? Wait...What? No, Nina, don't think about that.

This is the first time I've seen him since this morning. Waiting for Daddy, I had joined Eileen in the kitchen for a cup of coffee. "He actually said he wanted to be friends?" Eileen asked me looking up from her crossword.

"Mmhm."

"What did you say?"

"Nick saved me." My lips tingled remembering what else had happened.

"Well, that explains a lot."

"What do you mean?"

"Good morning, Lee!" Eileen said, looking past me as he made his way into the kitchen. "Feeling better?"

"What are you talking about, Eileen?" Lee refused to meet either of our stares focused on pouring his own cup of coffee.

"You seemed kind of upset earlier."

"Good morning!" Teagan bound into the kitchen with a face full of makeup, hair done, and dressed in a pale yellow T-shirt dress leaving little to the imagination.

Nick and Kai walked side-by-side up the stairs deep in conversation about what they needed from the parts store to finish working on one of the old Jeeps Daddy had been holding onto. Nick glared at Lee noticing how close he stood to me and quickly sidled up between us.

"Not so loud, Teagan," I hissed. "Unlike you, some of us actually like the peace and quiet of the mountains."

"You sure are a grump in the morning." Teagan leaned against the counter and let her dress rise a little higher. "Y'know, if I woke up with his head between my legs every morning, I'd be a lot nicer."

I choked on my coffee, the pen in Eileen's hand clattered to the floor, and the others froze. It felt like the world had stopped.

Did she just say that?

After a moment, Lee finally said what the rest of us were thinking, "Teag, what the fuck?"

"Well, it's true!" Teagan shrugged as if it wasn't a big deal.

"Sometimes, you need to just stay quiet." Lee guided her from the kitchen towards the stairs leaving behind the still-steaming cup of coffee.

"But, I—"

"No, you don't. We're leaving."

"Oh. My. God." Eileen said once they had left.

"Well, now that we're all awake. Who's hungry?" Kai suggested, but neither Nick nor I seemed interested in the idea.

"Babe, didn't your dad ask you to bring some logs in for Diana later? Why don't you do that and we'll figure out something to do for lunch," Eileen ushered Kai towards the stairs. Once he was gone, she turned to us. "You guys not hungry?"

"I'm good," Nick said and slipped his phone into his back pocket.

"Nin?" But, I just shook my head. "Well, if you change your mind, call me."

I tried to make a quick exit with Eileen, but Nick stopped me. In the moments after we kissed, I ran inside and locked myself in the bathroom. I took my time showering and getting ready, making sure he wasn't there when I finished. "We need to talk, Dee."

"Can't, gotta go."

"Where are we going?"

"Not we, *me*. I'm going to town with my dad."

"We need to talk about this when you get back."

"Nick, nothing happened."

"Nina, come on."

"We're not... We shouldn't do this. Okay? Just, leave it alone."

Nick held his ground for another moment, arms crossed firmly against his chest. He wanted to make me stay, to talk about it, but I'm not sure it would have helped. Finally, he stepped to the side.

Now, we are face-to-face again and all I can think about is finishing what we started earlier.

"What happened to you?" Nick asks following me into our room.

"Kai pushed me in the pool." I wrung my hair into a towel and tossed my cardigan onto the laundry room floor. I can see the ghost of a smirk on his lips. "Where'd you go?"

"For a run."

I pull out a clean pair of leggings and a tank top in desperate need to get out of these wet clothes. Without thinking, I pull my wet shirt over my head, but stop. Nick is still in the room. "Um," I look back at him. "I just need to change, then the bathroom is all yours." Nick half nods, his attention on the text he is sending. I change quickly and throw my wet clothes into the washer when he slams the bathroom door. Taking my book, I settle on the balcony under the blanket ready to take my mind off the events of the day.

But, before I get too deep, I see him in the doorway from my peripheral vision. "Are you coming to dinner?"

"I'm not hungry."

"Look, Nina..."

"Nick, it's been a long day." I can only hope my voice matches how exhausted I feel. "Can we please not do this, right now?"

He contemplates whether it's worth the fight, but decides to let it go, for now. I'm grateful when he leaves to join the rest of the family upstairs, but I can't help wonder what excuse he'll come up with when they ask why I'm not there.

§

"Knock, knock," Kai stands at the open door with a plate of food. "Figured you might be hungry."

"Hai portato del vino?" I ask and he lifts a glass filled with red wine in the air. "You may enter."

"I see you went shopping today." Kai motions through the window where shopping bags sit on my bed.

"You saw nothing."

"So all of those bags just appeared out of nowhere?"

"Exactly. We're keeping it a secret."

"Just like old times," Kai smirks. Even though he and I hadn't gotten along much growing up, my shopping trips with Daddy had always been a secret he kept from Mother. Why? I'm not entirely sure, but I appreciated it nonetheless. "What she doesn't know won't kill her."

"Or me." I smile as Kai's laugh booms around us. But, I know he didn't just come to bring me dinner, he wants something. Picking at the chicken breast, I ask, "What are you doing here, Kai?"

"I can't bring my baby sister dinner without strings attached?"

"Not usually."

He sighs, "Is everything okay, Nin?"

I raise a suspicious brow. "Did Nick say something?"

"No, but it's not hard to tell." Kai motions toward the plate in my lap.

"Don't worry about it, Kai."

"Are you guys fighting?"

"I said, don't worry about it."

"Look, I'm not trying to pry, but I don't want this to be another Lee situation. Yeah, this guy is cool and all, but if he hurts you or—"

"It's not like that."

"Then, what's it like?"

"Kai, just drop it. Sei così ficcanaso."

"Nina—"

"I said drop it." I'm tired of the constant game of 20 Questions when it comes to my relationship with Nick. Fake relationship. Fake, I remind myself.

"Well, if you decide you do want to talk about it, you know where to find me."

"Kai, you're the last person I would go to for relationship advice. I'd sooner humiliate myself and go to Dad."

"Offended!" I giggle at his outburst, but it fades when I see Nick through the window. We share a glance my brother steals his attention. With them being preoccupied, it gives me the chance to escape without having to answer anymore questions.

Upstairs is quiet, everyone turned in early tonight. So, I'm taking the opportunity to enjoy the stillness. I wash my plate and refill my wine glass before retreating to the patio to dip my feet in the pool. Finally, I recount the events of the day. I touch my lips remembering the sensation of Nick's lips on mine, completely different from anything I've felt before. And, it scares me. I cannot let myself feel this. I can't. He is only here for the money. He isn't here for me. I'm not even looking for anything either.

Right?

No. I'm not. I'm supposed to be focused on work, on building my company. I can't afford distractions. And so far, this entire trip has been nothing but a distraction.

Maybe if I act like it didn't happen things can go back to normal. Whatever that is. If Nick wants to talk, I'll tell him there's nothing to talk about. Because there isn't. Just a fluke, an accident. These kinds of things happen. We just need to forget it.

eighteen

I PULL A BOTTLE from the wine cooler and head for the patio to rejoin the others on the rooftop. My parents took Karol and Jack to dinner at the club which left us on our own. I helped Eileen cook a pasta dish while the boys worked in the garage. Dinner was quieter than normal, it's getting harder to ignore the tension between me and Nick. We've never talked about things, instead chosen to act like nothing happened. Which, I thought I was okay with. I thought that's what I wanted, I thought—

I swing the bottle in my hands when someone grabs my arm before I reach the rooftop stairs. My attacker throws his hands up in surrender. "Lee! What the hell?"

"What were you going to do, wine me to death?"

"It would stun you enough to get away. Maybe even break and I could stab you with the broken pieces," I say, taking a few steps back.

"Did you really thing some stranger was trying to attack you?"

"Strange times are these in which we live."

"Okay, Plato." He takes a step closer.

"What in the hell were you doing, anyway?" Another step back.

"You were taking a while, so I came to check on you."

"Do you need a play-by-play of what I do every minute that I'm gone? I went downstairs to use the bathroom and then I came back upstairs to get this bottle before I walked outside and almost brained you with it for being a creep."

"Come on, Dove, don't be like that." Another step closer.

"Don't call me that."

"You used to love it. Don't you think we can at least try and let go of what happened?" The distance between us closing. "I just want to talk, that's it."

"Lee stop." My back hits the wall, the stucco rough against my skin.

"C'mon, Dove," Lee whispers and pushes a piece of hair from my face. "Just like old times."

"Stop," I whisper, my voice quivers.

"Sure?" His lips hover over mine. When I don't say it again, he moves closer, his lips brushing mine. When I don't refuse, he keeps going. But, it's wrong. Everything about it feels wrong.

I push him away. "I said stop. This is not happening." I can only hope he doesn't notice the shake in my voice. My whole body vibrates from pure adrenaline as I back away from him towards the steps. "Stay the hell away from me, Lee."

On the rooftop, I ignore the stares from Eileen, Kai, and Teagan around the fire walking straight to Nick. I position myself between him and the corner trying to keep as much distance between me and the others. Deep, shaky breaths catch his attention. Setting his empty beer down, he touches my shoulder. "You okay?" I can only nod, but he knows better. He pulls me into a tight embrace. It's safe here. And slowly, I relax against him until I hear Teagan call out to Lee.

"What took you so long?"

"Mom was asking me something," Lee lies.

"Baby, I'm starting to get kind of tired." I can imagine

Teagan playing with the collar on Lee's shirt, her signature move. I've never understood why it worked on so many guys. "Aren't *you* tired?"

The rest of their conversation is a blur when I hear Nick whisper, "Did he do something?" I'm sure he felt my body tense when Lee returned. I swallow the lump in my throat. Do I tell him the truth? "Dee, you gotta talk to me. What happened?"

"Nothing."

"Don't lie to me, Nina. What did he do?"

"Just drop it. Please."

"Dee—"

"Please." It's the first time in two days we've had a conversation away from the others. We have been avoiding one-on-one conversations, afraid what might happen if we brought up the you-know-what.

"You gonna go after her?" I hear Eileen ask and I notice Teagan is gone.

"Probably should," Lee sighs. Before he leaves, he glances over his shoulder and I see him swallow the lump in his throat. Nick's arms tighten around me. I can imagine his jaw locked, gaze zeroed in on Lee, daring him to say something.

"I think we're gonna go too," Eileen says. "I'm pretty tired."

"Vacation is so hard, isn't it, babe?" Kai pokes her side.

"It's the absolute worst." Eileen feigns dismay before she takes Kai's hand pulling her to her feet.

"C'mon man, we'll walk down with you." Kai urges Lee towards the steps. "You guys coming?" Kai calls to us.

"You wanna go to bed?" Nick whispers to me and I nod against his chest. "We're right behind you."

§

The adrenaline finally subsides and I feel like I can breathe again. I trail behind the others, behind Nick, keeping as much distance between me and Lee as possible. We bid goodnight to the others and retreat to our room. Once the door shuts, we fall back into the same routine we have been in for days. Dancing around each other, getting ready for bed without a word. I climb into bed and turn my back to him ready to pass out.

His side of the bed dips and he tries to settle into a more comfortable position. He ends up on his back and after a moment, he speaks, his voice so soft I barely hear him. "I'm sorry."

"Nick," his name a sigh on my lips.

"Look, the other morning...it was way out of line. I shouldn't have done that. It was— I know it was wrong."

I try to hide my disappointment. But, why do I care? He should be sorry. We're not supposed to be doing things like kissing. Even I decided we should forget it, act like nothing happened. So, why does the thought of him regretting it upset me? "You don't need to apologize," I whisper and try to smile.

"I don't want to make you uncomfortable."

"It's okay, I'm sorry, too."

"No more weirdness?"

"No more weirdness," I promise, but I'm not sure I can keep it.

"I promise to be on my best behavior and get you through the rest of vacation without any more problems."

nineteen

I WOULD LIKE TO tell you things have gotten better, but I can't. Nick has stayed true to his word. He's been on his best behavior since our reconciliation in bed a week ago. When we are alone, we keep our distance — he's even stopped spending mornings with me. Things are still awkward and neither of us wants to be the one to bring it up. Instead, we do our best to avoid each other. Until now... I drop the steaming cup of coffee on his nightstand. My way of officially laying my arms down.

When he finally joins me on the balcony, he hesitates by the door for a brief moment. I don't meet his stare. I wait. I let him come to me. Gently, he lifts my legs to rest in my lap. Behind my book, the smallest pull on the corner of my lips.

"You read a lot of books," Nick finally says. I wonder if he reads.

"You don't?" Marking my page, I finally meet his gaze.

"Not as many as you and from the looks of it, you've read this one a lot. Who is your favorite?"

"Stephen King. Or Edgar Allan Poe."

"I don't know whether to be impressed or concerned."

"They're both misunderstood," I sip my coffee. "But, people categorize King as one thing, horror. Right? But, he's so much

108

more than that. Does his brain go down some pretty dark roads? One hundred percent. But, have you seen some of the people who live in this world? They're scarier than anything he could ever write. Most of the time, he's just telling the story of ordinary people and their struggles. In the end, good always overcomes evil." I sip my coffee and continue to match his stare. "Plus, he's funny."

"You think Stephen King is funny?"

"Just because he writes some fucked up situations doesn't mean he can't be funny. I cherish my relationship with Stephen King."

"You're a strange girl, Nina Villa."

"And for some reason, you're still here, Nick Davis."

He matches my smile with a dimpled one.

"Nick." His name sweet on my tongue, but a sigh follows. "I'm sorry. The last week was...I know I've been weird and awkward, even though we said we wouldn't. It's not your fault. Things are just...When we kissed—"

His phone rings inside, but Nick doesn't move. A silent invitation to continue, whoever it is can wait because we need to have this conversation. His eyes never leave mine, but I swallow back any trace of what I was feeling moments earlier. "You gonna get that?" I open my book, effectively ending the conversation.

"Probably just my brother."

"Vai a rispondere al telefono."

"Aren't you supposed to be reading?" He flicks my book on his way back inside. By the time he reaches the phone, whoever it is has already started calling a third time. "Damn, Alex. Where's the fire?"

"I started to think you were dead," his brother's voice echoes over the speaker.

"Not unless Nina plans on killing me like the people in her books."

"Shut up!" I shout from the balcony.

"Wait, what?" Alex asks.

"Nothing." Through the window, I stick my tongue out at him and he laughs. "What's up?"

"Happy birthday!"

Nick's eyes grow wide in horror. He panics trying to take the call off speaker. "You could have just sent a text," Nick hisses and looks out the window. He's looking for me, but I'm not there.

"Did someone say birthday?" Nick spins on his heel to greet me in the doorway. I make quick strides across the room and take Nick's phone. "Buongiorno, Alex! Thank you so much for calling, otherwise, I would have never known it was your brother's birthday. He must have forgotten to mention it."

"Of course, he didn't tell you."

"Nina, please. Please, don't do anything," Nick pleads.

"So, Alex," I dodge Nick's attempts to take the phone. "Tell me more."

And, he does. I don't know how long he spent sharing stories from their childhood, but I can't get enough. It's comforting. I want to meet their parents, meet Alex, and get to know them. I want to see the house they grew up in and spent their entire lives in. I want to see the giant magnolia tree in the front yard with a tire swing. The same one Nick fell out of when he was seven years old and broke his arm trying to help his brother face his fears of climbing a tree. Probably not the best way to get someone over that fear...

I catch him again. Staring. A blush flames my cheeks when he doesn't look away this time. Instead, that dimple appears in the corner of his cheek and I melt. "Well, I should probably let you go. I need to go figure out what I'm going to do for your brother's birthday," I say and hand Nick the phone with a wink.

§

Kai had already scheduled a tee time for eleven o'clock at the country club. Whether my brother knew it or not, I was thankful because it meant Nick wouldn't be sitting around the house on his birthday. I can imagine Nick walking on eggshells waiting to see if my brother is going to bring it up. But, Kai doesn't know. I can keep a promise, even if it's eating me inside. I've been chomping at the bit to tell someone, anyone, it's Nick's birthday. Who doesn't want to celebrate their birthday? There has to be some reason, but he refuses to tell me. "I just don't like to," he said and shrugged.

"That's bullshit."

"Don't make this a big deal. Please, Dee. I promise I am perfectly fine with treating it like a normal day." Clearly, he wasn't going to budge, but after the last week, I felt like I had to do something.

"Fine, Fossette. But, I'm getting you a cupcake and I'm going to celebrate. Deal?" I stuck out my pinky finger.

"Deal." Nick started to get dressed to meet my brother, but I sat in the same spot on the bed, waiting. Walking out of the closet, he saw me — pinky finger hanging in the air. I wasn't going to give up until he wrapped his finger around mine. He rolled his eyes, and a heavy sigh, but finally did.

"So, how are things?" Eileen asks. We've spent most of the day dressed in plush white robes with fresh glasses of champagne in hand. Between the facial and full body massage, I'm feeling like a brand new woman. "You guys have seemed a little tense."

"We're fine." I smile at the waitress handing me a fresh glass of champagne avoiding looking at Eileen.

"Just fine?"

"We're good, Lina. We were just working through some things, but we're good."

"You're not letting Lee get in the middle of things, are you?" Eileen had told me about a conversation she overheard yesterday morning between Karol and my mother. She had been cooking breakfast for Kai when Karol joined Mother for an espresso in the dining room. Mother spent most of the morning expressing her dislike of Nick. "Have you told her your concerns?" Karol asked. I had always liked Karol. She was one of the few who didn't give in to Mother and her tantrums. We have known the Madigans for many years. Our families met when Jack came to Daddy looking for an investor in his private airline company. The Madigan family had been in the airline business for over twenty years before that, Jack's father had started a private airline repair company after working on aircrafts for most of his life. Now, the Madigans own the largest private airline company in the world. So, Karol has been around to see the change in Mother from (supposed) loving wife and doting mother to the person we have the pleasure of knowing today. I think it's why Karol refuses to walk on eggshells around her. "I think you're overreacting just a tad, Bri."

"She could be with Lee. She could—"

"Do you want that for her? Bri, Lee is my son, and I love him, but we both know he and Nina were never going to last."

"A merge—"

"Can you not think about the money for one second?" Karol sighed. Eileen told me Karol hadn't realized Mother was still pushing the idea of me dating Lee — she can't let the idea of the merge go. Merging the Madigan company underneath Villa Inc. is one more thing to generate what seemed to be an endless stream of income for the matriarch, and she doesn't see that happening unless I marry Lee. "Your daughter was hurt tremendously by what Lee did. You should be happy that she found someone who seems to care about her." Eileen said Mother didn't give up though. She made it clear — she does not like Nick.

And now, Eileen is worried about Lee trying to weasel his

way into my relationship.

"No!" I sip my champagne. Of course, I'm not letting him get in the way. There is nothing to get in the way of. I just need to get through the next few weeks and everything can go back to normal. The more I think about it, I'm not sure I want to go back to "normal." After getting to know him, I'm not sure if I can let Nick just walk away.

"Nina."

"I'm doing my best! I hoped having Nick here would make it easier. And it has, some, but Lee doesn't make it very easy."

"Do not let him ruin this for you."

"Non sono sicuro che ci sia molto da rovinare."

"What's going on Nin?"

I sigh. Keeping this secret has turned out to be a lot harder than I thought. I can tell Eileen, right? Eileen will understand. She won't judge. I watch the bubbles rise in my glass and feel my nerves do the same.

"Look, you don't have to tell me, if you don't want. But, when you're ready, I'm here."

"There is something I need to tell you."

twenty

Nick

I CAN HARDLY ENJOY our day on the green. I keep waiting for Kai to bring up my birthday, but so far, he's made no indication of knowing. Nina kept her promise — I made her swear not to tell the others. I have a sneaky suspicion they will make it a bigger deal than is necessary and I don't want that. I am perfectly fine treating it like a normal day. I haven't celebrated my birthday since Mom passed. Birthdays were always her specialty — big parties with her homemade red velvet cake and Pop's secret recipe hamburgers. It just isn't the same without her.

Mom passed away six years ago after battling brain cancer. When she was first diagnosed, she kept it from me and Alex until she weighed out her options. She could go through multiple surgeries, radiation, and chemotherapy with no guaranteed outcome — she had been told the surgeon would never be able to get all of the tumor out, and chemo and radiation wouldn't stop it, only slow down the inevitable. Doctors gave her one year to live if she refused treatments.

Mom decided to take her chances. The night after she had decided to refuse treatments, she told us everything.

"Why are you refusing treatment?" Alex yelled. He couldn't understand why she wouldn't at least try to fight it. He looked to me for help, but I had nothing to offer. What was I supposed to say? It was her decision to make, as much as I hated it. "Get a second opinion!"

"I did. It's not going to stop it, Alex." She maintained a calm demeanor, just like she always did. "It would only prolong the inevitable."

To the surprise of her doctors, and us, Mom lived for another four years. Long enough to see me graduate high school and go to college and see Alex get accepted into Boston College. She suffered a lot in those four years. Headaches. Nausea. Mood swings. Memory loss. Trouble speaking. Trouble walking. Through it all, she always did her best to hide it from us, but it got harder as time went on.

Pop later told me about the day before she passed. She woke up without any pain. No nausea. She remembered everything vividly. It was one of the best days she had in over nine months. That day, he closed up shop early and took her to dinner at her favorite restaurant. They made love for the first time in almost a year. That night, she kissed Pop goodnight and fell into an eternal sleep. There was something different in the air the next morning. When I saw my brother's name on my phone, I already knew what happened.

"One under," Kai says, stuffing his club into the bag on the back of the golf cart. "You good, man?"

"Yeah," it wasn't convincing. "Yeah, just tired, I guess."

"My sister keeping you up too late?" Kai wiggles his eyes suggestively as he waves over the beer girl. I set up to finish the eighth hole. "How are things going with you guys, anyway?"

I put the ball into the hole, two under. "Fine, I guess."

"You guess?"

"Your sister is...complicated and that makes us complicated." We laugh and Kai hands me a fresh beer. "Hey, how long did it take you to speak Italian?"

"I can't speak it, actually. I can understand, for the most

part, put the pieces together, but I don't speak it. Nonna taught Nin what she knew and Dad taught her the rest. His dad was from Italy, so he made sure Dad and Uncle Drew knew the language. It didn't stick for me, but Nin picked it up right away. It gave them something special the rest of us didn't have."

"I didn't realize she was so fluent."

"You'll start to pick up on it. And, if she starts on one of her rants, just remind her to translate. That's what I do."

Taking a sip of beer, I contemplate asking him the question I've wanted to ask since we got here. I've tried not to pry into Nina's life, respect the boundaries she has set and the information she doesn't want me to know. But, it's hard when these things keep happening right in front of me. "Kai, can I ask you a question?"

"Go for it," he climbs into the golf cart.

"What's the deal with your sister and your mom?"

Kai doesn't answer. The drive to the next hole is quiet, at first, I think he didn't hear me, but then I see him chew on the inside of his cheek, his eyes slightly narrowed. He's trying to formulate an answer. He parks but doesn't get out, his hands still gripping the steering wheel. "I don't think I should tell you any of this. If Nin hasn't...I don't want to overstep that."

"I just...I see some of this stuff go on with them and it worries me."

Kai sighs. "Their relationship is very different. They have never gotten along, ever. The only time I've ever seen Mom somewhat invested in Nina was when she was dating Lee. When that ended—"

"Why does your mom love him so much?"

Without hesitation, "The money."

"So, she does only care about two things: you and money."

Kai laughs, but it's more of a scoff. "Trust me, our relationship has been different since I brought Eileen home. She wanted me to marry some trust fund brat, but nothing will ever compare to what I have with Eileen." He sighs. "Look, I don't know how well you knew Nin before this, but she is not the same person she used to be. I'm sure you heard the rumors, but that's just not her. Don't get me wrong, Nina had her fun. Partied hard, messed around, but a lot of those rumors were wildly exaggerated."

"People love to talk."

"Bet you'd never guess Teagan started most of them."

"Teagan?"

"Nin made it easy for people to believe she was this sex-crazed party girl living off Daddy's money, but if you paid attention, you'd realize it was Teagan. She would drag Nina to parties, feed her drinks, all to keep up appearances while Teagan slipped away with God knows who doing God knows what. Then, Monday morning she'd tell everyone what 'Nina' did."

"Why would she do that?"

"When you grow up in a family like ours, you learn to play the game. Everyone has something to offer." Kai sipped his beer. "The name Villa means a lot, it means you can do what you want, when you want. People like having that kind of access. Teagan loved it, especially when her family was in some legal trouble."

"What kind of trouble?"

"The kind you get in when you've been cooking the books and stealing money from your clients. Somehow, her dad was able to weasel his way out of it."

"How do you just walk away from that?"

"That's a great question. One you don't bring up and if you do, no one hears it. Teagan is great at playing the airhead, but she knows exactly what she's doing. When she and Lee started messing around, it wasn't by chance."

"You and Nina and your dad, you're not like these people. But your mom—"

"I used to be. I just realized there was more to life than a name and having expensive shit. Nina and I never got along, she was the wild child and I was the perfect one."

"What changed?"

"I brought Lina home." He smiles thinking about her. "Eileen doesn't come from money. She went to college on a scholarship and dropped out to go to cosmetology school. Her family runs a restaurant down in Tampa where she's from. It's not exactly what Mom had pictured for a wife."

"Speaking of, when you gonna put a ring on it?"

"When are you?"

My eyes widen.

"I'm joking," Kai laughs. "But, to answer your original question…Mom and Dad had me pretty early and they never planned on having more kids, one and done." A sad look crosses Kai's face. "Mom always made sure Nina knew she wasn't planned. And, Nin tried, she did…until one day, she just stopped caring. Like a switch flipped and she started doing anything and everything just to piss Mom off. I guess she thought if Mom was gonna hate her, might as well give her a reason."

"Your mom doesn't hate her."

"No, I don't think so, but she didn't know what to do with my sister. Dad was hardly home, she and I weren't close…it left Nina feeling lonely. I think that's why she did some of the things she did." Kai finishes his beer and climbs out of the cart. "Don't tell her I said anything. My sister tries to play the tough guy… She is tough, tougher than me, but let her tell you when she's ready. Just be there for her, Mom isn't making this very easy."

It's a lot to take in.

Don't judge a book by its cover, my brother's words echo in my mind. Alex has always had the biggest crush on Nina, always told me she was different from the way people portrayed her. I never listened. What did he know? He'd only met her once when she almost ran over him in the parking lot after a football game. Now I'm starting to wonder if maybe he was right.

"Can I ask you to translate something for me?"

"I make no promises it will be totally accurate, but I'll do my best."

"Fossette. Nina calls me that sometimes and when I asked her what it meant, she wouldn't tell me. Just please tell me she isn't calling me asshole or something in Italian."

A toothy grin spreads as Kai pulls his club from the bag. "Fossette means dimples."

twenty-one

Nina

EILEEN AND KAI SIT ACROSS the fire pit on the patio of the country club. "I can't believe you didn't tell us," Eileen shakes her head.

I chickened out — I couldn't tell her the truth about our relationship, so I broke my promise. I decided I'd rather face the consequences of telling them about Nick's birthday than answer one million questions about why I hired a boyfriend for the summer. It wasn't two seconds after I cracked that Eileen picked up her phone to call my brother. At the same time, I called Nick, furiously apologizing. I knew he was going to be upset, I just hoped he would forgive me. Once Kai knew the truth, he told Daddy who told Mother who booked dinner at the country club. "If you didn't want to tell everyone, you could have at least told us. We would have kept your secret."

"We see how well that went, don't we?" I giggle, but I was proud of them, they had kept it simple just like he asked.

"I'm sorry, I don't usually celebrate my birthday." Nick's hand rests on my thigh, my legs draped over his. He's had a problem keeping his hands to himself tonight, but so have I.

The second he stepped out of the bathroom tonight, it was like a switch flipped inside me. I'd never seen him in anything but T-shirts, jeans, and gym shorts, but tonight... Dark gray dress pants. Fitted white T-shirt. Dark gray blazer. Dress shoes. I fought the urge to cancel dinner, lock the door, and ravage him. "Too much?" he asked.

I pulled my bottom lip between my teeth shaking my head. "No, not at all." I took a step closer, letting my fingers smooth the collar of the blazer. My heels made it easy to look directly into his eyes. There was something new in those honey eyes. He was fighting the same urges I was — his hands balled at his sides afraid to touch me. Because once he did, we'd be having a different kind of feast. "You look very handsome," I whispered.

"So do you." He smiled when I laughed, breaking through some of the tension. "You look beautiful, Dee. Really."

"Happy birthday, Nick," I said softly and kissed his cheek.

I smile thinking of the memory only hours earlier. His thumb grazes the exposed skin of my thigh, igniting a fire under his touch. I try to contain the shaky breath behind a sip of champagne, but his smirk tells me he heard it. Without looking away from the conversation, his hand subtly inches closer to the hemline of my dress — a cream-colored plunge neck cloak dress, my hair pulled into a bun, a few strands falling to frame my face. My burgundy lipstick leaves a stain in the shape of a half-moon on the champagne glass. I try to focus on the conversation, but it's hard when all I can think about is his hand and all the places I wish it was touching me right now.

"Happy birthday, Nick!" Daddy says dragging me from my burning thoughts. On our way out of the restaurant, he and Mother were dragged into a conversation with one of the other members of the club. Apparently, they just escaped. Behind them, a waitress holds a cake loaded with sparklers sending flurries into the air.

Nick shrinks back into his seat and a blush creeps into his cheeks. All eyes on him. This is what he didn't want, a big spectacle, but I know my family and they couldn't let him get away without some kind of show. As we sing, my fingers weave through the hair at the nape of his neck and he matches my smile. I lean in close to whisper in his ear as the song comes to an end, "Make a wish, Fossette."

"I already have it."

§

I walk from the bathroom to the closet so I can change into something more comfortable. Removing my earrings, I see Nick leaning against the bedroom door, arms crossed over his broad chest. He stares at me, a small smile on corner of his lips. "Take a picture, it'll last longer," I laugh, but his expression doesn't change. "What?"

"Thank you for tonight."

"I'm sorry I told your secret."

"It was worth it. I haven't celebrated my birthday in years, but I'm happy the first time was with you."

My heart stops.

He crosses the room and takes my hands in his. "Can I do something?"

"What?"

"Just want to test a theory." His hands cup my cheek and he kisses me. It's soft — gentle. Testing the boundaries. I savor the feeling of his lips against mine, a hint of sugar from the cake on them. My hands grip onto the collar of his blazer pulling him closer and my mouth opens to him, his tongue sliding in to massage mine. A moan deep in my throat turns to a whimper when he tears his lips from mine. Without another word, he walks into the bathroom closing the door.

twenty-two

NICK HASN'T MADE A move since the night of his birthday a week ago and I haven't had the nerve to bring it up. When he came to bed that night, he cuddled up behind me, wrapping his arm around my waist and pulling me flush against his chest. We froze entering that new territory. As if he realized what he'd done, he started to pull away, but I held him in place and turned to face him. Our faces mere inches apart. The smell of whiskey and red wine mingled in the air between us. When I woke up the next morning, my head rose and fell with the rhythm of his steady breathing. I've fallen asleep in his arms every night since.

I wash out the popcorn bowl thinking about the past week. How good things have been. How much I like spending time with him, but then I think about the end of summer. This is going to be a lot harder than I thought. How am I supposed to just walk away? What if we don't walk away? This is getting too complicated.

I sigh taking a rather large gulp of wine. Nick left a few minutes ago to call his brother. Alex had called while we were finishing a movie and Nick wanted to make sure he was okay. It was two in the morning in Boston, a little late for a routine phone call.

"We've got to stop meeting like this," Lee says walking into the kitchen.

"Goodnight, Lee."

He grabs my arm when I walk past him. "Oh, come on, Dove. Don't be like that. I'm just playing around." I shrug his arm off when he drapes it across my shoulders and take a step back. "C'mon, Nin. I'm sorry."

"James…"

"Davina." The hint of a smirk on his lips. "Look, I'm sorry for what happened. I never meant to hurt you. I should've just told you, been honest when I wasn't happy. But, that's the thing…I was happy when we were together. It's when we were apart that I—"

"I don't care anymore." I'm two steps away from the stairs when he grabs my arm again.

"C'mon Dove, don't be this way." I cringe at the use of the old pet name. He pushes a piece of hair behind my ear, but I recoil from his touch my back hitting one of the large pale logs lining the stairwell. My chest tightens as he surrounds me. There's nowhere I can go that he wouldn't be able to stop me.

I try to push past him but he holds me against the log. "Would you get off of me?" His arms brace against the side of my head.

"He can't give you what you want."

"I'm so serious, James."

"Not like I can."

"I do just fine on my own, thanks."

Lee leans in close and whispers in my ear, "But, I can give you more." Before I can protest further, Lee kisses me. It's hard, full of desperation. He presses into me, his body melding into mine. I try to push him away, but his grasp is firm. He traps my hands above us and kisses down my neck, nipping at the soft skin. I hate that I'm starting to lose myself in the familiarity. A soft moan escapes my lips. "There she is," Lee kisses me again.

"I missed you, Dove."

It sends me into a spiral of emotions and when he tells me to follow, I obey. Lee holds a finger to his lips pressing me against the wall of the hallway. Mere feet from the room he shares with Teagan. Reality smacks me in the face when Lee opens the door to the spare room. What in the hell am I doing? I try to take a step back, but he has a firm grasp on my hand. "Come on, Dove," Lee beckons. "No one has to know."

"Is that what you used to tell Teagan?"

"That's not fair, Nina."

"What in the hell is wrong with you?" I rip myself from him taking two big steps back.

"You're turning me down?"

"This was never going to happen."

"Because he is so much better?"

"Stay away from me, James."

§

"Che cazzo?" I fall against the door out of breath. Did that actually happen?

"I'm starting to see why you left him." There's a smugness in his tone I've never heard before. I'm still trying to catch my breath when I open my eyes to find Nick sitting on the bed. "He didn't last very long."

"What are you talking about?"

"Don't play coy, Davina." My heart drops when he all but spits my full name. "It's all starting to make sense now. If you just wanted to make Lee jealous, why didn't you just say that?"

"Nick, that is not—"

"Come on, Nina. It's obvious. I saw you not even ten minutes ago."

Saw me? What does he mean he saw me?

"Were you spying on me?"

"Hardly." Darkened eyes meet mine. "You weren't exactly hiding. I came to check on you when you didn't come to bed, but you seemed to be doing just fine."

"Nick, nothing happened. I mean, yes, he kissed me, but we didn't— We didn't have sex."

"I'll be the good fake boyfriend you hired. When this is all over, you can go back to him."

"Zitto! Listen to me." I take his hands in mine. The need to make him understand courses through me. "Nothing happened. I stopped him before anything could happen, and I came back…to you."

And finally, it's like he sees me, and really takes in my appearance. My lips are swollen from Lee's attack, but I'm still put together as usual. My olive green button-up still tucked neatly into my jean shorts, hair still pulled into a loose braid, not a strand out of place. I visibly see his defenses fall. "Shit… Nina, I-I'm sorry. I shouldn't have just assumed—" I practically melt into his embrace. "I'm sorry. And, even if you did—"

"I don't. It's over, it's been over." I shouldn't have to explain it though, we're not together. Even if the lines are a little blurred at the moment…we're not together, but being in his arms feels so right. "I tried to stop him, tried to push him away, but I couldn't."

His arms tighten around me at my confession. "If he touches you again, I'll beat his ass."

twenty-three

WHEN I WAKE UP, I notice the sun is higher in the sky than normal for six in the morning and a glance at the alarm proves it true. 9:43 A.M. Shit, did I sleep through my alarm? I don't remember the last time I slept past seven. Beside me, the bed is empty. Why didn't he wake me up? A groan fills the space around me when I stretch. My phone vibrates on the nightstand next to me. Why is it on vibrate? I never have it on vibrate.

NICHOLAS DAVIS

Mornin' Dee

I turned off your alarm & your ringer. Get some sleep. You work too much.

Your dad and Kai wanted to go to breakfast, I think they're trying to pick my brain a bit more… I'll let you know when we're on our way back.

You're reading these, go back to sleep. I have coffee and breakfast for you. Don't get out of bed.

Is that an order?

Yes.

Yes, sir. ♥

Are you suggesting I have a black heart?

127

Maybe a little.

Offended.

Good.

Brat.

I can't fight a smile — I don't think I ever received a good morning text from Lee or JJ. And, he's bringing breakfast? And, he's flirting with me? I can't even be mad about him turning off the alarm.

NICHOLAS DAVIS
I'll be home soon.

My heart skips a beat.

I'll be home soon.

With that thought, I snuggle back into my bed. The familiar earthy scents of cedar and cardamom fill my lungs when I grip his pillow settling in for a long day in bed with my boyfriend.

Fake.

Fake boyfriend.

A long day in bed with my fake boyfriend.

§

I don't even remember falling back asleep. One minute, I'm watching *Supernatural,* and the next… Nick is staring down at me with a smirk and a coffee. "Just following orders, Fossette," my voice thick with sleep.

"Good girl." That goes straight to my core and suddenly I'm wide awake. His lips like fire against my forehead. Nick leaves the coffee on my nightstand and collects the rest of my breakfast. It's like he's oblivious to what his words are doing to me as he starts to pull take-out boxes from the bag. "Do you want breakfast on the balcony?"

"How about breakfast in bed?"

Darkened eyes dart up to meet mine. He stares at me like

he's trying to figure out what exactly I'm saying before a smirk tugs on the corner of his lips. I can see he's considering it, but he shakes his head. "I'll meet you on the balcony, Dee."

When he's gone, I let out the breath I'd been holding. Holy shit. What in the hell just happened?

§

"So, what did Daddy and Kai want?" I sip my coffee joining him on the balcony. The sun high in the sky confirms it's almost noon. Is this what normal people do on vacation — sleep until noon and eat breakfast on the balcony? I've never done this, but I think I could get used to it. Nick has laid breakfast out on the square wooden coffee table — avocado toast with a side of eggs and potatoes from Little Bird. They took him to my favorite restaurant without me? Rude.

"Just wanted to see how I'm liking it here."

"That all?"

"And you."

I rip open the hot sauce packet with my teeth and pour it on my eggs, ignoring his stare. I have to. From the way this morning has been going, I can't promise we'll be keeping our distance any longer.

"Asked about Pop and my brother." He takes a sip of my coffee. "Wonder what your dad would think if he knew I was describing myself. You think he'd still be okay with you dating someone who isn't making six figures a year?"

"Yes." Finally, I meet his gaze and it's softer. Like he really wants to know. Like he's really thought about this. I know Daddy would be okay with it. As long as I'm happy.

"He thinks you and Lee have a right to talk things over without me and Teagan getting in the way." It's more of a question than a statement. He wants to know if I think the same, if I want the same.

"I don't want him, Nick."

"I didn't say—"

"I don't want him. Not as my boyfriend, not as a friend. I want nothing to do with him."

"What do you want, Davina?"

You.

But, I can't say that.

"Eat your breakfast, Dee," Nick sighs. He kisses the top of my head lingering just a moment too long for it to be a friendly peck. "I'm gonna go find Kai. Help him in the garage."

twenty-four

I CAN HONESTLY SAY I haven't heard a word Eileen has said in the last two minutes. My attention solely on the man in front of me. I pull my lip between my teeth watching him toss the football across the driveway to my brother. The way his skin seems to glow under the sun. The way his arms flex with each toss of the ball. The way his legs move fluidly between catching and throwing stance, almost like a dance — like he's done this a million times.

"You're drooling." Eileen nudges my shoulder.

"Am not." But, I'm close. Nick meets my stare as he catches the ball. He sends me a wink before he returns it to Kai.

"Well, c'mon, before you start actually drooling." Eileen loops her arm through mine and pulls me from the garden wall.

Nick wraps his arm around my waist and presses a lingering kiss to my temple. He whispers, "See something you like?"

"I don't know what you're talking about." I smile up at him and stand on my tiptoes to kiss his cheek.

"Finally, Madigan!" Kai calls up the front steps. Lee glares from the front door as Teagan skips down the steps, oblivious as always. "I was starting to think you were gonna bail."

"In your dreams, Villa." Lee catches the ball my brother

throws his way tossing it between his hands. "Did you forget who won last time?"

"In *your* dreams, Madigan."

The football game is a Villa family tradition every year around the Fourth of July. Daddy started it years ago to get Kai out of the house. My brother was always doing something with Mother or watching TV, while I was out exploring. It was Daddy's way of getting Kai outdoors for a little bit. It used to just be Kai and me versus Daddy, but then we would bring friends over and it would be girls versus boys or kids versus adults. Mother never participates. Too likely to break a nail or get dirt on her clothes.

The game takes place in the sideyard, the only area relatively flat enough for space to run without trees in the way. The end zones have always remained the same: the stone steps leading around the house and the tree line fifty yards from the house. The line of scrimmage marked by a stake Daddy hammered into the ground the first game.

Nick maintains his hold on me, his arm slung over my shoulders, following the others into the yard. Lee tosses the ball back to Kai when he steps up to the front. "Okay, only one rule," Kai says. "No tackling. None of us are trying to end up in the hospital." That has always been the only rule we abide by because one wrong move and someone is going to need stitches. Once everyone agrees, Kai declares himself and Lee team captains. Kai picks first, "Nina."

"Thank you," I mouth to my brother.

"Eileen."

"Nick."

"That means I'm with you, baby!" Teagan jumps up and down, but Lee doesn't share her excitement stalking away from her.

"Sorry, babe," Kai fake pouts before kissing Eileen's cheek. "You know, I might let you score just to make up for it."

"Oh, please, I don't need your pity point, Villa." Eileen flips him off.

Kai laughs and joins us at the line of scrimmage. When everyone has settled into position, he explains the rules one more time. With the tension radiating between Lee and Nick, I can't blame him. Not a bad idea to remind at least one of them this is not meant to put anyone in the hospital. This is supposed to be fun and one wrong hit could send someone flying into a tree or split their head open on a rock.

"Hut-hut!" Kai runs backward looking for an opening. Nick runs towards the steps, but Lee blocks him. Eileen and Teagan both run toward Kai.

"Teagan, block Nina!" Lee yells, but Kai has already thrown the ball to me in the end zone. "Teagan, you need to block," Lee continues. "Eileen was already blocking Kai, so what does that mean? You block the open person."

"Sorry, I just thought—"

"Just do what I say!"

I almost feel bad for Teagan as she stalks back to the middle of the yard. She always hated sports. She did the bare minimum in gym class and refused to play whenever she came to Haven in the past. Why should we expect her to do anything more now? "Better luck next time," I say, tossing the ball to Lee and adding a quick smirk if only to irritate him further.

After we line up, I share an eye roll with Nick when Lee calls out, "Red 42!" trying to act like the quarterbacks he has seen in movies. "Hut!"

I block Eileen and Kai takes Lee, which leaves Nick wide open. From across the field, I can see Teagan's eyes light up stalking her prey.

"Poor Nick," Eileen giggles as we watch him raise his hands trying to keep as much distance between them as possible while still blocking her. With Teagan distracted, Lee has no choice but to toss the ball to Eileen. Kai picks her up, spinning her around so I can intercept the ball running into the end zone.

Nick kisses my forehead and takes the ball, "Nice job, babe."

I stare after him for a brief moment. Did he just... Did he say babe? The word bounces around my brain as we line up again.

Kai sets everyone in motion — Eileen runs towards me, Lee towards Nick. Teagan tries to block Kai, but he throws the ball over her head to Nick. The ball brushes Lee's hands before Nick catches it. Lee tries to grab Nick, but he is already in the end zone.

"What were you saying, Madigan?" Kai antagonizes him.

"It's okay, baby. We'll get it this time," Teagan says, but he ignores her. Lee hates losing. Hates it. He mumbles to himself walking back to the line and I have a bad feeling this is about to get ugly.

When Lee yells, "Hut-hut!" I block Teagan and Kai blocks Lee. Lee tosses the ball to Teagan, there's no chance Eileen will be able to get it behind Nick's block. Teagan catches the ball, but I grab it from her hands when she stops to celebrate. I quickly toss the ball to Nick who takes off towards the steps.

The world seems to slow down after that. Nick runs towards the end zone, Lee hot on his heels. I already know what is about to happen. I can see it in Lee's features. He's going to break the one rule. But, I can't get the words out. Lee tackles Nick just before they reach the end zone. Both tumbling towards the house, towards the stairs...

twenty-five

WHAT HAPPENED TO THE one rule? ONE.

It happened so fast, none of us could have been ready. No way Nick could have stopped it. He tumbles toward the end zone. I hear the impact — his head colliding with one of the rock steps. Not good. I don't even realize my legs have carried me to him until I'm already there. His eyes still closed as he sits up, but there is a trail of blood falling down the side of his face.

"Lee, dude, what the fuck?" I hear Kai shout. I agree. What. The. Fuck. "You know we don't do that shit here. Someone's gonna get hurt!"

I push Nick's hair aside accidentally grazing the wound. "Merda," I whisper between clenched teeth. Finally, he opens his eyes. "Stai bene?"

"English, please."

"Eileen, get my keys. Devo portarlo all'ospedale."

He pushes me away, "I'm fine, Nina. I'm not going to the hospital."

"You're not fine!"

"I've been hit worse on the field."

"You hit your head on a rock, Nick. We need to make sure you don't have a concussion. Stai sanguinando, what if you need stitches?"

"Nina, I don't—"

"Stiamo andando all'ospedale." No argument in my voice. Pure authority. This is not up for discussion.

Kai offers his hand to help Nick stand, but he waves it off. He stands only to stumble but catches himself on one of the boulders. He needs to goto the hospital.

"Sorry, man. I was just—"

"Stay the fuck away from him," I stop Lee from getting too close. "Qual è il tuo problema?"

Kai leads Nick towards the garage where Eileen waits with my keys and wallet. He's still fighting them, he doesn't want to go, but I don't care. He's going. I need to make sure he doesn't have a concussion.

"It's not my fault he can't take a hit, Nin."

"Can't take a hit? You tackled him nelle fottute rocce! We don't tackle, Lee. You know that. L'hai fatto apposta." He tries to reach for me, but I shove his hand away. Nick tries to move toward us, but Kai holds him back. There's no way he can confront Lee in his current state.

Lee tries to reach for me again, "Nina, come on. I'm sorry."

"Lee, lo giuro…if you don't back up—"

"That's not what you were saying the other night."

"You fucking wish."

"You're choosing him over me?" Lee still hot on my trail.

"You chose first, Lee." Just before I reach the garage, he grabs my hand. Without hesitation, I slap him and he staggers back a step, stunned. "Stay the hell away from us."

twenty-six

SINCE WE GOT BACK from the hospital, I have refused to leave his side, even after he fell asleep two hours ago. The hospital says they don't believe he has a concussion, but I still need to watch for the signs, just in case. They gave Nick eight stitches. Eight. I hope he doesn't hate me after this. I mean, he's going to have a scar on the side of his head now. Eileen brought leftovers from dinner down about twenty minutes ago, but I'm almost too tired to eat. The only thing keeping me going right now is coffee.

"No wine? That's not like you," Eileen jokes, but I'm not in the mood. So much is going on, so much I don't even understand. I can't even begin to describe the panic I felt when I saw Nick tumble into those rocks. The idea of something happening to him scares the shit out of me. "What is going on with you, Nin?"

"Niente," I snap and Eileen reels back. Shit, I didn't mean to snap at her. "I'm sorry, I just…I'm fine. Everything is fine, Lina. There's nothing you need to worry about."

"It's very obvious you're not fine. Maybe everyone else is okay ignoring it, but I'm not. And, I know it's not just about Lee." Eileen reaches over and holds my hand. I want to tell her. I need to tell someone, to finally get it off my chest. But, I can't.

What if it backfires? "You can tell me."

"We're not… We're not together."

"What?" Eileen laughs, but it fades when I don't join her.

"Nick and I aren't together." Saying it out loud…hurts? It physically makes my heart ache to finally say it out loud. It's like before, I could almost believe the lie, believe we were together. But, saying it out loud, makes it true.

"What?"

"He's pretending to be my boyfriend."

"What?"

"Are you a parrot?" I sip my coffee. For a moment, neither of us says anything as Eileen soaks in the information. "Mother was adamant I have someone here to make it less awkward. It didn't matter that I'm her daughter and didn't want to see my ex-boyfriend. She was gonna set me up with someone…the neighbor, actually. I couldn't let that happen."

"So you what — picked some random guy off the street?"

"Not exactly."

"Is he an escort?"

"No! Lina," I laugh. "No, he's Michaela's cousin."

"This doesn't make sense, Nina. You seem so great together."

"Well yeah, that's kind of the point." I shrug. "But, things have gotten…complicated." I look through the window. Nick is sound asleep, but the time on the clock means I needed to wake him soon. The doctor suggested waking him every four hours and monitoring him for concussion symptoms through tomorrow. "I think…I think I have feelings for him."

"As in *real* feelings?" I nod. "That's great!" Eileen's smile fades when I don't return it. "Isn't it?"

I play with the hem of the blanket. "I just wanted to get Mom off my back and keep Lee away from me. I didn't think it would turn into this." Eileen smiles, a knowing look on her face. "I know that look. What?"

"Did you tell him you love him?"

"What?" I scoff. "Lina, I don't—"

"Oh yes, you do. It's young and reckless." Eileen covers my hand again. "But, it's love, Nina. Trust me, what you two have going on is more than just a paid arrangement. I guarantee he doesn't even take the money."

"You're not mad?" I'm relieved at how well she seems to be taking the news.

"I don't think it's your best idea, but I get it," Eileen says behind her wine glass. "Your mom can be... Well, let's just say I get it. But, Nin, the two of you have something special. I can see it. He has been so good for you. You need someone normal, someone like him."

And, I think she might just be right.

§

Teagan skips into the kitchen. "Whatcha doing?" I ignore her. "Oh, come on! What's a little conversation between friends? I'm just trying to be nice."

"We see how well that worked out for me last time," I quip heading for the stairs.

"Nina, wait! I just want to talk."

"Not now, Teagan."

"Just two seconds!"

I'm going to regret this, but I turn to face her, "What?"

"I just wanted to...apologize. I never meant for any of it to happen this way."

I scoff, she cannot be serious.

"You know I would never do anything to hurt you. I mean, aren't you glad things turned out the way they did? If you had never broken up with Lee, you wouldn't have found Nick. And, you seem so happy together! I was hoping we could move past what happened before."

"This isn't high school, Teagan. You can't just go around

hurting people and think everything is going to be okay because you pretend to feel sorry. The high school popularity contest doesn't matter in the real world."

"That why you've used Daddy's name to get everything you want?"

"Used his…" I scoff. "And, what did you do, Teagan?" She doesn't answer. "Niente. Non hai fatto nulla. You didn't even graduate college. But, you got what you always wanted, right? You always wanted Lee, always. He never wanted you—"

"That's not true."

"Not even when I was fucking JJ did Lee want you. You were just convenient when I was busy. And, if that is the one thing you have over me, I can live with that."

"Lee loves me!"

"Ti ama? If he loves you, why did he try to sleep with me?"

"You're lying." Teagan knows better. I have no reason to lie, but she has to believe Lee loves her, because what else does she have? "You're just jealous."

I laugh. "That's nothing to be jealous of."

"Because you have Nick? You don't even know him, Nina."

"What's that supposed to mean?"

"Just be careful. You wouldn't want to get your heart broken again."

I narrow my gaze. The way she says it… Does she know something? The wall clock catches my attention. We should have left ten minutes ago to meet Kai and Eileen downtown at the Fourth of July festival, but I was running behind.

"Nina, we gotta go!" Nick's voice echoes from the foyer.

"Better go, wouldn't want to keep Nicky waiting," Teagan smirks and waves innocently. She's satisfied with herself knowing she's been able to get under my skin, even if only a little. With a little more pep in her step, she returns to the kitchen before I turn back down the stairs.

twenty-seven

"**WHERE THE HELL IS** she?" I hear Kai burst through the garage door. He and Eileen have been waiting for the past ten minutes, and if I take any longer we are going to be extremely late. At least, by Kai standards. I'm almost within view when he lets out an exasperated sigh — such a drama queen. "What's taking so long?"

"You can't rush perfection, Kai." I finally descend the stairs dressed in black high-waisted pants, a white blouse, and heels. My hair pulled back into a loose ponytail with pieces framing my face.

"This is what took so long? You just put on a pair of pants and —"

"You look great, Nin," Eileen hushes him.

"Sure, sure, you look great. Now can we go? We're late." Kai disappears back into the garage leaving the door open.

I roll my eyes, it's not like my brother gave me much notice about these plans for the evening. He notified me exactly an hour and fifteen minutes ago that I needed to get ready for dinner. I hadn't even showered from my afternoon run, an hour was not going to be enough time to pick out an outfit, shower, and do my makeup and hair. I was going to need at least twenty additional minutes. He should be happy I finished with five minutes to spare. "You know, I'm feeling a little overdressed," I notice Eileen's outfit — jeans and a flowing purple tank top with a kimono. "You told me to dress up, but you're in the same outfit from earlier. Should I go change?"

"No!" She practically shouts. "No, you look perfect."

"Eileen, what's going on? Where are you taking me?"

"It's a surprise!"

"You know I don't like surprises."

"Well, you'll just have to wait and see." Eileen loops her arm with mine and leads me into the garage.

§

The Golden Oak is Haven's grande dame hotel tucked away at the base of Haven Mountain. The resort is best known for its breathtaking mountain views, award-winning restaurants, and a ski lift to ski in and out with ease. The exterior of the resort is unassuming — a modest Tudor style. Each room a unique space with individualized layouts and designs because of the hotel's unique horseshoe shape. And, while the Golden Oak feels like a boutique hotel, the vibe is decidedly unpretentious.

As Kai pulled into the porte-coché, my favorite bellhop quickly opens the back passenger door. "Nin, it's so good to see you!"

"Andy, it's been too long!" No one looks twice as I hug him. This kind of interaction is the norm around here. "I didn't see you a few weeks ago."

"I was on my honeymoon."

"Ce l'hai fatta!" I've come to know Andy over the last six years since he first began working at the Golden Oak. Three years ago, I was in town with Daddy when we ran into Andy and his girlfriend. From the look in his eye, I knew Andy had met his person — it was the same look I could see now. "I'm so happy for you. I'm sure it was beautiful."

"Thank you. The honeymoon was in Greece. She refused to go anywhere else after you told us so much."

"Isn't it the best?" He agrees. Congratulating him one more time, I begin to walk inside only to realize I'm alone.

Where are Kai and Eileen?

Still in the car.

"Aren't you coming?"

"Not tonight," Eileen says with a bright smile.

"So, the surprise is...what exactly? I'm eating alone?"

Kai points behind me to the entrance of the hotel.

Nick walks out the open door — a brief smile in thanks to the doorman. His smile widens when he sees me. A small wave brings a smile to my lips and I return the gesture. A light brush against my arm tears my attention from him, Eileen is suddenly beside me.

"Do me a favor, just have fun tonight." Eileen squeezes my hand gently before her expression turns serious. "But, not too much fun and make sure you're home before midnight."

I roll my eyes. "Yes, Mom."

"Have fun kids!" Kai shouts from the car and Eileen climbs back into the passenger seat. As they drive off, a sinking feeling washes over me. Does Kai know the truth? Eileen promised she wouldn't say anything, she would let me tell my brother when I'm ready.

The feeling disappears when I see Nick again. Hands shoved deep in his pockets, he rocks back on his heels, a shy smile ghosting his lips. Screw it. I can worry about it tomorrow. Right now, nothing else matters except us.

"Hey," he says, his voice smooth like silk wraps around me.

"Hi," my voice soft. He takes a step forward, his eyes unwavering under the lights. "Nick, what's all this about? I thought—"

"I'm sorry," Nick interjects. Fingers sift through curls nervously. "I know I haven't been the easiest to deal with since

143

we got here. Hell, even before. And, there is a lot for us to figure out, and to learn about each other, but I thought we could start with a date."

"A date?" A smile on my pink-stained lips. "Like, a real date?"

"Yeah, a real date."

"Nicholas Davis is a romantic, who knew?"

"Don't tell anyone, it might ruin my reputation." His soft words danced across my skin as he whispers in my ear. "Shall we?"

twenty-eight

THE INSIDE OF THE Grand Oak was renovated two years ago to give it a more modern atmosphere, while still keeping classic ski lodge vibes. The lobby includes a large picture window looking over the mountainside, a double-sided fireplace, and a library with ample seating perfect for relaxing after a long day on the slopes. The renovations carry over into the rooms which were renovated at the same time, however they were given a slightly less modern feel maintaining that cozy mountain vibe.

Turning down the last hallway, Nick's hand moves from my back to take my hand in his. Our fingers immediately intertwine. We approach the restaurant, The Little Bird, and the hostess perks up. "Oh my gosh, Nina! I didn't know you were coming tonight. I would have prepared your normal table. I didn't—"

"It's okay, Adriana. That's what happens with surprises, right?" A sincere smile as I reassure her.

"We can totally move you—"

"No, it's fine. I'm sure wherever we're set up is perfect."

"You sure?" Nick asks.

"Positive." I squeeze his hand following Adriana to a table in the far corner. We slide into the round booth, leaving a small space between us — enough room to be comfortable, with the ability to move closer depending how the night progresses.

"I'll let Steve know you're here," Adriana says with a knowing smirk before she disappears.

"Kai said this was your favorite restaurant. So, I thought it would be a good choice. If I had known you had a certain table, I would've given your name."

"Nick, it's perfect." I kiss his cheek. "So, you enlisted the help of my brother?"

"Don't worry, Eileen supervised."

Steve interrupts us, "Nina, so good to see you! I didn't know you were joining us this evening."

"How are you, Steve?"

"You just know everyone, don't you?" Nick jokes.

"We all know Nina around here, but we haven't seen much of her this summer."

"I've been a little busy."

Steve looks between us and our hands that rest on top of the table. "I see that. It's nice to meet you..."

"Nick."

"Well, Nick. I hope to see more of you. Nin, the usual?"

"Just a glass of Cab, and he'll take an IPA," I order for us. When Steve leaves, it's time to ask the question I've been holding back. "So, what made you decide to take me out on a 'real' date?"

"Well, I really have seen a different side of you."

"You never gave me a chance."

"And, I'm sorry for that. I'm sorry for a lot of my behavior. I want us to get to know each other. Who knows, maybe we walk away from this as friends or maybe more?"

"Maybe," I say with a small smirk.

"But, I wanted to say thank you. You've done so much for me this summer, I wanted to return the favor."

"It was part of our agreement, Fossette."

"Fuck the agreement, Dee. I don't care about that anymore." Nick kisses the back of my hand. "I could walk away without a fucking cent and I'd be happy that I got to spend this time with you." His eyes never leave mine when he says, "I think we both know we haven't been pretending for a while now."

My heart stops.

We haven't been pretending for a while now.

Hearing him admit it makes my heart swell. Confirms everything I've felt. Every look, every touch, every word...

"You know, my brother had the biggest crush on you in school. Totally, in love with you. I thought he was seeing dollar signs and parties, but he always told me there was more to you. I guess, I just thought he was making shit up."

Steve returns with our drinks. "We ready to order?"

"Just a few more minutes," I say, taking a sip of my wine. When he's gone, I turn back to Nick with a smirk, "In love with me, huh?"

"Apparently, you almost ran him over once." He laughs when I choke on a sip of wine. "Some football game against Bridgeport, guess you just barely missed him in the parking lot."

"I am so sorry."

"Don't be. He came home and told Mom how the Nina Villa talked to him after she almost ran him over."

"Wait." The pieces fall into place. "I think, I remember him. Kinda looks like you, but taller...shorter hair?" Nick nods. "He and I talked earlier that night before I almost ran him over."

Senior Year. The Hills Academy Eagles versus the Bridgeport High Tigers. We crushed Bridgeport and our team was in the mood to celebrate. His brother had been walking through the parking lot without paying attention to where he was going and walked right out in between two cars into the middle of the road and —

SCREECH!

Alex jumped back from my Wrangler that had come to a halt mere inches from him. I sat behind the wheel, Teagan next to me, and Elizabeth in the backseat. We were dressed in cheerleading uniforms embellished with the word EAGLES. After a moment, my glare softened — recognizing him. There was no way I could forget that obnoxious Tigers spirit shirt from when I met him earlier that night — we had helped a Bridgeport girl who spilled red icee down the front of her white jeans.

"What, are you stupid?" Teagan shouted, ripping Alex's attention from me. "Watch where you're going!"

"Didn't see you," Alex said and took a step back, his eyes met mine again.

"Better watch yourself, Tiger," I winked at him before speeding away.

Nick's thumb grazes the top of my hand bringing me back to the present moment. "He never told me that."

"Well, he ran into me right after I had a fight with my boyfriend, at the time. And—"

"You had a boyfriend?" He sounds genuinely shocked.

Was it that surprising? Then again… Maybe it was. He went to Bridgeport and Rosecliffe. I'm sure he heard the stories. Everyone did. Even if most of them weren't true.

"Yes," I contemplate the answer. "It wasn't something I advertised. Not to mention, it wasn't the best situation. I was, um…I was dating someone who I shouldn't have gotten involved with."

"Oh, this oughta be good. Who was it?"

"You're actually going to judge me now." Nick puts his hand up, swearing no judgment. "Do you remember John Jansen?"

His eyes widen. "Nina! You didn't."

"Guilty."

"Is that why he got transferred?"

I sigh, "Mother found out and I had to tell Daddy. I begged

him not to turn JJ in. But, as mad as I was about it…I'd been looking for a way out. That doesn't mean I wasn't upset. I was, especially when I found out who told."

"Please tell me it wasn't Alex."

"No!" I laugh. "No, it was Teagan."

"Teagan? But, I thought you guys were best friends."

"We weren't best friends, we weren't even really friends. I mean, kind of, but… We actually hated each other. She only tried to be friends with me when her family had no money."

"So, how did we get where we are now?"

"What do you mean?"

"You and Lee and Teagan."

"Well, I told you Mother always wanted me and Lee to get together. And, I never was interested, but Lee was. So, when Teagan ratted me out, I wanted to take something from her, just like she took it from me." I chew on my lip. How much do I really want to tell him? I mean this isn't exactly first date material. "I proposed that Lee and I become friends with benefits. She had always been in love with Lee, so I knew it would kill her when she found out."

"So you weren't actually dating?"

"Not at first, but eventually. Then, I started to actually kind of like him. Thought we'd get married, have kids, the whole shebang."

"Until Teagan."

"Until Lee. He decided he didn't want to be with someone independent and goal driven. He wanted someone who didn't have any real passion in life." Nick presses a kiss to the back of my hand. "I knew, or at least I had a feeling about what was going on between them. I didn't want to believe it, but I knew."

"I'm sorry, Dee."

"Don't be. Getting rid of Lee was the best thing that ever happened."

"I'm sorry that I haven't made this trip any easier for you."

"I haven't exactly made it easy for you, either."

"So, let's start over." Nick sticks his hand out to me. "Hi, I'm Nicholas Davis. I work with my dad at the family shop and I used to think you were a stuck-up bitch, but I'm here to change that."

I laugh but shake his hand. "Davina Bay Villa. I come from money, but don't use it as a crutch. And, I kind of wish your brother had introduced us back in school."

"We ready to order?" Steve reappears with his notepad ready.

§

After dinner, we walk down Oak Avenue, his arm wrapped securely around me. Tonight has felt like a fever dream. I can't help but wonder when I'm going to wake up. When it's all going to end... But, I should enjoy it while it lasts. So, I ask the question I've been curious about from the moment I saw him shirtless the first time. "So, I have a question...I saw that you have a tattoo on your chest. What does it mean?"

"Why, Ms.Villa, have you been checking me out?" Heat rises in my cheeks. "It's the Tree of Life... Cycle of life, connection with God and the universe and...all that stuff."

There's more to the story, I'm sure of it. More that he isn't ready to share just yet. I don't want to push.

"I never pegged you for the basic tattoo trend kind of person."

A tight smile pulls at the corner of his mouth.

"Can I ask you another question?"

"You just did."

I stick my tongue out at him. "When we met, you looked so familiar, but I just... I can't figure out where we might've met before. We didn't go to high school together, but you did go to Rosecliffe. And, you studied architecture, I studied architecture. Did we meet there?"

He's quiet for a second too long as we walk down the street. "We probably ran into each other. Lee was in a frat, right? I hung around Sig Phi a lot."

"This had to be more than a casual run in."

"So, you can remember my brother at a football game, but don't remember me?" I laugh realizing how weird it sounds. "I don't mean to sound rude, but—"

"There are so many things I've forgotten because... Well, because I did party. I had fun in school, sometimes a little too much fun. And, some things are a little fuzzy."

"That's fair."

We come to one of my favorite spots in all of downtown — a courtyard with an unobstructed view of the mountain. No buildings, no ski lifts, nothing. I take a deep breath of fresh air and smile — there's a storm coming.

"So Fossette, how are you feeling about me now?"

A dimpled smile when Nick takes my hands in his. "Dee, I like you. Something, I never thought I would say, but—"

Nina, don't push it.

"Okay."

"Okay?"

There's so much I want to ask him. So much I feel like he's not telling me. I know we've met before, I can feel it tugging at me somewhere deep inside my mind... But, right now, maybe it's not worth digging. Maybe, I just need to let go. "I'm not looking for an undying love confession, Nick. We can agree to take it slow. Get to know each other, see what happens. We don't have to cement a future right this minute."

I smile at the thought of a possible future.

I pull my phone out of my purse and pull him close to take a photo. I capture a few selfies, but my favorite is the one where we stare at each other — a bright smile on my lips, his dimple on display. Almost instantly after I put my phone away, a few raindrops fall on us. Soon, it's pouring. I giggle and resist when he tries to pull me under a nearby shop awning. "Nick, c'mere!"

"Dee, you're soaked."

"Vivi un po'!"

Giggles echo through the courtyard as I dance in the rain. He's still fighting the urge to join me, but I know he feels it too...that invisible string pulling us together.

I jump when his hands graze my sides. He pulls me impossibly close, our bodies fit together like missing pieces of a puzzle. I meet his gaze and molten honey stares back. That feeling is back. The warmth that spreads wherever we touch. It draws us closer, inching until our lips just barely touch. It seems like forever, but finally... He kisses me. The first one is soft and nervous. Just like the one we shared on the Fourth of July. A smile on our lips when we pull away. By now, we're soaked to the bone, but I don't care. He kisses me again. This time, sure and honest, hungry. And in this moment, I know, I'm falling for Nick Davis.

Part Two

Love is patient, Love is kind. It does not envy, it does not boast it is not proud. It does not dishonor others, it is not self-seeking, it is not easily angered, it keeps not record of wrongs. Love does not delight in evil but rejoices with the truth. It always protects, always trusts, always hopes, always perseveres.

- 1 Corinthians 13:4-7

twenty-nine

"DADDY, CAN I ASK you something?" I ask, picking at my salad. He invited me to lunch at the Country Club, but if I'm honest, I've been distracted the whole time. I can't stop thinking about last night.

The date.

The kiss.

Dancing in the rain.

It was magical. But, it came to a halt when we got home. We walked through the door well past midnight trying to be quiet since everyone was already in bed, except one. Mother. Her shadow in the doorway of the theatre room, arms crossed tightly, a bright flashing light in the room behind her. "Davina, you're both soaking wet!"

"We got caught in the rain on the way to the car," Nick said, touching my lower back.

"Well, I hope you had a good time." Her eyes never left mine, locked in some sort of standoff to see who was going to crack first. Finally, "Run along then, you should change. Don't want to ruin the floors." It was the first time my mother has ever come close to showing the smallest amount of concern.

"G'night, Mrs. Villa," Nick pushed me forward.

Halfway up the stairs, I noticed he was no longer with me.

"Nick?"

"Run along, Nicholas," Mother hissed loud enough for me to hear. "Wouldn't want to keep Davina waiting."

"Coming Dee," he said after another moment.

"What was that about?" I asked behind the safety of our bedroom door.

"Nothing." Nick smiled and kissed me, but I didn't believe him. Something definitely happened. "Dee, it was nothing. Okay? Just your mom being your mom. C'mon, let's get ready for bed."

But, I didn't get much sleep last night. I couldn't figure it out. What was he doing down there? Did she say something to him? When I woke up this morning, he wasn't in bed. I heard hushed voices from down the hallway. I couldn't quite make out what they were saying, but it was obviously Mother and Nick. "Watch your mouth," Mother hissed, unable to contain her volume. But, that was all I could hear before Nick walked in juggling pastry bags and a tray of coffee.

"You're up?"

I debated asking him what in the hell was going on, but decided it might be best to let it go. I knew Mother didn't like him. She could only keep the nice act up for so long and I was surprised it had lasted this long. So, I let it go. "Bed was cold."

"I can fix that." Breakfast long forgotten as he climbed into bed and kissed me.

"Everything okay, Nin?" Daddy asks wiping his mouth with his napkin.

"Come hai fatto a saperlo?"

"Know what, Piccola?"

"Mom was the one."

A knowing smile spreads across his lips. "Haven't I told you this before?" I shake my head, I've never cared to ask. Daddy settles back into his chair. "Your mother wasn't like the other girls. She was feisty and no-nonsense, kept me on my toes, and I loved every second of it." A smile thinking back to when they were younger. "I think what solidified it for me was when Pop died."

"Because she knew she was about to get his fortune?"

"When Pop died, your mother was the only one there. I didn't hear much from my 'friends,' but your mother was there every step of the way. For no other reason than to make sure I was okay. In those moments, the money didn't matter to her... I mattered. She took care of us — me, Nonna, Drew. And, I knew, she was the one." His eyes are blurry when he opens them again, but he blinks away the tears. Daddy has never liked to talk about his family, it's always been a hard topic.

But today, he decided to tell me everything.

It was never the same after Pop died. Nonna's heart broken. She passed when I was eight years old. And Daddy's younger brother, Drew, O.D.'ed after his daughter was killed in a tragic boating accident.

Daddy grew up in a blue-collar family in Holly Hill, South Carolina. His father, Lorenzo Villa, was an Italian immigrant who had moved to the United States in search of a fresh start after his parents died in a tragic car accident. He met Natalie Jones on a job site and fell head over heels for her. They dated for three months before they were married and Daddy was born two years later.

Lorenzo worked many odd jobs throughout his life, mostly picking up carpentry jobs, a trade he learned from his father. Two years before Daddy started high school, Pop started his own home services company. The business took off quickly and he began operating throughout the entire state. The Villa family became one of the wealthiest families in the area. But even after the money came, Pop never stopped working.

Watching his success inspired Daddy to do the same. From a young age, he found ways to make money, whether it was mowing lawns or selling lemonade on the side of the road. In high school, he played football and baseball, but Pop made him get a job to understand what it meant to earn his own money.

After high school, Daddy went to Clemson University, but college didn't suit him. After sophomore year, he dropped out and started working at the family company. After two years, he opened his own business — a furniture store with handcrafted items by local vendors and himself. Three years later, he had acquired enough equity in the company that he was able to sell it and use the money to invest in other opportunities.

After Pop's death, he took over the home services company. Later, he sold Drew's share of the company after his passing and used the funds to start his investment firm. Thus, began the Villa Empire.

Mother grew up in a lower-class family, the Moores. Her father walked out when she was five years old, her sisters were two and nine months old. Her mother worked three jobs to make ends meet, but sometimes it still wasn't enough. There were plenty of nights she went to bed hungry so her sisters could have something to eat. Despite her home life, Mother never let anyone at school know what went on behind closed doors. Not until much later when Daddy finally discovered the truth.

When she was old enough, Mother got a job at the local diner. She worked most nights after school and during the day on weekends so she could still attend school activities. She had heard of the Alaric Villa, who hadn't? Football star. Baseball star. Son of Lorenzo and Natalie Villa, owners of Villa Home Repairs. Everyone had heard of him, but unlike her friends, Mother had no interest. They would melt at the mention of his name, not her. Needless to say, Daddy was a little surprised when she didn't try to jump his bones like every other girl. That's what made him want her even more, but she wanted better than some sports star who would burn out after high school. She wanted someone who was going to take her far, far away from their small town.

Finally, Daddy's senior year, he convinced her to go to the Homecoming dance. It was her junior year, their last chance to enjoy high school together. Even though she would deny it to anyone who asked, she was excited. She even worked doubles the weekend before to earn enough money to buy a new dress. After Homecoming, they started going steady and fell in love quickly.

"She realized I had a fighting spirit, much like Pop, and I was going to be successful, even if it meant she had to work a little while longer," Daddy says wiping the corner of his eyes.

Despite my feelings towards Mother, hearing their story was kind of romantic, but it makes me sad. Sad for my father because I realize she is not the person she once was. I've never known that person and I never will. The person I used to hope and pray for... She did exist, but will never be anything more than a story to me.

"You and Nick have something special, Nina. I don't know everything, and maybe I don't want to, but from what I can see, you have a man who loves you. Not for the money or your name, but for you."

A blush rises in my cheeks.

"I know you have been through a lot. I don't know if he knows everything, but the only way it's going to work is if you're honest with each other."

thirty

I SIT ACROSS FROM my brother with a shy smile. He was utterly confused when I asked him to go to dinner, just the two of us. Dinner started normal, he even told me of his plan to propose soon. He wants me to go with him to design the ring. But, when he brought up Nick, he noticed the slight shift in my demeanor.

That's when I told him.

"What do you mean you're not together?"

"Weren't together, big difference."

"You are now?"

"Yes, I think."

"And Eileen knew about this?"

"I'm sorry I lied to you, Kai."

Kai taps his fingers against his whiskey glass. "But, what about when he brought you here the other night? And, what about the Fourth of July, you guys kissed at the fireworks."

"Le cose sono diventate un po' complicate. None of this was supposed to happen. We were only supposed to keep it up until we left and then it would be like it never happened. He was just here to be my boyfriend when everyone was around, but... I didn't think about the consequences of having someone get so close."

"You like him, he likes you. Seems pretty simple to me."

"How do I know it's real? That when we go home, back to reality, it's not gonna fall apart?"

"You won't know unless you try, Nin."

"I don't want anyone else to know. Even when the summer is over, even if it all works out, I don't want Mom and Dad to find out."

"You can't expect me to keep this a secret."

"I've kept things a secret for you too, Kai." I smirk behind my wine glass. Despite my brother being a narc the first twenty-three years of his life, I have kept all of his secrets. "Need I remind you about Lucinda Brown?"

"No, I remember, thank you."

"So, just between us, right?" I stick my little finger out to him.

"What are we, five?"

"Yes, now come on."

Kai rolls his eyes but wraps his finger around mine squeezing it. "Happy now?"

"Yes, thank you," I laugh and take a bite of cheesecake.

$$ \S $$

"Che cazzo sta succedendo?" I say as we pull into the driveway. Just outside of the garage, Lee stands yelling at Nick while Teagan watches from the front steps. I practically jump out of the Jeep before Kai pulls to a stop.

"I've been calling you!" Eileen meets me outside the garage.

"My phone was on silent," I say and pull my phone out of my purse to see multiple missed calls and texts from Eileen.

"Lee, just take your girl and go inside. You don't want to do this," Nick says as we join them.

"How can you act so casual about this? You've been lying this whole time!"

"You have no idea what you're talking about. You really need to let this go."

"So, this isn't you?" Lee holds out his phone, on display a photo — a group of boys in front of the Phi Gamma Delta frat house. At the end of the line none other than Nick with a buzzcut and I know I've seen that boy in the photo before. But, the photo doesn't prove anything. We know he went to Rosecliffe.

"What's your point? I went to Rosecliffe, that wasn't a secret."

"You're a fraud. A liar. I knew something was up with you, I just couldn't prove it. When Jonas sent this the other day, I had what I needed to find who you really are."

Jonas. Does Nick know Jonas? Does he know Tobi too? Wait, didn't he say he hung around Sig Phi? Tobias was in Sig Phi.

"You're one to talk, Lee. Are you forgetting what you've been doing since we got here? Maybe even longer."

Lee's eyes widen.

"Okay, enough. What is going on?" I finally ask.

"You wanna tell her or should I?" Lee demands.

"I could ask you the same thing." Nick's smirk never falters. What in the hell is he talking about?

Lee's face contorts before he turns to me, practically yelling, "He's lying to you, Nina."

"For the last time, Lee, stay out of my business." I've had enough of him sticking his nose where it didn't belong. "You're really starting to get on my last nerve."

"He's not who you think! He dropped out of Rosecliffe, he—"

"I know who he is. I don't need your help, nor do I want it."

"You are so pathetic," Teagan scoffs as she descends the stairs. "Did you think bringing him here would make Lee jealous? Make him want you back?"

"Oh, here we go."

"Do your parents know?"

"Stay the hell out of this, Teagan."

"I'll take that as a no."

"That's enough, Teagan," Kai warns.

"Oh, so you know the truth?" Teagan laughs when Kai doesn't respond. "You're all in on it, aren't you? Well, I'm sure Mommy and Daddy would love to know who your new boy toy is. Especially, Daddy. I wonder how he'd feel to know his Princess isn't as innocent as she seems. To know she's been lying about her new boyfriend."

"Shut the hell up," I say through gritted teeth. I want nothing more than to slap the smirk from Teagan's lips. I take a deep breath, I refuse to let Teagan bait me. It has been a long time since my last fight, high school probably. It's not happening. I'm not that person anymore. These people bring out the worst in me, but that part of me is hidden behind a locked door. I won't be opening the door no matter how hard it tries to claw out.

"What are you gonna do, Nin? You wouldn't hurt a fly."

"I seem to remember quite a few people who would disagree."

"You're all talk."

"Wanna test that theory?" Voice velvety smooth. I know better than to make the first move. "C'mon, Teaggy. After all these years, after everything we did... Go ahead, hit me. I'll give you one good shot before I beat the shit out of you."

Teagan considers it. She can get at least one hit in before I beat her ass. Lee shakes his head telling her this is not a good idea. He knows it will end badly for one of us, and it's not me. I can see the wheels turning in her head. Teagan glances at Nick who has his arm ready to grab me, just in case. It won't do any good, she doesn't know that though. Teagan turns as if she's going to go inside and I deflate. I turn to Nick ready to figure

out what in the hell is going on when —
SMACK.
The sting is in my cheek.
Everyone freezes.
Nick tries to grab me, but I'm quicker. I lunge at Teagan.
We fall into the grass, Teagan's head landing centimeters from the concrete. Teagan cries when I punch her. She tries to hit back, tries to push me off, but I'm stronger. Teagan scratches my neck and cheek, leaving trails of blood, but it doesn't phase me. She cries out and rips the necklaces from my neck using them as a whip, but I take them from her hand and toss them somewhere behind us.

"Are you just going to stand there?" I hear Eileen yell, but no one makes a move to intervene. Years of fake friendship and animosity have finally boiled over the surface and they don't want to be caught in the crossfire.

"I find it best not to get in the middle," Kai says.

"Help me, now!"

Within seconds, I'm lifted from the ground. Nick's arms wrapped securely around me as he carries me away from Teagan. When he sets my feet back on the ground, he tries to check on me, but I push him away.

"Lee doesn't want you, Nina. He never did. Not everyone wants you," Teagan yells past Lee. "And clearly, neither does Nicky. I mean, he seemed to enjoy our time together."

Time together? What in the fuck does that mean? This bitch needs to learn to stay away from—

"Nina," Nick warns and I glare up at him. "Don't. She's just fucking with you."

"You missed a good show."

This fucking bitch.

"Don't let her bait you."

"You should've seen him when I started to take off—"

I break free and lunge again. This time, the part of me deep inside pushes its way to the surface. I shove Teagan into the side of the house — my fingers wrap around her throat. "Stay the hell away from him, you bitch. You can have Lee, he was a shitty boyfriend. But you will stay away from Nick. Do you hear me?"

She claws at my fingers. For the first time, I can see the fear swimming behind Teagan's eyes. She is truly afraid and she should be. She nods quickly and slumps against the side of the house when I release my grasp.

thirty-one

I HISS, TOUCHING THE scratches on my shoulder, deeper than I thought. My purple camisole has been pulled from my shorts and my white jacket is covered in grass stains and blood. I won't ever get that out. My knees are covered in dirt and grass, a cut on my right shin. I touch my neck where my necklaces used to be and sigh. I don't recognize the woman in the mirror — this is not who I am anymore. I haven't been that person in a long time. I haven't let myself get that far out of control and I'm not proud of it. I hate that I let Lee and Teagan bring this side out of me.

From my peripheral vision, I see him in the doorway. He's quiet. I'm sure he's mad. What he just witnessed is evidence of the Nina Villa he's heard so much about. The one he's been waiting to make an appearance. This is the proof he's searching for. I finally look away from the mirror to meet his gaze ready to see the "I told you so" look, but it's not there. No, he is genuinely concerned.

"Are you alright?"

"Bene."

"Here, let me help." Nick reaches, but I step back. "C'mon, Dee. We need to get you cleaned up." He wets a washcloth and lifts it to my cheek waiting for the okay. When I don't pull away, he wipes gently. After my cheek, he pushes the jacket from my shoulders and grimaces. "What are her nails made out of metal or something? Where are the band-aids? We need to cover these." I motion to the linen closet.

After he cleans and covers the scratches on my shoulder, he brings pajamas for me to change into. He kisses my forehead and starts to leave, but I stop him. "What happened, Nick?"

"What do you mean?"

"Teagan...she said you were together. Nick, I can't go through this again. What was she talking about?"

Nick takes my hands into his. "Nina..."

"Just answer the question, Nick."

"Eileen and I were watching TV, waiting for you to get back. Eileen had to take a phone call and Teagan came in. She was fine, at first. Nothing out of the ordinary. But, then she started getting close, too close, and saying how convenient that you and Lee were gone. She tried to take her clothes off, but I stopped her. And then, Eileen and Lee walk in fighting about God knows what. And well, you know the rest." He cups my cheeks. "Nothing happened, Dee. I promise."

A knock at the door before Eileen barges into the room, "What the hell was that?"

I stand in the bathroom door, but Nick takes a subtle step in front of me. His fingers lazily intertwine with my own between us.

"Seriously, Nina? You just beat the shit out of her."

"She had it coming," I say unbothered.

"You just got into a knockdown drag-out with someone who used to be your best friend. That's a little cause for concern, don't you think?"

"Hey, Slugger!" Kai wears a proud smirk when he joins us. "You got her pretty good, definitely gonna have a black eye and some bruises. Pulled a few extensions out too."

"Kai," Eileen hisses. "Not helping."

"I'm just glad she finally put Teagan in her place."

I roll my eyes trying to hide my smile.

"C'mon, babe. Let's go, give them some space." Kai winks at me before he pulls Eileen out of the room.

"I know you worked hard on these bandages, but I think I'm gonna take a bath," I say when they're gone. "I need some... space." I kiss Nick's cheek, but as I begin to walk away, he holds me still. His breath dances across my exposed skin and his hands lightly trace my curves sending a shiver down my spine. He presses light kisses along my neck until our lips brush and I feel him smile.

"I'm right outside."

"Thank you, Fossette."

thirty-two

IT'S JUST LIKE WHEN he saw the house in Haven for the first time, I wonder if the shock and awe factor will ever go away when it comes to these kinds of things. Maybe, or maybe not. I don't mind, it's kind of cute. I like being able to share the experience with him. I booked the presidential suite at the Four Seasons Denver — it's more like an apartment than a hotel room. Even Eileen seemed surprised when we walked in, apparently, Kai doesn't book such rooms when they go out of town. "We all need our space, I don't want to be in the same room when my brother decides to get handsy," I said when Eileen scolded me.

After the fight with Lee and Teagan, things have been even more tense around the house and I've packed our schedule to keep us anywhere else. I even tried to avoid Eileen for a few days, not looking for another lecture. We have since apologized and all has been forgiven, but I was tired of having to leave the house to feel like I could breathe. I needed a vacation from vacation and Denver seemed like the perfect place. Not too far from Haven, but far enough to get away for a few days and let everything calm down.

"Pretty cool, huh?" I join Nick at the floor-to-ceiling windows overlooking downtown and the mountains.

"Gorgeous." But, he isn't looking at the view anymore.

"I thought you might like it."

"I like it a lot." Nick pulls me close and kisses the crown of my head. "What is all this for, Dee? I know you wanted to get away from Lee and Teagan, but even this is a little much."

"I just thought we could celebrate your birthday while we're here."

"My birthday was almost three weeks ago."

"But, now I can celebrate it as your girlfriend...your real girlfriend."

Nick laughs and kisses me.

"If you two are done, we'd like to eat something," Eileen interrupts us.

"Yeah, yeah, we're coming, Lina," I say without looking, but neither of us moves. I roll my eyes when Eileen clears her throat. "Okay, okay." I kiss Nick again and drag him away from the window to follow Eileen.

§

I planned four days in Denver. On our first day, I booked tickets to the Colorado Rockies versus Chicago Cubs game. Our seats directly behind first base. "Where's your man, Nin?" Kai asks.

"Rizzo? He got traded."

"Don't you remember her one million text messages about it?" Eileen teases earning a glare from me. I've never been into sports, unless it came to Anthony Rizzo...or Tim Tebow. I'd be lying if I said I haven't had a thing for the first baseman after Daddy dragged me to a Cubs-Rockies game years ago.

"You gonna stand for that?" Kai asked Nick.

"I know where she sleeps at night," Nick said and kissed me.

On our second day, I planned a private tour of Stranahan's

Whiskey for the boys. I would go for a hike while Eileen spent the day at the spa, but she refused to go. She didn't want me to go hiking alone. I won't tell Eileen this, but had she just asked, I would've gone to the spa instead.

"How was the spa?" Kai asks when we meet them for dinner.

"I wouldn't know," Eileen rolls her eyes. She immediately regretted her decision the second we reached the trail.

"What do you mean?"

"Eileen went hiking with me," I chime in.

"I would have rather been by the pool."

"I told you to stay back, but no, you didn't want to let me go alone."

"What if you had been kidnapped?"

"Oh, don't be so dramatic, Lina." I roll my eyes and pop a piece of bread in my mouth.

On our third day, Nick and I went hiking in the Rocky Mountain National Park before we met Kai and Eileen for dinner. Just before we left for drinks at The Cooper Lounge, Michaela called. A manufacturer giving her issues and kept pushing back the delivery date, if they pushed back any further the project would have to be delayed. Within thirty minutes, I had it resolved, but then Michaela started asking for more.

"C'mon, Dee, we gotta go," Nick says walking into the suite office.

"Solo un secondo."

"Nope, time is up."

"Nick! How is Denver?" Michaela shouts through the phone.

"Stealing her, Michaela. I gave you thirty minutes, now she's mine."

"Wait, I just have one more—" But, Nick hangs up before she can finish.

On our fourth day, I left the day open for anything Nick

wanted to do. We spent the morning in bed watching TV and talking. By lunchtime, we finally pulled ourselves out of bed to meet Kai and Eileen. For dinner, I surprised him with dinner at the Flagstaff House in Boulder. The restaurant originally built as a summer cabin was later turned into a restaurant that offers some of the best views.

I try not to laugh too loud as we walk into the suite after dinner. I know Kai and Eileen are already in bed, it's well past one in the morning. Walking into the bedroom, I step out of my heels kicking them toward my suitcase. I pull pajamas from my bag, but a hot shower sounds miraculous. I strip out of my satin drape blouse and faux leather pants and wrap a towel around my frame. As I turn the dial waiting for the water to warm up, I wonder how we got here.

Elevator, Nick would say. I smile at the thought, such a smartass. But that's not what I mean...

Speak of the devil.

Nick walks into the bathroom still dressed, but his eyes darken when he sees me in just a towel. His attention quickly diverts to the sink.

My fingers flick through the falling stream to see if it's warm enough...not quite. The thought comes back to me. How did we get here? I don't mean the room, but how did we make it to this moment? We're dating... I think? I'm still not completely sure, but it's nice. We're taking it slow and I'm okay with that. We still have so much to learn, we're letting each other in little by little, but I might be falling for him.

Can I be honest? That's scares the shit out of me.

"You okay?" I ask when I catch him staring again, but his mind seems to be somewhere else. When he finally meets my stare, I smile and ask again, "Fossette?" Nick crosses the bathroom and closes the space between us. At first, his kiss is soft and tender, the smallest hint of hesitation. If the line is crossed, what happens next? I push him away gently, "Nick, are you sure?"

He captures my lips in a crushing kiss. It's demanding and possessive. Hungry. Deep. The kiss of a man who isn't going to stop until he's had every part of me.

Locked in a hungry embrace, he pushes me into the open shower, we're immediately soaked from the falling water. No more hesitation, this is what we've been waiting for. He pins me against the wall, taking both my hands into one of his above our heads. A soft moan when his lips meet the sweet spot where my neck and collarbone meet. His teeth graze my skin.

I claw at his soaked shirt, pulling it over his head. It falls into a wet heap on the shower floor, next to it my towel. He takes the opportunity to take in the sight of me. His rough hands explore my soft, tanned skin leaving a trail of fire in their wake. I've never felt so comfortable in front of a man before. His stare makes me feel sexy, beautiful. His appetite insatiable as he explores every inch of my body. Touching me. Tasting me. Teasing me. Pushing me right to the edge, but never letting me fall. He lifts me with ease, carrying me into the bedroom.

I reach for him as he crawls onto the bed. My fingers trace the tattoo on his chest. I have so many questions about it, but that can wait. My mind moves to the feeling of his growing erection. Goosebumps rise across my skin, anticipation growing inside me — an ache between my thighs. I want him.

No, I need him.

Nick brings my hand to his lips and kisses my fingertips. I can't help but laugh at the sensation and it makes him smile. He pushes a wet strand of hair from my face, "You're beautiful, Davina." A deep blush rises in my cheeks and he kisses me again. Slow and tender, his hands exploring my body again. He fondles my breast, pinching and squeezing my nipples with a rough grip. When I try to reciprocate, he holds both my hands again. I'm sure he can feel my heart beating against my chest. "Stay," his voice soft, but commanding, when he releases my hands.

"Yes sir." It's meant to be teasing, but the way his eyes darken I know I've crossed into new territory. His eyes never leave mine when he steps off the bed yanking me to the edge, hooking my legs over his shoulders when he kneels before me. "Nick," I gasp when his teeth graze the sensitive skin on the inside of my thigh.

A fire ignites with the first lick of his tongue.

I can't contain a moan as he feasts on me and he growls in approval. One hand pins my hips to the bed; the other, I'm sure, leaves bruises on my right leg. When his tongue slides inside me, the sound that rips through my throat is unlike anything I've ever made. I forget how to breathe, how to speak... Nick moves like we have all the time in the world, like he could do this for hours, and I find myself thanking God for this man and his mouth. A soft moan against me when I plunge my fingers into his hair and tug. I feel that familiar ache inside my core. I'm so close to falling over the edge when his fingers replace his mouth, pumping inside me, as he sucks on that sensitive bud just—

My climax tears through me lighting every nerve on fire. He continues feasting on me, pinning me to the bed so I can't escape his assault. And after, only after I come again does he finally let up.

"Such a good girl," he whispers in my ear and I swear I almost come again at the words alone. He smiles against my skin, "You like that, huh?"

"Nick, please."

"Not yet, baby. We have plenty of time."

I whine.

"Demanding, aren't we?" He kisses me briefly, letting his tongue swipe across mine so I taste myself. I let myself stare as he steps off the bed. Unbuttoning his jeans, he shoves denim and cotton down his legs — his considerable length springs free. The rip of foil sends a pulse through me. Another pulse when he climbs on top of me again. His nose trails along my jaw before he kisses the soft skin behind my ear. "Are you sure?" he whispers. "I don't want—"

I kiss him — I want this, want him, want every part of him...every inch in me until we're one. Hooking my right leg around his waist, he pushes into me, slowly, savoring it. He smirks when I dig my shoulders into the mattress and arch into him. The only thought I have is the feeling of him as he sinks deeper inside me.

"Please," I beg in a whisper, needing more. That single word is enough for him. The way he soothes every craving I've ever had doesn't slip past me. No man has ever made me feel the way he does right now. He pulls out slightly before thrusting back in slower, deeper inside me, if it's even possible, and the sound it pulls from me...

"That's my girl," his voice a low growl. "You feel so fucking good, Dee."

The heat slowly builds inside, the tightening of a coil begging to be released. But, it's different. This isn't like the other times, it's hotter, brighter than before. He moves unbelievably slow, savoring the feeling of me around him. "Nick," a plea, but my voice so high, barely above a whisper, I'm not sure he hears me.

"What do you want, beautiful?" He pins my hands down, firmly grips my right leg hooked around his waist, and then... he waits. I try to squirm under his hold, try to create any kind of friction between us, but he holds me impossibly still. He wants me to beg. Beg him to move. Beg him to give me what I want, what I need. "Tell me, Davina." His teeth graze my jaw. My throat. "What do you want?"

"Please, Nick. You have to...I need— Ho bisogno di te."

He goes mad. The sounds echoing in my ear animalistic. With each pounding stroke, my nails dig further into his skin as I move my hips in time with his. I'm slowly losing control, but I lose every bit of it when he stares into my eyes and says, "You're mine." A fire so hot burns inside of me when my release comes — a blinding white heat. I try to scream, but nothing. He pounds into me, hard and fast. Nick holds back his own roar building in his chest as he comes, filling me to the hilt. He bites down on my shoulder leaving his mark — a searing brand.

The sheets damp with sweat. The room smells of sex. The only sound our panting breaths. Our bodies sticky, but I don't care. I run my fingers through the soft curls they viciously attacked moments ago. He smiles down at me, a lazy, sedated smile, but it makes me smile back.

"You like Italian, huh?"

"Shut up," he laughs and I swear it's the most beautiful sound I've heard.

thirty-three

MY LEGS AND LUNGS scream. I haven't stopped once. Not since I hit the trailhead. Six and a half miles of pure elevation gain, beautiful lakes, and rocky terrain. Apparently, no one else was up for the challenge, I've only seen two other people on the trail all day. I wipe the sweat off my brow reaching the summit of Mount Sopris.

Hello, old friend.

A wave of nausea rolls through me — from the run or events of this morning, I'm not sure. But, I can't hold it back any longer. I empty the little contents of my stomach on the side of the trail. My heart still races when I lean back against a boulder trying to catch my breath.

Inhale.

Exhale.

Repeat.

It's okay.

No, it's not.

Let him explain.

He did.

He did explain.

He explained how last night was a mistake.

Nick was gone when I woke up this morning, probably to

work out — a gym is the only thing the suite was missing. I made a cup of coffee before I packed our bags. We were supposed to meet Andrew at the airport in an hour. It seemed like forever when I finally heard him enter the bedroom, holding a fresh cup of coffee from downstairs. Okay, so maybe he didn't go to the gym. Where was he? As if he could read my mind, he said, "Kai and I grabbed breakfast, then Josh called. Sorry." His smile didn't quite reach his eyes handing the coffee to me and where he would have normally kissed me, he didn't. Something was wrong.

"Everything okay?" I asked watching him fiddle with the lid of his coffee cup.

"Fine." He smiled, but it wasn't convincing.

"Nick, what's wrong?"

He sighs, "Look, Dee... Last night, maybe we should've waited."

And, there it is. The moment I've been waiting for — when magic runs out.

"It's just... We're still getting to know each other. We don't know what's going to happen when we go home. I think— I think we should take it slow."

"Prenderla con calma?" I repeated his own words. Take it slow? "You are unbelievable. I asked you! I asked if you wanted to and—"

"I'm sorry." Nick reached for me, but I swatted his hand.

"Non avresti potuto dirlo ieri sera?"

"I'm sorry! I was so caught up in the moment, and after dinner, I felt like—"

"Cosa? Like you had to put out?"

"No, that's not what I meant. Nina, I just— Look, I know it's not a good reason. I'm sorry. I just think we need to slow down."

"Cazzate, Nick." I threw the shirt I had been folding into my bag. "Why don't you tell me what's really going on?" He swallows the lump in his throat. "Tell me what the fuck is going on."

"Dee," Nick tried to take my hand into his, but I retreated a few steps. "I'm sorry, I just think... Maybe, it was a mistake." Pain gripped my chest. *Mistake.* Surely, I misheard him.

His eyes widen as if he realized what he said. "Nina, no, that's not what I meant. I just meant— Please, don't. Don't do this. Don't build the walls back up. You know that's not what I meant."

"Actually, I don't think I do." I zipped my suitcase, but my burning stare never left his.

"I'm sorry. I didn't mean it like that. You have to believe me. I just don't want to mess this up. And, there's things that you don't—"

"A little late for that, don't you think?" I pushed past him leaving the room, but he was hot on my heels. Kai and Eileen walked through the front door blissfully unaware.

"We brought coffee!" Kai lifts a tray of coffee and a bag of donuts high in the air with a toothy grin. "We have to be at the airport in thirty minutes."

"Everything okay?" Eileen asked me, sensing the tension.

"I'll be downstairs," I walked out the door without another word.

And I haven't spoken to any of them since. The plane ride was quiet, not even Kai or Eileen attempting to talk. The moment we got home, I changed into hiking clothes and left. I needed space.

You're missing something. There's something you don't know.

§

I don't think I realized what was happening, not until I was already falling toward the ground. Maybe it's the lack of sleep or I just wasn't paying attention, it doesn't really matter. What matters is the pain shooting through my left leg as my ankle twists one way and my leg the other, the jagged rocks dig and scratch my skin as I land. The pain almost unbearable when I try to push from the ground but fail. My heart beats in my ankle, in my thigh... This is not good. The sun will set within the next hour and I have no reception which means I'm on my own. Just like I wanted...

Everything begins to hit me chipping away at the wall around me blow by blow.

Lee.

Teagan.

Mother.

Lying.

My ankle.

Nick.

His secrets.

Our mistake.

I let the tears fall freely for the first time in a long time.

I'm not sure how long I've been sitting here, but I know the sun is lower than before. I need to get moving or I'll be trying to hike back in complete darkness. Probably not the smartest idea. I wipe my eyes and examine the damage done. My ankle is swollen but seems manageable. I can move it without too much pain. The real damage is my leg. A deep bruise has already formed on my left thigh. Blood covers my leg from a gash in the middle of the bruise; it's deep, but I don't think it needs stitches, thank God. Small scratches and gashes litter the rest of my skin. It's going to be a long walk back, but I don't have a choice. I need to wrap the biggest cut, I can't risk something getting into it. I peel my tank top off turning it inside out hoping I don't run into anyone else on the trail.

"Fuck," I hiss wrapping the shirt around my thigh. A small whimper when I tighten the knot. I just need to make it a quarter mile to the car.

Pushing up from the ground, I remind myself it's not that bad. I don't need stitches. I just need to get to the car and then home. I can do this...

thirty-four

I UNDO THE KNOT in my tank top and peel it off my leg and fuck if I don't want to just chop off my leg because I'm sure it would be less painful than this. I begin pushing my shorts down my legs, but the bedroom door opens. His gaze immediately lands on my left leg — a large purple bruise on my thigh; inside the bruise, a deep gash. Dried blood around the edges. Smaller bruises pepper the rest of my leg. Closing the door, Nick rushes to my side. "Shit, what happened?" He tries to look at the wound, but I ignore him. "Do you need to go to the hospital? That looks bad, it might need stitches." I continue to ignore him walking — limping — towards the bathroom, but he grabs me. "Nina, what happened?"

"Sto bene."

"Look at your leg! I didn't even know where you were. What—what if it had been worse?" I push past him, a rush of pain with weight on my leg. "Let me help."

"Nick, just leave me alone." But, he doesn't budge. "Please, I need a shower. I just need twenty minutes...alone." My eyes well as my leg throbs. "Nick, please."

"Dee, I'm sorry, okay? I didn't mean to sound like an ass, I just—"

"A mistake, yep, got it."

"No, we just…We don't know each other. I mean, we just started whatever this is. And with Lee—"

"Are you fucking kidding me?" I scoff. "You don't trust me at all, davvero? That's why you think it was a mistake. You think I'm going to up and leave you for Lee."

"No."

"Then what is it?"

"I don't know. I just…I…" His jaw locks like he's trying to hold back whatever he wants to say.

"What? You just what?"

"Can you blame me? It's not like I didn't hear the rumors. With your reputation—"

"Excuse me?" Venom wraps around the word.

"Look, you had a reputation in high school and at Rosecliffe. You—"

SMACK!

The sound of my palm colliding with his cheek echoes in the stillness of the room. "Come ti permetti!" I try to move past him, but he grabs my hands.

"Davina, stop." His features dark, he's trying to contain the anger brewing. I try to push past him again, but he refuses to let me go. "Listen to me," he growls.

"Fuck you, Nick." I finally move past him and grab my purse from the closet. I open my checkbook and furiously begin to fill out a check. "Questo è quello che vuoi, giusto?"

Nick's anger deflates. "Dee, stop."

"Don't call me that." I rip the check out and try to hand it to him. "This is what you came for." He refuses. "Take. It." I push it into his hand and he crumples it.

"Nina, please."

I open the bedroom door, "I think you should go."

"Nina…"

"Fuori."

"Nina, please, let's talk about this." Nick says and closes the door softly.

"Get the fuck out of my house."

"You don't even know what is going on in your house."

"What is that supposed to mean?"

"Your mom—" But he stops.

Mother? Did she do something?

"Go on. My mother what?"

"Nothing. Just forget it."

"Non fermarti ora. Spit it out." My leg begins to tremble, but I'm not sure if it's from the pain or anger. What could Mother possibly have done now? *You're missing something. There's something you don't know.* What isn't he telling me? "If you have something to say, then say it, Nick. I don't have time for the games." He still refuses. "Did she say something to you? Threaten you? Nick, whatever it is, I can handle it. You just have to tell me."

He chews on the inside of his cheek. "I can't, Dee."

I don't miss the way his voice cracks. I want him to tell me. I can help him fix this, whatever it is. I just need to know what we're up against. I'll go to Daddy if I can't handle it. Tears brim my eyes, "Fine, then leave."

"Why are you so fucking stubborn?"

"Guarda chi sta parlando!"

"I said, I was sorry, Nina."

"Why can't you just admit you were wrong about me? I'm not the girl you thought and that scares you! You want to keep me in this box so you have an excuse why this can't work. Is it so awful to admit you have feelings for me?"

"That's not it."

"You said you wanted to try, but you didn't. You didn't try. The second you realized this could be real, you called it a mistake." I try to hide the tears clouding my vision, the breaking in my voice. This is exactly why I didn't want to let him in, why I have refused to let anyone in. "All I'm asking is for you to be honest with me. What did I do?"

"It wasn't you, baby. Please, don't think that. It's me."

"Oh great, the 'it's not you, it's me,' line."

"I have some shit to work out, but that doesn't mean I don't want this. We can still try, okay? We can still work this out. I just need time. We just need to take it slow."

"I don't think we can."

"Nina…"

"You need to leave, please." I don't want him to leave. I want him to tell me what the fuck is going on. Tell me the truth. I want to fix it, I want to make this work. Whatever the reason, I don't care. But, if he can't be honest… I open the door, if he won't go, I will. "You know something, I think you're right. This was a mistake. I should've never asked you to come. Pack your things and take the check. I want you gone by the time I get back."

Within seconds, Nick is there — he slams the door and pushes me against the wall. Emotions high. Dark eyes stare down at me and when I try to push him away, he shoves me back into the wall. He crushes his lips on mine. This is not the same as last night, he is not gentle as he devours me. He shoves my shorts and underwear down my legs. I whimper when he grips my legs wrapping them around his waist, hands grazing the cuts and bruises. He pins my hands above our heads and nips along my neck. He bites down on the skin of my collarbone before kissing down my chest. I try to create the desired friction between us, but he's not in a giving mood. He kisses the swell of my breasts before his tongue trails upwards ending with a soft nip on my ear. "Stay still. Do you understand?" I let out a shaky breath in response, but it's not what he wants. He pulls away to look me in the eye. "Do you understand, Davina?"

"Fuck you."

A dangerous smirk.

"Not until you say it." Nick moves his hips against me and I can already feel how hard he is through the thin fabric of his shorts. "Davina, do…you…understand?"

"Yes," it's breathless.

"Yes, what?"

"Yes…sir."

In one swift motion, Nick is on his knees, my legs hooked over his shoulders, his hands bruise my hips as he begins an unrelenting assault. Waves of pleasure and pain course through me as he feasts. My fingers find purchase in his hair when his fingers push inside me, curling. I feel it, that blinding heat building in the pit of my stomach, but he rips his mouth from me with a *tsk tsk*. "I told you not to move," Nick says from between my thighs.

He lets my right leg fall from his shoulder, but my left leg remains. His fingers ghost across the injuries and he cocks his head to the side — *Are you okay?* And I'm reminded why I've fallen for this man. Despite everything, he's worried about my well-being. I could tell him about the pain ripping my thigh to pieces, about the fire searing across my skin — from both pain and his touch — but, I won't.

A quick nod, almost unnoticeable. A feather kiss against the inside of my thigh and my leg falls from his shoulder.

But, he's not finished.

His grip is rough as he kisses up my body — tongue gliding, teeth scraping, until we are eye level. He kisses me and my mouth opens to him, his tongue sliding in to massage mine — a moan deep in my throat when his fingers push inside me again. But, they're gone just as fast and he pulls away from me to lick his index finger with a moan of satisfaction. It might be one of the hottest things I've ever seen. Nick dips his tongue into my mouth so I can taste myself. He pushes me towards the bed, my thighs knocking against the mattress, but he stops me before I can fall. He bites down where my jaw and neck meet. "Do not move," his words caress my skin before he turns and bends me over the edge of the mattress. His shorts fall from his hips and his knee widens my stance.

A guttural moan echoes between us when he pushes inside me, my breath escapes in a gasp. My fingers grip the comforter doing my best not to move as he begins to pull out slightly, thrusting back in deeper. Don't move, I repeat to myself. Don't move. Because fuck, I don't want this to ever end. One hand buries in my hair, the other grips my throat bowing my body so my back is flush against his chest. He can't thrust, but his hips make the slightest movements against me that send me spiraling.

His hand grips my throat, his teeth scrape against the shell of my ear. "You're mine," the same words from last night. He licks down the column of my neck to my shoulder making sure to leave another bruising claim on my skin.

Nick guides me back to the bed and before I have time to adjust my grip, he's pounding into me. Harder. Faster. The tension building inside my core almost unbearable, the pleasure tightening every muscle in my body. Just before I fall over the edge into that blinding heat, he pulls out. My back hits the mattress and he guides me further up the bed. "I want to see your face when you come," he says before thrusting back into me. A silent curse under his breath when a guttural moan escapes my lips and I'm teetering on the edge. When he lifts my right thigh to create the sweetest angle before he pulls out and thrusts back in deeper, my body bursts. Nick silences the noises I make with a kiss, pounding into me.

His right-hand grips the sheets to ground himself. I stroke his face and force him to look at me. His eyes tell a different story than his animalistic behavior. And, his movements begin to slow, savoring the feeling of me around him. I kiss him. Softer than before. Slower.

"Nina," his voice a low growl, he leans his forehead against mine.

"Va tutto bene, baby." I caress his cheek and kiss him once. "It's okay." His face contorts and his body grows rigid when he comes. I run my fingers through his damp curls, caressing the side of his face — we share slow, languid kisses as he comes down from his high.

My head on his chest, I listen to the sound of his heartbeat. We don't talk, even if we should. There's still a lot left unsaid, but in this moment I know we won't be the same again. Eight billion people in this world and I can't bring myself to want to be with any one of them except the man next to me. Whatever happens from this moment on, I am his and he is mine. I can only hope it's enough to weather the storm ahead.

Nick kisses the top of my head as the rhythm of his heartbeat lulls me to sleep.

§

I wake gradually the next morning, but the room is still dark. How long have I been asleep? I reach for him, but the space beside me is empty.

I'm wide awake.

I'm alone.

His things no longer in the closet or on his nightstand. When I see the one item he left, a sob wracks my chest — alone on his nightstand is the crumpled check.

I should've known this was coming. I told him to leave, but I thought... I fight the tears building behind my eyes. I've done it again — given myself over to someone only to have my heart broken. How could I be so stupid?

The time on the clock catches my attention.

3:47 A.M.

When did he leave? It couldn't have been that long ago. I wipe my eyes and search for my phone. It's placed neatly on the dresser next to my now-folded clothes. My leg throbs reminding me I still have another problem to deal with, but it's going to have to wait. I dial his number and it goes straight to voicemail. "Shit." I pull on a pair of shorts and a sweater. I almost trip over my own feet pulling on a pair of boots as I run out of the room. I need to get to the airport. Fast.

thirty-five

DADDY SITS ACROSS THE table at The Vintage House. I ordered only a kale salad and declined when he suggested adding a sandwich. I'm not hungry. I haven't been hungry in the last few days since Nick's sudden departure. "Davina?" When I look up, I'm met with a sympathetic smile. "Stai bene?"

I know I have to tell him. I have to be honest. He isn't going to be happy, but he needs to know the truth.

"Nina, I'm worried about you. You come home covered with bruises and a huge gash in your leg, Nick leaves in the middle of the night, and you've barely eaten or spoken since. What's going on? Did you guys break up?"

I can't hold back the laugh.

"This isn't funny, Nina."

"Daddy, ti ho detto, he had to go take care of something for work."

"Davina Bay, non mentirmi. I heard you fighting, I think everyone in the house did."

"Non era niente."

"Didn't sound like nothing."

"We...We just—"

"Tua madre ed io siamo preoccupati per te."

"Mother, worried about me? That's funny."

"She cares about you, Nina."

"That's why she spent years telling me I was a mistake? She never wanted me, right? She only wanted Kai. Her planned child. Look, Daddy, you want me to be honest? Nick wasn't my boyfriend. I hired him."

He laughs. Why is that everyone's reaction? But, his laugh fades when I don't join him.

"I offered him money to pretend to be my boyfriend to keep Mother off my back."

"You can't be serious."

"She told me I needed to get over Lee, I needed to move on. She was going to fix me up with the neighbor kid so I wouldn't be alone while Lee and Teagan were here." I watch his face slowly set to stone. "I brought someone you wouldn't know. Someone who could be whoever I needed them to be. Nick wasn't fond of the idea, but I guess a free vacation and money can persuade anyone." The table next to us has started to listen. I roll my eyes when the woman quickly averts her gaze. "We ended up getting pretty close. We— I started to feel something more... I thought he did too, but he told me that it was a mistake. Something about Mother and my reputation. It was all too much for him." I wish he would say something, anything, but he just stares. "Something happened out in Denver and I don't know what it was, but something changed his mind about me. And for days, I've been trying to figure it out, but I can't. The only thing I know, Nick doesn't want to be with me. Whether it's something Mother said or did, or maybe he can't get past my reputation, I don't know. But, I'm tired of lying. I can't do it anymore. I'm sorry, Daddy. I didn't want to lie to you, but at the time, I didn't feel like I had a choice."

Daddy stands from the table without a word and leaves.

thirty-six

THE FRONT DOOR OPENS and I can hear Michaela mumbling to herself about how I'm going to kill her if I find out she left the door unlocked. But, she's one hundred, no ninety-nine percent sure it was locked last night. By now, she's realizing all the lights are and there aren't any messages on the phone. That's unusual. "Hello?"

"Don't you know the last thing you're supposed to do is say 'Hello,' if you think a killer is inside?" She jumps at the sound of my voice when I walk around the corner. A hot cup of coffee in my hands. She still holds her keys between her fingers like a tiny sword.

"Nina!" She practically tackles me, almost spilling my coffee. I've missed this. I feel like I haven't seen her in forever. She quickly pulls away from the embrace, skeptical. She's trying to figure out why I'm here. I'm not scheduled to be back for at least two more weeks. "Wait, Nina? What are you doing here? You're not supposed to be here. Wait, what day is it? Did I miss something?"

I sip my coffee, "Came back a few days early."

"When did you get home? Alex said Nick showed up in Boston last night."

"He left a few days before I did."

"Are you going with him? Oh my gosh, can I come?"

"Um, no."

"No, I can't come?"

"No, I won't be going to Boston."

Her excitement fades. "Wait, did something happen? Something definitely happened. What happened?"

"Here, this is for you." Ignoring her questions, I pull an envelope from my back pocket. "Thanks for taking care of things while I was gone."

"What is this?"

"Just a little something to say thank you."

"Nina, no. I can't take this. I was just doing my job."

"Please, I appreciate it." I push it into her hands. "Now, I already started arranging a few meetings for the end of this week. Kathleen seems pleased with how you've handled things, so I'm going to let you keep leading that one. Can you finish scheduling the rest? I need to make a few phone calls."

I smile trying to put on my best face, but she doesn't believe me. She knows better. I return to my office before she can ask anymore questions. As soon as the door closes, the smile falls. This is going to be a lot harder than I thought. Trying to act like nothing is wrong, like I don't have this constant ache in my chest. Only one way to ignore it — work. Work is the only way I can keep my mind from wandering.

thirty-seven

"HEY NINA, THIS IS Alex, Nick's brother. We talked in Haven. Um, I hope this isn't too weird. He doesn't know I'm calling. Can you call me?" I listen to the voicemail again. It has been two days since Alex left the message. I've considered ignoring it all together, but I'm worried something might be wrong. What if something happened to Nick? Surely, Alex would call Michaela, right? Just before I call him back, my phone rings. I wonder if his ears were burning. "Hey, Alex."

He stumbles around on the other end. A chair scrapes across the floor. Jumbled footsteps. A hushed apology.

"Damn, dude, calm down." Butterflies fill my stomach at the sound of Nick's voice. I haven't heard his voice in over a month. I've missed it more than I care to admit.

"I just need to take this phone call, I'll be in my room," Alex says, obviously trying to get away from his brother.

"I didn't come here to work while you sit on the phone. Who is it? The girl from the bar?" A scuffle on the other end. "Look, it's cute you want to talk to my brother, but we have things to do. He can call you back tonight when we're done."

I hold my breath.

"Dude, I think she hung up."

"Or, she doesn't want to talk to you," Alex mumbles.

"Just hurry up so we can— Wait, this says…Nina." Oh my gosh, Alex is such an idiot. Why would he put my name in there? Everyone knows you're supposed to put a fake name. "Alex, what in the hell are you doing?"

"Give me the phone."

"How did you get her number? What did you—"

"Nick." It stills him.

Nick sighs, "I'm sorry, I'll take care of it."

"Nick, dategli il telefono."

"English, please." There's a smile in his voice.

"Give him the phone. Please."

After a long pause, Alex is back, "I'm sorry." A door closes loudly in the background and I know Nick is gone.

"What do you need, Alex?"

"Um, I just…I-I want to know what happened."

"Shouldn't you be asking your brother about this?"

"He won't talk to anyone, not even me. My brother always talks to me! We don't hide things from each other." I pick at the fresh paint on my nails. "Look, I know something happened. He's been acting out since they got here."

"Alex, just let it go."

"He's been out partying and getting into fights. Sometimes, he doesn't even come home."

"I don't feel comfortable talking to you about this." How am I supposed to tell him what happened when I don't even know what really happened? I'm still trying to understand what changed between us in a matter of hours. I notice a blonde head peek inside the door. She's carrying food from Java Fountain. "I'm sorry, I have to go." I hang up before Alex can say anymore.

"Who was that?" Michaela asks.

"No one." I can't remember the last time I felt so many emotions in one phone call. My body vibrates with adrenaline. What did Alex expect from that phone call? If his brother wants to go out and party, there's nothing I can do about it. If he wants to hook up with a new girl every night, nothing is stopping him. When he left Haven, he left me.

"You good?" Michaela falls into the chair across from me. "Look kinda pale."

"What do you want, Michaela?"

"Well, you've been locked in here all day without food or water," she sets a fresh iced water and salad in front of me. "So, I figured you could use some."

"I'm fine, Mic."

"Keep telling yourself that."

"I just need to finish these last few things, otherwise we won't get the furniture for Sarah, and then— Shit! I need to send Hannah the design for approval."

"Nina, stop. I already took care of Hannah and we have until tomorrow to order for Sarah." Michaela pushes the food closer, "Come on, eat."

I relent opening the salad and take a bite. "Happy?"

"Yes, thank you."

"What else?"

"Huh?"

"You're doing that thing when you need to tell me something," I say while taking a bite of salad. Michaela has never been very good at hiding things. She's always the first to crack when it comes to family secrets. If you don't want the rest of the world to know something, don't tell Michaela. "Your nose flares, you chew on your lip, and crack your thumbs."

"I do not!"

"Dai, versa il tè." She hates how well I know her. Taking a sip of water, I continue, "C'mon, spill."

"Well, you know, the wedding is coming up in like two weeks."

Seriously? That's what this is about?

"Are you still going?"

"Of course, I'm going." What kind of question is that? Of course I'm going to Elizabeth's wedding. It's Elizabeth. My best friend. My sister. Nothing could keep me from this wedding.

"Well, you know...It's just that..."

"What? Spit it out, Michaela."

"Nick is going to be at the wedding."

Oh, right. That.

thirty-eight

I **HAND THE VALET** my keys with a smile and thank the doorman as I enter the hotel. The front desk girl recognizes me; apparently, I designed her cousin's home in Charlotte. She continues gushing about how much she loved the aesthetic even after she passes me the room key. "I'm sorry, hun, I'm talkin' your ear off and I'm sure you wanna get upstairs before the events."

"Nonsense. I appreciate it," I smile. "But, I do need to meet the bride a little early, so I should probably go." I thank the girl again and almost make it to the elevator without incident. I hit the call button just as someone yells my name.

"Hi, Jenny." I embrace her and the older man next to her. Jenny and Patrick Davis — Josh and Michaela's parents. Patrick owns a local accounting firm in Winchester and Jenny is a school teacher at Winchester Elementary. While they live humbly, they do well in the financial department. Probably why Mother didn't fuss when Elizabeth started dating Josh. It doesn't hurt Josh makes almost six figures a year at the marketing firm.

"We're glad you made it. Will your parents be here?"

"Unfortunately, they won't. But, I'm sure they will make it up one way or another." Their gift would have been great anyway, but now Mother would make sure Elizabeth received an even better gift since they won't be here.

"Elizabeth was looking for you, did you get a chance to speak with her?"

"Pat! Jenny!" I hear someone call to them. Turning, I see a man around the same age walking towards us. He has similar features to Nick — dark brown hair, chiseled jaw, and gruff voice, but his eyes are the color of the ocean. I'm sure it's Jimmy Davis. I stand to the side as Jenny and Patrick welcome him. I notice the tattoos covering his left arm extending further under the sleeve of his T-shirt.

"Jim, this is Nina. Elizabeth's sister," Jenny introduces us.

Jimmy and I share a knowing look. And to confirm what he already knows, Jimmy asks, "As in Villa?"

"The same," I say with a shy smile and shake his hand.

"Nina, you know Michaela and Josh's cousin, Nick? Well, this is his father."

"It's nice to finally meet you."

"You too, sweetheart." Jimmy squeezes my hand before finally releasing it.

"Well, if you'll excuse me, I need to go, Elizabeth wants to meet before dinner. I need to get some work done and want to get a run in beforehand." I press the elevator call button again, the doors open immediately.

"Of course, I'm sorry to keep you. I'm sure Elizabeth will have you very busy this weekend," Jenny says as I step inside.

"Very," I give Jenny a small wave and share one last look with Jimmy before the doors close between us.

§

700 Drayton is one of my favorite restaurants in Savannah. Not just for the food, but the warm, bohemian atmosphere carried over from the hotel. I love admiring the different art

covering the walls — my favorite is the large leopard painting that hangs in the far back room where they've set smaller tables for other guests attending the rehearsal dinner. The wedding party will occupy a long table that has been set in the main dining space.

Employees scurry around finalizing last-minute touches before dinner. A young waitress bumps into me almost knocking the wine glass from my hands. "Oh my gosh, I am so sorry. I wasn't looking and—"

"It's okay, I was in your way." I laugh and check my outfit to make sure no wine spilled on me. "Just yell at me to move next time."

The waitress blushes and runs off for the pre-shift meeting.

I use one of the mirrors in the lobby to double-check my appearance. I readjust my high-waisted black pants and straightened my blouse, a satin emerald color that matches my eyes. I apply a fresh coat of nude lipstick popping my lips just as Elizabeth and the wedding planner descend the stairs. The planner goes over the evening's schedule for the millionth time. Elizabeth dismisses her mid-sentence when they reach the lobby. She sighs when the planner is gone, "This is too much."

"Isn't that why you have a wedding planner?"

"I just want it to be perfect, Nin. It feels like I'm going to mess up. There is so much that could go wrong."

"It's going to be great, Elizabeth. You just need to relax." I pull her to the bar and ask for a glass of white wine.

"I don't think I should."

"Oh, I definitely think you should." I tip the bartender and hand Elizabeth the glass. "Drink. Ti sentirai meglio." Elizabeth practically downs the entire glass. "I didn't mean chug it, but sure." We fall into a pair of leopard print chairs in front of the fireplace. "I'm sorry Mom and Dad couldn't be here."

"I get it," Elizabeth shrugs, playing with the hem of her

white dress. "Are you getting along?"

"Not exactly, but I know they still wanted to come. Regardless of what is going on between us. Daddy just couldn't get away from work."

"It's okay, it just means we get a better gift."

"That is the upside," I laugh.

"Hey, Nin," Elizabeth says after a moment. "I'm sorry I didn't ask you to be my maid of honor, you're my sister. You've always been here for me and you guys took me in when everything happened. No questions asked. I just…I'm sorry."

"Elizabeth Regina Cain, don't you dare. This is your day and it should be exactly how you want it. Lola has been a great friend to you. I'm glad you asked her."

"You are?" I roll my eyes, of course, I am. I don't need to be her maid of honor to know how she feels about me. "I just worry. I don't want you to be upset, you're my best friend and—"

"Elizabeth, stop. I promise, I am not upset."

"Thanks, Nin. Ti amo."

"Ti amo di più," I smile, but it falls when Elizabeth dabs her eyes. "Are you crying?"

"No, ugh!"

"Happy tears are the only tears I will accept this weekend."

"It's all just so much…I just can't believe it's here. This is everything I've ever wanted, but…"

"But?"

"I wish my parents were here."

I squeeze Elizabeth's hand gently. "They're here. Just in a different way. But, they're here."

"I don't know what I'd do without you."

"Crash and burn?" Elizabeth finally laughs. "I'm happy for you. You and Josh, you're great together."

"Kind of like you and Nick?" Elizabeth smirks and my eyes grow wide. "Michaela hasn't been able to stop talking about it. And then, Josh was telling me some more after his trip to Boston. Did you know Nick called him while you guys were in Denver? He won't tell me what that's about."

Nick called Bub? Wait, does he have something to do with the sudden change? Surely, Bub wouldn't have caused this.

"I know you've been busy, so I didn't want to bother you. I was kind of waiting for you to tell me, but I couldn't wait any longer."

I down the rest of my wine.

"What happened between you two?"

"Well, we're not together. Obviously."

"But, from what I hear, you make a good pair."

"It doesn't matter. He has a new girlfriend in Boston."

"That Sheyenne girl? She is not his girlfriend. Josh asked him about it when he was in town last week. Nick seemed pretty adamant nothing was going on."

"Well, I don't care." I sound almost convincing. "He can have a girlfriend if he wants to. We aren't together."

"That's not what I heard."

"It was a fluke. A mistake." I know I'm trying to convince myself just as much, if not more, as I'm trying to convince Elizabeth, but neither of us believes it.

"Josh and I didn't always get along, either. Look at us now! We're getting married tomorrow."

"And that's what we should be focusing on."

"Look, Nin, I love you, but you're so fucking stubborn." I raise a surprised brow, Elizabeth rarely cusses. "If you two would just talk about whatever is going on, I think you could make it work."

"Not if he's hiding something from me."

"Is he?"

"Yes."

"How do you know?"

"I just do." I run my fingers over the rim of my empty wine

glass. "I can just tell. One minute, we're having the best sex of my life and the next—"

"TMI," Elizabeth giggles.

"He comes back with coffee and tells me it was a mistake." I shake my head. "But, he said the weirdest thing, something about my mother. I think she has something to do with this."

"Would you be surprised?"

"No," I sigh. "Not at all."

"Do you think it was Lee?"

"Could've been both."

"I wish they would fuck already."

"Elizabeth!"

"Oh, come on. Your mom has been on his dick for years. One of these days, I'm telling you, it's gonna happen."

I shudder at the thought. "I haven't had enough alcohol for this conversation."

Elizabeth laughs. "Just promise, you'll think about it. If you think Nick isn't telling you something, talk to him. Make him tell you. If you were half as happy as it seems, isn't it worth it? At least to figure out what really happened?"

Elizabeth is right, I know that, but I don't think this weekend is the right time to handle the situation. This is supposed to be about her and Josh, not the mess Nick and I have created. Once this is all over, maybe I'll consider finally confronting him about whatever it is he's been hiding from me the past month and a half. But, what about that girl? The one in Boston. Sheyenne, I think. What's the point in trying to resolve this shit if he's already moved on?

"Nina, you deserve to be happy. Your life doesn't have to revolve around work. You've proven yourself already. Time and time again. You're more than a name." Elizabeth wipes a tear that rolls down my cheek. "It's okay to let someone in. Someone who will love you like you deserve...because Lee was not it."

"You can say that again."

"Just promise me, you'll think about it."

"Promise me, you won't meddle."

"I can't promise that." Elizabeth winks before she returns our glasses to the bar. I wipe my eyes and straighten my outfit before meeting her at the door. Elizabeth begins relaying everything the planner said as she loops our arms and we cross Drayton Street towards Forsyth Park. I'm thankful for the useless information as I try to keep my mind from wandering to a certain someone sure to be waiting at our destination.

thirty-nine

I SIT WITH JENNY on one of the nearby benches surrounding the Forsyth Park Fountain. The wedding planner explains how things will work during the ceremony and pairs up members of the wedding party: Selena, Elizabeth's friend from college, paired with Elijah, Josh's fraternity brother; Michaela paired with Daniel, Josh and Elijah's college friend; and Nick, the best man, paired with Lola, the maid-of-honor who hasn't made it into town yet. Nick assures the planner he can manage to show Lola the ropes, but Elizabeth has other plans. "Nina!" Elizabeth interrupts my conversation. "Can you stand in for Lola?"

"Elizabeth," a warning.

"Elizabeth, come on. I'll be fine," Nick sighs.

"Please, Nin? Just so Nick has a partner for tonight. So, he knows exactly what to do tomorrow." If looks could kill, Elizabeth would be missing her wedding tomorrow. "Pleaseeeee!"

You have no idea how badly I want to throttle her, but it's hard to stay annoyed when she gives her best puppy dog eyes from across the fountain. "Excuse me, Jenny," I sigh.

"Oh, no. You're perfectly fine, sweetie." Jenny tries but fails to hide a smirk.

"Qualsiasi cosa per te. Sappi solo che ti prenderò calci in culo," I say, joining them at the end of the aisle. Hopefully, the smile on my face tells Elizabeth what I said was anything but nice.

"Do I even want to know?" Elizabeth asks.

"Ti amo." I know she understands that.

The wedding planner pushes me towards Nick, but neither of us makes a move to stand closer. "Come on, you two. Act like you like each other."

"Yeah, act like you like each other!" Michaela yells from the altar earning a glare from both of us.

C'mon, just do it, Elizabeth says with her eyes urging me closer.

I'm about to take the first step when Nick holds his arm out to me. I hesitate, but take it and that familiar spark spreads the moment we touch. I know he feels it too, how could he not? The space disappears, his hand resting on top of mine over his arm. He leads me down the aisle. The walk feels longer than a few seconds, it feels like an eternity. The universe giving us a chance to talk for the first time in months, yet neither of us does.

"You dyed your hair," he finally whispers.

"Observant." I stopped coloring my hair and let my stylist dye it back to my natural dark chocolate color and added extensions giving it the length I have missed since I cut it off in college.

I see the corner of his lips tug upwards and I can't stop my own from doing the same. "It's good to see you, Dee."

"Is it?"

Our eyes meet for the first time when we reach the end of the aisle, but we don't say anymore. A brief smile before he turns to take his place at the altar. No dimple.

"Not a word, Michaela," I whisper when I meet her smirk.

"I didn't say anything."

§

Elijah leads me out of the restaurant by the arm. I'm exhausted and have another long day ahead of me. "It's only 7:48, anyone up for another round?" I hear my brother ask when he and Eileen reach the sidewalk where the others wait. Is it really only a quarter 'til eight? It feels like it should be closer to ten o'clock.

"You should meet up with us this year, it's a lot of fun," Elijah says, pushing a piece of hair behind my ear.

"I don't know, Eli. You guys are there on Christmas, I don't think I can do that."

"You can bring Nick if you want."

"Elijah!" I smack his chest playfully.

"I'm just saying, you guys aren't very good at hiding it."

"Nothing is going on."

Elijah leans in close and whispers in my ear, "You might wanna tell him that." He motions down the steps where Nick glares at us. He quickly averts his gaze.

"Nina, finally!" Elizabeth tears me away from Elijah and pulls me down the stairs. "We're going to Savoy for drinks."

"You guys go have fun. I'm going to bed."

"Nonsense! You have to come."

I don't want to go out, especially if Nick is going. But, it's no use arguing against Elizabeth. She won't take no for an answer. "Fine, but only because it's your wedding. I need to freshen up first, I'll meet you there." Elizabeth is wary, she's worried if she lets me go upstairs I may not come back down. "I'm right behind you, leave Elijah here if you don't believe me." I don't miss the way my words catch Nick's attention nor the glare he shoots at the dirty blonde. The way he's trying to replay the night's events to see if there is something he missed. Something between me and Elijah.

Elijah and I became fast friends when Josh introduced me

JENSEN PARKER

to him and Daniel almost three years ago, but that's all we've ever been, friends. Sure, he's handsome. They both are, but I've never been interested in either of them. Daniel had just started Kelly when we met and Elijah was in a relationship that ended about six months ago. And don't think Daniel and I haven't noticed the way he's been staring at Selena all night. We made sure to give him crap for it at dinner just before Elijah mentioned the annual Christmas trip he and Daniel take with their friends to the mountains near Asheville.

"C'mon, Liz, she'll be there." Josh pulls Elizabeth towards the awaiting van.

"Promise?" Elizabeth asks.

"Promettere."

"Oh, you said it in Italian, that means you're serious!" Elizabeth giggles before Josh finally pushes her into the van.

§

I'm about to ask the valet to get a ride from the hotel shuttle when I see Nick sitting on one of the benches near the entrance. The plaid shirt hugs his broad shoulders, sleeves rolled precisely to his elbows. I've spent most of the evening trying not to stare at the way it showcases the strength of the muscles underneath or the way the colors bring out the faintest bit of hazel in his eyes. His leg bounces absentmindedly and a rogue curl falls in his face illuminated by his phone as he types and erases a message five times. "Shouldn't you be at the bar?"

It startles him, but he doesn't miss a beat. Nick jumps to his feet and stuffs his phone into his back pocket. "Figured we could walk together."

I don't know if that's a good idea. A walk leads to talking and talking leads to—

"It's just a walk, Dee." The nickname sends a shock through my system. I've missed it. I chew on my bottom lip, debating

210

the offer, but he's right. It's just a walk.

My feet thank me for changing into a pair of sandals as I walk toward the street. Elizabeth will send a search party if we don't get there soon. Looking over my shoulder, he's still standing near the benches, "You coming, Fossette?"

A smile with the faintest dimple.

The September night is cool against the warmth radiating through me when our arms brush. Luckily, the walk to Savoy is a straight shot from the hotel, but it takes longer than it should have because our pace is slower than normal. Not many words are shared, but Nick finally takes my left hand in his right. The heat rises in my cheeks when he intertwines our fingers. His grip tightens as we cross Liberty Street and I squeeze his gently in return. He presses a light kiss to the back of my hand and fire ignites where his lips touch my skin.

As we approach the bar, he slows our pace even further — he's trying to say something, but stops, unable to find the right words.

"Thanks for walking with me," I cut him off.

"Oh, um, yeah. You're welcome."

His phone rings, but he ignores it.

"Nina—"

"You should probably get that." But, he still doesn't move to answer it. "I'll see you in there."

The air inside is warm, but not as warm as Nick's touch. I maneuver through the crowd to meet the others in the back corner where they've taken over a few tables. "Everything okay?" Elizabeth greets me just before I reach the tables, she hands me a glass of champagne.

"What do you think is going on with him?"

"Nick?"

I nod as we watch him pace outside the bar. He looks upset, his hands tug the ends of his curls, his jaw locks as he holds back what he really wants to say. Whoever is on the other end of the phone has caused a definite change in his demeanor. Our gaze meets through the window and he sighs. He seems to agree to whatever it is the person wants. When he finally enters the bar, I try to swim through the crowd to confront him, but Josh beats me to it.

"C'mon," Elizabeth pulls me by the arm. "Let Josh handle it for now. Worry about it later."

When I glance back, Nick is staring straight at me, but he breaks our stare to finally meet Josh with a sigh. I'm left with more questions than I came with. What the fuck is going on?

forty

THE REFLECTION IN THE elevator doors allows me to apply a final layer of lipstick, a warm peachy nude color. With a step back, I meet the stare of the girl in the mirror — she wears a plunge neck cabernet chiffon dress with long sleeves and a thigh split, dark hair falls down her shoulders in loose waves, minimal makeup, the way she likes, and nude heels accentuate the tanned leg that peaks through the slit in her dress. "You can do this, Nina," I whisper to her, to myself.

The elevator doors open to the lobby and I'm immediately greeted by a panicked wedding planner. "Thank God, you're here!" The planner drags me out before the doors can open all the way. "She hit the wall." This has turned out to be a lot harder than Elizabeth thought. The weight of her parents not being here finally hit her and the wedding planner's attempts to calm her down only made it worse. Pushing me towards one of the side hallways, the planner makes a quick escape out of the hotel to handle the rest of the wedding party.

Elizabeth paces trying to catch her breath. Tears brim her eyes threatening to ruin the hard work of her makeup artist, but she's doing her best to hold it together. "You okay?" I ask, but she shakes her head rapidly. "Can you tell me what you're feeling?"

"I miss them, Nina." Elizabeth clings to me. "I always pictured them here on this day, and I guess... I guess it didn't hit me until now." I take the tissue from her hand and dab the tears from the corner of her eyes. "I'm so nervous, what if I mess up? What if I fall or trip?"

"Relax." I squeeze her shoulders. "Take a deep breath." I inhale and then exhale once and then again with her. "You're going to be fine. Just keep your eyes on Josh, don't worry about anyone else."

"Can I ask you a favor?"

"No, I won't help you escape," I smile.

"No, not that!" Elizabeth laughs. "Will you walk with me? I don't think I can do it alone. And, you're not going to be up there. I'm sorry, I should've asked—"

"Yes."

"Really?" I nod and Elizabeth hugs me, tighter than before.

§

Elizabeth has a death grip on my hand as we walk through the park. One more turn and we will be standing face-to-face with her soon-to-be husband. She slows to a stop and takes a deep shaky breath. This is the moment we've been waiting for, even before the night of the 2015 Christmas Ball. It was obvious they were made for each other. They just needed a little push in the right direction from yours truly.

I fix the curl of her hair letting it rest gently on her shoulders and adjust the veil so the faux white flower pieces sewn into the fabric are on display. Her dress is the last one she had tried on, she didn't even want to, but I made her. The second she stepped out of the dressing room, we knew it was the one. Long sheer sleeves, elegant floral lace, and a flattering a-line v-neck were the total opposite of every other dress she had tried on, but she beamed with an excitement I hadn't seen with any of the others. I adjust the clasp of her necklace — the same one her mother had worn on her wedding day — and finally, meet her brown eyes.

Faintly, I hear the wedding march begin.

"Don't let me fall," she whispers.

"Never."

"Okay ladies, it's time," the wedding planner approaches.

We share one last smile before turning the corner and my breath hitches meeting his whiskey-colored eyes. That familiar warmth spreads through my entire being when he smiles at me. God, I miss him.

"You're staring," Elizabeth whispers without missing a step.

"I know." I can't help it, not when he looks so handsome in that sand-colored tuxedo with an olive-colored tie. The way it brings out the color in his eyes… I rip my gaze from him when we reach the altar. I have a role to play. "I know where you live, Joshua," I warn, earning a laugh from the crowd.

"Love you too, Nin," Josh says without missing a beat and kisses my cheek.

I share a final look with Nick taking my seat next to Kai. I wonder if he's imagining us in the same place. Because right now, that's all I can think about.

§

I step out onto the balcony of the ballroom taking a breath of fresh air. Nick and I have been actively avoiding each other for most of the evening, but every chance I get, I steal a glance. And every time I think about going to talk to him, I remember what Michaela told me a few days ago. Alex isn't the only person Nick has been hanging around in Boston — some girl named Sheyenne has entered the picture. They met during one of his late-night escapades Alex had tried telling me about. Yet, Alex failed to mention this Sheyenne girl to me. "He didn't want you to know that part," Michaela said when I questioned it. So, now I'm left to wonder if everything that happened in Haven was in my head. Did I imagine it all because he was able to forget it so quickly?

"I'm glad we get the chance to finally meet," I hear someone say — their voice rugged and warm. Jimmy Davis. He settles up next to me with a fresh glass of champagne. "I've heard a lot about you, Nina."

"Likewise." I smile taking the champagne. "It's nice to put a face to the name, Jimmy."

I wonder how much he knows — if he knows Nick didn't take the money even though it was right in his hands. I can only hope it didn't put them in a tight spot, especially with the time off they've had in Boston. I'm tempted to ask him about Sheyenne, what does he know about that relationship? Instead, I swallow my questions with a rather large gulp of champagne.

Something catches his attention inside the ballroom, but he says, "Nick would kill me if he knew I was saying anything, but whatever happened in Haven...it rocked him."

"I'm not sure I know what you mean."

"I think you do." He turns to look at me, but I refuse. My gaze fixed on the park below us.

"There you are!" Kai exclaims joining us. He looks between me and Jimmy, "Am I interrupting something?"

"Kai, this is Jimmy. Nick's dad," I introduce them.

Realization crosses my brother's face. "Nice to meet you, Kai Villa."

"Likewise," Jimmy says as they shake hands.

"I feel like I already know you."

"I wish I could say the same, but Nick hasn't told me much about his trip out West."

I tuck a piece of hair behind my ear suddenly feeling uncomfortable. I try to excuse myself, but Kai wraps his arm around my waist. "No? Well, he and Nin had a great time. You could never tell from the way they've been avoiding each other today, but—"

"Kai," I warn.

"I should thank you, Nina," Jimmy draws my attention away from my brother. "Taking him with you...it was good for Nick. Best thing that could've happened, really. He would run that garage for the rest of his life, but I know that's not what he wants. Not really. You brought a spark back I haven't seen in a long time."

Kai gives me a knowing look.

"And, I don't know what happened while you were gone, but I can see that—"

"There you are!" Alex joins us — apparently, everyone has been looking for me. He extends his hand out to me in a small bow, a twinkle in his cerulean eyes. "May I have this dance?"

"You'll have to excuse me," I say to Jimmy. "I promised Alex we'd share a dance before the night ends."

"Be my guest, I know he's been waiting for this moment for a long time," Jimmy smirks at his son. Jimmy laughs when Alex groans in annoyance and winks at me before I'm pulled back inside to the dance floor.

"Your dad is sweet," I say as Alex pulls me close. He's slightly taller than Nick, maybe two inches? Bright blue eyes, like his father, but dark brown hair like his brother — shorter, but I'm sure he'd have the same curls if he grew it out.

"He's embarrassing."

"You know, I do remember you."

"Is that a good thing?"

"I should be asking you that question. Not only did I almost run you over, but I was a mess after fighting with my ex."

"Yeah, but I learned who you were that night. I mean, not everyone would have helped that girl who spilled red icee down her shirt."

"It was her pants, actually."

"Just checking to see if you really remembered," Alex winks.

"How could I forget?" He twirls me under his arm and pulls me back in, but he looks past me. I know what caught his attention without having to look. I'd seen his brother standing with Elijah and Daniel the second we walked back inside. Felt his gaze on us the entire time. "Alex," I bring his attention back to me.

"Sorry," Alex smiles.

"Michaela told me...about Sheyenne." Alex visibly swallows. "I want you to know, I'd never do anything to jeopardize your brother's happiness. I've had my heart broken, had someone betray my trust... If this is what makes him happy, then I'm happy."

"She's just a friend, Nina."

"Sure about that?" But, he doesn't answer. "That's what I thought."

"I'm sorry, Nina," he whispers, pulling me closer and I rest my head on his chest. We stay like that until the song ends. He bows kissing the back of my hand and I curtsy briefly.

Alex leads me towards the table Kai and Jimmy have claimed where it's obvious Kai has been spilling secrets. He looks like a toddler caught red-handed with a Sharpie next to doodles on the wall. I roll my eyes and take a sip of champagne. I don't have it in me to bring an end to his meddling.

As the evening begins to wind down, I order another champagne from the bartender who smiles in thanks when I stuff a twenty dollar bill into the tip jar. Rule number one at any event with an open bar: make nice with the bartender. I'm about to leave when a man approaches — I'm pretty sure he is one of Josh's co-workers, but I honestly can't remember. I've met so many people in the last two days, they're all starting to blur together. I don't know what he's talking about, I stopped listening two minutes ago, but I smile as if I'm interested. My smile falls behind my glass when I scan the room for anyone to save me.

Don't get me wrong, this guy — what's his name? — is sweet and all, but I don't want to have to deal with this. I wonder if Elijah will pretend to be my boyfriend so I can get away from him. Without warning, his hand lands on top of mine and I'm well aware of the stark contrast between his hand and the ones I've been dreaming of every night.

Wait...no. I am not supposed to be thinking about the difference between Nick and other guys. That is over. Dead and gone. He's with Sheyenne now...but, it's hard not to think about it when every time he touches me, a fire ignites under my skin.

Okay, seriously. Where are the guys? Elijah...Alex... Daniel...Anyone.

"Would you like to dance?" Homeboy asks extending his hand towards me. Shit, what is his name?

"Hey, baby." It's like my prayers have been answered when I hear that voice. He kisses my cheek and I relax under his touch. "I'm sorry, I've been so busy tonight."

"Oh," the guy looks between us. "I'm sorry, I had no idea."

"I'm sorry...Sam." That's his name. Sam.

I don't miss the way Nick's hand lingers on my waist as he watches Sam scurry away. His lips turn up into a smirk matching my own when he finally meets my gaze. "What?"

"Oh, niente," I laugh taking a sip of champagne.

Over the speakers, a soft piano melody plays and other couples move to return to the dance floor. His fingers grip my waist pulling me closer, his breath warm against my ear, "Do you wanna dance?"

Yes. Yes, I do. He has no idea how badly I want to dance, but what happens after? Do we go back to avoiding each other? Do we pretend like there isn't an elephant sitting in the corner, waiting to be acknowledged?

"Yes."

Nick kisses my temple before leading me to the dance floor. That familiar warmth grows in my chest when he takes me into his arms, one hand in mine, the other resting on my lower back. I notice other guests have started to stare, but when I meet his stare, everyone else disappears. It's just us on the dance floor as the singer softly relays his love the best way he knows how.

His left hand holds mine to his chest as we sway. I rest my chin on his shoulder inhaling the comforting scent of him. It transports me back to the night of his birthday. We couldn't keep our hands to ourselves all night. Cedar and cardamom surrounded me the same way they do now. *I'm happy the first time was with you,* he said when we got home. And, the way he kissed me... I hate how much this is affecting me.

"Come back to me," he whispers with a lingering kiss.

A brief spin out...in...back into his arms. Our faces mere centimeters apart. The heat between us grows with each beat and I'm falling more in love with the man in front of me. A man I've never really known. One who has never known me, not really. Has never given himself the chance to know me. But, something deep inside yearns for him.

The music slows and he dips me. His breath tickles the exposed skin of my neck and his lips brush over my collarbone. When we stand, we are closer than before. Our noses touch and time stands still when his lips brush mine...

We're walking a thin line that neither dares cross.

A new beat.

Moment gone.

forty-one

WEDDING GUESTS WAVE GOODBYE to Elizabeth and Josh as they depart for the airport. I stand near my brother who's chomping at the bit to get back inside and enjoy a few more rounds at the bar. I can't blame him, he's been busier since coming home from Haven. It's pretty obvious Daddy wants to start the transition sooner than later, finally take some time off for once in his life. Kai doesn't think he's ready to give it all up yet, but he doesn't know Daddy like I do. He's tired and he's not getting any younger. If he wants to enjoy the life he's built, now would be the time.

"You guys up for a nightcap?" Kai asks. I'd been too lost in thought to notice the car had finally turned and the crowd had begun to disperse. The night's events replaying on a loop in my mind. The dance with Nick left me confused — more than confused.

"Count me in," Alex chirps and Michaela agrees.

"Sure, why not?" Nick checks his watch. "Still pretty early."

"I think I'm going to turn in, I'm pretty tired," I decline with a small smile and Eileen yawns in agreement. "It's been a long day." I just want to be alone.. The past forty-eight hours have been a complete whirlwind.

"Oh, would you two live a little?" Michaela huffs.

"I'll see you in the morning for breakfast."

"What about you, babe?" Kai asks.

"Fine," Eileen sighs. "But, just one."

Michaela squeals with delight leading the group toward the lobby doors. I don't even make it through the front door before a familiar warmth blooms under my skin. Nick's grip is light, I could easily slip my hand from his, but I let them hang between us.

"You okay?" he asks.

"Just a little tired. It's been a long few weeks."

"What if I grab something and meet you upstairs?"

"Nick," I sigh. "I don't think that's a good idea."

"Dee..."

"Look, I'm sorry. I just... Maybe we should just leave it. I don't—"

He kisses me. Hard and breathtaking, it reignites the fire in my chest, the same one left to smolder. His fingers tangle in my hair and pull me impossibly close — almost like he's forgotten how good it feels. How warm and soft...I want more. I need more.

But, we can't have more.

I push him away, gently, and take one step back. When he reaches for me, I shake my head and run for the elevators.

§

"Nina, open the door," Nick's voice comes from the other side of the door. How does he know my room number? I didn't—

Michaela. Of course, she would give it to him.

"Dee, please." His voice is soft, pleading. I stare at this side of the door weighing the options. I want to open the door. I want to let him in, but I shouldn't. How can I let him in when he has a girlfriend in Boston? That doesn't make me any better than Teagan…

I already miss the feeling of his lips on mine.

I'm going to regret this.

It's going to end with heartbreak, but who's, I'm not entirely sure. With a deep breath, I unchain the door. Meeting his stare through a small crack, I'm goner and he knows it. Nick pushes the door the rest of the way. He kisses me and kicks the door.

"Nick," I mumble against his lips. "Nick, wait." I can't do this, it's not right. I don't want to be like Teagan. I tug my fingers through my hair trying to find the words. "I-I can't, I can't do it. I won't put someone through this. I have been here and I won't do it."

"What are you talking about?"

"Your girlfriend."

"What girlfriend?"

"That girl in Boston, Alex told Michaela you're seeing someone."

He almost laughs. "Sheyenne? Nina, Shey is not my girlfriend. We're just friends."

"That was her last night, wasn't it? At the bar. You got a phone call—"

"No, Nina." It's stern. "No, that wasn't her."

"Who was it?" His eyes shift around the room trying to look anywhere but me. "Why did you act so weird? I mean, when we walked to the bar, things seemed okay, but after that, you got the call…You were weird."

"I-I…" Fingers scrub down his face and pinch the bridge of his nose. "It was… Look, it wasn't her. Can't we just leave it at that?"

"Who was it, Nick?"

He hesitates, "Alex."

"Okay," I scoff. "Say that I believe you, that it was Alex — who was in the bar, by the way. That doesn't change the fact that you've been seeing this girl."

"I'm not seeing anyone. Shey is nothing but a friend. Just someone to talk to. An outsider's perspective on things, I'm just trying to figure everything out."

"Interesting way of doing it."

"She is not my girlfriend, Davina."

Then, why does everyone else seem to think otherwise?

"I wouldn't put you in that position. Not after everything you've been through." His stare is unwavering when he says it and I believe him. I know he's lying about the phone call, but I believe this. I have no choice because when he kisses me, I can't stop myself. It's soft and slow, giving me the chance to ease into it, but I'm tired of waiting. I twist his tie in my fingers pulling him further into the room.

Nick presses me against the wall, hands pinned on either side of my head. His mouth over mine in a hard, possessive kiss. Shifting both of my hands into one of his, high above my head, his other hand slides down my body. A soft moan falls from my lips when his rough skin finds my breast through the fabric of my dress, his thumb teasing my nipple to attention.

"Nick," I whisper when his mouth finds my neck. "Please."

He lifts my feet off the ground. My legs around his waist, his hands on my ass, he carries me to the bed. He sits on the edge of the bed and tugs the zipper of my dress down, his mouth covering every inch of skin he exposes. I push his jacket from his shoulders and use his tie to pull his mouth to mine again.

He swiftly lifts me from his lap and sets me on the floor, my dress pooling at my feet. Wholly naked, I watch him make haste work of his dress pants, his tie, his shirt. His breaths come out in hard pants as he stares at me, never wanting to forget this. His hands trace my curves before he lifts me wrapping my legs around his waist — one hand on my back, the other grips my ass. I stare into those whiskey-golden eyes I've missed so much.

"I've missed you," he whispers. A piece of my heart mends at the confession. Nick buries his face into the crook of my neck. "I've missed you so much, Dee."

I tug the end of his hair so I can see his eyes when I say, "Show me."

His mouth collides with mine, his tongue plies my mouth, tasting of whiskey. He drops me onto the bed, his knee dipping between my thighs widening them. Interlacing our fingers beside my head, he stares into my eyes as he slowly guides himself into me and I swear I've never felt anything more intense. "Nick," I breathe, his name a prayer on my lips. When he pauses to let me adjust, I feel everything click into place. This is home, anywhere with him...is home.

Slowly, he begins to move his hips thrusting deeper, harder. Goosebumps rise across my skin as his free hand traces down my side until he's lifting my left thigh off the bed. The sound he makes is almost enough to make me come. Nick nips softly at the skin of my neck, and I gasp when he sinks his teeth in. After a brutal assault, his tongue laps the same spot — he wants to make sure there will be evidence in the morning.

"Nina," he whimpers, almost inaudible. My fingers dig into his back and I move my hips in time with his. His fingers bruise the skin of my thigh, and with slow, sensuous strokes he drives deeper. I hold his gaze, unable to look away. I study every part of his face, committing it to memory. Every movement, every breath, every moan... That burning pressure explodes deep inside my core. Nick captures my lips in a bruising kiss swallowing the moans of my release, his own not far behind. I hold him as he stills, relishing in the feeling of his skin on mine.

We remain like that for a while, skin to skin, until Nick shifts his hips drawing a moan from me.

"You know how to wreck a man, Davina Bay." I run my fingers through the soft curls on top of his head, longer than before, I twist one around my finger. He leans into my touch and when he meets my gaze again, I hear the words left unsaid.

I miss you.

I need you.

Forgive me.

forty-two

FOLLOWING THE HOST THROUGH the maze of tables, I can see Mother smile at her phone, but it fades when she remembers where she is. I'm sure she wishes she brought a jacket to fight the cool of the late September evening, but the weather is no match for the demeanor of the man next to her. I can't remember the last time he was this mad. He says something to her, but she rolls her eyes and turns her phone upside down on the table. Just in case. "Davina has always done things we never understood or agreed with, but you were always there for her, even when I wasn't. Don't stop now," I can hear her say as we get closer. They haven't seen me yet.

"This is different," he says and is about to say more, but their conversation halts as I appear at the table. "You're late."

I try to ignore his clipped tone. Try not to let it affect me, but I know he sees right through me. Daddy turns away, because if he doesn't, he might see the pain behind the mask. He might be willing to let it go and he doesn't want to. He isn't ready. He isn't ready to understand why I did it because that might open up a can of worms he's kept tucked away for a long time.

"How was your flight, Davina?" Mother's attempt at conversation makes my skin crawl.

"Delayed. Weather out of West Palm."

Daddy still refuses to look at me. I can't remember a time when Daddy and I barely uttered a word to each other. Even when he had to clean up my messes, get me out of trouble... He was always there. But, if one good thing has come out of this, he and Kai have gotten closer.

"So, we haven't seen you since before the wedding, how was it? We're sad we couldn't make it, but you know how that goes," she tries to move the conversation along.

"Elizabeth understood."

"Your brother mentioned you left Savannah a little early. Why is—"

"Excuse me," Daddy interrupts springing from the table when his phone rings.

An uneasy silence settles over the table after he leaves. I'd rather drink bleach than sit here with Mother. Yes, that sounds dramatic, but it doesn't make it any less true. I don't know why I came tonight. I don't want to fight with either of them. And while Mother seems to be trying the cordial route, I know it can only last so long. I start scrolling through my phone — a new photo message appears. I open it, but wish I hadn't when a photo of Nick and me dancing stares me in the face. Below it, a message:

LINA
I heard you're back. Call me when you're ready.

Yes, I left Savannah early. Sue me. I guess Kai hasn't totally abandoned his favorite former pastime — narcing. You would think I'd murdered someone with the family news coverage on it.

I left Savannah the morning after the wedding. I quietly packed my things, folded Nick's clothes, and left without saying goodbye. I thought I could get away without anyone noticing, but I didn't count on Eileen seeing me from the table

I was supposed to be sitting at that rainy morning. She was at breakfast with Kai, Michaela, and Alex when I made my escape. It's not like Nick didn't do the same in Haven, not that any of them know that. So, I guess that makes me a bitch — at least, in their eyes.

I flew to West Palm Beach and stayed there for almost two weeks. I turned my phone off, Michaela could handle the business. After two weeks, I figured it was time to head home, but I was honestly scared to turn my phone back on. After a flood of texts, emails, and missed calls, I only opened one message.

DADDY
Dinner when you decide to be an adult and come home.

"Just give him some time, Davina," Mother says. "He'll get over it."

Time? He's had sixty-seven days, how much time does he need? I scoff. "And, why are you okay with it?"

No one else seems to notice how well Mother is taking the whole thing. I knew Daddy would be mad, but I didn't think between the two, she would be the one who was nice about the whole ordeal.

"I'm not," her voice sharp. "But, I'm not going to hold it against you. I know we haven't always gotten along, but I would like to think we're more alike than you know."

"You and I? Okay."

"I just don't understand why you thought you had to hire some boy to be your boyfriend."

"You don't understand? You invited my ex-boyfriend to our house. If you hadn't done that, we wouldn't be in this position. Did it ever occur to you that the rest of us don't want to spend our time with Lee?"

"Don't blame me for your actions, Davina Bay. You chose to bring that boy, no one else."

"I don't have time for this." I throw my napkin on the table.

"You rush to get into bed with someone you don't even know, someone you...hired," she says the word quietly, scared someone might hear. "And, somehow it's my fault?"

"Nick slept on the floor for days. We kept our distance. But, things happened. Mistakes happened."

"You've made a lot of mistakes, Nina."

"And, I don't regret any of them."

"Not even what you did to that poor cop?"

"That wasn't my fault."

"No?"

"Teagan stuck her nose where it didn't belong."

"He should have been arrested."

"It was consensual."

"That doesn't make it legal. Sleeping with a minor—"

"I wasn't a minor."

"Oh, please. You think I don't know what you were doing well before then?"

"You couldn't have cared less. I could've been dead in a ditch and you wouldn't have noticed. You never cared about me or what I was doing. You only cared about—"

"Davina Bay," Daddy's voice halts the argument. "Ti scuserai con tua madre, ora."

"No."

"Apologize."

"No apology needed," Mother assures him. Her smile is sickening. "Is everything okay?"

"Nothing Kai can't handle."

"Oh, Davina! Did your brother tell you? It looks like your father may get to step down sooner than we thought."

"Goody," I can't contain my grimace. I already knew this was coming, it was clear to see in the way Daddy has been handing more responsibility over to my brother well before we went to Haven. And, I'm happy for my father, he deserves to enjoy the life he's built. I just hope I get to enjoy it with him.

The waiter appears to take our order, but I'm not hungry. I don't want to give myself any reason to stick around longer than I should — I order a whiskey neat. When the waiter finally leaves, only silence remains.

"Nina, I know this isn't what you want to talk about, but we're just trying to understand," Mother says when she can't take it any longer.

"How many times do I have to explain it?" It's getting ridiculous at this point. The answer isn't going to change no matter how many times they ask. "I wanted you to leave me alone. I just wanted to be able to go on vacation without hearing about Lee and how great he is. But, not only did I have to hear about him, I had to see him. All because you had to invite the Madigans back to Haven."

"They've always come out to the summer house, why should that change now?"

"Because we broke up! You want to invite Karol and Jack? Fine. I can deal with that, but not Lee or Teagan."

"It's time you moved past this, Davina. The way you hold on to the past is not flattering."

"I have moved on, but that doesn't mean I want to spend time with him." I thank the waiter for my drink before he scurries away, sensing the tension at the table. "If you hadn't invited Lee, I wouldn't have brought Nick. And, if not for that, I may not have met him."

"Michaela is his cousin, I'm sure she would've hooked you up eventually."

"Come fai a saperlo?"

"Would you please speak in English? You know I cannot understand—"

"How did you know Michaela is his cousin? I never told either of you that."

Panic. That's the only word I can use to describe the look

on my mother's face. And finally, Daddy joins the conversation, equally as interested to know how she knew something he didn't.

Mother's voice wavers, "I don't know, you must have said it."

"This is the first I'm hearing about it. How did you know, Bri?" Daddy asks, but she refuses to answer. "Brina."

"Fine, I looked into him. Okay?"

"You looked into him?" Even Daddy seems surprised.

A million thoughts race through my mind... Does Nick know she looked into him? Is that why he started acting so weird? Did she say something to him? Do something?

"What were you looking for?" I hiss.

"Nothing, I just wanted to know some more about him. You know, Davina, it's a good thing you didn't end up with him because he lied about everything. He dropped out of RU, he—"

"You're unbelievable. I know. I know everything! I didn't tell you because I knew you would react this way. I found someone who didn't want anything from me, he didn't care about our name or what I—"

"Didn't want anything from you?" Daddy's anger turns on me. "Lo stavi pagando!"

"He didn't even take the money!"

"Quiet, people are staring," Mother threatens.

"He didn't take the money," I say again. Quieter. Calmer. "I know you're mad, Daddy, and I am sorry." My voice cracks behind the tears welling in my eyes. "But, I would do it again. I just...I couldn't do it alone. I couldn't spend the summer with them. And, yes, it was about the money, at first, but he didn't take it."

Daddy says nothing.

"When did you look into him?" I turn back to Mother, but she doesn't respond."Mother. When?"

"Right before he left, I was—"

"Why'd you wait so long? If you were actually concerned, you would have done it in the beginning."

"Davina, I just wanted what was best for you."

"You wanted what was best for you."

"Davina," Daddy warns.

"After everything you put me through—"

"I was just looking out for you," Mother half pleads.

"You were looking out for you!"

"That's enough, Davina. This is not the place." Daddy looks around at the other club members, apologizing.

"Fine, I was looking out for me and your father and your brother. I didn't have to look out for you, Davina. You didn't need me. You never needed me."

"Yes, I did! I needed you, I needed my mom, but you didn't even want me." I reject my mother's hand when she reaches across the table. I share a look with Daddy, the cracks forming in his rough exterior. But, I'm not sticking around to see how long it takes to finally break. I stand from the chair, "If you'll excuse me."

forty-three

I HAVEN'T SEEN MY parents in over a week, not that I want to after our last confrontation at the club. To be fair, I haven't seen much of anyone the past week. Keeping to myself, my work…The way I like things. But, when I got the call from Alex about not being able to get in touch with Jimmy, I figured I could use the company. I'd go check on him, maybe spend a few minutes with someone normal.

I've knocked on the front door of the Davis residence for what feels like the hundredth time now with no answer. A truck is parked in the driveway, so I'm almost positive someone is home. I glance through one of the windows again, but nothing has changed — still dark and silent on the other side. Looking around, I notice the side garage door propped open, a light on.

I pull my cardigan tight against the October breeze and make the small trek across the driveway. I let myself inside with a small knock to signal my entry, but there's no answer and from the looks of it no one inside.

"Mr. Davis?"

A light hangs from the hood of a car and tools are scattered around it, signs of his earlier presence — where is he now? Surely, he couldn't have gone far. I dial Alex's number, to suggest putting a locator app on his dad's phone the next time they're together. Just before I cross the threshold, a small reflection catches my eye.

Holy.

Shit.

"Jimmy!"

On the other side of the garage, Jimmy lays unconscious on the floor. I touch his neck searching for a pulse, but I have no idea what I'm actually supposed to do. They don't exactly teach CPR in design school and I skipped that day in health class. Kind of starting to regret that now.

"Shit." Panic grips my chest. I cannot freak out. I cannot panic. Panicking is only going to make this worse. If I panic, who is going to call the police, who is— Shit. I need to call 911. Okay, it's fine. Everything is fine.

Wait, did his chest just move? That's a good sign.

Nina focus.

9-1-1.

§

I hate hospitals. Uncomfortable plastic chairs. Nauseatingly sterile air. Loud fluorescent lights. Sickness. Death. I just hate it. I'm trying to stay calm, but it's becoming harder with each passing minute. It feels like days have passed since they told me to wait, but in reality it has only been about two hours. Michaela has been trying to comfort me, but I shrug her off every time.

Elizabeth stands in the corner on the phone trying not to disturb anyone else in the room. "We don't know yet, still waiting on the— They're not here yet. Alex text Mic about an hour and a half ago, they were getting on the plane."

"Davis?" an older man in a white coat enters the waiting room. His name badge reads Dr. Erin Andress. I stand to meet him. "Are you family?"

"She's his daughter-in-law," Elizabeth ends the call. "His son is on the way."

"We're his nieces," Michaela adds.

"Should we wait for your husband, Mrs. Davis?" Dr. Andress asks me.

"No, I'll fill him in," I say.

He doesn't quite believe me, but instead of arguing, he leads us to a more private room. "Your father-in-law suffered a massive heart attack. He bumped his head pretty good with the fall, so we'll be monitoring him for any signs of a concussion. And, we will need to monitor his heart for a bit, but I expect he should make a full recovery. I don't think surgery is required at this moment, but if he doesn't make some lifestyle changes... It will be inevitable, but right now, it seems damage wasn't too severe. He's very lucky."

"Can we see him?" Elizabeth asks.

"He may still be a little groggy, but you can go in if you like. I'll have one of the nurses show you to his room."

"Thank you, doctor." I offer a small smile before Dr. Andress nods and steps out of the room.

"Mrs. Davis has a nice ring to it, huh?" Michaela giggles when the doctor is gone. I roll my eyes and leave her and Elizabeth with their daydreams.

§

When I walk into the room, I can hear the steady beep of the heart monitor — it sounds normal. His eyes are closed as if he were asleep, but it startles me. I take a step back, the image of him lying on the ground lifeless flashes before my eyes. It's gone just as fast, but I don't think I'll ever forget it.

"Hey, Uncle Jim," his eyes open when Michaela touches his hand.

"Well, hey girls, what are y'all doing here?"

"Just wanted to make sure you were okay."

"Healthy as a horse." Jimmy laughs when Michaela and Elizabeth roll their eyes. "How'd you know I was here?"

"Nina found you."

At the sound of my name, Jimmy looks behind them where I stand in the doorway.

"Hi, Jimmy," I finally step further into the room and his smile grows. "Alex asked me to stop by, check on you. He hadn't been able to get a hold of you."

"Oh, Nina. I'm sorry."

I look at my watch, the plane should have landed by now. "The boys should be here soon."

"They're coming? Well, I know Nick'll be happy to see you. He was so happy to see you at the wedding. I don't think I've ever seen him more in love."

"I wouldn't say that." I share a look with Michaela and Elizabeth.

"Trust me, I know what it looks like." Jimmy readjusts in bed to sit up straighter. "Look, Nina, Nick has trouble letting his guard down. I think it's a Davis man trait, but it got a lot worse after Evie passed."

"Who's Evie?"

"His mother."

"Aunt Evie died when Nick was in college," Michaela adds. "It hit us all pretty hard, but he took it the worst."

My heart sinks. "When did this happen?"

"The anniversary was last month, six years now. Nick's junior year of college...pretty early into the year, too," Jimmy sighs, a hint of guilt in his tone. "It was hard for me, at first. I struggled to keep up with the garage. So, Nick left Rosecliffe. I promised him that I would get back on my feet and he could go back to school, but he took over and just stayed."

"I'm so sorry, Jimmy."

"It's all part of life." Jimmy touches his hand to his left

pectoral patting the skin softly through the hospital gown. The same place where Nick's tattoo is... "We keep her close, the boys and I got matching tattoos a few years back. Evie was very deep in her relationship with the good Lord and she always wore a necklace with the Tree of Life to remind her of where we come from. So, we each got a tattoo of the Tree."

Tears prick the corner of my eyes. Why didn't Nick tell me this? And then I went and called this tattoo with so much meaning basic...

Oh. My. God.

I know who Nick is.

forty-four

THEN

"**I NEED SOME AIR.**" I push through the crowd without looking back. The alcohol courses through me. The air thick and the music too loud. I need fresh air. I can hear them yelling for me, but I don't care. I need to be anywhere but here right now. A couple blocks the door — the boy's mouth open so wide it looks like he's trying to swallow her face, but he's too busy enjoying himself to notice she isn't even kissing him back. She offers me a grateful smile when I push him aside to open the door, he offers an obscene gesture I return before stepping outside. "Fuck," I mumble taking the a large breath. The air is thick, humid, but I don't care. Anything is better than inside the small house.

I stumble reaching for the railing of the steps, plopping onto the first step. My eyes close as the concrete cools my skin, but there's something warm against the side of my thigh. My fingers graze warmth, it's something covered in... fabric? What the hell?

I jump from the steps almost falling, but something catches my wrist. A hand. A warm hand, the skin rough and worn, sends a trail of heat blazing across my skin. "You're okay, I gotcha."

"I'm sorry," I giggle, the alcohol still coursing through my veins. It's not funny, but it is. "I didn't mean to sit on you."

"Y'alright?" His voice warm like a warm blanket.

"Bene, bene. Needed some air, troppo caldo." Christmas lights hanging on the porch illuminate his face. He's handsome — sharp jaw, slight stubble, freckles, buzz cut... But, it's his eyes that draw me in. Even in the dark, I can tell they're gorgeous.

"Nina?"

"Hmm?"

"Your name is Nina?"

"At your service." My attempt to curtsy falls flat sending me stumbling again, but I catch myself just before I fall into him. I adjust my dress — the olive green garment leaves very little to the imagination, tanned skin exposed beneath thin spaghetti straps and a v-neckline. The dress hugs my body like a glove, like it had been made for me, because it was. Looking up to thank him for helping me, I recognize him. "Hey! I've seen you before, you're in some of my classes. You're cute."

He laughs and I swear my insides melt.

"What's your name?" I sink back onto the step.

"Nick."

"What are *you* doing out here?"

"Wondering why I came out tonight."

"Non sei l'unico," I whisper more to myself than him.

"You seemed to be having a good time."

"Watching me?" A flirtatious smile.

"Not exactly."

"Well, I didn't see you. I definitely would've danced with a cutie like you." I laugh because it's true. Had I seen him inside, I definitely would have stuck by his side. "You just need to learn how to have a little fun. If you want, I can teach you."

"I'll keep that in mind for next time," he says, twirling car keys on his finger.

"You're leaving?"

"Gettin' to be that time."

I stand from the stairs and trip on my heels. He catches me, again. "We've got to stop meeting like this," I giggle.

"You sure you're okay?"

"Peachy." After a long deep breath, I straighten my dress and stare at the door. I really don't want to go back inside. I rode with Teagan, and Lord knows she won't want to leave yet. I refuse to ask Lee, he'll want to stay the night, and I just want to be left alone.

"Gonna be okay in there?"

"Of course! Not a party without Nina Villa, is it?" He studies me for a moment, like he understands what I'm really saying. I'm sure he's heard the rumors, who hasn't? But, the way he looks at me, it's like he sees beyond the mask I've perfected. Like he sees the lie. "It was nice to meet you... Um..."

Shit, what was his name?

Without warning, Teagan bursts from the house. She's so skinny, there's almost no definition to her. Not even the tight black dress shows off much of a figure. I keep telling her she needs to eat, but she just rolls her eyes. One of these days, it's going to catch up to her, I swear. "There you are!" She stumbles, gripping onto me. "What are you doing out here?"

"Talking with my new friend." I point to the boy. "Isn't he cute?"

"Sure. Whatever. C'mon, let's go inside. Tommy promised he would play my song!"

"I don't want to," I whine. "I'm tired, Teag, and have family brunch in the morning. Can we leave?"

"The party is just starting!"

"I wanna go home."

"Don't be a grandma, Nin."

"You know," the boy interrupts. "I was about to leave, I could drive you home if you want."

"She's fine, thanks." Teagan tries to pull me back to the party.

"Actually, that would be great." I push her away.

"You don't even know him."

"That's never stopped you, Teag." I smile to myself when Teagan storms inside before turning to the boy. "Sorry about her. She's a drama queen."

"She gonna be okay?" He extends his hand to me and I try to ignore the warmth that spreads when our hands touch. It's obviously just the alcohol.

"Fine," I wave off the idea of Teagan. "She just hates when I leave her alone. Very clingy." The warm sensation spreads further when I lean him as we walk down the driveway.

§

The ride is quiet except the sound of Breaking Benjamin playing softly on the radio. I hum along to the beat of "Breath," not missing the small smirk on his lips. When we pull up to the front gate of the Villa Estate, I clumsily reach over him to put in the gate code.

"A gentleman," I giggle, taking his hand when he opens the car door.

"Do you have a key?"

I reach below the door mat and find the spare. "Daddy musta known I was coming home tonight." I start to open the door, but freeze. This is the part I always dread. No one does stuff like this for free, and I know he must want something in return. Taking a deep breath, I plaster on a fake smile and turn to face him again. "Do you want to come in?"

"No, that's okay." A soft smile in return, his hands pushed deep into jean pockets. "Goodnight, Nina." Without another word, he retreats back to his aqua colored Mustang — interesting color choice — and leaves me standing alone on the porch.

"Goodnight..."

Shit, I still can't remember his name.

forty-five

SINCE THE NIGHT OF Phillip's party, I haven't been able to stop thinking about mystery boy. I want to get to know him more, he isn't like the rest of the guys here. Not even Lee treats me with the same respect as this guy. But, when I woke up the next morning, everything was a bit fuzzy. I still can't remember his name. Even his face is trapped in a haze. I've spent the past week waiting to run into him again, but I haven't seen him. He hasn't been to class and he wasn't at Phillip's party on Saturday.

He isn't the only one.

Tobias has been missing too. Tobias Greene — junior at Rosecliffe, Sigma Phi Epsilon brother, and friend. We became friends through Lee, but he isn't Lee's biggest fan. Then again, neither am I. But, his sudden absence tells me he knows something.

§

"There you are!" I quicken my pace to meet Tobias across the quad. "Where have you been? You disappeared."

"I was helping a friend with some...stuff."

"Anyone I know?"

244

"Nope, don't think so." His smile doesn't quite reach his blue eyes and he looks exhausted. But, he changes the subject, "Hey, Lee was looking for you."

"He'll find me eventually, he always does."

"Why don't you just let him down, Nin? If you don't want to be with the kid just tell him."

"That's kind of what I wanted to talk to you about."

"I am not going to pretend to be in love with you."

"Not that! Weirdo. I was hoping you could point me in the right direction though. There was this guy at the party and—"

"Imagine that," Jonas quips, earning a warning glare from Tobias. I hadn't even noticed him standing there. Jonas Moreno — junior at Rosecliffe, Sigma Phi Epsilon brother, and not-friend. Jonas and I have never gotten along, but we tolerate each other for Tobias.

"He actually dropped me off at home, but I can't remember his name. I know he told me, but it's a little fuzzy."

"I'm surprised. I'm sure you said it enough that night."

"Do we have a problem, Jonas?"

"Just stating the obvious."

"I think you have me confused with Teagan."

"Drop the innocent act, Nina."

"You're not really one to talk, are you? Mister Two-Girls-One-Cup Remake."

"Okay, enough," Tobias tries to cut us off.

"I'm sure Lee would be interested to know you're looking for some guy from a party when you're supposedly dating him." Jonas means for it to be a threat, but I don't care. Let him say something to Lee, he'd be doing me a favor.

"Casual sex to let off a little bit of steam doesn't mean we're together."

"I said enough." Tobias steps between us. "Nin, I don't know who you're talking about. Do you remember what he looked like?"

"You all look the same," I joke.

"Ha. Ha. Well, do you remember what he was wearing?"

"Jeans and a hoodie, maybe a jacket? It was kind of dark and I'd been drinking. But, he definitely had a buzz cut."

Tobias shares a knowing look with Jonas, "Davis?"

"Doesn't sound right."

"Ethan?"

"No, definitely not."

"Sorry." Tobias keeps looking at Jonas — a conversation I'm not privy to. "Could've just been a friend of one of the guys."

"No, he goes here. I'm sure of it," I sigh. "He's in one of my classes, but he's been missing."

"Sorry, wish I could help." Tobias smiles, apologetic.

"It's okay, maybe I'll run into him again."

Jonas mumbles something I can't quite hear, but I don't get the chance to ask him to repeat it before I'm being lifted off the ground. Lee laughs behind me as I try to squirm from his grasp. I glare when he finally sets me back on my feet, straightening my hair and sweater, but it doesn't matter because he slings his arm around my shoulders messing up my hair again. "Tobi, where you been? You fell off the planet for a while," Lee says, meeting my attempts to move away with a tightening grip.

"Had a few things to take care of."

"Where have you been?" Lee asks me.

"Sono stato occupato."

"Yeah, *real occupato*," Jonas adds earning a glare from me.

"Want to grab lunch? My last class got canceled." Lee expects me to say yes, but it's the last thing I want to do. "We can go to Java, get you a coffee and then grab lunch at the club."

If I say no, I'll never hear the end of it. He'll follow me wherever I go anyway, so I might as well just say yes. "Fine."

I release myself from his grasp and hug Tobias. "Good luck," he whispers.

"Lunch on Thursday?"

"Sure."

Before I'm fully out of the embrace, Lee pulls me down the sidewalk. "What did he mean by good luck?"

"Oh, a class project. It's dumb."

"Sure that's the only thing bothering you?"

"Yes." I step away to put some space between us.

"Just seems like you've been avoiding me."

"Maybe I have."

"Why would you want to do that?"

"Because you're annoying." Lee laughs and wraps his arm around my waist to pull me close again.

forty-six

NOW

ALEX GETS HERE FIRST. He's shocked by the sheer size of the room his father has been placed in — it's more like an apartment than a hospital room. Upon entering, there's an area with a couch and dressing room for family members who stay overnight. Then, the patient's quarters. Two large windows overlook a lake nearby. A large plush couch between the windows, a lazy boy recliner in the corner, and built in cabinets frame the flat screen across from the bed. Behind the bed, a tufted wall with an intricate pattern, and wall mounted vital monitors. A desk opposite the windows. A large bathroom with a walk-in shower opens to a closet for patient belongings. But, Alex doesn't ask questions. Doesn't ask how his father got placed into a room like this. His eyes wander the room, but he falls into the recliner and joins the conversation as if he's been here the entire time.

I'm trying to follow the conversation myself, something about a string of murders in a prominent family in the southern part of the state. In recent news, the story the father had told was beginning to unravel and fingers were being pointed in his direction. Apparently, Jimmy was a big true crime buff like the rest of us. But, I can't help wondering where is Nick? Shouldn't he be with his brother? I can't imagine he would skip—

"Took you long enough!" Alex interrupts the story to point out his brother has finally joined us. And, he's not the only one. Just past him, a girl stands with a bright smile as she waves to Jimmy.

"Who's that?" I hear Michaela whisper to Elizabeth.

"I'll give you one guess."

She's not exactly what I imagined, in fact, she's the opposite. Short dress. Heels. Makeup. Nails. Her boobs practically fall out of the A-line dress, the hemline reaches just below her butt. I hope she doesn't plan on bending over anytime soon. She exudes a high maintenance attitude, it reminds me of my mother.

When she smiles, her teeth are radiant against ruby red lips that match the color of her dress — a warm combination against her cinnamon skin. She smiles at Jimmy before turning it to Nick, who doesn't reciprocate. No, his eyes are still on me. They flicker briefly to my left arm before meeting my gaze again — a question. *Did you get a tattoo?* But, I don't answer. My glare flickers between him and Shey — a question. *Is that who I think it is?* But, he doesn't answer.

"Well, hello Shey," Jimmy says, interrupting our silent conversation. "I didn't realize you were coming."

"When I heard the news, I got so worried! I just wanted to make sure you were okay."

"That was kind of you."

"Nice room you got, Pops," Nick says, trying to steer the conversation. "How'd you get put here?"

"Not sure, but not gonna question it."

"Until the bill comes."

Jimmy shrugs and stares at me when he speaks again, "Said it's been taken care of." The flaking nail polish on my fingers becomes the most interesting thing I've seen all day. I didn't want him to know what I had done, but I guess it's pretty obvious. Yes, I told the hospital to move Jimmy into the private wing. I wanted him to be comfortable and the thought of him potentially having to share a room was unfathomable. Besides, what if the boys wanted to come and visit? They needed to be comfortable too. "I'm just grateful."

Elizabeth clears her throat to get my attention. She raises her eyebrows in question — am I ready to go? Yes. I need to get out of here. A single nod springs her and Michaela from the couch.

"Well, we have to get going." I reach across the bed to hug Jimmy tightly. "I have a bunch of work waiting for me. Call me if you need anything, big or small, I don't care." I instruct Alex the same as he engulfs me in a hug.

When I finally turn towards the door, Shey squirms under my glare. She tugs at the end of her dress, but it doesn't go any further. We are nothing alike, that much is obvious. I wonder if she knows what happened in Savannah. I wonder if she even knows the truth about who I am.

When I meet Nick's stare there are so many things swirling behind his eyes, so many things left unsaid. I wonder if he wishes we were alone like I do. He begins to say something, but Shey steps between us, "Hi! You must be the girl Nick has told me all about." She extends her hand towards me. "I'm Shey."

"Shey, don't—"

"Davina," I interrupt him. I don't return her smile, but I do extend my hand.

"It's so nice to meet you. I feel like I already know you."

"I can't say the same." A tight smile spreads across my lips. "If you'll excuse me, I have some things to take care of."

She steps out of the way allowing me to pass, Elizabeth and Michaela follow.

forty-seven

THE HOSTESS LEADS ELIZABETH and Eileen to my table, they order a glass of wine each as they wait for me to finish an email. The past week has been hell, why are there so many people who want to start projects all of the sudden? I shouldn't complain, but I'm running out of hands to get work done.

"Sorry, finishing notes from my last meeting."

"Isn't that Michaela's job?" Elizabeth asks.

"She's on site in Asheville. So, today, it's my job."

"We really need to get you a pause button."

I stick my tongue out. "I didn't work on vacation."

"That's a lie," Eileen interjects.

"Fine, I didn't work *as much* on vacation," I correct putting my computer away.

"Why don't you hire another person to help?"

"I will, soon. I just need to get through this year."

"If you're seriously considering another office, you're going to need to hire a few more people," Elizabeth says, taking her wine from the waitress.

"It's just finding the time to sit down and interview them." I take the fresh glass of wine with a smile. "Anyway, where's Kai? I've been trying to call him all day."

"He's with your dad, some luncheon in Charlotte with the

board," Eileen says. "Have you talked to him?"

"Daddy? No, not really. He's still pretty mad."

"He'll get over it. I mean, how long did it take him to get over JJ?" Elizabeth asks.

"A while, but at least he talked to me back then."

"I don't remember him ever mentioning it... Almost like it never happened. But, I do remember the screaming match between you and Brina." I share a smile with her, that was a fun night. Daddy had been away on business when Teagan told Mother about John, she and I spent most of the night going back and forth.

"That was a little different," Eileen said.

"Was it?"

"I mean, you didn't hire him."

"Actually," Elizabeth sips her wine. "I think John might have been worse, we were still in high school."

"Wait! Were you underage?" Eileen's eyes grow wide at the thought. I thought Kai told her about that?

"Depends what you consider underage," I shrug behind my own glass.

"Davina Bay!"

"He was only four years older than me, I didn't think it was a big deal. Pop was ten years older than my Nonna. Hell, Josh is four years older than Elizabeth."

"They aren't in high school."

"Have you seen him?" Elizabeth asks.

"Jay?" I shake my head. I haven't seen John Jansen in almost seven years. Not long after a steamy night in his patrol car, I came home to news that Mother had found out about my not-so-secret boyfriend. Someone had seen us. Someone had followed us and taken photos as evidence. I called Daddy and came clean about what I had been doing. I asked him to do whatever he could to stop Mother from turning John into the police. Since I was eighteen and there was no evidence anything happened prior, Daddy pulled some strings and John was transferred to a unit in Raleigh, North Carolina. But, he had made me promise to not contact John again.

John "JJ" Jansen grew up in another suburb just west of Winchester. His family well known in the community for their service to the Sheriff's Department. He had no other plans than to follow in the footsteps of the men before him. Join the police, start a family, and live the rest of his days sipping sweet tea while his wife cooked dinner and his kids played out in the yard.

By chance, he met a girl at a party when he was in the academy. Some of his old high school friends invited him to attend their frat party. He thought she looked young, but he didn't question it, girls didn't always look their age. They spent the night together and he knew she was the one. What he didn't know, she was the daughter of one of the wealthiest families in the country, and sixteen.

"You know who that was, don't you?" his friend asked the next morning.

"Said her name was Nina."

"Yeah, Nina as in Davina Villa."

The next time John saw me, I did my best to avoid him. He did the same until I came into the kitchen looking for a drink. "You didn't mention you were underage," he said casually before I could leave.

"You didn't ask."

"I'm in the academy. If they found out—"

"What they don't know won't hurt 'em." Pulling my lower lip between my teeth, John could only see me under him like I had been the first night. I snaked my arms around his neck and instinctively he pulled me close when my lips found the sensitive skin of his neck.

"Your dad would kill me."

"What Daddy doesn't know, won't hurt him."

How we had never been caught was beyond my comprehension, we had never been very conspicuous in the two years we were together. I would go to his house in broad daylight, we would ride around town together, we even had sex in his patrol car on more than one occasion.

By my eighteenth birthday, he wanted to tell my family. He wanted them to know how in love he was, but I refused. I didn't want them to know, because that would mean coming clean about everything. He knew they were pushing me to go to Boston for school, the program was better than anything Rosecliffe could offer, but he was being selfish. He didn't want me to leave him. He hoped if they knew about our relationship, they'd let me stay. I could go to Rosecliffe and earn my "little degree" before I settled into our life together.

Somewhere, deep down, I think he knew it was never going to work. Davina Villa is not one to be tamed. I'm not a housewife and I had no intentions of becoming one, but I give him credit for trying. When he threatened to tell Daddy, I broke up with him. He got spooked — worried it would ruin his family reputation. I could have easily had him arrested, claiming he had been sexually assaulting me. Coerced me into it. So, he was left dealing with the heartbreak he'd brought upon himself while he heard the stories of my wild nights as a free woman.

Four months after I broke up with him, he got a call about a beach party — a bunch of seniors trying to enjoy what little childhood they had left before college. Neighbors across the lake had made the call. John saw me before I saw him, in fact he made eye contact with Elizabeth first. She glared at him, daring him to come near us. She had been the only one who knew about our relationship and she had always disliked him.

"I got these girls," John said to his counterpart. "Send the rest of 'em home."

"Just let them go?"

"They're just kids trying to have a good time. Give 'em a warning and let 'em go." John turned his attention to the three girls in front of him. Elizabeth glared at him and Teagan batted her eyelashes innocently, but I refused to look at him.

"I'm really sorry, Officer. We were just trying to have some fun. Please don't tell our parents." Teagan practically fell to her knees pleading with him.

"You're free to go, ladies. In the future, if you're going to throw a beach party, do it where there aren't so many residences, huh?"

"Yes, of course. Thank you so much! Let's go girls." Teagan had started to push me and Elizabeth away, but he stopped us.

"Actually, I need to speak with Ms. Villa. I'd be happy to take her home afterwards."

"I can drive," I finally said.

"You probably shouldn't, you have been drinking after all. Wouldn't want to end up with a spot on your record, would we?"

"Are you threatening me?"

"Not at all."

"I'll take the car, Nin," Elizabeth interrupted us. She knew John wasn't going to give up until I agreed to talk to him, but I know she still regrets not sticking around. Wonders if she would have been able to prevent what happened next.

When they left, John dismissed the other deputy — he was going to take me home, I'd had too much to drink. The other deputy was suspicious, but didn't question it. As soon as John turned back to me, I knew I was in for a fight. We hadn't spoken since I told him to 'fuck off' and hung up. But, the yelling didn't come. He was quiet as he asked me to explain to him what he had done wrong.

"Look at what you're doing, John. This! Right here. You want to control everything I do."

"That's not true." He reached for me, his thumb grazing my

cheek. "I miss you, Nina."

"Funny way of showing it."

"What was I supposed to do? Did you want me to show up on your doorstep and profess my love for you?"

"You didn't even try."

"You didn't want me to." My lack of a response was enough for him. "Get in, I'll take you home." He pushed me towards the door, but I planted my feet. "Nina, please get in the car."

"Make me."

John's body stiffened at the challenge. We shared an intense stare, neither backing down. He knew better than to take the bait, but he was losing his resolve. I don't know why I did it, I guess because I was lonely those few months without him? I had grown used to having someone there and missed the warmth of his touch. He pushed me against the car and crashed his mouth to mine. His hand shuffled for the door handle and he pushed me inside covering my body with his own.

The reignited flame was put out a month later.

"Honestly, I don't know that I want to see him again," I say while taking a sip of my wine. "It was fun while it lasted, but that'd be like opening Pandora's box."

"You sure it doesn't have to do with a certain someone?" Eileen's tone suggestive.

"No...I don't know, maybe. I mean, I was over Jay before, but sometimes, when things with Lee would get rough, I'd think about it. But, I haven't in a while." I swish the wine around my glass. "In the end, I was kind of relieved that Teagan told my mom. It was easier to end things that way than if I had to do it myself."

"He was kind of possessive."

I think back to the many fights with John, each one usually stemming from his behavior towards me. "Kind of?"

"I was trying to be nice."

"What about Nick and this Sheyenne girl?" Eileen finally asks the question everyone wants to know.

"He says they're just friends, but I don't think *she* got the memo," Elizabeth giggles. "Josh said she was up their ass the whole time he was at the house the other day. Freaked out because they were working and she decided to sit on the workbench wearing white pants."

Oh no, I already see where this is going.

"Got a big ol' grease stain right on her backside." Elizabeth smirks behind her wine glass. "That's what she gets for wearing white pants around a garage."

"Is Nick leading her on?" Eileen asks the question I want to know.

"I don't think so. I mean, he's been practically avoiding her since they got back. Alex has been the one dealing with her. Nick's been in the garage most of the time, Josh goes over to help when he can and he says Nick doesn't know why she's here, but he doesn't really care. To Nick, they really are just friends."

"She thinks if she sticks around long enough he'll give her a go."

"Precisely."

"Nin, have you talked since he got home?"

"No, but I talked to Alex yesterday." I've called Alex every few days to check in on his dad — make sure they don't need anything. Each time, I'm told I've already done enough.

"Don't you think you should?" Elizabeth asks.

No.

No, I don't think I should.

There is too much to talk about, too much to deal with. I'd rather not.

"There's a lot you guys need to talk about it. I mean, you still haven't even told us what happened in Haven. So, I know you haven't talked to him about it."

Typical Elizabeth, calling me out.

"Alex says he's fine. I told him to let me know if they need anything. Nick's busy, I don't want to get in the way."

"Honestly, Nin, I think you're the only one who wouldn't be in the way."

forty-eight

I HAVE WRITTEN AND deleted text messages to Nick over and over again for the last hour. I can never quite find the right words — I mean, what am I supposed to say? We haven't spoken since Savannah and I don't want to have that conversation.

That's a lie.

If it wasn't for Sheyenne, I probably would have driven over there already. Regardless of what anyone says, she showed up while his dad is in the hospital. She flew from Massachusetts to South Carolina at the drop of a hat. You don't just do that for someone who is only your friend. Someone who you just met. The whole thing just doesn't sit right with me.

But, I'm worried about Nick. I know he isn't taking care of himself. I've heard enough from Elizabeth and Alex to know he's barely sleeping, barely eating, and working nonstop.

So, against my better judgment...I call.

I don't think he's going to answer. It's been ringing for what seems like an eternity. Where is the voicemail? And then, "Hello?" He doesn't know it's me, that much is obvious by his tone. His voice echoes slightly, he must be working.

"Hey."

There's a scuffle on the other end. I imagine him rolling out from underneath the car he's working on to see if his ears are playing tricks on him. When he speaks, his voice is closer, "Dee?"

I smile at the nickname. "Hi, I uh...I just wanted to check on you."

"Oh. Um, we're good. Yeah, things are fine."

"That's not what I meant, Nick."

I wonder if anyone has checked on him during all of this. Of course, everyone wonders how Jimmy is and if he needs anything. But, has anyone checked on the boys? Even when I talk to Alex, I'm mostly asking about Jimmy.

I start to ask him again, but Nick cuts me off, "Can I see you?"

$$\S$$

He parks outside my office thirty minutes later, but he doesn't come inside. From the hallway, I can see the same Gulfstream Aqua Mustang from years ago parked along the curb and imagine him debating whether he is actually going to come in. He doesn't know I've seen him. I won't blame him if he doesn't go through with it. To be honest, I was a little shocked when he asked, but I couldn't say no. I wanted to see him too. I mean, is it a good idea? Probably not. It has the potential to make things much worse. What did he think was going to happen tonight? Could we really just push everything to the wayside and act like there aren't about five different elephants in the room? Even if we tried, things are bound to come up.

If he did leave, I wonder what excuse he would try to use? Alex needed help. No, Alex would never cover for him, not to me. The hospital called. No, I would call Jimmy, check on him. He needed to finish working. That's the most likely one.

In my office, my cell phone rings and I'm sure it's him calling to tell me he can't make it, but through the front door I see him finally get out of the car. He still doesn't come inside. I'm about to go outside and drag him inside when my office phone rings. I roll my eyes and return to my office to put out whatever fire awaits me.

Natalia.

Fuck. What now?

Natalia tells me we've run into a small situation at the house one of our crews is working on. What kind of situation? Issues with the flooring, paint, and cabinets. Construction needs another week to get it done.

I hear the front door open — either Nick finally decided to come inside or I'm about to be murdered.

I return my attention to Natalia. If I'm going to be murdered, let me at least tell her how to handle the situation first. "That's unacceptable. This project will be done by Tuesday, no exceptions. Do whatever needs to be done to make it happen. Pay them overtime, for all I care. I'll take the hit. This cannot be extended." I rake my fingers through my hair when Natalia sighs. The crew isn't going to like it. I don't care. Finish the job. Whatever it takes.

Natalia ends the call and I'm left more stressed out than I was ten minutes ago. Turning my chair, I throw my planner back on my desk and rub my eyes under my glasses. A heavy sigh, I mutter to myself in Italian before remembering I am not alone.

"Hi," he says, his smirk growing.

"Hey," I sigh. "I'm sorry, things have been crazy around here."

"I see that." Nick sits in the chair across from me. Still an obvious tension, but we are doing our best to ignore it.

"How's your dad?"

"He's alright. Trying to adjust. How are you?"

"Busy. From the looks of it, you have been too." I motion toward his grease-stained clothes.

"Sorry, I should've changed, but I didn't feel like answering a bunch of questions." Questions from both Alex and Sheyenne. I wonder if Sheyenne would've tried to tag along if she knew he was leaving.

"Nick, it's okay. I don't mind."

Nick rubs at the stain on his hand — where he hadn't been able to wash the grease off completely. Why is he here?

"Can I ask you something?" I finally ask and he looks up from his hand. "Why did you want to see me?"

"Look, maybe I should just go. I can—"

"Nick, don't." I walk around to sit in the chair next to him. "I'm just trying to understand. We haven't talked, not since you left. Hell, even before that. I know something was bothering you, but I just—"

"Dee, I'm sorry. I was a dick. I shouldn't have left you like that. You didn't deserve it."

"It's okay, I just want to know why."

"It's not okay, Nina! None of this is okay." Nick chews on my bottom lip and I take one of his hands threading our fingers together. "I'm sorry for what happened between us. I'm sorry for everything. I never meant to hurt you or put a wedge between you and your dad, I know how much he means to you. And then your mom and Lee—"

"Nick, let's not do this." I remove my glasses and rub my eyes. I don't have it in me to fight about this right now. "At this moment, I don't care what happened in Haven or in Savannah or a week ago. I just want to be with you. Okay? I'm worried about you." I run my thumb over the stubble that has started to grow on his cheek. "Parlami."

Ever so slowly, he begins to let the walls around him crumble. The past three months have been anything but easy. "I can't do this, Nina." He's fighting back the tears welling in his eyes. "Not again."

"Can't do what, baby?"

"I should've been here. I should've been with him. If you hadn't found him, I can't even think about what might've—"

"Don't do this to yourself, Nick. Don't worry about the what ifs, focus on the fact that he's gonna be okay. He's healing."

"They're talking about complications now. He's not gonna be the same. He can't run the garage, I'm gonna have to take over again."

"No." I won't let him. I won't let him go back to that garage. "No, he can hire someone. You've got to live your own life, Nick."

"You don't get it, Nina."

"You want to be there for him, keep an eye on him. But Nick, he doesn't want that for you. You know that. He wouldn't have pushed you to come with me if he did."

"You know about that?"

"He may have mentioned a few things at the wedding."

"Of course he did." Nick rolls his eyes. He takes my hand that had been caressing his cheek and presses it to his lips.

A blush creeps into my cheeks. "How about we go get something to eat and not talk about things?"

"I need to tell you something first."

"I don't want to talk about it. Any of it. I want to act like nothing is wrong, like we don't have a million things to talk about."

"Nina, there is one thing I need to tell you."

"Forget it, for now. Tonight, let's just not talk about how fucked up we are. Okay?"

"Nina, I just…It's about your mom and I really think you should know." I give him a warning glare from across the desk packing my things into my purse. He is not going to win this battle. "Fine, okay, whatever."

"Good. Now, we should probably get you a different shirt. I think that shop on Turner Street is still open. Then we can head to The Gathering Place, have you been there before?"

"No."

"Oh, it's so good."

"What if we run into someone in town? Your family, perhaps."

"Non c'è motivo per cui non possiamo essere amici, right?" I heave my bag onto my shoulder. When he doesn't respond, I look at him, "What?"

"English, please." His smirk makes me blush.

Oops.

"Plenty of people are friends with their ex. I mean, fake ex? — I don't know what to call us."

"Whatever you say, Princess," he laughs.

"Just do that more often, and we'll be fine, Fossette."

"What? Agree with you?"

"Yes."

We laugh and the last of the tension finally seems to disappear. Nick's hand lands on the small of my back as we leave the office. But, my mind wanders to what he said moments ago. He has to tell me something about my mother? It reminds me of what he said in Haven... As we walk down Sparrow Street towards Turner, I'm starting to think she really is the reason he left Haven. She admitted to looking into him. Did she do something? Say something? The thought doesn't leave my mind even when he begins telling me about spending time with Alex in Boston, intentionally leaving out the parts with Sheyenne.

forty-nine

HAVE I BEEN ACTIVELY avoiding my parents since dinner at the club? I plead the fifth. I'm not looking for another argument or twenty questions about whyI hired Nick. The answer has remained the same no matter how many times they ask. But, I've avoided them far too long and Elizabeth knows it, so she asked me to drop wedding photos at the house. I refused at first, but Elizabeth wouldn't give up until I agreed.

The Villa Estate is empty, no sign of either of my parents. I silently thank the Lord, because that means I can get in and out without any interaction. Dropping the photos on the kitchen counter, I'm about to leave when I see the fire roaring outside. I look up at the ceiling as if God himself is staring down at me with a smirk, proud of himself for not letting me escape that easily. "You just couldn't let me have this one, could you?" I ask aloud.

"Bri?" Daddy calls when I open the patio door. "Oh, Davina. Pensavo che tu fossi tua madre."

"No, but I was looking for her. Elizabeth gave me some wedding photos for you."

"Set them inside, I'll be sure to tell her you left them."

I fight the urge to go back inside, drop the photos, and run. I'm tired of dancing around him, walking on eggshells, I want to hash things out once and for all. "Daddy, can we talk?"

"I'm not sure there's anything to talk about."

"Beh, non sono d'accordo."

"Davina, I am not in the mood for this."

"All due respect, I don't give a shit." I sit in the chair next to him. "You have been mad at me since we left Haven. It's the middle of October, you cannot seriously still be holding this against me."

"I'm sorry, Piccola." When he finally looks at me, the cracks in his armor are growing bigger. "But, you have to understand where I'm coming from. You bring this boy into our home and you don't even know him. You pretend to be dating him, you—"

"Oh, Davina! You're here." Mother joins us ignoring the obvious tension. "I see you have the photos from the wedding. Let me see!" I hand her the photos without looking away from Daddy. "Oh, they are just beautiful. You walked her?" She holds up a photo of me and Elizabeth walking down the aisle.

"Since Daddy wasn't there, she asked me to do it."

"You look stunning, just beautiful." Mother pauses coming to the next photo. "Oh my, is that Nick? Doesn't he look handsome?"

I don't miss the way Daddy rolls his eyes at the mention of Nick.

"Mother, I need to go."

"Oh," she holds up a different photo of Nick and me dancing. Why would Elizabeth include that photo in their stack? She should know better. "You're just glowing."

"Please, make sure you let Elizabeth know you got the photos. She's been bugging me to drop them off."

"Of course." Mother continues to shuffle through the photos. "Oh, I heard you saw Lee recently."

"What?"

"Yes, he mentioned he saw you."

"No, I— Oh, you mean when he broke into my house?"

"Ha fatto cosa?" Daddy's attention is fully on me now. He's probably wondering why I didn't tell him. I thought about it, but we aren't exactly talking right now. Besides, I handled it.

"Well, I guess it's not really breaking in when you know where the spare key is, but…I told him to fuck off."

"Language, Davina," Mother warns.

"When did you see Lee, Bri?" Daddy asks.

"Oh no, darling, I haven't. Karol was telling me about it."

"Ooookay, well as much fun as I'm not having, I have to go now." I can feel the tension mounting between my parents. I'd rather not be around when Daddy decides to push the topic.

"So soon?"

"Yeah, I have plans that don't include talking about my stalker ex-boyfriend." I smile at Daddy when he chuckles.

"Well, if you get the chance, give him a call. I know he would love to hear from you."

"That sounds awful, so I won't be doing that." I make my way toward the patio door. "And, if you do see him again, make sure you remind him of what I told him the last time I saw him." I smirk. "Goodnight."

Behind me, I hear Daddy say, "Stop trying to push her on him, Bri."

"I just want her to be happy," she whispers.

"I don't think her idea of happy includes Lee."

At least someone around her understands that.

§

Five days earlier, I returned home from the office late and had an early morning flight I was not looking forward to, but duty called me down to Sullivans Island. I pulled a bottle of water from the fridge and walked into the pantry tossing leftover pad thai into the microwave. Scrolling through my phone, I swore I heard the front door open and close.

I listened for any other sound, but the house was still. Quietly, I opened the microwave door and set my phone down on the counter. I reached inside the knife drawer and gripped the wooden handle of a knife.

Tiptoeing, I glanced out of the pantry, but saw no one. The house remained quiet. The only sound the *tick-tick-tick* of the clock. Nothing out of place, but something *felt* off. Through the living room, I froze when I heard something on the stairs in the foyer. Using the fireplace to conceal myself, I waited until they reached the top of the stairs. Adjusting my grip on the knife, I stepped out and my heart jumped seeing a man.

"Damnit, Lee!" I let out the breath I had been holding. "Che cazzo?"

"Hey, Dove." Lee stood in front of me with a wide smirk. Clean shaven and his hair gelled back, but the top buttons of his shirt undone and sleeves rolled up, he looked unusually casual.

"I could've stabbed you."

"Oh, so scary." He feigned being scared seeing the knife in my hands.

"It's not much, but it's sharper than you."

Lee mocked me. "I'm just glad it wasn't your gun."

I hummed in response and set the knife securely on the foyer table. "How did you even get in here?"

"Time for a new hide-a-key spot." Lee held up my spare key.

"Pretty sure I can still call the cops for breaking and entering when you come in uninvited."

"Oh, come on, Dove. Don't be hasty." Lee wrapped his arm around me, but I shrugged out of his grasp.

"You need to find someone else to stalk, like your girlfriend. Remember her? About yea high, black hair, and—"

"It's not stalking if you know the person."

"What? Yes, it is." I stepped back. With each step closer, I took two back. "What do you want, Lee? I'm not in the mood for your bullshit today."

"How about tomorrow?"

"How about never."

"I just want to talk. I heard you and Nick broke up. But, you can't call it a breakup when you weren't really together in the first place, can you?"

I wanted to slap the smug look off his face. "Did you just come here to insult me?"

"C'mon, I'm just playing around."

I had run out of space, my back against the stone of the fireplace. He leaned in close, his breath fanning across my face. He placed his hands on either side of my head. This was all too familiar, like a bad case of déjà vu.

"I'll remind you what it's like to be with a real man."

"You? Un vero uomo?" I laughed, my heart racing in my chest. I cursed myself for putting the knife down. "That's cute, but I think it's time to go home. I'm sure your girlfriend is wondering where you are."

"Teagan and I broke up, actually." I can tell by the way he said it, he thought it would change things.

"Oh, did she dump your sorry ass when she realized you were cheating on her?"

"I'm not...I didn't cheat on her! What did he say to you?"

The look in his eyes scared me. I had never seen that look before, like a wild animal caught in a snare. "What are you talking about?"

"Nick. What did he say to you?" His eyes blazed.

"Nick didn't say anything to me. Why would he?" I was confused. Was there something Nick knew? Was this what he had been trying to tell me before? "This has nothing to do with him. You tried to sleep with me in Haven. It's pretty obvious you're fucking around on her."

"Nina, please. I want you. No one else. Seeing you with him, it made me realize you were the best thing that ever happened to me. I can't stand the thought of you with someone else. Especially not him."

"That's when you realized?"

"I wasn't the best boyfriend, I know that, but I can do better. I want to do better, for you." Before I could protest, Lee crashed his mouth to mine in a bruising kiss. I tried to push him away, but his fingers tangled in my hair holding me steady.

"Lee, stop," I said against his lips and pushed him away. I wiped blood from my lip where he had bitten it. "What is wrong with you?"

"Don't be so dramatic, Nina."

"Go home, Lee." I stopped him when he tried to say something else. "I said, go."

"We can make this work. We can—"

"Lee, if you don't get the fuck out of my house, I will cut your dick off and feed it to the alligators in the lake. And, if you ever come here uninvited again, this," I picked up the knife. "This will be the least of your problems."

Lee's jaw locked, he squared his shoulders and took a deep breath puffing his chest. Neither of us had any intention of breaking the stare, neither wanting to be the first to give in. But, after a few moments, he finally did. The key clattered to the ground near my feet when he threw it. A moment later, the door slammed echoing around me.

fifty

"YOU'LL NEVER GUESS WHO came to visit the other day." Elizabeth sits in the chair across my desk.

"Let me guess." I rest my chin atop my bridged fingers pretending to think. "Was it Jack Skellington telling you what to get me for my birthday?" Elizabeth rolls her eyes. "No? Hmm, Santa Claus checking in to see if you deserve to be on the nice list this year?"

"I'm always on the nice list."

"So, not Santa then?"

Elizabeth rolls her eyes ignoring my question. "We invited Nick over."

"I see why you're always on the nice list. Your charity work is out of this world."

"You're insufferable." I duck when she balls a Post-it note throwing it at me.

"I love you too."

"Sheyenne showed up," Elizabeth continues her story. "I was hoping he'd come alone, but I guess she heard him talking to me the night before and made sure she was ready to go when he left."

"Sounds like a personal problem." My focus remains on my email where plans for a new build await approval.

271

"You didn't tell Nick you've been sick?"

"It's not anyone's business, is it?"

"He seemed pretty worried when I brought it up."

"Can't be too worried, he hasn't said anything to me." I finally tear my attention away from the computer. "Elizabeth, I'm fine. I went to the doctor like you asked, okay? They said it's just stress and fatigue. Gave me something to help me sleep because apparently that's important." She doesn't seem convinced. "I'm fine. I just have to take it down a notch."

"You're not pregnant, are you?"

She cannot be serious.

"It's not that far-fetched. You guys slept together. You could be! I mean, you've had the worst mood swings and you've been throwing up! You have all the symptoms and—"

"Elizabeth, I am not pregnant. Mother Nature called about a week ago."

"You're sure?"

"I think it would have shown up on the blood tests."

"They checked?" She deflates when I nod.

"You seem disappointed."

"The thought of a little Nick or Nina running around makes me happy." Elizabeth laughs when I toss the Post-it note back at her and turn back to my email. "Uncle Jim gets out tomorrow."

"Does that mean Alex is going back to school?"

"According to Sheyenne, he is. But, Nick doesn't seem so sure."

"What does that mean, according to Sheyenne?"

"Well, she didn't let him say much. Whenever we'd ask him a question, she'd jump in and answer it for him." I'm sure he loved that. "I could tell he was about to blow, but Josh kind of intervened. He asked her the question we've all been wanting to know."

"Which is?"

"Why is she here when Nick has made it abundantly clear that they are not together."

I try not to react, but I find myself giggling at the thought. Bub has never been very subtle.

"She says they're not together."

"Yet, she shows up anyway."

"Personally, Nin, I think she wanted to meet you." I give her my full attention. What does that mean? "She says we need to focus on what he really wants, instead of telling him what he wants. We're all obsessed with this idea of you and him, so caught up in your fake relationship that we can't see the truth."

"Which is?"

"According to her, he doesn't want you."

A stab in the heart.

"Nick doesn't agree."

"Elizabeth, I don't—"

"He didn't hesitate to tell us that, Nina. And, I know him, he isn't going to do something he doesn't wanna do. He wants to fix things with you, he wants you. I just... Something is holding him back and I don't know what it is."

"I do." Her interest peaks. "Well, sort of. Maybe. I think it has something to do with my mother. I don't know what, but he said it in Haven and he said it the other night. Something isn't right, Elizabeth. And, Lee made a comment about it the other night."

"What do you think she did?"

I shrug, "I have no idea, but I know she told Karol that she didn't like Nick. Didn't think he was good enough."

"Since when does she care?"

"Since I'm not dating Lee anymore."

fifty-one

"HAPPY BIRTHDAY, NINA," THE waitress said, setting down a stack of funfetti pancakes — they were my favorite birthday treat when I was younger. It was tradition for Daddy to take me out for a birthday breakfast at Honeybee's Cafe before work or school every year. The waitress, her name tag pinned to her sweater read Tessa, sat next to Daddy. Theresa "Tessa" Bennett had been our waitress at Honeybee's Cafe for over fifteen years, even though she had moved from waitressing to running the place five years prior. When the former owner decided to sell the restaurant, he first offered it to Tessa, but she declined. There was no way she could afford it. When Daddy heard, he offered to invest in her and the business. She wanted to refuse, but he wouldn't hear it. After two years, she became full owner. "And, this is for you," Tessa handed the morning newspaper to Daddy.

"Thanks, Tess." I began cutting the short stack into bite-size pieces, but I don't miss the way the gap between Daddy and Tessa seemed to shrink.

"I can't believe our little girl is all grown up, Ricky. Feels like just yesterday you were bringing her in for the first time, now she's eighteen and soon off to college." Tessa touched her heart, her eyes shimmering under the fluorescent lights.

"Hasn't she always been?" Daddy asked.

"That she has." Tessa squeezed his hand gently, a lingering smile between them. I smirked behind my coffee at the interaction. I always thought Tessa had a thing for Daddy. I wouldn't object, even if Tessa was secretly a bitch, anything was better than my mother. "Well, I'll leave you to it. Just holler if you need anything." Standing, Tessa dusted off her jeans before she disappeared into the kitchen.

"Not a word," he said, turning his attention to the newspaper.

"I didn't say anything, Daddy," I stuffed a piece of pancake in my mouth, a satisfied smirk on my lips.

"Just eat your pancakes."

§

"Daddy?" What was he doing here? We aren't exactly on the best terms, I figured he wanted to put breakfast on hold this year. So, I'm rightfully confused seeing him sitting in our normal booth at Honeybee's Cafe. Daddy folds the newspaper and looks up at me over his glasses. "You're here?" I sit across from him.

"It is your birthday."

"But—"

"There she is!" Tessa bursts from the kitchen door dressed in jeans and a loose T-shirt. Her graying hair pulled into a loose braid of her shoulder. She sets a stack of funfetti pancakes on the table and refills Daddy's coffee. "Happy birthday, Princess. Holler if y'all need anything." I don't miss the small squeeze on his shoulder before Tessa leaves.

"I thought you were still mad at me. Why would you want to do this?"

"Because Nina, I'm trying to move past it." He puts his glasses away. "Avevi ragione. It's the end of October and this is long overdue."

"Daddy, mi dispiace."

But, he holds his hand up in pause. "Nina, I don't understand, and maybe I never will, but I'm trying. I want you to be honest with me about all of it."

I nod in understanding.

"Did you know him before?"

"We met in college, if he is who I think he is. He brought me home one night after a party. We didn't do anything, he just made sure I got home. He was a gentleman and he was nice. And, I liked him."

"Quindi, perché sei uscito con Lee?"

"I'd only met Nick once, but I couldn't remember his name and it wasn't like we swapped life stories, so I didn't have much to go off of when I was looking for him. It was like he fell off the face of the Earth."

"Until now?"

"Until now," I confirm. This was the first time I was admitting it out loud. I have always been grateful for the cute stranger who offered to drive me home from Phillip's party.

Here are the things I already knew...Nick had gone to Rosecliffe and studied architecture. The photo Jonas sent to Lee proves he ran around the same circle we did. Which means we more than likely ran into each other, had probably even attended the same parties. Here is what I didn't know... after the death of his wife, Jimmy struggled to keep up with the business and Nick decided to push pause on school and help around the garage. Nick dropped out of Rosecliffe — an abrupt departure.

I am so sure Nick is the same boy from the party. The boy I had been looking for but never found. The one who could have stopped me from ever dating Lee, ever going through that heartache.

"I looked for him, but he was just...poof. Gone. I think,

276

after talking to his dad, that was around the time he dropped out because his mom died."

"His mother died?"

"It makes sense. I never saw him again, until he spilled coffee on me and then when he walked into my office with Josh."

"Did you know it was him?"

"No. I mean, I thought he looked familiar, but I didn't know." His silence begs me to continue. "When we met this time, he didn't seem to like me. So, I thought he'd be a good fit. You guys didn't know him and he didn't like me. I thought it would be easier to cut ties at the end of the summer, but things changed."

"What changed?"

"We became friends. He realized I wasn't the spoiled brat who got everything and everyone she wanted. And, I realized he just needed someone to help him pull the stick out of his ass and have a little fun."

"You'd be the person to do it," Daddy laughs. "So, where do you stand now?"

"We still haven't talked about what happened."

"What did happen, Piccola?" I'm not sure I can tell him. But, this is supposed to be about honesty, right? He can't get too mad if I'm honest. "Don't you think you guys should talk about it?"

"There's a lot to talk about. Especially if he is who I think he is. I don't understand why he wouldn't have told me. But, a lot is going on right now, his dad was in the hospital—"

"L'ospedale?"

"Jimmy had a heart attack."

"Is he okay? Nick, I mean."

"We had dinner not long ago, he's coping, but—"

"You had dinner?" He is rightfully confused. "You had dinner, but you haven't talked about things?"

"He just needed a friend."

"Siete amici?"

"We're trying."

"But, don't you think you should talk things over before you put a label on it? What if you want more than just friends, or what if he decides he wants something you don't?"

"We'll talk. When the time is right."

"The time will never be right, Davina." He covers my hands. "Take it from me, there is no right time. You need to talk to him. I want you to be happy, and if that's him, then I want you guys to figure this out." He smiles at me. "I will always love you, Davina. Even when you do things I don't agree with or understand. Sei ancora la mia bambina."

Tears brim my eyes, for the first time, it feels like things are going to work out.

"I am sorry for how I reacted. I love you very much and I know things haven't always been easy, but we're gonna get through it."

"Thanks, Daddy."

"Now, one more question." He squares his shoulders and looks me straight in the eye. "Do you love him?"

I'm taken aback. "What?"

"It's a serious question, Nina."

"Does it matter?"

"Of course, it matters."

I'm hesitant. There is no going back once I cross this line, when I finally say it out loud. "I mean, it feels different. Non lo so."

"It is different, because you love him."

"But, Lee—"

"You didn't love Lee, Piccola. Not in the same way."

"What am I supposed to do?"

"Well, that's up to you, isn't it?"

§

I end the FaceTime with one of my past clients in Nashville. They just sold their home and are in desperate need of help on a fixer-upper they just purchased in its place. Opening my email, I ask Andrew if he is available November 1st for a flight to Nashville. If it was up to me, we would leave in the morning, but I know my clients would rather spend Halloween with their kids than going over design ideas.

"You have a visitor," Michaela singsongs walking past my office to her own.

Without looking, "Busy, take a message."

"Should only take a few minutes." At the sound of his voice, I look up from my computer.

What is he doing here?

"What's all this?" I point to the load in his arms.

Nick holds up my black and white striped knitted cardigan, the one I had been wearing the day I found Jimmy. "Well, figured I should return this. You left it at the hospital." But, it's the bouquet tucked in the crook of his arm that catches my eye. White roses, sunflowers, mums, and daisies. "And, I might've heard it was your birthday."

I blush when he sets the bouquet in front of me, next to it a coffee from Java, and a cupcake from Dani's Cupcakes. I pick up the bouquet and take a deep breath inhaling their fresh scent. "These are stunning."

"I didn't mean to bother you, I just wanted to wish you a happy birthday."

"I could use a quick break." I sit in one of the chairs in front of my desk picking at the cupcake. "Sit, I have a few minutes." I don't, but I'm not ready to let him go. For some reason, this feels like more than just a casual birthday drop in. It feels like goodbye. "How have you been, Fossette?"

"Fine, just busy. Dad got home last week. He's started going for walks in the morning with Alex and he hates it."

"That's not surprising," I laugh. I think about the conversation with Daddy from this morning. We should talk, but it's not a good time. I don't want to spend my birthday rehashing the last few months. And, I have one million other things to deal with on the other side of that screen on my desk. The silence envelopes us, neither knowing what to say, afraid to say the wrong thing. "Well, thank you for returning my sweater and the gifts, but I need to get back to work. I have to get ready to go to Nashville."

"Yeah, I should probably get back to the garage."

"Nin," Michaela knocks on the door. "Angela's calling. Said it's a 9-1-1. I tried, but she won't talk to me."

I sigh and meet Nick's stare. "Sorry."

"It's okay. We'll talk later."

I want to believe him, but I don't.

Nick pulls me to him tightly, almost like he's memorizing the feel of me against him. He presses his lips to the crown of my head, lingering there longer than just a friendly peck. "Happy birthday, Princess," he mumbles against my skin and leaves.

fifty-two

FIVE WEEKS LATER

"DADDY!" I BURST THROUGH the door of his office followed by his assistant. I've never seen her before, she must be new, some impression I'm making on her. That thought long forgotten — the scene inside my father's office makes my blood boil. What is he doing here?

"I'm sorry, Mr. Villa. I couldn't stop her," his assistant panics beside me.

"It's okay, Jenna. Just close the door on your way out." Daddy reassures her and she looks between us before quietly closing the door.

"Che cazzo ci fai qui?" I hiss.

"Nina." Daddy tries to stop me, but I've already reached my target.

Nicholas Davis.

He sits in the leather chair across from my father refusing to cower to the ticking time bomb in front of him. His lips pulled into a firm line, he tries to exude an air of confidence, but I see through it.

"How can you sit here like you haven't been lying to us — to me — for months?"

"Nina, per favore," Daddy pleads.

"Pensavi davvero che non l'avrei scoperto? Did you think

281

you could play nice and maybe, if I found out, I would just forgive you perché eravamo 'amici?'"

"Davina. Abbastanza."

No. He deserves this. He deserves every ounce of my wrath. How could he do this?

"Sei un bugiardo."

"He didn't lie."

Why is Daddy trying to defend him?

"You have no idea what you're talking about, Davina."

"So, he hasn't been hiding the fact that he knew Mom was fucking Lee?"

Daddy sighs. "Yes, that is true, but..." He shares a look with Nick. "Only because I asked him to. He told me and I asked him not to say anything to you."

"Stronzata," I scoff. "You expect me to believe that?"

"He wanted to tell you, but there was never a right time."

"There were plenty of times!"

"Nina, I can assure you, Nick wanted to tell you. But, you were just starting to get along with your mother again and I didn't want to—"

"So?"

"So, I didn't want to ruin that."

I scoff again. "Okay, let's pretend I believe you. Now what?"

"Well, I've suspected it for a while. And now that I know for sure, I'm handling it." Daddy nods towards Nick, "Thank you." And, immediately I understand what he is doing. Daddy is giving him an out. He's trying to save what little is left of our relationship. He thinks if Nick leaves now there will be hope for us.

Nick shares a look with me when he stands from the chair, but I don't give him a chance to say anything. "Just because you told him doesn't mean anything to me. You should've been honest with me. After everything... You should have told me."

"You don't understand, Nina," Nick says. "I tried, I did, but

282

you didn't let me—"

"Capisco perfettamente." Nick starts to argue but holds his tongue. I don't think he wants to get into a screaming match right here with an audience. Anything he has to say is going to do just that. Besides, I don't want to hear it. Why would I? He gives a final nod to Daddy and leaves. "You can't honestly be okay with this," I say before the door closes.

"I'm not."

"Te l'ha detto davvero?"

"Yes, Davina. The only reason he didn't tell *you* is because I asked him not to. I didn't want anyone to know before I was sure." Daddy's poker face has gotten better over the years, but I'm sure he is lying. Too bad he will never tell me. "I had to be sure, this is a serious accusation."

"How long?"

"I've suspected it for a while."

"Con lui?"

"Not with him, but in general." He motions for me to sit, but I refuse. "How did you find out?"

I had been working out when the doorbell rang. I ignored it, hoping whomever it was would get the message and leave, but they were persistent. "I really need to change that damn gate code," I said to myself. Why didn't I change it two years ago? Opening the front door, I'm met with the last person I expected to see, "What?"

"Well, hello to you too."

"Why are you here, Teagan?"

"Aren't you going to invite me in?" I rolled my eyes, but stepped aside. "You working out?"

"No, I just like being sweaty." Teagan followed me into the kitchen and climbed onto one of the island bar stools. She seemed a little nervous, rightfully so considering the last time we were around each other I had her pinned by her throat. "So, what do I owe the displeasure?" Teagan looked upset.

"Geez, take a joke, Teag. What's wrong?"

"It's not that. I just... I-I broke up with Lee."

I'm not sure what kind of a response she was looking for, if it was sympathy she wouldn't find it here. "I'm sorry, I guess? I won't say I told you so, but..." I'm surprised when Teagan laughs. "Did he cheat?"

"Do you really have to ask?"

"Well, I was hoping I was wrong. You're taking it better than I thought you would."

"So are you."

"Not like him cheating on you affects me."

"Well, yeah, it kinda does."

"What are you talking about?"

Teagan's jaw dropped. "Holy shit. You don't know."

"Teagan, what are you talking about?"

"Lee was screwing your mom." The glass bottle slipped from my hands shattering against the white concrete beneath my feet. "I thought you knew, I thought— Wait, Nick didn't tell you?"

"What do you mean Nick didn't tell me? I haven't seen him since my birthday." It's three weeks until Christmas and I haven't seen or heard from Nick since he left my office.

"Nina, he knew. That's why your mom—"

"Are you fucking with me?"

"I thought you knew."

"I have to go, I need to go see my dad. Make sure he knows."

"I'm sure Nick told him."

"If Nick didn't tell me, what makes you think he told him?" I wasted no time leaving to confront Daddy about the news I just learned.

Daddy pinches the bridge of his nose before he massages his forehead. If you're listening God, please let this be the final nail in my mother's coffin. I can only hope for my father's sake. I can't imagine what he's going through. I can't imagine the person I've spent the last thirty years with acting the way my mother has. "I have no reason to lie to you, Davina."

"Teagan is a lot of things, but she wouldn't lie about this."

"Your mother was blackmailing him and I had to handle this as delicately as possible. I don't want her to find out he told me."

"What do you mean she was blackmailing him?"

"Remember when she told you she looked into him? Well, I guess she's been using that against him. She found out who he was well before you even told me."

Is that why he left?

"It's why he left Haven." Daddy rubs his tired eyes. "He found out about your mother and Lee, and in return, she looked into him. He was gonna tell you and she couldn't have that happen. So, she threatened his father's garage, his brother's school...you."

"Me?"

"You were a weak spot she knew she could exploit."

That doesn't mean he should've kept it from me. I could've helped him. I could've gone to Daddy, we would've figured it out. If he had just told me the truth—

"Nina," Daddy leans forward. "That boy was trying to find a way to protect his family. You can't tell me you wouldn't do the same."

It's all starting to make sense. The hushed conversations in the hallway. The glares. The way she didn't seem shocked when she found out the truth. The mysterious text messages in Denver and the phone call in Savannah — it was her. She's been threatening us and Nick was trying to keep her at bay. This whole time, it was all her.

"So, I'm supposed to just forgive him for breaking my heart because Mother blackmailed his family?"

"You are part of his family."

fifty-three

I AM UNBELIEVABLY LATE — it's obviously going to be one of those days and it's the worst day for it. I almost missed my first meeting, forgot half of my suitcase, and I have to drive out to Bridgeport before meeting Daddy at the airport. I forgot Alex had invited me to visit until he text me exactly forty-one minutes before I was supposed to be there. I have exactly no time to do anything before I'm supposed to be on a plane to Denver.

"Nina!" Jimmy opens the door before I even reach the top step and pulls me into a tight embrace. He looks much better than he did the last time I saw him. He's lost some weight and he has color in his cheeks again. "I'm so glad you made it."

"I'm happy to see you on your feet." I pull my wool coat tight against the breeze longing to get inside, heat radiating from the open door. "I hear you're doing four miles every morning with Alex."

"And, it's awful."

"He's not much of a morning person," Alex says behind Jimmy. I melt into his warm embrace against the cold.

"Well, come on in. We have plenty of room," Jimmy says and follows Alex back inside.

The warmth of the house calls to me, but my attention is

on the garage across the driveway. I know he's in there — his Mustang is parked in the driveway. It's been a week since I stormed into Daddy's office and as the days have gone by, I find myself dialing his number every time I need someone to talk to. But, I never hit send.

In the blink of an eye, he's there. He stands in the door wiping his hands on a grease-stained rag. We stare at one another, locked in a silent battle, but when Alex calls from inside, I finally surrender.

§

Jimmy offers some of his homemade sweet tea and I can't resist. "Boy, you better not be spilling family secrets," Jimmy calls from the kitchen hearing Alex whispering. I couldn't resist when Jimmy offered some of his homemade sweet tea, but apologized because he wouldn't be able to tell me the secret ingredient that makes it so good.

"Never." Alex and I share a knowing smile, he had just told me the 'secret ingredient' was honey. He found the recipe for his father to create a healthier alternative to the loads of sugar that goes into making sweet tea. But, according to Alex, it tasted better with honey anyway!

The Davis home is much smaller than anything I've ever lived in, but it's cute and cozy. An agreeable gray wall separates the living room from the eat-in kitchen. Peaking around the corner, a weathered oak four-seater sits under a chandelier, a single stack of mail in the top left-hand corner. I am a little surprised by the decor, I was expecting it to be a little more... bachelor?

Green tea, baby blue, and white accent pillows are tossed on a gray couch. A jute rug lies beneath a distressed white coffee table. To the right of the couch, a recliner that doesn't quite fit the aesthetic, most likely a more recent addition.

A wood desk chair sits next to the Austin stone fireplace, it looks like it belongs to the vintage writing desk nearby the hallway just off the front door. Two windows on either side of the fireplace overlook the sideyard — a red vintage Ford truck pulls out of the garage and takes off down the road.

A fire warms the living room, family photos sprawled out on a wood mantle. One photo, in particular, catches my eye: a young boy with a head full of dark curls and a polite smile stares into the camera. His eyes the color of whiskey, warm and charming. His arms around the neck of a twenty-something brunette with the same color eyes. She smiles brightly at the camera. I touch the face of the boy, I would recognize those eyes anywhere.

"They were best friends," Alex swallows. "When she died, it was hard on all of us, but it was extremely hard on him. I lost my mom and I was scared I was gonna lose my brother too." The memories swim behind his eyes, the fear still very real. "But, the shop, it gave him something to stay focused."

"Alex—"

"Here we go," Jimmy returns with the sweet tea. His smile falters slightly noticing the tension between us. "Everything okay?"

"Fine! Fine, I was just looking at your photos," I glance back at the photo before excusing myself to the restroom. I need a moment to recompose myself.

"What was that about?" I hear Jimmy ask just before I close the bathroom door.

§

Leaving the bathroom, I notice the door across the hall is open. I know better than to intrude, but I'm curious. When is the next time I'll be here? Probably never. What's that saying about curiosity? Oh, curiosity often leads to trouble. I think

Alice was on to something when she said that.

Peering inside, the room is simple and clean. If not for the large metal letter on the wall, it would look like a guest room. A person's bedroom can tell you a lot about them — a reflection of who they are and I feel like I'm invading the deepest parts of him. The more I look, the more of him I see in everything.

A record player atop the oak dresser holds a vinyl, *Boston*, the self-titled debut album of one of my favorite bands. More records fill the bottom shelf of a bookcase in the far corner. I run my fingers along the worn spines of the books two shelves higher: Hemingway. Tolstoy. Fitzgerald. Crichton. Grisham. Another shelf is lined with gold-plated trophies and awards for football, baseball, and basketball.

MVP — Bridgeport High Football.
Athlete of the Year — Bridgeport High Baseball.
Heart Award — Bridgeport High Basketball.

Thirteen awards in all, not including a Salutatorian medal. Nerd.

I imagine him painting the single dark gray wall behind the bed with his mom on a Sunday afternoon. Breaking Benjamin plays softly in the background as he tells her about the coming week. The soft blue and gray plaid comforter reminds me of his plaid shirt I had worn in Haven and the others he has been favoring during the colder months.

On his nightstand, a brand new copy of *The Shining* by Stephen King. I open it to the last marked page, 426, and start to read...

"The tub lady scarred me for life."

"Shit!" I drop the book at the sound of his voice. "Dammit, Alex, don't do that." I kneel to retrieve the book from under the bed. Finding the marked page, I'm about to return it to the nightstand when I notice something now sticking out of the pages. Releasing it, my heart sinks.

A photo.

From his birthday.

My head thrown back in laughter, my leg draped over him. Nick's eyes crinkled, a toothy grin as he stares at me. His hand on my exposed thigh. Dimple on full display. Who took this? It had to be Eileen, but why didn't she show me?

"He misses you." Alex stands over me.

"Alex...Please don't." Blinking back the tears, I use the photo to bookmark page 426 and return the book to its original place. I wipe my eyes and push past him without another word.

Returning to the living room, I settle on the couch next to Jimmy and we fall into easy conversation. I can't deny I feel more comfortable with the Davis family than I ever have my own most days. They're normal. Something I have never experienced. It's a nice change to be around a family that doesn't worry about what to say or do to impress others. Though, I do feel like Alex is trying to make a good impression. From my peripheral, I watch him subtly pick up things that are out of place or clear clutter that covers some of the surfaces. When Jimmy goes into the kitchen to refill my tea, I gently stop him.

"You know, Nina," Jimmy says when he returns. "There is something I've been wanting to talk to you about. Nick told me about your mother..."

"Jimmy—"

"Let me say this," he stops me. "Nick is a very loyal person, sometimes to a fault. When Evie..." Jimmy clears his throat. "Well, he took it upon himself to take care of us. I should have stepped up and taken care of them, but I couldn't. Her passing was bear. Cancer is a cruel thing."

The pressure builds behind my eyes. I try to swallow it back down, but it continues to grow. Alex keeps his gaze in his lap, holding back his tears. The death of Mrs. Davis still obviously affects them. I can't even imagine that type of loss.

"Nick is very much like his mother. He's a kind soul, and when he loves, he loves hard. He wants to protect those he loves. When Nick found out about your mother and this Lee fellow. He confronted her. And—"

"Dad, don't," Alex stops him.

"She deserves to know, Alex."

"You promised him."

"It's okay, Jimmy. You don't have to. I-I know he meant well. Even if it hurt me." Even if I'm still pissed off, I've started to understand why he did it. The time on the clock catches my attention. "Shit, I have to go. I'm supposed to be at the airport in twenty minutes. I'm so sorry."

"Of course, you're a busy woman," Jimmy concedes. "Where ya headed?"

"Daddy and I are flying to Denver."

"Denver?" Alex helps me slip back into my coat.

"He's working on making final transitions for Kai to take over by January and I'm looking at office spaces."

"A new office? That's great, Nina!" Jimmy's smile is sincere. When we step outside, a sudden clang and a mumbled curse from the garage catch our attention. Jimmy sighs, "I should go help him."

"He's been keeping up, everyone knows what happened," Alex argues.

Even if it's true, it doesn't help subside Jimmy's guilt. I think he and I share the same concern — worried Nick will fall back into his old routine. Worried that he will return to nonstop work inside the garage. The doctor ordered Jimmy to take a few weeks rest, which meant no work. Which means the load lands on his son. "Well, shouldn't you be going?" Jimmy asks me.

"He's probably going to leave without me at this rate." I feel the same sense of safety when I hug Jimmy that I feel when I hug my father.

Alex hugs me tightly. "Thank you for everything."

I kiss Alex's cheek before I run to my car hoping I'm not too late.

fifty-four

I PULL A BOTTLE of water from the fridge and turn on the TV. I have less than thirteen hours before I need to leave again. I could go for a run — I wasn't able to get one in earlier because of how hectic today has been. And after this afternoon, I could use it. I could just work out here, then I don't have to leave the house again... But, some fresh air sounds amazing. I'll just go to the trail not too far away — the one on the other side of the lake.

In case you haven't figured out by now, I didn't make the flight to Denver. I got the call from Daddy about fifteen minutes from the airport that they were leaving, Andrew would be back in the morning to pick me up. *Don't be late this time.* His tone joking, but I know he was serious. We have a lunch meeting I cannot afford to miss.

I change into a pair of teal-colored leggings and a black sweater pulling my hair into a high bun. Pouring the rest of my water into a bottle I can carry on the trail, I listen as two news anchors go back and forth about something that happened in Congress today. Same shit, different day. The sun is going to be setting soon which means I need to get moving unless I want to be running in the dark. Switching the TV off, I head for the door and—

Shit.

Running back to the kitchen, I grab my phone off the counter. Okay, now I'm ready.

§

Hot puffs of air form a cloud around me as I crest the hill. Wiping the sweat from my face, my pace slows seeing someone up ahead on the trail. Why is someone just now getting started? The sun has practically set below the horizon, there's no way they can hike this trail in the dark. Hearing me, they freeze and I've come face to face with the last person I expect to see here. "Nick?"

As if my voice unglues his feet, he races towards me pulling me into a soul-crushing hug. His chest heaves with a sigh of relief. "Nina, thank God."

"Nick, what's going on?" I ask when he refuses to let go. "Is it your dad? Did something happen?"

"What are you doing here?"

"What do you mean? I went for a run."

"Where's your phone?"

"It died." I dig my phone out of my leggings pocket, hands trembling as my adrenaline continues to course through my body even though I'm not running anymore. Something is wrong, I can see it on his face.

"You didn't go to Denver?"

"I missed the flight." Deep in my heart, I think I know what he is about to tell me, but I don't want to believe it. Hot tears burn my eyes, but I refuse them. Not when I don't even know for sure what's happening. My throat thickens, "Nick, what's going on?"

His face contorts into a pained expression, eyes glassy as he stares at me. I've never seen him like this before and it scares the shit out of me. He takes a deep breath and I see a single tear roll down his cheek. "Dee, there was an accident." I shake my head. "The plane..." His words falter and another tear falls. "The plane... They don't know what happened, but the plane...it went down."

I shake my head, unable to accept the words. That cannot be true. "Nick, no. You're wrong. This has to be a mistake."

"Your dad... Your dad's gone, Dee."

I furiously wipe the single tear that falls down my cheek. "No. Nick, no. I just talked to him. He's fine. I'm flying to Denver tomorrow."

Nick shakes his head, but I can't believe it because that means... That means my dad is gone. He can't be gone — I just talked to him. His lip trembles when I meet his stare again and a sob racks my chest. "I'm sorry, Dee." Nick catches me before I hit the ground and I cling to him. "I'm so sorry, baby." He holds me for dear life, trying to hold me together as my world falls apart.

fifty-five

"NINA!" NICK REACHES FOR me across the center console of my Jeep, but I've already slammed the passenger door. I don't want to hear whatever excuse he is about to give. There is no excuse. Looking over my shoulder, I glare at his Mustang as it pulls further up my driveway, more specifically at the two people inside the Mustang. "Nina, it's nothing," Nick says standing in front of me. He bends down so he is eye level with me and forces me to look at him.

"You brought her to tell me that my dad just died, Nick! How is that nothing?"

"Because!"

"That's not a reason!"

"I needed someone to be there if I found you. I just spent hours looking for you. Why do you think I did that? It wasn't for shits and giggles, Davina."

"Fuck you, Nick." He refuses to let me walk away. "Let go of me." And, he does because he isn't going to force me to stay. "Get the fuck off my property."

"Nina—"

"Go." It's harsh, probably too harsh, but I don't want *her* here. And if Nick is here, that means she is here. "I don't want you here." He takes a shaky breath trying to contain his composure, but it's slipping.

"Oh, Nina, thank God!" Eileen rushes out of the house straight into the crossfire. She fusses over me and hugs me tightly, but my eyes never leave his, not even when she hugs him. "Why are you guys standing out here? Come inside. Elizabeth and Josh just arrived with some food."

I glare at him daring him to accept the offer.

"I should probably get home," Nick says. "I'm sure Pop will want to know Nin's okay."

Nin.

Not Nina.

Not Dee.

Not Princess.

Nin.

He's not supposed to call me Nin.

"Do you need to borrow my phone? You can—"

"Eileen," I snap.

"It's okay, Lina. I need to get them back anyway." He motions towards his car where his brother and Sheyenne watch the scene unfold. I take a step back when he reaches for me. "I'm sorry."

"I'm gonna go find Kai." I turn on my heel to go in the house because all I want right now is to crawl into his arms and let the walls come down. And, if I stand there any longer, I'll lose my resolve. I'm still mad at him. Still hurt. Too many lies and secrets. I'm not hurt by what Brina did, but it hurt my brother. And now, our dad is gone. I'm the only one he has left and I can only imagine the mess that awaits me inside.

§

I didn't sleep last night. I couldn't. I went through the motions of my nightly routine — shower, comfy sweater, skincare, and a glass of wine by the fire in my room. I did my best to avoid the others, I had a lot of information to process before the sun rose today. Around two in the morning, I finally turned off the television. The news had spread globally: Alaric Villa was dead. Everyone wanted to know what came next. What did this mean for the companies? Was Kai ready to fill his father's shoes? Would I have a role to play in the company? The news media had spent hours trying to determine the answers as photos of our family flashed across the screen. I hated how they seemingly ignored the fact two other people had died in the crash. What about them? What about their families?

I wanted to hear them say their names too.

Andrew Collins.

Phillip Gable.

The cause of the crash remains undetermined, but it's speculated to be pilot error. I refuse to believe it. Andrew had flown that route too many times, he could do it with his eyes closed. Phillip, too. Somewhere deep in the back of my mind, a horrendous thought took root. Brina. Could she have done something? Had someone done something?

Daddy told me he was filing the divorce papers when he returned from Denver. He already told Brina it was coming. I wouldn't put it past her to do something to stop the divorce from happening. After all, becoming a widow looked much better than a divorcee.

I dialed and deleted the familiar number six times before I finally hit send on the seventh time, and it went straight to voicemail. That's the moment I finally let myself break. The walls crumbling down. It felt like someone had a hold of my heart and squeezed it mercilessly. I gasped for air in between sobs. His voice on the recording the straw that broke the camel's back — the weight of the last six months finally chipped enough away and I crumbled.

He's gone.

The one person I had always been able to turn to, the one who loved me unconditionally... Gone. My dreams reduced to a pile of ash and smoke on the side of a mountain. He would never get to hand over the business to Kai or watch Kai follow in his footsteps. He would never see Kai and Eileen get married and start a family. He wouldn't be there to walk me down the aisle. He would never meet his grandchildren or see them take their first steps or graduate college. He would never get to enjoy a real vacation, one where he wasn't managing Brina's emotions and a million work calls. He'd never enjoy a life free from Brina. The more I thought about everything he was going to miss, the harder I sobbed. It didn't seem fair in the moments when he was going to start living life, it was ripped away from him.

When the sobs finally subsided, I sat on my balcony. It was cold, but not unbearable — it helped me breathe again. The weight on my chest never lifted, but I could at least take a breath. By the first break of dawn, I finally started to rebuild the walls and pushed everything back into place.

I had a job to do.

The sounds of someone walking around upstairs tells me Eileen is up. Kai probably won't be getting up until Elizabeth and Josh arrive with food around noon. I can imagine Eileen's shock when she walks into the kitchen to find a fresh pot of coffee. She will find my room empty — bed made and curtains drawn. Maybe I went for a run, she'll think, but by now she has heard the muffled sounds of my conversation with the Colorado State Police. On cue, her feet pad against the oak flooring of the stairs leading down to the lower level. Just as I hang up the phone, a knock on the door. "Morning, Lina."

"Morning?" Eileen peeks her head inside, utterly confused. Surely, this isn't the same Nina Villa who just received the news that her father was dead less than twelve hours ago. "Nin, what are you doing?"

I shrug nonchalantly. "Just taking care of some things. I had to meet with a client and—"

"Wait, you're working?"

"I started working on the funeral arrangements. I need to go meet with the director this afternoon, and set something up with the priest. I already spoke with the police about getting—"

"Nina, it hasn't even been twenty-four hours."

"Someone has to do it, Eileen." I look up from my desk for the first time, lips pulled into a firm line. "And, I refuse to let Brina handle any of this. The sooner it's done, the sooner we can get through it... Start moving on."

My phone rings and I answer on the first ring. Eileen remains in the doorway, unsure what to do. After a moment, I mute the call, "Do you need something else?"

"No, guess not." Eileen is dumbfounded. She stands in the doorway a moment longer watching as I continue my conversation as if arranging my father's funeral was normal conversation.

fifty-six

"**YOU DON'T NEED TO** be so harsh, Nin," Elizabeth scolds me from the doorway of my office. I glance at her over the edge of my computer monitor, my fingers continue typing the email I'd been answering. She wants me to say something, anything; wants me to feel bad for what I did less than thirty minutes ago, but I don't. Realizing I'm not going to give her what she wants, Elizabeth sits in the chair across from my desk with a sigh. "I know you're upset and you're just trying to cope with all of this, but don't take it out on us."

"I'm not."

"You threatened to fire Michaela because she was doing her job."

"I told her to leave, she didn't—"

"As your best friend, I'm telling you right now, you were wrong. Whether it's Michaela, me, Josh... We're just looking out for you. I get it, you're trying to avoid what's going on, that's fine, but don't be a bitch."

My fingers halt at the final word. Did she just call me a bitch? Her face remains stoic — waiting for the explosion, but she won't get it. Elizabeth has always been a straight shooter. It's one of the things I love most about her, but I hate when she's right. And, she's right. I have been a bitch.

"Just like the night of the accident. You went off on Nick because—"

"Elizabeth..."

"Do you know he and Alex got into a fight that night? Alex has a black eye because Nick punched him. Not to mention the shit he said to Sheyenne. Look, I get it, you're upset because she showed up, but that wasn't Nick's fault. Do you know how devastated he was when he found out about the accident? Thinking you might have been on that plane... It scared the shit out of him. And, whether you want to believe it or not, he loved your dad as much as the rest of us. He's grieving too."

Tears sting my eyes.

"You have a lot going on right now, but you can't take it out on the rest of us — we're just trying to help."

She's right, I know she's right. I haven't been myself, but I don't know what else to do. I've barely slept since the accident, every time I close my eyes I see it. The crash. The smoke rising from the burning ashes, the shredded scraps of metal scattered amongst the mountainside. I can't understand what happened, how it happened. Nothing about it makes sense. The police have ruled it a tragic accident caused by a mix of pilot error and weather conditions.

"I'm sorry," I whisper rubbing my eyes. "I don't mean to be so harsh, I think it's the lack of sleep and just trying to deal with everything."

"I know."

"I'll call Michaela, apologize."

Elizabeth offers a weak smile.

"Why did Nick punch Alex?"

Elizabeth sighs and relays the story Josh told her. "Nick was still heated from your argument when he got home. Alex, being Alex, decided to push the topic. I guess, in the midst of it all, Nick said some things to Sheyenne, called her out about showing up here. Tried to say your fight was because of her. Alex made a few comments, said it's Nick's own fault you didn't want him around..." Elizabeth shakes her head and rubs her tired eyes. "What actually led to the punch isn't super clear, but regardless, Nick punched him."

"Fuck," I whisper into my hands. Another thing to add to the list of problems I've caused.

"Alex is okay, he's not mad. Sheyenne is licking her wounds, apparently she booked a flight home to Boston in the next few days."

I don't ask the question I really want to know — how is Nick? I know he's beating himself up for punching Alex and saying those things to Sheyenne. He loves his brother so much, I can't imagine how he felt when he saw Alex's bruised eye.

"I'm gonna grab a coffee before we go to the Church, you want one?"

"I could use about ten."

§

Where in the hell is she?

Elizabeth left to get coffee twenty minutes ago. We need to leave or we're going to be late. I'm giving her one more minute before I leave without her. But, I don't want to do this part alone. I'm not sure why, but something about it freaks me out. I can't take Kai, I've learned the past two days, he cannot be entrusted with these kinds of situations. Just before her minute is up, I hear the front door open.

"Elizabeth, what is taking so long? I need to get going. I have to—" I drop my purse when I meet the smoldering gaze from a lifetime ago. Surely, this is some kind of nightmare I'm about to wake up from. A hallucination from lack of sleep... I almost don't recognize him. He has definitely filled out, his face slimmer and more manly. Gone is the baby face John Jansen I knew years ago. His brown eyes almost black. His hair darker than I remember, slightly longer, but styled to look as though he had done no work at all. "Jay?" His eyes light up at the sound of his name — a siren song beckoning him closer.

His hands open and close repeatedly at his sides. Like he's fighting the urge to reach out and touch me. "Hey, beautiful."

The term of endearment feels wrong coming from him. He isn't supposed to call me that anymore, it's reserved for another. "What are you doing here?"

"Can't I come see an old friend?"

"That's what we're calling it now?"

Elizabeth tries to hide my laugh behind a cough earning a small glare from John.

"I figured you could use all the support you could get." He picks my purse up from the ground and hands it back to me. "I'm sorry about your dad, Nin."

I look past him to Elizabeth, a silent conversation between sisters. This is weird, right? She shrugs.

"You said you're on your way somewhere? I'd be happy to accompany you." My eyes back on him, the wheels turning. I'm trying to figure out what to do with him. As far as he knows, as far as anyone knows, there isn't another man in my life. So, did he come because my dad just died or to finish what we started years ago without the threat of prison. "If you want company, that is."

Elizabeth answers before I can, "Actually, I'm going with her and—"

"Fine," I sigh. "You can come." I take the coffee from Elizabeth, stopping her protests, "It's fine, Elizabeth. I'll be fine."

"Nina, I—"

"I'll call you later, okay?"

I have a bad feeling about this. Nothing good can come from his return. Nothing. I don't miss the glare Elizabeth shoots at John, his smile practically splits his face in two following me towards the car.

fifty-seven

WALKING OUT OF MY bedroom, I see John making himself comfortable on the couch, his feet propped on the coffee table — at least his shoes are off. I don't have it in me to fight with him about where he puts his feet, even if it pisses me off. In the short amount of time I spent getting ready, it seems like everyone dispersed: Elizabeth paces the patio on the phone as Eileen watches, but Josh is nowhere to be seen.

"Dude, get your feet off the table," my brother snaps when he joins us. I snicker behind my water bottle swallowing two Tylenol. I'm going to need it if I have any hopes of getting through this meeting.

"Oh, Nin! There you are," John says, jumping to his feet. "You look gorgeous."

I roll my eyes and rinse out the glass water bottle putting it in the dishwasher. John has been overly helpful since he made his grand return two days ago. Any time one of us needs something, especially me, he is the first to jump into action. And, he's always complimenting me. It's sweet, I guess, but it's starting to grind my nerves.

"What time do we leave?"

"We," I motion between me and Kai, "are leaving now. You are staying here."

"I don't mind driving. I know how hard this is going to be, you guys might want—"

"I think they can manage, John," Elizabeth says, coming back inside. She hates that I've let him hang around, but what am I supposed to do? It's not like he's harming anything. He's just annoying.

"What did Alex want?" Josh asks when he returns from downstairs.

I'm not surprised it was Alex on the phone. He's been calling at least once a day to check on us.

"He's not coming," Elizabeth sighs.

"What do you mean he's not coming?" Josh's jaw tightens, his eyes narrow towards his wife.

"Alex is gonna see what he can do, but doesn't look promising. Not with..." Elizabeth motions slightly jerks her head towards John and it all clicks into place. They're talking about Nick. And, he's not coming...to the funeral?

"You sure you don't want me to drive you?" John takes my hand into his gaining my attention. "Really, it's no trouble."

"I can manage," I say and slip from his grasp. Like a sad puppy, John watches us leave, but I don't miss the steady glare Elizabeth has on him like a hawk stalking its prey. She's daring him to try and come with us so she can strike. Suddenly, it feels like I'm throwing John to a pack of savage hyenas. "Behave yourselves," I call over my shoulder following Kai down the hall to the garage.

Before we pull out of the garage, I send a text to the three of them...

ME
Try not to kill him.

LINA
No promises.
SISSY
What she said.
BUB
no comment

fifty-eight

BENJAMIN CAMPBELL, LONG TIME attorney of the Villa family, is not looking forward to going over the last will and testament of Alaric Villa. He told me Daddy had visited him two weeks prior to the accident asking Ben to make changes to his will and to expedite the process. With the changes made, Ben was sure World War III was about to break out. Normally, this would be done later, but Daddy had made it clear it was to be done as soon as possible after his death. "I think this will be easier if you let me get through everything and then we can discuss further, if you have any questions."

"Of course," Kai says wanting to get the show on the road. He and I left a large space between us and Brina. In fact, Kai asked me if it was possible to do this without her, but I had already asked Benjamin and he said no.

"Where to begin," the attorney shuffles through the papers. He slides his glasses over his eyes and finally decides on one of the pages. "How about we start with the kids?" He takes our silence as acceptance. "To Kai James Villa...Villa Inc., you will ascend to replace your father, Alaric Villa. However, both children, Kai and Davina, will share ownership of all family companies and their assets. You can decide amongst yourselves how your sister is to be involved. Also, Kai, you will begin to receive monthly stipends from your inheritance equaling one-third of the family fortune. A separate fund has been set aside for you to use for your future wedding and college for future children."

Kai nods. That was painless. Why does Ben seem so nervous?

"To Davina Bay Villa...One-third of the family fortune, which you too will receive in monthly stipends. You will share ownership of all family companies and their assets with your brother, Kai Villa. A separate fund has been set aside for you to use for your future wedding and college for future children. You have been named the new owner of the home in Haven."

I nod, there was nothing shocking about that.

"The Santorini, Napa, Key West, and Paris homes are to be sold."

Okay, that's a little more interesting.

"To Brina Arrow Villa, and Alaric made this very clear...you will receive a monthly stipend to cover your living expenses at a modest amount, but nothing else."

Kai and I share a surprised glance.

"Excuse me?" Brina's voice rises two octaves.

"Need I remind you, you signed a prenup before you and Alaric were married. The prenup was clear: you were to only receive a monthly stipend to cover living expenses at a modest amount if you were to divorce or anything were to happen to your husband. Mr. Villa made it very clear, you—"

"I didn't agree to this in the prenup! I would have never agreed to that. These must be the recent changes he made."

"Actually, no. I have a copy here, that's all you were ever meant to get. But, there is more." Ben cleans his glasses before he flips to the last page. "If you choose to remarry, that is fine. You will still receive monthly stipends. However," Ben looks up from the papers holding eye contact with Brina as he says the rest. "If that person is any of the men you had an affair with during the course of your marriage to Alaric Villa, the monthly stipends will cease."

"Beh, questo non lascia molte opzioni," I mumble with a small smirk to my brother.

"How many affairs did you have?" Kai looks at her in disgust.

"Only the one!"

"Oh, so you weren't fucking my ex-boyfriend?" I finally address her.

"You little bitch, you turned your father against me. We never had any issues until you were born."

It's like a punch to the stomach. I turn away from Brina, I don't want to give her the satisfaction of knowing her words affect me.

"This is not her fault." Kai puts himself between us. "You did this to yourself."

"Kai, I never—"

"Is that all?" Kai turns his attention back to Ben.

"No," Ben flips back a page. "In other more recent changes, Alaric asked that the half of the final one-third of the family money be donated to charity. Kai and Davina are allowed to decide which one. The other half will be set aside for grandchildren. And," Ben sighs, he looks at me, "the final thing to note, Alaric appointed you, Davina, to be the executor of the estate."

fifty-nine

THE CHURCH FALLS INTO a hushed whisper. I sit next to Kai at the head of the first row. John keeping a watchful eye from the second row. He tried to sit next to me, but Kai refused. He was going to be sitting next to his sister and, "I'll be damned if John Jansen is going to head the family row," he said. I tried to hide my smirk when John retreated to the second row, but found it hard when I saw Elizabeth giggle a few seats away next to Eileen.

"Would you mind moving down?" One of the ushers asks us. Behind him, Brina glares at us through her black veil, daring us to refuse in front of everyone. Just before I can argue, Kai stops me — he motions for Elizabeth and Josh to move down the row leaving a noticeable space between us and Brina.

Throughout the service, Brina sobs for everyone to hear. I can't contain an eye roll when she lets out a sob every so often just to make sure everyone knows how upset she is. Kai sheds a few tears, but he manages to contain himself.

I don't cry.

I can't.

My nerves eat away at me. I'm thinking of what is coming. I don't want to do it, but Daddy requested it. Trust me, I thought about asking Kai to take my place, but I know he would refuse.

It has to be me. My heart races when the usher approaches and offers to escort me to the altar steps.

When I approach the pulpit, the nerves seem to disappear. The thought of speaking to the crowd intimidated me, but the moment I see them, I feel a blanket of comfort fall around me. I smile looking at the faces of those who loved Daddy almost as much as I did. Members of the fire and police department line the perimeter of the church. Business partners, old and new, with their wives peppered throughout the crowd. My favorite high school English teacher, Mr. R, and his wife with their newborn son next to other teachers from The Hills Academy. Lindsay and other members of the cheerleading squad. Diana. Tobias with his wife, next to them other members of Rosecliffe University fraternities. Tessa and the rest of the Honeybee's staff. Michaela next to Jenny and Patrick. Jimmy and Alex next to them.

But, the one person I wanted to see most isn't here. A tear rolls down my cheek realizing he really didn't come. I had hoped Alex would have been able to convince him, but it looks like he still refused.

I didn't exactly make him welcome either.

"Thank you, all, for coming today." I grip the pulpit a little tighter. "It really means a lot to me and my brother. We know how loved our father was in the community and to see all of you here, it reminds us of how special he was. Not just to us, but everyone. It's funny they asked me to do this, I didn't think I would be able to. Even though I run a whole company, I am not great at speeches, just ask Mr. R over there." A small laugh from the audience and Mr. R agrees. "But, we're just gonna see how this goes."

I share a smile with my brother before I began.

"Alaric Tobias Villa was born November 27, 1968, in Holly Hill, South Carolina. He was very proud of where he came from, proud of his roots. If you didn't know, my grandfather was an Italian immigrant who came to this country looking for a better life. He met my grandmother, they were married, had my dad, and the rest is history. Normally, these are supposed to be about all the great things the person accomplished, but you guys know all of that. You watched him build this empire from the ground up.

"I got my ambitious spirit from him, I'm sure of that. I would've never started my own company had it not been for him. And, I know Kai wouldn't be the man he is without our dad. They weren't always close, but Kai is so much like Daddy, whether he knows it or not. I'm happy that he's going to continue Daddy's legacy. I know he was so proud of how well Kai has done in the company so far." I smiled at Kai seeing the tears roll down his cheeks.

I glance at Jimmy. "You know, you never think you're going to face Death so early. But, in the last two months, I have twice. I got lucky the first time, but I guess, Death doesn't like to be cheated." My attention is pulled to the back of the church as the doors open. Tears build behind my eyes when Nick walks through the door. He stands at the back, his hands pushed deep in the pockets of his jacket. When our eyes finally meet, a smile tugs at the corner of my lips. He returns it.

"A few days before the accident, I was talking to my dad. We talked about a lot of things, some I had no idea he even knew about. In case you didn't know, I was kind of a wild child growing up." The audience laughs. "No, really. Poor Daddy, I know he was glad when I grew out of that phase. But, recently, I did something pretty reckless and stupid. I was sure he was never gonna forgive me, but he did. That's the power of a parent's love, I guess.

"I think we take our parents for granted. We think they will always be here... I did. Hell, I was supposed to be with him that day, I was supposed to be on that plane."

I meet Nick's stare again and I can see the fear in his eyes.

The same fear I saw that night when he found me on the trail. And suddenly, it all seems so stupid. The fighting, the grudges... I don't want to hold on to it anymore. What if I had been on the plane? I wouldn't have ever been able to tell him how I feel...

"But, I was running late, and everyone knows, I never do that." Everyone laughs, but I'm only looking at him. "Daddy couldn't wait anymore, so he left. I never would have guessed something like this would happen, especially to him. Andrew and Phillip had flown that route thousands of times. What could go wrong? What was so different *this* time?" For the first time, I spare a look at Brina, but she refuses to break character. "We never know who Death is going to visit next. So, if you walk away from this remembering anything, please don't hold on to meaningless shit. You need to let it go." I meet his stare again. "Love each other. We're not promised tomorrow. So, make the most of what you have now, because you don't know when it'll be gone."

sixty

THE WEIGHT OF THE last week is finally starting to catch up with me. I've been able to stave it off, but now that everything is done, I have nothing to keep me preoccupied. Being executor of the estate is something and work will keep me busy, but will it be enough? I don't know. I'm afraid for the moment when everyone is gone and the silence surrounds me.

Movement behind my second monitor catches my attention. Glancing up, I see John sitting in the chair across my desk, a steaming cup of coffee in hand. I don't acknowledge him. Instead, my focus returns to the email to the attorney.

I'm sure John can see the walls surrounding me. They weren't building, they're already built. I know he hoped this wouldn't happen, hoped he could have helped prevent it. Figured I was going to need someone there to help ground me, but that's not him. "Figured you could use some of this," he says and pushes the mug towards me.

"Thanks."

"We just finished cleaning up."

"Okay."

"Everyone's about to leave, you wanna come say goodbye?"

"I already told them goodbye."

John sighs, "You need anything?"

"Nothing you can give me."

I can see the lightbulb flash above his head. Treading lightly, he makes his way around my desk. He takes in the workload surrounding me — multiple windows open on the desktop screen, another two open on my laptop, a copy of designs printed out underneath. It's no wonder I'm always stressed. He rubs my shoulders, the muscles wound tight under the skin. But, his touch does the opposite of what it's meant to. "Why don't we go somewhere? Get away from here," he whispers in my ear. "After everything you've been through, you could use a vacation."

"A vacation?" I pull away from him. "Do you know how much shit I have left to take care of? I can't just disappear. In case you forgot, my dad just died. I have to take care of the estate. I have to help Kai with the company. I have my own business to run. I can't just run off with you."

"I'm just saying, it would be good for you. We could go out to Napa or take a trip to Paris, you always loved that."

"You cannot be serious." My fingers tug at my hair. "First of all, I'm not going on vacation with you. Second, who's paying for it?"

"That's not fair, Nina."

"Am I wrong?"

"I'm just trying to help."

"You have done enough. Thank you."

"So, that's it, then?"

I scoff, "What did you expect, Jay?"

"I'm not like the others Nina, I don't expect anything from you. I just wanted—"

"You haven't shown your face in years. Years. Now all the sudden, you show up after my dad dies. Were you scared of what might happen if you showed up before then?"

"It's not like that, Nina."

"Then tell me what it's like because from where I'm sitting, it doesn't look very good."

"I'm sorry I haven't been here. I didn't know what to say. Every time I picked up the phone, I got scared. And when I never heard from you, I don't know, I guess—"

"You coming here, it doesn't change things. I've moved on and you should too."

"Where is he, then?" My face hardens. "You moved on? You found someone else? Why isn't he here?"

"That is none of your business."

"You're still the same starry eyed girl I met all those years ago. You have no idea what the real world is like. But, you're about to find out now that Daddy won't be here to fix it all for you."

"Fuck you, John." I stand from my desk. My jaw locks, there is a lot more I want to say, but it's not worth it. "It's time to leave the past in the past. We were not good for each other, and I think you know that."

"We're great together."

"You can't honestly believe that." Disbelief. Utter disbelief. "Ending things was the best thing that ever happened. I'd been searching for a way out, but didn't know how to do it. If not for Teagan's big mouth, I don't where I would be right now. I knew you'd never let me go."

"I would've never held you back."

"I don't believe you. You never wanted me to do any of this." I motion to everything around us. "You wanted me to be someone I'm not. Stay here, buy a house, raise a few kids. You didn't even want me to go to college. It was never in your plan to share the world with me." I feel a little bit of the weight lift off my chest. "Now, I think it's time you go."

"That's what you want?"

"Yes," I don't hesitate. "I appreciate you being here, but you could've just sent flowers. It would've meant the same."

"I'm sorry I couldn't be who you needed me to be." I roll

my eyes, I'm in no mood to listen to whatever else he has to say. "Can I ask you something?" When I don't respond, he continues, "Who is it?"

"That's none of your business."

"Is it Nick?" I chew on my bottom lip but still refuse to answer. "He's a good guy, Nina. Whatever is keeping you from him—"

I hold my hand up silencing him. "Just go."

sixty-one

Nick

THE HOUSE COMES INTO view at the end of the magnolia lined driveway. It sits back at least half a mile from the gated entrance inside a community along the edge of the lake. There's at least two acres of land surrounding the house — a beautiful structure made of stone, stucco, and wood. The driveway comes to a fork — the left leads to a three-car garage, the right leads to an uncovered parking area where three cars remain. No sign of Alex and Pop, though. I recognize two of the cars — Josh and Kai. The third must be John's, he finally got rid of the Coupe. I had been telling him for years to sell it, but he loved that car, just hated the bill that came along with it.

I sit inside my 1968 Mustang at war with myself. Why am I here? She clearly has everyone she needs. John has stepped in to fill the role I couldn't. She just lost her dad and knowing Nina, she hasn't given herself time to grieve. She's been occupying her time with the funeral arrangements and handling everyone else, but now that's all over. She'll have to face it now and I don't want my presence to upset her further.

Taking a deep breath, I pull the keys from the ignition and finally get out.

Baby steps.

Fingers strumming against the Gulfstream Aqua paint,

I think about that look on her face when I walked into the Church today. She looked so relieved. Happy, even, that I'd come. I had tried to find her before they left for the cemetery, but he was there leading her out the door.

"Fuck it," I whisper to myself and make the trek to her front door. The front door is solid black with two large paneled windows on either side. To the left is a wall of windows blacked out by privacy screens; on the right, more windows behind a bench that looks like it's more for decoration than sitting on the front porch. This time I'm able to make out a Christmas tree through the privacy screens. Before I can knock, I see Elizabeth walk past the front door, she stops when our eyes meet through the window on the right side of the door — the privacy screen not put down yet.

"Nick?" She opens the door in a rush. "Thank God, I thought you weren't ever going to show up."

When they rushed Nina out of the service, I didn't follow. I didn't go to the burial or come to lunch. Instead, I went to visit someone I haven't seen in a while. "Hey Mom," I whispered, running my fingers over the cold stone. I traced her name.

Evie Joanna Davis
Beloved Wife, Mother, and Daughter.
April 08, 1973 - September 07, 2013

"I miss you. There has been so much going on and I wish you were here. You'd know the right thing to say. Right thing to do." I tried to blink back the tears brimming my eyes, but a few escaped, warm against my skin. "You were right about her, I should've given her a chance... I just wish I had listened to you before. Maybe it would have saved us all a bunch of heartache. You would've loved her... I love her." I gripped the headstone a little tighter. "That night, right before you left, that night...I saw someone different. She wasn't— She wasn't who they said. But, then you were gone and I couldn't see past that. I was drowning and felt like I didn't have anyone on my side. When I thought about her, all I could see was something keeping me from being with you.

"All I've done is hurt her. I should've told her, I should've just been honest about her mom, I should've been there for her with all this funeral stuff. I shouldn't have left her alone, but she was so pissed. I can't blame her. And now he's here. She doesn't need me, she has him. I don't know what to do. I just want her to be happy, whatever that means." I felt a little better getting it off my chest, but another thought crossed my mind making my insides twist into knots. A gentle breeze passed over me, as if Mom was there giving a gentle squeeze, letting me know it's all going to work out. "I'm gonna talk to her. I promise. But, there's one more thing I need to do."

There was one more person I needed to talk to before Nina.

"I didn't want to be in the way," I say hesitating just outside the door.

"You're not in the way, Nick. She'll be glad to see you." Elizabeth hugs me tightly.

"How is she?"

"She's...well, she's Nina." We laugh and I notice she tries to hide the tear that escapes the corner of her eye. "Come on, I know Kai will want to see you." I finally step across the threshold and Elizabeth closes the door softly. She disappears into the living area to the right of the entryway, but I don't follow. My eyes wander every inch of the entrance to Nina's home — it is nothing like I had imagined. And yet, I can see her in everything — the sense of warmth it brings.

In the foyer, built-in bookshelves next to a streamlined staircase lead down into a lower level. The shelves are filled with photos, books, and random decorative items. A warm almond color on the walls and wood mantle of the double-sided stone fireplace. A painting of a woman sits on the mantle

— the straps of high heels dangle from her finger, her long hair and dress hang a second behind in the wind, her toes dig into the sand as she walks towards the beating waves of the sea. You can't see her face, but when I look at it...it's her. Above the foyer, an iron ring hangs from planks of white oak on the ceiling. At the opposite end of the room, a grand piano sits in front of large windows. Does she actually play or is it mere decoration?

To the left of the entry, a hallway that had been behind the privacy screens leads to various doors. A small alcove houses an entry table, the photo on top begs for attention. I've never seen one like it before, not even at the house in Haven. At first glance, it seems like a normal family photo, but if you look closer, it's quite the opposite. The Villa family poses in front of the mountains, but they don't hold on to one another like a normal family. Brina's lips pull into a firm line, the edge of her lips quirked into a smile I've seen on more than one occasion. A hint of annoyance on Nina's face as she stands next to Brina, Kai next to Ric.

From the corner of my eye, I see someone race by — a blonde blur I recognize as Elizabeth rushes down the stairs.

"We flew to Haven solely for that picture," Kai says from behind me, a fondness in his voice. Taking the frame, his fingers ghost over the photo. "Nin was so mad, she had a game and didn't want to miss it. They were undefeated, but Mom refused to let her go. They ended up losing, so you can imagine that conversation." Kai laughs softly. "It's the only family photo where she and Mom are next to each other. The photographer said it would look better that way. I'm surprised she hasn't destroyed it after what happened." He gently sets it down next to the bouquet of white roses, peonies, and hydrangeas. I try not to laugh, but I can't help it when Kai does anyway. "I always knew we had problems, but..."

"I'm sorry, Kai. I should've told you."

"No," Kai's voice is stern. "Don't blame yourself. You did what you thought was best and I don't hold that against you. Nina just needs time...but, she doesn't blame you."

"Kai," Eileen interrupts us. "You ready to get going?"

"Probably should. I know she's ready for some peace and quiet." Kai glances at the photo one last time before he excuses himself.

Eileen watches him disappear into the guest bedroom at the top of the stairs. Apparently they've been occupying Nina's house since the accident. The news of his mother's affair and now the accident has taken its toll. Unlike his sister, he isn't good at hiding his feelings. With a sigh, Eileen turns to me, "It's good to see you. I'm sorry, I missed you at the funeral. I didn't see you come in, but Elizabeth said you were there."

"I was late."

"You were there, that's all that matters. Come on," Eileen ushers me past the fireplace into the living area. "We have plenty of food if you're hungry."

"It's 'bout time you showed up," Josh says from the refrigerator where he and Michaela pack away food. I notice everyone is accounted for, except two. If everyone was leaving, I hope I can still get time with Nina if there isn't someone to distract John. "Where'd you run off to earlier? Didn't see you at the cemetery."

"Had to make a stop."

"Nin should be up in a few. She's just taking care of some business," Elizabeth reappears with a suitcase.

They cannot be serious. "She's working?"

"Takes her mind off things," Kai says when he returns with two suitcases.

"If she wants to be alone with—"

"No," Eileen interrupts me. "No, Nina has been hosting all of us since the accident and we should give her some space. You're fine, Nick." When Eileen hugs me, I give her a reassuring squeeze. "We're happy you're here. Thank you."

"Take care of her," Michaela whispers, hugging me next.

"You heard anything yet?" Josh asks.

"I'll call you tomorrow." My answer confuses the others, but it tells Josh everything he needs to know. After a quick embrace, he leads Eileen and Michaela out the front door.

When they are gone, Elizabeth sighs. "Look, Nick, the other night...she was just upset. She didn't mean to blow up on you. I think it was just a combination of everything and— And, then he shows up."

"It's okay. I won't stay long. I'm sure they want—"

"He's gone, Nick. Left about an hour ago." Elizabeth smiles when I perk up. She hugs me tightly. "I know it's been rough, but having you here means a lot."

"Tell Lina I'll be out in a minute," Kai instructs Elizabeth when we part. When she's gone, he looks around the house and checks the stairwell. Sure we are still alone, he says, "Look, I know things got off to a rocky start, but if there's one thing I know...you and Nina have that spark. We all see it. Dad, too. And, I know you wouldn't be here if you didn't love her." Kai takes a deep, shaky breath, he rubs his eyes trying to hold himself together a little longer. "Nin has been the glue holding all of this together. She's done all of this by herself, I don't know how. I don't think I could have done it."

"I'm sorry I wasn't here."

Kai shakes his head, "I understand why, but you're here now and she needs you now more than ever. You're a good guy, Nick. I'm glad she has you."

"If you need anything—"

"You're already here."

When Kai leaves, the house falls into a comforting silence and I take the opportunity to explore. The first thing I notice is the floor — concrete, an interesting choice — it encompasses the entire house. The living area is an open space where the great room, kitchen, and dining room meet. Warm, soft colors and different shades of wood cover the home. White oak ceilings flow from the foyer into the living area meeting white ceilings outlined with large white oak beams. Along the back wall, paneled windows offer expanding views of the backyard and lake.

A fire roars in the fireplace that stretches into an opening in the ceiling — clerestory windows on either side allow for more natural light to flood the room making it feel bigger than it already is. I don't know how I missed them in the foyer. A large flat screen, hung above the mantle, plays a Hallmark movie. Blankets sprawl on the gray couch and an empty wine glass sits on the solid wood coffee table. In another small alcove with more windows, a large Christmas tree decorated in white and gold. Matching Christmas decorations are scattered tastefully throughout the house, but not overly done. I wonder if that is by choice or because of the accident. It's hard to imagine Nina as one of those people who over-decorates for Christmas.

The kitchen is state of the art. The refrigerator made to blend in with the cabinets. A glass-front hutch opposite the refrigerator showcases serving dishes, cookbooks, cutting boards, and glasses. But, it's the countertops that capture my attention. Bright white contrasts the warm, dramatic veining of the Calcutta marble and the off-white cabinetry. The expansive island houses six black and white bar stools. It's immaculate, but what is the point in having such a grand kitchen if you never used it? Has she ever used it? I can't remember ever seeing her cook before.

A bump out on the left side of the kitchen houses the dining room with a long black farmhouse table. Another iron chandelier extends the length of the table. To the right of the kitchen, a glass panel door separates the large walk-in pantry. The same cabinetry, tile backsplash, and black metal accents carry from the kitchen. Down the hallway just off the kitchen, a wine cellar behind a similar glass panel door. Across the hallway, a home gym. But, it's the closed door at the end of the long hallway that calls me. I refuse. For now, it is off-limits.

On the wall, next to the hallway, a collection of black and white photos. Each photo a moment of her life frozen in time. Nina at college graduation. Nina walking Elizabeth down the aisle. Nina, Elizabeth, and Michaela on the beach. Nina, Elizabeth, Kai, and Eileen in front of a large castle, mouse ears on their heads. Nina and Eileen in a lagoon surrounded by snow. Nina harvesting in a vineyard. Nina playing with a red panda. Nina and Ric at a Christmas event. Nina standing with a shovel on a construction site.

"Snooping?"

I jump at the sound of her voice. How long has she been standing there? My heart sinks when I see her by the fireplace. She looks paler than I remember, still wearing her long black dress from the funeral, but her hair has been pulled into a messy bun and her makeup gone exposing the dark, puffy circles under her eyes. She looks like she has been crying, but she wears a smirk trying to mask it just a little longer.

"I didn't mean to, I was just—"

"I'm joking." The smirk slips into a smile. "What's the point of putting them up if not to be looked at?" She holds her hand towards me. "How about a tour, so you can gawk at the rest? I mean, I snooped in your room. It's only fair."

I smile at her admission. When I returned to find the photo marking my place in the book, I had one guess as to who had been in my room. "Nina Villa, a snoop? I would've never guessed." She rolls her eyes and leads me down the same hallway I had refused to enter moments earlier.

Entering her room, I'm floored by the size — I swear, it's bigger than my entire house. A wall of paneled windows showcases the landscape outside. Along the back wall, a wood platform king bed stands against a blue-gray wall. Different shades of blue throw pillows against white sheets and a comforter with black trimmings, a blue throw blanket across the foot of the bed. A blue and ivory colored ornamental rug against the dark concrete floor. Above the bed, a painting of magnolia flowers. A marble fireplace with a wood beam mantle across from the foot of the bed. A sitting area nearby with white arm chairs, paperwork sprawls the floor. Just off the fireplace, a door matching the windows leads to a balcony overlooking the lake. A black trimmed mirror and a single photo of Nina, Ric, and Kai sits atop a gray chest next to the bathroom door. I'm amused and surprised to find no private laundry room.

The concrete floor runs into the bathroom ending at more paneled windows behind a soaker tub, a large walk-in shower housed by glass walls next to it. Fresh peonies and a candle rest on a marble table next to the tub. The same countertops from the kitchen rest on a floating white oak vanity.

That's where I find her.

Nina stands in front of the bathroom mirror analyzing every inch of her reflection as she removes her jewelry. Under the light, I can finally see the weight of the last few months catching up to her. Her emerald orbs have dulled. Dark, puffy circles underneath them. Her skin is paler and small stress lines have started to form on her forehead. She closes her eyes and takes a deep breath. I know she's trying so hard to hold it together just a little bit longer. Without thinking, I wrap my arms around her and pull her tight against my chest. She clutches to me like a much needed life raft.

I don't know how long we stand here, but when our eyes finally meet in the mirror, I can see the walls being pieced back together. I kiss her temple and squeeze her reassuringly.

She pulls away from me. "Can you help with my dress?" Goosebumps erupt across her skin as my fingers search for the zipper. A shiver down her spine dragging the zipper down her back. I push the sleeves of her dress down and kiss her shoulder, my lips lingering on her skin. "Nick," she whispers. It's not an invitation. When I step away, she lets her dress fall into a heap on the floor.

After a moment, I follow her inside the adjoining room. "This is your closet? This is as big as our room in Haven."

"You'll never get used to these things, will you?" Nina smiles.

"What, no private laundry here?" She points towards another door I hadn't even noticed. "Unbelievable." Nina shrugs digging through one of the many drawers. And for the first time, I'm able to see the artwork I'd only caught a glimpse of at the hospital — on her left arm in black ink a hummingbird surrounded by peonies. "You got a tattoo?"

She only smiles and pulls on striped pajama shorts and a Rosecliffe sweater.

"Why a hummingbird?"

"They're small, but fierce. Extremely hard workers. But, don't do well in captivity, they like their freedom."

"Sounds like someone I know."

Letting her hair fall from the bun, she reaches her hand out. "C'mon Fossette, I owe you a tour."

sixty-two

Nina

I SHOW NICK THE house and answer all of his questions. Did I decorate it? Yes. Did I design it and have it built? Yes. When? Almost three years ago. What was my favorite room? The living room or the library, maybe my office. Did I actually cook? Sometimes. Twenty-Questions: House Edition, I jokingly called it. As he follows me up the stairs, he has one more question. Motioning towards the piano, "Do you play?"

"Yes, but I'm very out of practice." My fingers ghost over the keys. "Brina made us take lessons and even though I wasn't the best, I loved it. I guess it's the one thing I have to thank her for." I smile as his fingers linger next to mine, playing a note. Middle C. Looking up from our hands, our faces are closer than I anticipated. When he starts to close the space between us, "Nick, we shouldn't."

"Probably not," his words dance across my skin, but neither of us moves.

Just before our lips touch, "Nick."

He stops — he knows I'm right, this is not the time. He kisses my forehead and takes a step back. "How about a drink?"

"Sure," my voice barely a whisper as I move past him to the kitchen. I see the surprise on his face when I take two beers from the fridge. "I keep telling you, you don't know me." I wink handing him a bottle.

"How are you feeling, Dee?" He asks after a moment, but I don't answer. My finger traces the neck of the bottle as my gaze narrows on him.

The world seems to still.

How am I feeling? I spent the last week handling the funeral of my father while also trying to manage the emotions of everyone else. I feel like I've been run over by a truck ten fucking times. I feel like I'm alone in the world. I feel hurt and betrayed by the man in front of me. I feel confused by all the emotions running through me when I see him sitting in my home — the way it feels normal and makes everything feel complete. All I want to do is curl in a ball and cry, but what good is that going to? The rest of the world doesn't stop just because mine is crumbling to pieces.

The silence becoming almost too much to bear, he starts, "Are you—"

"What are you doing here, Nick?" The question startles him and me. But, it's the one thing I want to know. "Why are you here? You haven't been here this whole time and you decide to show up now?"

"I wanted to check on you."

"Well, as you can see, I'm fine."

"Nina." He is cautious. "Nina, don't do this." But, the walls are already up. "Don't push me away. Don't act like everything is fine when—"

"Everything is fine! I'm fine. It's all fine."

"Stop it. Don't dismiss this."

"I'm not dismissing anything! Quite the opposite, actually. I'm the one taking care of everything. The one making sure shit isn't falling apart. Because the second my dad died... The second he was gone, it's like everyone forgot how to function."

There's a fire inside me trying to get out. I've been withholding it for months, but I don't think I can do it anymore.

"I am not them. I am not him, Nina. I don't want anything from you. I don't expect anything from you. I just want to be here for you. I want to give you what no one gave me." Ever so slowly, he pulls me into his chest and wraps his arms around me. With each word, I feel the walls crack. I've been holding back — taking care of everything and everyone else instead of myself. "Dee, it's okay to let it out," he whispers, but I shake my head against him. "I know what it's like, but you can't hold it in."

"You don't know anything."

Except, I know he does.

"I've been here. I've been in your position. You don't have to do it alone." He kisses the crown of my head. "I'm right here, baby."

"Don't."

"Nina—"

"Basta fermarsi!" I push him away.

"I'm sorry, Nina. Is that what you want to hear? Because I am, I am so sorry."

"Sei dispiaciuto?" My voice a low hiss. When he tries to say more, I stop him. "Don't. Don't you fucking dare."

"I'm sorry for everything, but mostly, I'm sorry that I wasn't here for you."

"You're right, you weren't here. But, you know who was?" Of course he knows, how can he not? Everyone saw John at the funeral. Subtly, his jaw tightens. Apparently, I've struck a nerve. Good. "John fucking Jansen."

"Well, where is he now? Because from where I'm standing, I don't see anyone but you and me."

"I don't have time for this, Nick."

"You can't keep running!"

"I wasn't the one who ran!" My blood boils. He really has the audacity to do this after the day I just had? He couldn't even wait until tomorrow? He couldn't let me get through this day first? "Vuoi andarci? Bene, parliamone. Where do you wanna start?"

"Nina—"

"No, you obviously want to get this out. Quindi, parla." His silence only infuriates me more. "Sputa fuori, Nick."

Nothing.

"No? Bene, I'll go first." I pace the kitchen. "How about we start with my 'reputation.' That was such an issue for you, right? *Davina Villa*, party girl, slut, trouble maker...the list goes on and on. Just another trust fund baby living off Daddy's money, fucking her way through school." I watch him swallow the lump growing in his throat. "But, you know what, I can't blame you considering how we met the first time."

"What do you mean? We met at the coffee shop, we—"

"Don't you fucking lie to me, Nick Davis. Don't you dare," my voice deadly. "Your dad told me about your mom. How you left school unexpectedly. How you never went back because you were helping him. You looked so familiar, but it wasn't until he told me that I finally realized who you were." He can only stare at me. "You took me home from Phillip's party and then, you were just...gone. I never saw you again."

"I didn't have a choice!" He sounds defeated. "My dad and Alex, they needed—"

"I looked everywhere for you. I asked Tobias, Jonas... They all lied to me."

"I asked them not to say anything to anyone, not just you. I didn't want to be a burden. I didn't want pity. I wasn't like you, I was there on a scholarship, there was no way I could keep up with school and the garage and my family."

"I would've been there for you."

"You didn't even know me, Nina."

"But, I wanted to!" My voice echoes in the open space. "I wanted to know you. You have no idea how nice it was to be treated like a normal person. You didn't care who I was or about my reputation. At least, I thought you didn't, but I was obviously wrong."

"I didn't."

"Bullshit, Nick. You've held those rumors over my head since before we met. You want me to be *that* person. You want me to be that girl, so you have an excuse to run. But, I'm not her." I step back when he moves towards me. "Is that why you helped me? Davina Villa offered you the chance to live the Villa lifestyle, get paid to do it, and who knows maybe she'd even put out."

"It wasn't like that, Nina."

"But then, you got mad because Lee kissed me."

"It's hard not to when he was fucking you with his eyes twenty-four-seven."

"So what! I wanted nothing to do with him."

"Could'a fooled me."

"Are you fucking kidding me? Oh mio dio. Nick, what did I ever do to make you think I wanted him?" But, he doesn't answer. "I didn't want him. I wanted you!" Tears make my eyes shine. "I shouldn't even have to explain myself. We weren't even together!"

"I know that."

"Davvero?!" I spit the word at him. "Do you?"

"Yes!"

"Could'a fooled me." I throw his own words back at him. "Being with you was... Even when it was just pretend, it was special. I never felt that with John or Lee." I wipe my eyes. "And then, the most unexpected thing happened...I actually started to fall for you."

Tears brim his eyes.

"But, it was all just a mistake, right? You still thought I was her, the girl from the rumors. You just couldn't let it go."

"That's not true."

"Perché te ne sei andato?"

"Nina, I was scared," he sighs. "I was scared of you, of us, and I was scared of what your mom would do to my family. Not just if I told you, but when she figured out what was going on. I couldn't risk her doing something to any of you."

"You didn't have to worry about her."

"Yes, I did. She had threatened my family, Nina. She threatened you! You can't tell me you wouldn't do the same. She had me investigated. She threatened Alex's education and my dad's livelihood... You. She threatened you. She would ruin you."

"My dad would never allow it."

"Your dad was pissed when he found out the truth. There was no way we came out of this unscathed. I did what I had to do to protect my family."

You are part of his family. Tears well in my eyes thinking of the words my dad had said that day in his office. Looking into Nick's eyes, I know they're true.

"You didn't even say goodbye. You just left in the middle of the night. Who does that? I don't even know why I tried to come after you."

"You did the same damn thing in Savannah!"

"Oh, vaffanculo, Nick."

"Wait, what did you just say?"

"I said, fuck you."

"No, before that." I know what he means, but I don't budge. "You came after me?"

I sigh, there's no use trying to backpedal now. "I woke up and you were gone. No matter how mad I was, I couldn't let you leave that way."

"Why didn't you tell me, Nina?"

"Would it have changed anything?" I wipe my eyes. "I tried to call, but you didn't answer. I got to the airport, but it was too late. You were gone...again. And when Michaela told me you met Sheyenne... What was I supposed to do, Nick? I couldn't—"

"Be honest, Nina. Be honest with me, honest with yourself."

"Onesto? Be honest about Sheyenne!"

"We are not together!"

"Then why is she here?"

"I don't know!" Nick takes a deep breath trying to regain composure. "I was with her when I heard about my dad, she just showed up. Uninvited."

"That's the worst excuse I've ever heard."

"I think she just wanted to meet you, the girl I've been so hung up on."

"Stronzata! That is bullshit, Nick."

"You wanna talk about bullshit?" He follows me when I try to walk away. "What happened in Savannah, Nina? Why did you leave when you had two more days planned? Michaela told me you skipped out on meetings and work. You went ghost."

I refuse to answer as I try to push past him, "Ho finito."

"Answer the question, Nina." Nick still blocks me. "Answer the question!"

"Because I was scared!" I take a deep breath. "I'm scared, okay? Is that what you want to hear?"

"Scared of what?"

"You!" My lip trembles. "Scared of this, us." I close my eyes, trying to hold back tears, but one falls anyway. "Being with you scares the shit out of me. I am so scared of being hurt again. I didn't know what to do."

"I got accepted at BU."

What?

I can tell by the look on his face he didn't mean to say it, but now it's out in the open. I'm not sure I'm even breathing as I try to piece together what he just said. Boston. He applied to Boston? He moving to Boston? All of this... This confrontation, trying to figure this out for what? So he can leave. "Boston?"

Nick reaches for me, but I retract.

"I'm supposed to start next semester, but I'll rescind. I can get back into RU, finish my degree there. We can make this work, I don't have to go, Nina. I'll do whatever you want. Do you want me to leave? Because I will walk out that door, right now, you don't have to ever see me again. Or, do you want me to stay? Because, that's what I want. I want you, but I will do whatever you want. You just have to tell me."

Listening to him, I realize I have to let him go. He can't stay here, I won't let him. There's a reason he applied to Boston and not Rosecliffe. I believe him when he says he wants to be here, be with me, but I can't ask that of him. I won't ask it. My heart aches because I know neither of us is what the other needs right now. Letting him go... It's best for both of us. I shake my head, "No."

"No?"

"No, we can't make this work." I watch him deflate. "I won't ask you to do that, to stay here. You deserve this opportunity. Non puoi essere bloccato qui."

"Nina, we can do this."

"Nick—"

"You are so stubborn. Why are you pushing me away?"

"Because I love you!" I choke back a sob. I wasn't prepared for this. I wasn't prepared to lay everything out on the table. Softer, "I love you, Nick. But, I refuse to be the reason you stay. The reason you don't experience the things you want in life. The reason you don't chase your dreams. If you want to stay here, you stay because you want to, not for me." His lip trembles as I take his hand in mine and intertwine our fingers. "There is so much out there for you. And, as much as I want to, I can't give it to you. Not right now." A tear falls down my cheek. "So, you have to go."

Nick smiles and rests his forehead against mine. "You have no idea how long I've wanted to hear you say that." He wipes another tear as it rolls down my cheek. "I'm sorry, for everything. I should've been honest with you. I should've told you when I found them, I know that. I was just so scared, your mom... I didn't know what she was truly capable of. When I found out she looked into me, knew who I was... I wanted to tell you. So many times I thought about it, but your mom's threats were always in the back of my mind. I didn't think it was going to be so difficult to let you go. I wanted to tell you everything in Denver, but your mom's texts were this constant reminder not to fuck up. Not to say anything if I didn't want anything to happen.

"So, I decided it was better to end it early, before either of us could really get hurt. I didn't plan on having sex with you, Nina. I wouldn't do that to you. But, when I saw you standing there... God, you looked beautiful. And, when you smiled at me, I was a goner. When I woke up the next morning, I called Josh and I told him everything. I told him about your mom and Lee, the threats, Denver...you.

"I had a choice to make and I made the wrong one, but I can't change the fact that it happened. Had I known you came after me...I would've stayed. I would've told you everything right then and there — I almost did that day in your room. I was so close to telling you, but I got scared and I took the easy way out. I said things I didn't mean because I knew the only way you'd let me go was if I hurt you. You didn't deserve that, Nina.

"When Eileen called me about the accident, I lost it. I couldn't fathom the idea that you might be gone. I didn't care that you were mad at me. I had to find you. I needed to know you were here, you were alive. I went out of my mind trying to find you. And when I couldn't find you..." Tears roll down his cheeks. "I didn't want to be the one to tell you, I didn't even think about Sheyenne being there, I just got in the car and drove. I shouldn't have left you. I should've been here, should've helped you through this. It shouldn't have been him.

I should've fought harder for you."

"It's okay, Nick," I whisper and he leans into my hand on his cheek.

"That night we met at Phillip's party, I saw you in a different light. One that didn't add up to all the things people said about you. But, that was the night my mom died. I was supposed to go home that night, but I went to the party instead. When I got the call from Alex the next morning my world fell apart and I couldn't see past my grief. I blamed you. I blamed you for keeping me from her, even though it wouldn't have changed anything had I been there. Spending this summer with you reminded me of that. My mom would've loved you. She always told me to give you a chance, I wish I had listened."

I laugh, "She sounds like a smart woman."

"I love you, Davina," Nick says without hesitation. He pushes a lock of hair behind my ear before kissing me — his lips are soft, vulnerable against mine. "I love your passion." A quick peck against my forehead. "I love your smile." A peck on my cheek. "I love your heart." The other cheek. "I love your soul." He kisses me again. "When I saw you dancing in the rain that night in Haven...I knew, I was in love with you." Nick dips his head to the sensitive spot behind my ear, a tender kiss. His words barely a whisper, "I meant it when I said, you're mine."

"You don't know how long *I've* waited to hear that."

sixty-three

THE SUBTLE MOVEMENTS OF a person next to me pull me out of my dreams. There's a weight settled over my waist, a hand splayed across my stomach underneath my sweater. His breath tickles the back of my neck before his lips brush against the skin. "G'morning," he whispers. I groan in protest and turn in his arms to bury further into his side. "C'mon baby," he tries to rouse me, but I still refuse.

Last night was the best sleep I've gotten in months. When the dust had settled, we spent the rest of the night cuddled on the couch watching *The Santa Clause*. The last thing I remembered was E.L.F.S. breaking into the police department, but the credits rolled as Nick carefully lifted me from the couch to carry me to bed and I refused to let him leave.

When I think he's finally going to settle back in for a long morning in bed, my phone rings. He reaches over me, taking it from my nightstand. "It's your brother."

"What?" I answer the phone.

"Well, good morning to you too," Kai laughs on the other end. He's in better spirits today.

"What do you want?"

"You coming to the board meeting?"

"Shit." I totally forgot. This is the first one with Kai as head of the company and me as his partner.

"I'll take that as a no."

"I'll be there." I rub my eyes looking at the clock. "What time does it start?" I throw the blankets off and storm into the bathroom. I have an hour to get dressed and be in Charlotte. No time for a shower, I douse my hair with dry shampoo before pulling it into a bun. I discard my pajamas on the floor of my closet changing into a pair of black faux leather pants, a tan turtleneck sweater, and boots, making a mental note to pick them up later.

Nick is half asleep when I return to the bedroom. A lazy smile spreads across his lips when I tug gently through his curls. "There's plenty of coffee and food, if you want something, I'll be back shortly." I lightly trace the scar on his forehead. "You'll be here?"

"If you want."

"I do."

He kisses me, slow and steady, when a moan resounds in my throat, he moves into action. His lips leave a blazing trail down my throat finding the spot he knows I like best, the one only he knows, but I push him away.

"I have to go."

"Fuck the board."

"I don't think that would be very pleasant. I'd rather save that for someone else." My smirk grows when he rolls his eyes. "I will come right back after the meeting and I'm all yours."

"Promise?" His teeth nibble the same spot and my body starts to melt into him as one of his hands grazes the skin of my stomach under my sweater.

"Sì, lo prometto, ma devo andare," I whimper and pull away from him. After a chaste kiss, I retreat to the safety of the door. Before I can leave, he calls my name. "What?"

"I love you, Dee."

"Ti amo, Fossette."

sixty-four

TOWN SQUARE BUZZES WITH excitement setting up for the festivities later tonight. I sit in one of the booths outside of Java Fountain in the makeshift heated outdoor space. It's an unusually bitter cold morning, I wear my black overcoat and a scarf to fend off the breeze. But, not even the cold weather can keep me from an iced coffee. Alex makes fun of me when he sits down, it's thirty-three degrees, why am I drinking an iced beverage? "Iced coffee is a way of life. You either get it or you don't."

"You know, I've never been here."

"Scusi?" I touch my heart, offended.

"Not a big coffee person, I guess."

"Shamey, shamey. How can you be a law student and not drink coffee? That defies all logic, Alex." I giggle when he rolls his eyes. "Well, what'd you get?"

"Just a coffee."

"Just a plain coffee? You're doing it wrong! Here," I hand him my coffee. "May I introduce you to the Iced DV."

"Of course you have your own drink." Alex rolls his eyes before he takes a small sip, letting the semi-sweet mixture fill his senses. "Oh wow! This is so good." He takes another large gulp.

"And now, you owe me another coffee," I say as he drains the cup.

Watching Alex order two new coffees, I notice how much he looks like his brother, only taller. He fusses with a few pieces of hair that fall into his eyes. He's overdue for a haircut, his hair now has a small curl at the ends. I barely recognize the boy I met years earlier at the football game. "So, when do you leave?" I ask when he returns.

"Tomorrow."

"New Year's Day?"

"Yeah, I need to try and get my job back. Then, go into the admin office when they open back up and make sure everything is squared away."

"You missed quite a lot of time."

"My professors were understanding, but I'm gonna have to retake a few."

"You okay with that?"

"Sure, it was worth it. I should be able to still graduate on time, that's all I really care about." Alex plays with his straw, his mind wandering somewhere other than our conversation.

"What's on your mind?"

"Straight to the point, I like it," Alex sighs. "Well, I guess I'm just trying to understand why you guys won't even try."

"Alex..."

"He would stay here, Nina. He can easily get back into Rosecliffe. You guys could finally be together."

"I want him to go."

"But, why?"

"He needs to go. He needs to get out of here, experience what the world has to offer."

"Why not try long distance?"

"Alex," I sigh. "I cannot be who he needs right now. I'm still building and expanding my own company and I have to help Kai. I'm still developing Michaela and gonna be hiring more people. I just…I can't offer myself to someone yet."

Alex stares intently as he swirls the coffee in his cup.

"He deserves to finish school, get his degree. To figure out what he wants in life. I won't take that from him." I cover his hand and give it a gentle squeeze. "This isn't me choosing my career over your brother. I would give it up for him, but he'd never let me. And, honestly, I need time. So much has happened in the past six months. I don't think I can be who he needs me to be, right now. I have a lot to figure out."

"You are nothing like I thought." I raise a suspicious brow, but Alex is quick to reassure me. "I just mean, I used to be so in love with you. Well, I guess, the idea of you. I realize, I never really knew who you were. It's crazy how things worked out."

"I was not the best person. Sometimes, I wish I could go back and change things. But, then I wouldn't be who I am. I'm just sorry I never got to know either of you before now."

"I think it worked out for the best."

I wink at him. "BU has a great architecture program. He'll be able to get a job anywhere."

"With DV Designs?"

I roll my eyes. "I guess, we'll see what happens."

"Oh, Michaela mentioned at Christmas you have a speech coming up at some conference. What's that about?"

"Una bocca così grande. Does she ever keep anything to herself?"

"You know who you're talking about, right?"

We laugh.

"I haven't decided if I'm gonna do it. I mean, standing in front of a bunch of people who think if they listen to me they'll find some get rich quick idea. I don't know if that's for me." I shrug. "If I can find something interesting to talk about, I might consider it."

"You've led a pretty interesting life, I think you can find something. I mean, from party girl, to fake boyfriends, to your mom sleeping with your ex...the list goes on and on."

"Thanks for reminding me." I check my watch, "Shit, I gotta go. I'm supposed to be picking up food for Elizabeth."

"Thanks for the invite," he jokes.

"Trust me, I don't want to go. I think picking up the food was Elizabeth's way of making sure I come."

Alex pulls me into a tight embrace.

"Tell them I said, Happy New Year." Alex knows I mean Nick. I haven't seen him since he left my house the morning after Christmas. When I returned from the board meeting, we agreed he would stay until December 26th. Then, we would go our separate ways...for now.

When the day finally came, I was woken up by a kiss goodbye. "I love you, Davina Bay," he whispered and kissed me one last time. The sound of the front door echoed straight into my heart. But, I didn't cry. We're doing the right thing for both of us. And, the thought that one day we might find our way back to one another brought a smile to my lips.

"Happy New Year, Nina," Alex whispers and squeezes me gently bringing me back to the present.

"Happy New Year, Alex."

Part Three

"There are all kinds of love in this world, but never the same love twice."

- F. Scott Fitzgerald, "The Great Gatsby"

sixty-five

TWO AND HALF YEARS LATER

I FOLLOW MICHAELA AND Elizabeth out of the restaurant along the Boston Harbor. Turning down Atlantic Avenue, I tighten my ponytail through the baseball hat and slip sunglasses over my eyes. The closer we get to the hotel, the more my nerves grow — they've tripled in size from the time I woke up. I have spoken to many different groups, including women's conferences, business conferences, and college classes, but it doesn't matter how many times I do it, I still get nervous.

"Relax, Nin, you're gonna be fine," Michaela says over her shoulder. I always get like this before a speech. Halfway through lunch, they both noticed I started to grow quieter as the time ticked by.

"Are you still meeting up with Alex tonight?" Elizabeth asks, trying to take my mind off things.

"Supposed to," I shrug, I'm thinking about canceling.

"Is that why you're so nervous?" Michaela asks. "You think a certain someone might tag along?"

I roll my eyes. Alex and I have talked regularly through the years and he kept me up-to-date on what was going on in the Davis family. Jimmy has semi-retired, hiring a few of the local boys who were looking for a job. They've been able to triple business at the shop. He visited Boston every few months and

349

the boys would come home for a short time on breaks. Nick graduated a week ago, but refused to walk despite Jimmy's best attempts to convince him. He has gone on multiple interviews, has been offered most of the jobs, but has yet to find the right firm. Alex has enjoyed having his brother in the same state again, they spend most weekends together and with some of Nick's architecture friends. Alex started dating someone, Anna Grant, a chemistry major; they actually met through one of Nick's friends, Dean Monroe. Alex has always made sure to remind me that his brother still hasn't found anyone else. Each time, I roll my eyes and say goodnight before he can say anything more.

As we approach the Boston Harbor Hotel, I notice a couple on the other side of the street. The man looks familiar, too familiar. His hair a little longer than the last time I saw him, curls more defined. The girl is petite, long brown hair sweeps side-to-side with each step, but I don't recognize her.

"Nina? You okay?" Michaela waves a hand in front of my face.

"Huh? Oh, yeah. I thought I saw something." When I look down the street again, the couple is gone.

"Everything okay?" Elizabeth calls from the entrance of the hotel.

"She just spaced out. The nerves are definitely getting to her." Michaela pushes me towards the door. "C'mon, we need to get you ready. We don't have much time!"

§

After my speech, I don't want to do anything but go back to the hotel and soak in the bath. The pain in my head intensifies with each step — a mix of lack of sleep, food, and the blaring sound on stage. The Tylenol started to wear off halfway through my presentation. When I open the door to my dressing room, I'm caught off guard by the large bouquet on the makeup table. Red roses, white hydrangeas, and white peonies. I smell one of the roses and smile when I see the hidden card tucked down between the stems. I trace the curve of his handwriting, but then my mind returns to the couple on the street.

"Whoa!" Elizabeth gasps walking into the room. "Who are those from?"

"Secret admirer." I tuck the card into my purse.

Elizabeth quirks an eyebrow. "How intriguing."

I slouch into the makeup chair and swallow another dose of Tylenol. "I'm exhausted and this headache won't give up. I might have to cancel on Alex tonight."

"Have you been sleeping?" Elizabeth frowns when I shrug. "Nin, you need to take some time to unwind. You've been going nonstop."

"Yeah, yeah. I will." I wave my hand. "I just need to finish the Denver office and get New York started."

"Denver, Charlotte, and now New York, you're never going to rest."

"I'll be fine, Elizabeth. I appreciate the concern, but I need to be there. Charlotte and San Diego are good, but Denver isn't quite there yet. I promise after New York, I'll take a vacation. Okay?"

"But, then you'll find another and—" Elizabeth is cut off when Michaela busts through the door. "Everything okay, Mic?"

Michaela holds up a finger trying to catch her breath.

"What is it?" I press. "I have a hot date with a bottle of champagne and a bathtub. I don't want to keep them waiting."

"I-I j-just ran here because I ne-needed to m-make sure you were s-still here."

"Well, I'm here. Che vuoi?"

"Y-you have g-guests!"

I share a confused glance with Elizabeth.

Michaela holds up her finger again before she runs out of the room. I roll my eyes and start packing my things. I want to be ready to leave as soon as these "guests" are gone. Michaela returns seconds later, Alex and a petite brunette follow her into the dressing room. "Hope you don't mind we crashed your speech," Alex says.

"Alex?!" I hug him. "Che ci fai qui? Pensavo che tu fossi occupato."

"I still have no idea what you're saying."

"I'm just excited to see you! What are you doing here?"

"Anna's a big fan. I couldn't disappoint her." Alex motions toward the brunette.

"This is Anna?" I'm shocked, I swear Anna was a redhead. "I'm so happy to finally meet you. I have heard so much about you!"

"It is so nice to meet you!" Anna shakes my hand, but everyone can see the internal scream she holds in. Her words fly by a million miles a minute, I can hardly keep up. "I just think you are the best. The way you built your company... it's so inspiring. I used to think about going into fashion and design, but science has my heart. I think you're so talented and real. You just tell it like it is. I love that."

I wave my face, heat rising in my cheeks.

"When Alex and Nick said they knew you, I couldn't believe it. What are the odds?"

"Any friend of the Davises is a friend of mine." I wink at Alex.

"Woah, someone must really like you." Anna points towards the bouquet.

"Who are those from?" Alex asks.

"Secret admirer," Elizabeth chimes in. The way she says it, I know she has an idea of who this "secret admirer" is.

"Do you have something you wanna share with the class,

Nina?"

"There's no card," Michaela searches the bouquet.

"There wasn't one," I shrug. "Probably just a good luck bouquet from the organization. It's nothing special."

"Some bouquet," Alex pushes. "They must be glad you came."

"Are you hungry?" I ask Anna intentionally avoiding Alex's stare. I can feel his eyes on me, but I still refuse to meet his stare as I finish packing up my bag. "I can see if we can move our reservation up at Davio's."

"Starving!" Anna seems oblivious to the knowing looks of the other three people in the room. That or she is good at ignoring them.

sixty-six

THE MOMENT I WALK into the space, I know. This is it. DV Designs: New York. Twenty stories above Columbus Circle, the empty floor has a breathtaking view through floor-to-ceiling windows — panoramic views of Manhattan below my feet. In the reflection, I watch the realtor pace the elevator bank on his phone. Michaela and Elizabeth stand inside a corner office overlooking Central Park. Wren, my new assistant and intern, types furiously on her phone nearby. A small sense of pride overwhelms me. Somedays, I still can't believe I've made it this far. After a moment of taking it all in, I join Michaela and Elizabeth. "Pretty cool, huh?"

"This is incredible!" Michaela gawks. "Do you see this view? I'd kill for this office. You're going to have the best views in the city."

"He was right about this one," Elizabeth says as we walk out of the office. We've looked at five other locations, but this is the first one I liked.

"What would you do with the space, Michaela?"

"Me?" Michaela has helped me design hundreds of projects, and has even given input on the Denver office, but this is different. I'm opening the floor for Michaela in a way I haven't before. "Well, I uh...I would make this your office

354

and I would..." I motion for Wren to take notes as Michaela describes wall placements, light fixtures, paint colors, and other decor.

"You think she's caught on, yet?" Elizabeth asks when we leave them to join the realtor.

"Nope," I laugh. "You were right, this is the best one. It was a bit deceptive online."

"You know how that goes," the realtor says. "I'll draw up the papers."

"Can you give us just a few more minutes?"

"Of course, take your time."

I stare out over the city again. This has been a long time coming. A New York office was one of my biggest goals when I started DV Designs, but I have one thing left to do. "Hey, Mic," I call from my place at the window. Michaela stops her directions. "Do you want it?"

"What do you mean?"

"Do you want to run the New York office?"

Michaela laughs, but my face doesn't change. I'm serious. Michaela's face falls, she doesn't think she is ready to run an office. She doesn't have the same experience I do or any of the other office directors. I know that, but I know she can handle it. "You're not serious, Nina."

I only smile.

"Nina, I can't just move to New York. What about you? What about David? What about Denver and—"

"You have been with me for the past five years, Michaela. You can do this. You've been doing it." I can see the struggle inside Michaela. "You've always wanted to move here, this is your chance. I already talked to David, just say the word, he's ready."

"You talked to David?" A swell of energy bubbles inside Michaela's chest. "He said okay?" A delighted squeal fills the office, "Thank you! Thank you! Thank you!"

"You're so oblivious," Elizabeth says with a small laugh.

"Does this mean I can have Michaela's office now?" Wren asks.

"We'll talk about it during your review," I wink.

"Shall we, ladies?" The realtor motions towards the elevator. On the ride down, he explains he will have the paperwork drawn up and sent to me for review tonight. I thank him when we part at the front door.

"So, what's the plan?" Elizabeth asks as we step out onto Columbus Circle. Michaela straggles behind us, her eyes sweeping through the oncoming crowd over and over again. She checks her watch, flustered.

"I was thinking Manhatta for dinner," I say.

"Manhatta? Nina, that's almost impossible to get into."

"Is it? Seemed pretty easy when I called earlier." My smile fades noticing Michaela's continued strange behavior. "Reservation is at eight." I share a confused look with Elizabeth before I finally ask, "Mic, are you okay?"

"Yeah, yeah." Michaela tears her eyes from the crowd "Why do you ask?"

"Are you looking for something?" Elizabeth asks.

"No, of course not. Why would you think that?"

"Because you're acting weird," I say.

"Am not. I'm just—" Michaela is suddenly distracted by an incoming text message.

"Acting weird." I finish for her and laugh. "Whatever, handle whatever it is you have going on. We have some time before dinner, so I'm going for a run."

"Can we just meet you there?" Elizabeth asks, looping her arm with Wren. "I wanted to run down to SoHo before everything closes."

sixty-seven

CENTRAL PARK IS MY second favorite place to go for a run. There is something magical about the quiet green space nestled in the middle of the bustling city. It brings a sense of peace when there is none outside of it. It's part of the reason I like to stay at the Plaza Hotel, where I'm greeted by the park each time I walk outside. I make a mental note to have Wren schedule a meeting regarding a condo for when I'm in town.

I ran around the pond, past the zoo and carousel, through the maze of statues and memorials. I slow as I descend the Bethesda Terrace steps. Stepping through the stone archway, a familiar tune echoes through the Arcade. I recognize it as the song that played when Nick and I danced at Elizabeth's wedding. A single violinist sits in the middle of the Arcade. The only person around — an odd sight for the normally busy tourist attraction. I sit on one of the stone benches just behind him.

My mind wanders to Nick. What is he doing right now? At dinner, Alex said he had an interview with a firm. I enjoyed my time with Alex and Anna the other night, I was glad I didn't bail. We spent the night laughing over glasses of wine and when the restaurant closed, the couple walked me back to the hotel where we shared one more drink in the hotel bar. I wonder if

Nick got the job? Where would he be moving to next? Would I see him again or would our only communication be through flowers and cards, maybe the occasional text?

A tear lands on my hand at the crescendo. I didn't even realize I had started to cry. I wipe my eyes and roll my shoulders trying to regain composure. I clear my throat and wipe under my eyes again. Checking my watch, I should get back to the hotel so I can shower before dinner. My run isn't going to last as long as I would have liked, but I had to help Kai when I got back earlier before I could leave. I stretch my legs preparing to finish my run. From the corner of my eye, I see someone else has finally joined from the fountain. They drop a few dollars in the violinist's case and whisper something to the artist.

I turn from my stretch and run straight into them. "Oh my gosh, I am so sorry, I—" My words falter when I meet their warm gaze.

"Hey, Princess."

sixty-eight

"NICK?" I TAKE THE opportunity to look him over — he's dressed in dark gray slacks with a blazer over a blue button-up. His hair slightly longer, the ends curled in a small tuft that I want nothing more than to run my fingers through. Slight stubble shades his jaw, more defined. When our eyes meet again, I feel that familiar warmth spread through my chest.

The song picks up again.

"Posso avere questa danza?" Nick extends his hand to me, his smirk fading into a soft smile. I laugh, but take his hand and let him lead me in a small sway.

"Have you been studying Italian?"

"I may have taken a few lessons."

My heart swells at the thought. When we have kids, I can teach them Italian without leaving Nick in the dark. The opposite of how it had been with my parents. He would be able to—

My smile falls. I'm getting ahead of myself. What is he even doing here?

"Hey, come back to me." His thumb grazes my cheek.

"Nick, what are you doing here?"

"I was in town. Heard you were here. Wanted to see you."

"In town?"

"I had an interview. Alex didn't tell you?"

No, Alex did not tell me, which is honestly kind of shocking. Usually, he's chomping at the bit to tell me anything that has to do with his brother.

"But, what are you doing *here*?"

"Michaela may have mentioned you were out for a run." His stubble scratches my face when he leans in. I can feel our hearts beat against our intertwined hands. "And, it's not hard to guess where you'd go for a run in the city."

"It's not a small park, Fossette," I whisper.

"No, but you've mentioned the Bethesda Fountain before. Something about a chair, or something?"

My laugh echoes through the empty arcade. "Chuck and Blair, Chair from *Gossip Girl*?"

"I could never forget Chuck and his redemption arc."

"It's the best."

Nick smiles and spins me under his arm before he pulls me close.

"What are you doing here, Nick? Really."

"I wanted to see you, Dee. I miss you."

"We haven't spoken in months. What makes you think you can just show up and—" I gasp when his lips crash against mine. Desperate and needy. He invades all my senses. My heart pounds in my chest, my knees weak. I can only focus on the feeling of his mouth against mine. With every breath I take, earthy scents of cedar and cardamom fill my lungs. It's intoxicating and inviting.

When we part, he wastes no time, "Ti amo, Davina. And, I know we have so much to figure out, but if there's one thing I know, it's that I love you."

"I love you, Nick." His smile grows at my admission and he brushes his lips against mine again. "But, you're in Boston. Your job, your life..."

"Will always be with you. My life is wherever you are. I'll

find a firm. I'll go back to working on cars. I don't care. I want you, Nina. I'm ready for this part of my life."

My fingers play with the lapels of his blazer, I close my eyes and inhale deeply. When I reopen them, whiskey-colored orbs stare into mine. "You're sure? Like one-hundred and ten percent?"

"More than. I want this. I want us." Nick brushes a piece of hair from my face and kisses me briefly. "I'm sorry we've spent so much time apart. I know we needed it, but none of it matters if it's not with you." He captures my lips in a possessive kiss. It's demanding and hungry. A moan resonates deep in my throat when he threads his fingers in my ponytail and tugs, his lips leave a burning trail down the skin of my jaw.

"Nick, I have dinner with Lydia and—"

"Cancel."

"Come with me and after dinner, I'm all yours."

"All mine?" His teeth graze the skin just below my ear, the sensitive spot where my jaw and neck meet.

"Yours."

"Promise?" He sticks out his left hand out between us, pinky finger hanging in the air. I roll my eyes, but wrap my finger around his.

"Promettere."

"Good, because I have an idea." The gleam in his eyes tells me I'm going to be late for dinner.

sixty-nine

Michaela

"WHERE IS SHE?" ELIZABETH checks her watch again. Staring down the street, there's no way to tell which car belongs to Nina. One million black SUVs on the street and not a single one has made any indication of stopping. "If this was us, she'd have our heads."

"If this was one of us," I motion between myself and Wren, "she'd have my head. If it was you, she wouldn't care."

Elizabeth rolls her eyes pulling up the "Find My" app on her phone. Nina's little blue dot radiates from a block away. It approaches quickly as the SUV finally pulls up. The driver opens the door and Elizabeth takes a step back when it isn't Nina stepping out of the car. "Nick?"

Nick helps Nina out of the SUV smiling down at her when she kisses him in thanks.

I'm the first to greet them, feigning shock, "Nick? What a surprise! I didn't know you were here." Nina doesn't buy it. From the look on her face, I know she is well aware I helped set this up.

"You can stop the act, Michaela. He told me everything," Nina smirks. "Where's Lydia?"

"Upstairs, we wanted to make sure we wouldn't lose the table since someone was late."

"Don't blame me, it wasn't my fault this time."

I glare at Nick. "So, you're the reason we've been left to starve?"

"We had other things to do first." Nick presses his lips to Nina's temple.

"Not that I'm not happy to see you, but what are you doing here?" Elizabeth asks.

"We'll explain everything," Nina says. "But, can we go upstairs first? I'm famished."

"I want to know everything."

"Yes, I promise, just go." Nina urges us towards the door, but Nick holds her back a step.

"I love you," he whispers.

"I know."

Just before their lips meet, I interrupt, "Let's go Han and Leia, we're withering away to nothing here!"

Nina rolls her eyes, mostly at my *Star Wars* reference. She gives him a chaste kiss and they follow us inside. In the elevator, Nick presses a kiss to the crown of her head when she leans back into his chest. He always has some type of hold on her, their fingers intertwined as Nina leads him into the restaurant. She only lets go to embrace a very pregnant Lydia.

"Who is this?" Lydia asks, looking straight at Nick.

"Lydia, this is Nick," Nina steps into his side. His arm wraps around her shoulders, and her hand rests on his chest. Only then do I notice a slight gleam on her hand. The setting sun streaming in through the windows reflects off the blue-green emerald with a diamond cushion as it demands attention against the fabric covering Nick's chest. Nina shares a smirk with Nick before she meets our stares. "My husband."

Thank you!

Did you enjoy *Until Now*? Please consider leaving a review on Amazon, Goodreads, etc! It doesn't matter the length, anything helps spread the word.

Interested in more? Scan the code above to sign up for my newsletter

WHAT'S NEXT?

The *Strangers* Series will continue with a stuck together, enemies to lovers romance featuring Michaela and a mysterious Villa family friend.

acknowledgements

I loved every second of writing this book... even the hard parts. Every sleepless night. Every tear. Every bottle of wine. Every cup of coffee. It was all worth it.

There were times I never thought I would get here, but I made it! If only the little girl who used to write secretly from the safety of her bedroom could see me know.

For years, I have wanted to publish a novel, which is something I only recently told my friends and family. No, I take that back, my best friend has known for a while. When I came up with the idea for this book, I knew it was going to be the one I finally published. This was something special I wanted to share with the world.

There were times I considered giving up. The first draft was ROUGH, I mean rough. The second was... still rough. The third and fourth drafts looked (kind of) close to where we are now, but not quite. It actually was the feedback from my beta readers that led me to create the book similar to the one hold in your hands now. And then...one day while working out in the yard, I decided to change the whole thing from third person to first person (which later changed to singular first person). Needless to say, it's been a lot of work, but I loved every minute of it.

§

First, I need to thank the Lord. Without Him, none of this

would be possible. He has blessed me with an incredible gift and I'm happy to have the opportunity to share it.

Second, I need to thank my husband. His patience and love during this whole process has been above and beyond. Truly, I don't think I realized how much time and energy was required when it came to writing a book. There were plenty of nights he went to bed alone while I stayed up writing, editing, designing... Kind of like right now. He's snoring away in the bedroom while I write this with our puppy at my feet and glass of Bonita Bonita that I should've finished by now. John, you have been so supportive and I'm so grateful to have you by my side... I love you to the moon and back. ♥

Third, I want to thank Jayden / Jordan / MAB (whoever you are). You're the best sounding board a girl could ask for. Romance is not your thing, that's why I love coming to you with ideas because you give me an outsider's perspective. Thank you for letting me text you at all hours of the day with ideas, excerpts, and rambling thoughts that make absolutely no sense until I figure out WHAT I'm trying to say. Now, we just need to work on that endorsement from Apothic (LOL) ... WHAT'S THE TROPE?! (P.S. I tried to think of a clever Cleopatra joke, but couldn't)

I need to thank my family and friends who have cheered me on along the way... or at least since they found out I was writing a book. I've always been very reserved when it came to sharing my work, but your love and support during this has been exactly what I needed. Some people to mention... My mom (who actually read it, even though she never reads LOL), my dad, and my step-mom. Stephanie Yelland. Ashley Brown. Brooke. Kay. Charla. Megan. Bonnie. BG. Raina. Robbie.

And, I guess I should thank my old job. When the idea for this book came to me, I had recently quit my management job and wanted something mindless (and trust, this was mindless). I was standing behind the reception desk of a salon in Chicago, Illinois. Now, I won't say I spent the rest of my shift piecing things together, but... let's just say it was a slow day at work.

Crafting a novel requires a lot of trial and error and feedback... I was very lucky to receive feedback from some generous and talented writers: Kate Gegas, Grace Rose, Becky Taylor. Hope you're ready for Book No. 2 ;)

My ARC team, you guys have been the best. I appreciate you more than you know.

I'd also like to thank two fellow authors: Michaela Jean Taylor and Allison Paige.

Lastly, I'd like to acknowledge another independent arist... Alexandra Kay. If you don't know her or her music, you should. Her journey is part of the reason I decided to finally pursue the self-publishing route (because, I wanted to avoid it). She was dropped by a label twice, but has become a very successful, totally **independent** artist. And, if she can do that in the music world, why can't I do it in the book world?

Honorable mention to my accountant, Lynda. Thanks for answering all my text messages when I was trying to figure out WTF I was doing (especially during tax season). This whole starting a business thing and trying to do the right thing when it comes to tax info is not fun.

And finally, my friend and photographer... Briana. You always know what I'm looking for. @EastlynPhotography.

There were so many of you who showed support during this journey, I can't even begin to name all of you, but just know I appreciate and love you.

Here's to the next books in the *Strangers* Series and many

others (because I have **plenty** of ideas)... I hope y'all are ready.

- Jensen

about the author

Jensen Parker is a former retail store manager and real estate professional turned contemporary romance author. She is an avid lover of traveling, coffee, and wine. When she isn't writing, you'll find her reading, playing with her animals, spending time outdoors, or trying (key word) to catch up on so much needed sleep. Jensen first began writing at a young age and has continued to hone her craft throughout the years, including classes and programs at Harvard University and Loyola. Though she will always be a Hoosier at heart, she currently resides in South Carolina with her husband and their fur babies.

For sneak peeks, giveaways, and more, sign up for Jensen's newsletter! https://www.jensenparker.com/subscribe

Follow her on social media!

Instagram : instagram.com/jensenparkerauthor

Facebook : facebook.com/jparkerauthor

Twitter : twitter.com/jensenpauthor

Goodreads : goodreads.com/jensenparkerauthor

Amazon : amazon.com/author/jensenparkerauthor

TikTok : tiktok.com/@jensenparkerauthor

"I urge you to live a life worthy of the calling you have received. Be completely humble and gentle; be patient, bearing with one another in love."

- Ephesians 4:1-2

Milton Keynes UK
Ingram Content Group UK Ltd.
UKHW042139020823
426203UK00005B/279